The Silver Lady's Men

ANTON SAVANYU. She was his greatest triumph, his truest tragedy. . . .

AUSTIN FLEMING. His love was a dark, forbidden curse that dared not speak its name. . . .

CAPTAIN LACY HAWKINS. She was the prize jewel in his crown of ruthless ambition, a pearl with a price he had yet to pay. . . .

ALEX COULTER. Lust was his armor, love a weakness he could not afford.

Silver Lady

SILVER LADY
NANCY MORSE

PUBLISHED BY POCKET BOOKS NEW YORK

A POCKET BOOKS/RICHARD GALLEN *Original* publication

**POCKET BOOKS, a Simon & Schuster division of
GULF & WESTERN CORPORATION
1230 Avenue of the Americas, New York, N.Y. 10020**

ISBN: 0-671-83504-1

First Pocket Books printing March, 1980

10 9 8 7 6 5 4 3 2 1

POCKET and colophon are trademarks of Simon & Schuster.

Printed in the U.S.A.

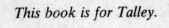

This book is for Talley.

Chapter 1

The early morning sun filtered through the tall cypresses, shading the vineyard estate called Chateaudun, which lays deep within the Lyon region of France, nestled away in the Rhone River Valley. Only the longest, most persistent yellow-white rays made their way through the treetops to fall upon the lawn that sprawled beneath Danielle Fleming's window, catching the morning moisture on select blades of grass in glints of brightness.

She tugged lightly at the trousers she was wearing. Just a trifle too tight, she thought, but then, what could she expect from boy's breeches that refused to take a woman's hips into consideration? She would have to speak to her brother about ordering a special pair just for her, to accommodate the slight curves her body had begun to develop.

When had she first noticed the subtle changes? She could not really remember. With a growing curiosity she had watched the contours of her own body alter and swell. She could only guess at its meaning, but it filled her with a sense of apprehension, as though perched precariously on some thin delicate line. At times it would leave her frightened, but . . . excited. Yes, she would think of what the future would bring. And lately, she had extended thoughts of her future to include the man she was waiting for, the man who waited for her.

Instantly, her eyes narrowed to glassy slivers and her fists clenched at her sides. No, she would not think about that now, she decided firmly, taking herself in hold.

Quickly, her small, slim hands worked the buttons of the

Silver Lady

linen shirt Austin had given her. Even that was noticeably snugger, buttons faintly straining when she breathed deeply.

Austin had encouraged his sixteen-year-old sister to wear his clothes. Dressed in that manner she could ride with him without being hampered by cumbersome clothing which, he reasoned, would only have rendered her powerless at an age when she had the greatest need of developing her strength.

Upon hearing his reasoning, Danielle had instantly abandoned all inhibitions and had taken to wearing men's clothing when riding as though it were perfectly normal to do so. Immediately, she had felt immense relief from the restrictions of her feminine garb which, although perfectly suited for dimly lit parlors and dinner parties, had no place atop a saddle. Her total abandonment to the newly afforded freedom fascinated Austin, and when they rode together, he would watch from the corner of his eye, catching glimpses of her as she pranced Destiny around him, coaxing the slender bay mare to draw away in short sprints, then fall back beside him.

The small cloth-visored cap she wore, to keep her hair from falling into her eyes, served to enhance the lovely delicate features of her face: her straight nose, small chin, full child-woman mouth that held a budding promise perpetually poised on its lips. But it was her eyes that one first noticed about her. In the dimness of a fire-lit room, they brooded beneath thick black lashes, yet caught in the reflection of a lamp or gazing upon a glittering bright day, they shone like bits of brown-yellow amber polished to brilliancy. And because they slanted just slightly at the corners, they evoked the look of a gypsy. Piled atop her head, beneath the cap, lay an abundance of dark auburn hair . . . hair that caught and held sunlight, turning captured rays from shades of palest gold to rich burnt copper—deep dark fullness that a man could lose himself in.

She teetered on the threshold of womanhood, sometimes stepping over the precarious line emerging as a sensual woman one moment and in the next slipping back into a playful child, eyes mischievously teasing, laughing, playing at being grown-up. All the while a kind of wildness persisted, a recklessness that her brother, Austin, did not understand. He could see it creep into her eyes. He could sense it smoldering beneath her, straining at her supple young muscles, washing a faint flush over her face. Somewhere inside her lay a stubbornness declaring itself resolute by the tilt of her chin. With a taste for devilish exaggeration, Danielle took a singular delight in sashaying forth, dressed as a boy, for all the world to see. Perhaps that was why she was smiling to herself as she adjusted a silk scarf around her neck on her way out of the bedroom.

Each morning, Sophie Le Hoult left the stillness of the big house to work in her garden. Snipping here, clipping there, she coaxed eruptions of brightly colored flowers with her careful ministrations. With magic hands she worked over each leaf and stalk with such a precise tenderness that even the most stubborn bulb was forced into a splendid explosion of color and aroma. Bent over her labors, the early morning sunlight was shielded from her eyes by the familiar wide-brimmed straw hat. She looked positively quaint, Danielle thought as she watched silently from a hall window.

Danielle found herself wondering why she sometimes detected a hint of sarcastic venom in her grandmother's usually pleasant voice whenever certain names fell from her lips. Some of the names were imprinted on Danielle's memory by the stories she had heard. Stories of her mother, Laura, of whose image only fragments remained, particularly came to mind when Danielle faced herself in a mirror and saw strange resemblances of a woman she hardly knew.

Somehow Danielle had always felt that the stories were only half-finished—partly told. For some inexplicable reason, she had always felt the strange uncomfortable presence of words left unspoken.

"Don't be absurd," Austin would chide whenever she hinted that there was perhaps more to it than either of them knew. "You are letting your foolish romantic imagination run away with you, Danny."

Yes, she supposed she was at that, Danielle was forced to admit. She quickly slipped past the window and headed toward the kitchen. Snatching an apple from a basket of fruit on the kitchen table, she let herself out the door and nearly fell over the old woman in the process.

"Why, Grandmother!" she exclaimed. "What are you . . . I mean, we don't usually find you in this part of the house so early."

"And I'll take it you certainly were not expecting to see me here today, young lady, or you would not be dressed in such a scandalous manner with the serious intention of going outdoors," the woman saucily replied.

"Oh really, Grandmother, must you be so predictably . . . womanish?" she asked, with a mischievous glint in her eye.

"Honestly, dear, you can be so impossible at times," sighed Sophie. "If your idea of being a woman is to go recklessly riding over the countryside dressed in that outlandish costume, then I fear I shall never understand you."

"Now don't go getting upset over it," Danielle teased back. "*Besides,* what is 'being a woman,' as you put it?"

Sophie nudged past her. "I dare say, child, I have seen you flutter your lashes at enough men to know that you do not ask that question of me as seriously as you pretend to. I think you know very well what being a woman is, if I know you at all. And don't you stand there with your pretty little head tilted at me in that way, with such . . . such . . . naive defiance."

How she loved this woman who had been her friend from the very first day her father had brought her to France . . . to Chateaudun. She was a lively woman who knew how to consistently outguess her, and who occasionally threw Danielle uneasily off her guard with a hardness, the reason for which she could not guess.

"I don't suppose it has occurred to you, my dear, that most any young man in the province would be reluctant to marry a woman with whom he had to share his clothing."

"Well then, you and all the young men in France need have nothing to fear from me," Danielle replied, shooting a sidelong glance at Sophie, "for I do not ever wish to marry." She took a loud bite on the apple sending little squirts of sweet juice into the air. "From what I have seen of that type of arrangement, it appears to be one-sided in its fairness—to females in particular."

"And just what would you propose in its place?" huffed Sophie.

"Surely there *must* be an alternative," Danielle said. "I plan on choosing my lovers myself and never becoming a slave to just one man. Why should a woman confine herself to the existence of . . . of . . ." She could not find the word she needed.

"An intellectual idiot?" suggested Sophie.

"Yes, yes." Danielle agreed growing mildly agitated, amber eyes widening. "Or become a mode of pleasure for some unimaginative man at that! It seems a fate worse than death!"

"I quite agree with you, my dear," Sophie replied after considering the question. "But nevertheless, men do serve a certain basic purpose after all, and you really must try to keep that in mind. Especially when the urge overtakes you to parade around in your brother's trousers." She flicked an annoyed glance down at them, and her voice lost its playful tease. "I dare say Austin has had his hand in all of this."

"You mustn't blame Austin for this, Grandmother," Danielle said quickly, coming to her brother's aid. She knew how easy it was for Sophie to become angry at Austin, sometimes for no apparent reason. "And besides, he's on your side . . . to a degree at least. He keeps telling me how I must settle down and begin to think of marriage. I'm certain I am the victim of your little conspiracy." She laughed and put a slender arm around Sophie's shoulders, hugging the woman close to her.

"Yes, well, I'm sure Austin wants to see you married for all the wrong reasons," Sophie replied coolly.

Abruptly, Danielle broke away letting her arm slide to her side. Sophie watched her steadily while pretending to busy herself with the freshly cut flowers she had brought in from the garden. Did she imagine it, or did she perceive the slightest shadow pass over Danielle's smooth white face? Did she really see that small hint of a flash in the girl's tawny eyes, or was it just a trick of the morning sun filtering in through the open window? In an instant it was gone, leaving the old woman wondering and slightly uncomfortable with the uncertainty.

"I know both you and Austin have my best interest at heart," Danielle said, "but the whole business of courting is such a trying experience, and the thought of being bound to one man forever, as his possession, is too unthinkable. Why should I subject myself to that?"

"Why, indeed," snorted Sophie, now visibly perturbed by her granddaughter's stubbornness. "As unfortunate as it may be, it is quite difficult, Danielle, even for a woman of your obvious resources to get along in this world quite by herself."

"But, Grandmother," she exclaimed, "I could never forfeit myself to the mundane whims of some country gentleman whose hunger for adventure does not exceed the bounds of his own estate. And those city dandies. . . . Oh, they are appealing to look at, I'll grant you that. But one can so easily see through all that pomp and pretense. I am continuously embarrassed whenever one of them tries to lure me off into some darkened corner to relieve me of my virtuous upbringing. Each wants to be the first, as though the privilege of christening a virgin were somehow like a stamp of possession."

"How horribly prehistoric you make it all sound, my dear. One would hardly know from hearing you speak that this is 1871."

"I'm glad you find it so amusing," Danielle snapped. "But the fact remains that it is difficult for me to hide the feelings of distaste that overwhelm me when I am forced to play that horrid game. Oh, I say all the correct things and I'm quite adept at flirting and playing the perfect little fool. But what of *me?* Where is *my* satisfaction? What are *my* rewards for the lengths I go to to achieve such an utterly dishonorable facade? And it *is* dishonorable! You know that as well as I do!"

Her eyes were flashing now, and Sophie noted with disapproval that the anger-caused flush in her cheeks only made her that much more beautiful. She watched Danielle's mouth, one moment full and pouting, the next moment curled back over small white teeth, mouthing words that Sophie had heard before, from another time, from another's lips.

For a fleeting instant time stood still for Sophie Le Hoult and she was taken back to a time years before when her own daughter, Laura, had stood before her so defiantly, her own golden eyes flashing, desperately trying to make Sophie understand why she was leaving France to follow her young American husband, a widower, through the severities of an untamed land called Arizona—a land for which only he was equipped to survive.

Sophie had never seen her daughter again even though Richard Fleming had promised they would return. She had not come back. All that excited hunger for life lay buried beneath a pile of large stones, bleached white by the perpetual glare of the sun. It had proven too much for Laura in the end. Unable to resist, she had broken beneath the unyielding rigors, remaining behind with the land that had claimed her. Years later, Richard Fleming returned to France a wealthy man, having amassed a sizable fortune from his mining ventures. Tagging along at his side was a small wisp of a girl he had come to deposit safely with Sophie before returning to his savage homeland. In place of Laura, Richard had brought their child.

Sophie had never really liked Richard but she had found herself powerless to dissuade Laura from marrying him and running off to America. In the end, Sophie had relented and given Laura her love and her blessings, preferring to send her daughter off with a loving goodbye rather than risk leaving an unfavorable impression on the young woman's mind which could easily have been heightened by the thousands of miles that would separate them. She had even gone so far as to act as legal guardian to Richard Fleming's year-old son, Austin, by his previous wife.

The frail little boy had been hardly capable of making the hazardous journey much less living out in the middle of the hostile wilderness, and Sophie had made the offer without having to be asked, knowing that in doing so, she made it that much easier for Laura to leave her. "Don't worry, Sophie," Richard had told her so long ago, "you'll have her back again." It was a promise never kept and the light in Sophie Le Hoult's world went out. A faith broken as easily and swiftly as a dried twig over a knee.

And so, it was only natural for Sophie to cling so tenaciously to the one thing that remained of Laura—the one legacy Laura had sent back in her place—Danielle.

It was with growing apprehension that Sophie watched Danielle now, pacing about the kitchen like a restless angry cat. The sound of her voice, harsh and slightly husky from emotion, brought Sophie back to the present. "Men are not my masters," she said defiantly. She rose impatiently on her toes to look out the window. The sun had risen higher in the sky and Destiny was waiting for her at the stable. When she turned back to the room her face wore a worried expression. "You know, Grandmother, some women are braver than men. Men, for the most part, are—"

"Cowards," Sophie interrupted in a whisper.

The two women looked at each other. Yes, they understood one another, but only Sophie realized why. They were very much alike and Sophie felt as though she were gazing in a mirror at a reflection . . . beyond Danielle . . . past Laura . . . at herself in her youth—her long forgotten, disillusioned youth. But it was Danielle who stood before her at present, dressed like a boy and yet undeniably a woman. Young, beautiful, reckless Danielle.

"Don't be late, dear," Sophie said, forcing a casual tone to her voice.

Danielle's expression lingered in the old woman's eyes. The moment passed as quickly as it had taken to occur, but each woman knew their bond had been strengthened by it. Instantly Danielle returned to her lovable mischievous self, laughing as she danced out the door. "I can hardly wait for this evening when Austin returns from Paris. Do you suppose he has brought me back a present? Oh, I've missed him so!" The door closed softly behind her.

Sophie frowned and walked from the room.

If Danielle had known Austin would be back from Paris so soon she would not have stopped by the river to allow Destiny to graze on the tender grass at its edge while she slipped off into a daydream beneath the cool shade of a cypress tree. Austin's carriage was sitting in the coachhouse next to the stable, where Johnny the stableman also waited, sponge and blanket in hand for the mistress' sweating mare. When Danielle reached the house, she was panting heavily from her run across the immense expanse of lawn. She knew Austin would be in the study so she went directly there. She could never understand how he could coop himself up in that dark stuffy room, she thought as she stopped briefly to catch a glimpse of herself in the hallway mirror. Removing her cap, she ran her fingers through waist-length hair, tossing long loose strands over her shoulders, sending them cascading down her back.

More and more lately Austin had been dividing his time between the apartment he kept in Paris and the old wood-paneled study. Danielle shuddered slightly when she thought of that enormous room, dimly lit by a single lamp, its walls made up of huge wooden shelves polished to a high mahogany luster, upon which lay row upon row of books. Sometimes he would sit there for hours reading, eyes straining against the darkness long after the sun had gone down. He's probably in there right now reading, Danielle thought to herself as she adjusted her scarf about her slender white throat. She would just have to go in and divert his attention.

A strange little smile spread across her lips when she recalled how easy it was for her to distract Austin. Lately he has even begun to look at me differently. So he has finally realized that I am no longer a child, the girl thought triumphantly, forcing the wicked smile from her lips as she entered the study without knocking.

Austin Fleming's handsome face was twisted with rage as he stared down at the letter he held stiffly in his clenched hand. His brown eyes scanned the pages, burning across each line with incredible speed, absorbing every word. The fine lines that framed his mouth and sprang up at the corners of his eyes when he smiled had hardened into tight little grooves. Together with dark, closely knit brows, he looked menacing. His entire face was a frown, a hardened frown that caused Danielle to gasp slightly when she opened the door to his study and saw him sitting there.

It was only the sound of it that caught Austin's attention. He didn't know how long she had been standing there, but suddenly, upon hearing the sharp, quick intake of breath, he looked up and saw her.

Her cheeks were still flushed from the brisk morning ride through the vineyards and she looked absolutely dazzling. But the apparent ease and innocence with which she exerted this unmentionable power over him caused him to glare at her.

"Danielle, how many times must I ask you to knock when you enter this room?" He spoke more harshly than he had intended. Then, realizing how much he had missed her the past few days, he rose and went to her. Folding the letter and tucking it away in his breast pocket, he placed both hands on her shoulders and planted a firm warm kiss on her forehead. "I'm sorry, Danny," he apologized. "The ride back from Paris was long and tiring and I'm worn out. You must excuse my terseness."

"Of course I forgive you, brother dear," she said, turning her childlike gaze upon him, melting away any lasting trace of anger he might have held over her for invading his sanctuary unannounced. "You do look a bit tired. Would you like me to pour you a brandy?" she purred.

He knew why she was being purposely sweet to him. "I'm afraid you'll just have to wait until after dinner."

"Why, Austin, I really do not know what you mean," she

replied coyly, tawny eyes darting about the room for a hint of a ribboned package. Seeing nothing, she looked back to him. "What was that you were reading?"

The abruptness of the question startled him. "That was . . . It was nothing . . . Just a solicitation, of no importance."

"Austin, you really are much too obvious, and such a poor liar in the bargain. I doubt that *nothing* would cause you to look so horribly morbid."

"I think I would like a brandy after all," he said quickly. "If you'll pour me one, perhaps I can be persuaded to give you your present now instead of after dinner." He raised his eyebrow at her to see if this would take her mind off the letter folded neatly in his coat.

She poured the amber liquid into the short-stemmed crystal glass and handed it to him. "Oh, I don't know, I can probably wait until later."

She was playing with him. She did not really care what was in the letter that he was trying so hard to keep from her, but she did take a kind of delight in seeing him trying to outwit her in such a foolish way. She was about to continue the game when Austin produced a small package wrapped in silver foil. Greedily, she reached out for it.

What a spoiled child she is, Austin thought, mildly irritated at himself for encouraging it in her. But beautiful women were made for beautiful things, he reminded himself, and she was indeed a beautiful woman. Oh, how aware of that he was.

He watched her graceful hands unwrapping the paper to expose the plain white box inside. Forcing the lid back with a nudge, her eyes widened at the sight of the silver necklace lying on a bed of rich black velvet. Its stark brilliance against the soft ebony fabric stunned her, forcing a slight gasp to remain in her throat.

Fashioned into a chain of tiny links, the sterling metal shone brightly, almost overbearingly, Danielle thought. It sparkled in spite of the dimness of the room, catching flicks of the lamp on its polished surface. Then she noticed the small heart-shaped lavalier made of the same luminous substance. It had been molded so delicately, its simple fluid lines almost in direct contrast to the silver links that held it securely in place. It almost looked like it was trapped there, chained to a captor. There could be no denying that together, sterling links and silver heart, it was the most beautiful and strangely contradicting thing she had ever seen.

"Austin," she whispered. It was all she could think of to say.

"Here, let me," he said softly, taking the necklace from the box and placing it gently around her neck. When it was clasped, he grasped the heart delicately between his fingers and placed it on the pulsing spot at the base of her throat. Almost instantly he could feel the metal warming beneath his fingers, and the sensation caused his touch to linger in that spot longer than his better senses would normally have allowed.

There was something about seeing her wearing that necklace that was so right. The sterling silver used to make it had come from a place neither of them had ever been to—taken out of the ground by men whose faces they would never know—heated, melted, forged into shape by hands of strangers. All nameless men, from nameless pasts, who worked the mine—*her* mine, the Lady Laura.

The Lady Laura. The ultimate fruition of their father's dream had grown in size and scope to provide enough wealth for him to live in opulent style in America, while his son and daughter were equally well cared for back in France. Ultimately, that grand style had claimed Richard Fleming's life, and a small girl living in France had unknowingly become the heiress to one of the largest silver fortunes in the new world.

Austin knew he could not keep it from Danielle forever, and was even surprised that he had thus far managed to. He had wanted to tell her this evening, coinciding his news with the arrival of the necklace from America, having traveled to Paris himself to fetch it.

Reluctantly, Austin watched his sister skip out of the room to find the nearest mirror—such a delightful coquette. Wouldn't she just love to hear that in America she is regarded as one of its wealthiest women? Austin could just visualize the way her eyes would sparkle at the knowledge that her name was well known in a land she had never even seen, and the way her delectable little mouth would open in a wide 'Oh' of wonder. But he dared not tell her just yet.

His hand reached for the letter folded in his pocket. No, there were certain other matters to be settled first. The letter that had arrived in that morning's post from his man in St.

Louis left little doubt in Austin Fleming's mind that he could not put off his visit to America any longer. Without knowing what really awaited him there, he somehow knew that upon his eventual return to France, Danielle would finally have to be told the truth. The truth about the silver necklace she wore about her throat, the truth about why her years in France were rapidly drawing to a close, the truth about the Lady Laura, the truth about . . .

Well, all things in their time. She was still merely a child, after all.

Chapter 2

Amber eyes shiny from tears, Danielle hugged Austin close and long, refusing to let go of his neck, even as the train signaled its departure, spitting great bursts of smoke at their feet. "Austin," she cried, "I feel your going to America is somehow the last of us as we are now. I mean . . . Oh, I don't know what I mean, but it frightens me." She sobbed dismally, tears spilling from her golden eyes down her flushed cheeks.

"No, no, Danny," he murmured, lifting her chin up to meet his gaze. "The time will go quickly and I'll be back before you know it. Besides, by then you'll have a fiancé and won't want me around any longer."

Oh, how could he tease her this way, she thought angrily. Couldn't he see how upset she was? What an insensitive brute he was at times!

Austin did see and grasped her firmly by the shoulders, shaking her lightly, noting the way her eyes blazed while her lips continued to pout. Kissing her on the mouth quickly, but forcefully, he turned on his heels and fled after the train that was preceding him out of the depot.

When Danny met him at the same train station three years later, it was apparent that three years had effected many changes on each of them, mostly those brought about by a natural progression of age. At nineteen, Danielle was even more stunningly beautiful, and at twenty-four, Austin was more aware of it than ever.

Danielle found it difficult to look into his eyes, although she tried to hide her discomfort with a grand display of feigned gaiety. Austin cursed himself for allowing his emotions to show. He was embarrassed by his lack of control and sought to make up for it by oversimplifying his greeting, and when he should have taken her into his arms . . . when he longed to take her into his arms . . . he, instead, had just taken her hand and given her a light kiss on the cheek.

The ride back to Chateaudun was uncomfortable, although pleasant enough, considering the wealth of small talk at their disposal. They avoided meeting each other's eyes, almost in secret compliance.

Later that night, Austin took Danielle into the study and closed the door behind them. Then he revealed the most fabulous tales she had ever heard—tales about silver mines and fortunes. He even teased her about being an heiress, an important woman in America. He furthermore had the nerve to pat her on the head in a way that annoyed her instantly.

The city of St. Louis was bristling with electricity the spring of 1875 when Austin returned, this time with Danielle. From regions as far south as New Orleans and as far north as Canada a throng of people assembled, filling the hotels, streaming in and out of restaurants and saloons, strolling down fashionable avenues and boulevards, and stumbling out of back alleys—cowboys jostling shoulders with gentlemen, the finest southern ladies and the bawdiest barroom girls frequenting the same shops.

Even the Seventh Cavalry was represented, having just completed a reconnaissance mission into the Black Hills of the Dakota territory. Everywhere was sprinkled the blue of uniformed men, adding their numbers to the crowds. But it was not the tales of hostile Indians out West that drew the throngs. It was something else, and each life, directly or indirectly, gravitated toward it. A single word sat poised on everyone's lips. Like a sultry siren it lured some men to their pinnacles, others to their graves. Tempers flared hotly over it leaving destruction in its wake, while soft cool lips whispered eternal promises in return for it.

Gold. That beautiful mystical magnetism that drew all men to it. Such was its power that at one moment a man could be the immigrant son of an illiterate peasant, ragged and raw, and the next, if his deerhide pouch bulged with the yellow sparkling dust, could be an important man, the toast of the town of St. Louis or Chicago or New York.

Most men who found it squandered it quickly on a

sky-wheeling drunken spree. Others parlayed their meager fortunes into more wealth and power. Everyone had an opportunity to sift out as much gold as the nameless creeks would allow.

Gold—too many men's greed and too many men's obsession.

Emmett Fleming reserved rooms for his family and for his niece and nephew at the Hotel Pierre, an elegant structure in the heart of the city which boasted of numerous guests—the famous and the infamous. While Austin dispensed with the formalities of registering and arranging for a messenger to inform their uncle of their arrival, Danielle slipped off to the side to look around.

The furnishings were splendid, to say the least, with floors heavily carpeted in rich red-piled velvet, and the walls adorned to the ceiling in mirrors. There was no mistaking the expensive opulence of the main lobby that sprawled beneath the glittering brilliance of a massive crystal chandelier suspended above it all.

The lobby was filled with activity and those who entered appeared to be oblivious to the elegance around them. They did not stroll. They did not venture outside for a cup of tea on the garden patio the way people in France were so apt to do on a sunny afternoon. Instead, the women bustled past her and the men walked about briskly as though they were all late for an appointment.

Danielle wandered back to the desk while her brother concluded arrangements with the clerk. Austin lay the quill-tipped pen across the page of the register and stood back to watch the clerk turn the big book around and examine the signature.

"*Monsieur Fleming.* Of course, sir. We have your rooms all ready for you."

There was no mistaking the obviously obsequious tone, and Danielle turned away from him with a frown. It was the same tone she had heard used by every other person with whom they had come in contact since they stepped foot on these shores: the stationmasters, the coachmen, the maitre d's, the business associates. How suddenly polite and gracious people became at the sound of the Fleming name. Smiling briefly at the desk clerk she followed Austin up to their rooms.

In spite of it, it really was intriguing—the sights she had seen so far and the names she had heard were as if it were all

right out of a dream. Just now she overheard two men
speaking about the Seventh Cavalry—another mystery to her.
Why, this city is positively throbbing, she thought.

If Danielle were not a stranger, she would have realized the
sizzling atmosphere in St. Louis was in some way connected
to the presence in town of all those soldiers.

She would have recognized in a flash the name of the
colorful commander of the Seventh, General George Custer,
who, a year earlier, with his own regiment, ten others, two
infantry companies, a three-inch Rodman gun and three
Gatling guns, a train consisting of one hundred wagons, that
many Indian scouts, white scouts, guides and a handful of
interpreters, all by Presidential order, on the morning of July
2, 1874 had marched out of Fort Abraham Lincoln in the
Dakota territory, in column, heading southwest toward the
Black Hills.

They rode through a region of the country that had seldom
been seen by anyone other than the Indians, their wagon
wheels churning over areas where dinosaur bones jutted out
of rocky crevices. The geologists accompanying the train were
disgruntled at the sickening thought of leaving behind all
those treasures of the past. The troopers complained bitterly
of the tiring pace, made intolerable by the heat of the treeless
prairie. Temperatures rose over one hundred degrees and
tempers flared equally as hot, but the column had pushed
onward.

After three weeks on the march the column had pulled up
to the approach of the Hills, camping for the night at the site
of Inyan Kara, an extinct volcano at the western edge of the
range. The Crow and Pawnee Indian scouts refused to go a
step further, becoming greatly agitated when the column
packed up its gear in the morning and continued its march.
Afraid of what would happen to them if they passed through
the Hills, vilifying the sacred place of the Sioux, they
cautiously held back as the last wagon disappeared in a cloud
of hot dust.

Three days later the company entered the Hills, and the
sight that overtook them moved the aesthetic senses of even
the most toughened soldier. There, growing wildly and
untouched, the land was covered by wild flowers in bloom
with currants and huckleberries, strawberries and gooseber-
ries, ripe and succulent. The game was abundant; the air crisp
and clear. It was as near to perfection as one could possibly

get. The atmosphere was relaxed and conducive to easy careless living until a week later when they found what they had come looking for. Gold. The miners exploring French Creek had raced back to camp shouting of the find at the tops of their lungs. In no time, small joint stock companies were formed by the troopers and talk was that gold, in paying quantities, could be found in every stream that ran through the Hills. An urgent message was dispatched at once to bring word of the discovery to those waiting back East.

By the middle of summer the column headed out of the Hills, camping briefly at a place called Bear Butte, then pushed hard to cover the distance to Fort Lincoln as quickly as possible. The ride back had been even more difficult than the one there. Compared to the lushness of the Hills, the prairie seemed even drier and hotter and dustier than before, with signs of hostile Indians all around.

The sensation had preceded them, and by the time they arrived, hundreds of citizens were busy making preparations to go to the Black Hills to seek their fortunes, while hundreds of others were busy scheming ways to make their fortunes by supplying the food, horses, wagons, equipment, guns—whatever was required by those men who were willing to risk their lives at the hands of hostile Sioux Indians.

From all over the country men began to pour into the territory and their increasing numbers created the one major embarrassment the United States Government could not explain—that the Black Hills of the Dakotas were the property of the Sioux Indians, not the United States.

Zoe Fleming squealed with delight when another column of soldiers rode into the city, their horses kicking up huge swirls of dust. She called Danielle to the window with frantic hand movements.

"Oh, Danny, look at this! You must come here!"

Zoe Fleming had matured into a lovely young woman, so different from the gangling little cousin Danielle remembered from many years ago. But she was just as bubbling, just as flowing with effervescence as she had been then, in spite of the sad circumstances of their previous meeting.

It was almost as though Zoe could not help herself, and Danielle found it absolutely refreshing. She also found it easier to be herself around someone who, to her utter pleasure, possessed a devilry equal to her own.

Zoe had inherited her mother's fair complexion and pale blond hair, but her hazel eyes were a gift from her father. She was quite a beauty at the age of eighteen, with many beaux, and hinted to Danielle in excited whispers that there were so many young men about town these days—mostly army officers, dashing and oh, so gallant.

Aunt Jane and Zoe had come to Danielle's room shortly after she had made herself comfortable, bringing with them a young black woman whom they introduced as Dossie and who, they informed her, quite matter-of-factly, would be acting as Danielle's personal maid.

The girl could not have been much older than Danielle or Zoe. She was very pretty with dark flashing eyes and black, tightly curled hair cut close to her head.

Without waiting for instructions, she quickly unpacked Danielle's baggage and saw to her toiletries, while Aunt Jane rattled on about how happy she was to see Danielle, and did she have a good trip, and she hoped her stay in America would be a pleasant one.

Yet, the woman could not hide the disapproving frown on her dour face when she spotted a dress with a plunging neckline that Dossie was hanging in the armoire. It was one of the latest Parisian creations that Danielle had bought during one last shopping spree in Paris before boarding the ship for America.

"Mother, won't you be late for your meeting?"

"Oh my, yes, Zoe, I'm so glad you reminded me. I'm so sorry, dear," she said to Danielle. "The ladies of the Auxiliary Committee are meeting at the church this afternoon and well, as coordinator, I really must be there."

Stiff petticoats rustled beneath her plain brown linen dress as she hastily gathered her things and prepared to leave.

"And remember, dear, we shall expect you and your brother to dine with us in our suite this evening. Oh, and, Zoe, be sure you stop off at Mr. Dietrich's to see if those bolts of fabric have come—the ones I ordered last month."

The door closed behind her, but they could still hear her voice, issuing orders as she scurried off down the hall.

Zoe rolled her eyes toward the heavens in mock exasperation, and the two young women laughed out loud in mutual sympathy. Then, whirling her skirts about her, Zoe flounced onto the bed.

"Dossie, put those things down right now and come here

with us," she said, pulling her white gloves off and patting the bed beside her.

"Sure thing, Miss Zoe." The black girl flashed her a bright smile.

As Danielle soon came to realize, Zoe Fleming was an ardent admirer and active pursuer of the opposite sex. And it was obvious that her relationship with Dossie went further than that of mistress and maid. They appeared to be genuine friends, sharing the deepest secrets each had to hold. However, it was Dossie who was clearly the more intelligent of the two, in spite of her subordinate position.

Unlike Zoe, she had never had proper schooling, nor were her manners quite as refined. Also unlike Zoe, she possessed a sensitivity and an awareness which surprised and delighted Danielle. Dossie's intellect extended beyond the narrow confines of her immediate world, and Danny quickly learned that Dossie had a feeling for things that went far deeper than her background and upbringing would have encouraged or allowed. She tolerated Zoe's forgetfulness and even helped conspire with the girl on elaborate ways to steal away at night when everyone else was asleep to meet whatever young man was waiting in the shadows beneath the window. She even gracefully put up with Zoe's constant ribbing—retaliating with teasing of her own, though always careful not to hurt or embarrass Zoe.

Several hours later Dossie began to fidget nervously and Zoe demanded to know what the matter was.

"It's just that if your mama comes back and finds you didn't go over Mista Dietrich's for them bolts of cloth, she's gonna be frightful mad."

"Oh, you're right," Zoe whined, reluctant to get up and leave. She sat for a moment contemplating the force behind her mother's anger should she not obey. Then, with a shrug of her slender shoulders she jumped up. "Okay, I'll go and see about the cloth. But, Dossie, you take Danny over to the millinery shop on Rue Des Mares and pick out some nice hats and I'll meet you there in about forty-five minutes. Oh, and Danny, be a dear and stop by my father's office on the way. Dossie will show you where it is. Be sure that my father doesn't keep that handsome brother of yours away from us tonight or I shall be very upset. See you later!" With a wave of her hand she was out the door singing softly to herself all the way down the hall.

Danny did not have much of an appetite by the time dinner rolled around. After checking in and then being whisked around town by Dossie and Zoe, her entire system seemed to be a bit out of sorts. Nevertheless, she arrived at her aunt and uncle's suite promptly at eight on the arm of her brother.

Zoe's eyes lit up when they were shown to the parlor. She ran up to them, taking Danny by the hand and reaching up to place a kiss on Austin's cheek. Danny smiled at Austin's blush, but Zoe never even noticed it.

Dinner was pleasant enough and in the short span of two hours Danny learned all about the Women's Auxiliary Committee—of which Jane Fleming was founder and chairwoman—whose principal aim and exhaustive effort were devoted to converting the more hedonistic element of the city to the truer, more spiritual pleasures of the Christian church. She also learned of her cousin's reluctance to leave the bristling atmosphere of St. Louis to return to the monotonously drab existence in Colorado.

"But surely Bennett, Colorado, must be as grand as St. Louis," Danny surmised, wondering why Zoe's obvious love of city life would extend to one city and not another.

"You see," Emmett Fleming spoke up, "Bennett is not as . . . well, it's not quite as, shall we say, civilized as St. Louis is. Bennett is still a pretty raw city by these terms, so I'm afraid Zoe doesn't get much opportunity to go there."

"That's right, Danny," Zoe agreed. "Father doesn't think Bennett is the kind of place a lady should frequent, and he forbids me to go there." There was a note of bitterness in Zoe's voice.

"Actually," Emmett said, ignoring his daughter's remark, "I have my firm's headquarters in Bennett, but we live about forty miles west of there. I also travel to St. Louis quite often on business and I bring my family along with me." He glanced at Zoe who remained tight-lipped. "So, I wouldn't feel too sorry for Zoe if I were you, Danielle. She has plenty of opportunity to taste big city life. Perhaps she has failed to mention that she has also been to New York *and* Chicago *and* San Francisco *and* Paris *and* London."

Danny could tell by the way he patted Zoe's hand and smiled at her that he wasn't really angry. What she did not know, and what Zoe herself could not have known in spite of her whining protests, was that Emmett was aware that at times he was a little too strict with her. He really wouldn't have been if it were not for the fact that there was so much to be protected from in this still untamed country. And at times that meant alienating his only child because of the forceful, but necessary, restrictions he placed on her.

It was clear by Emmett's eagerness to change the subject that they had covered this ground many times before. Danny was slightly annoyed when it suddenly occurred to her that people always seemed to be quickly changing subjects around here. Why, just that afternoon while out shopping, they had nearly been run down by a horse and rider. When Danny had questioned Dossie about the strange coloration of the horse—dappled with black and gray splotches across its rump—the girl diverted the question. And then, when Austin had come to call for dinner, she had questioned him about his afternoon with Uncle Emmett. He appeared to be downright evasive. He had just side-stepped her questions entirely. Instead, he had circled her waist lightly and whisked her out the door. He had mentioned something about leaving St. Louis in a few days in an effort to change the subject, and when they reached Emmett's door, it had seemed to Danny that Austin was too eager to get inside.

Zoe left the table and went to the fireplace where Austin stood admiring a painting above the mantle. Danny felt her annoyance diminish as she watched her cousin flirting with Austin. She excused herself from the table and joined Emmett on the sofa.

"Uncle Emmett, how long will the train ride take to get from here to Bennett? After that dreadful ocean voyage and the long train ride from New York, I don't think I could withstand another grueling ride."

"Well, ordinarily it would take about a day." Emmett hoped she had not noticed his qualification.

But Danny was her usual alert self despite her weariness. "Ordinarily? What do you mean? I assume we'll be traveling by rail to Bennett. That *is* what I was told." She cast a quick look across the room to where Austin stood at the fireplace, one arm resting on the mantle, deep in conversation with Zoe.

"Yes, I know, dear," Emmett said, "but, um, we had a little . . . well, we had some trouble over that way and the rail was torn up some. We'll have to go by wagon, I'm afraid."

"Wagon!" Danny's eyes flared and her mouth fell open.

"I'm sorry, Danielle, but I'm afraid there's nothing we can

do about it." His voice had a tone of finality about it, and Danny knew it was useless to argue.

"But what happened?"

Emmett Fleming frowned. "The fact is the rail was ripped up about eighty miles out of Bennett so the only way to get into the city for now is by wagon or horseback."

"Who on earth would do such a thing?"

"*Indians.*" Emmett said the word with an obvious contempt that he made no attempt to hide.

Danny studied the situation in her mind. "Do you suppose it will be safe for us to travel by wagon if the Indians are angry?" She rose from the sofa and began to pace the floor in front of Emmett. "They could attack the wagons, couldn't they?"

"That would be unlikely." Danny turned as Austin approached.

"And why not, may I ask? If they ripped up miles of iron rail, who's to say they would not attack a wagon train? Surely there'll be some things of value in those wagons—provisions maybe. Why, I heard someone say that the Indians are starving. Perhaps they would rob us for the food."

"Where did you hear that?" Emmett asked.

"This morning I overheard one man tell another that the Indians are starving on the reservations, that they are being forced to relocate, sometimes traveling hundreds of miles away from their homes, and how—"

"That's very touching, dear, but the fact remains that it was Indians who tore up that track, and because of them, you'll be traveling to Bennett by wagon."

She turned to Austin. "Well, you still have not told me how you know we won't be attacked."

"Because, Danny, we'll be escorted to Bennett by an armed unit. The men of the Seventh Cavalry are returning to their posts out West and Emmett has arranged with the Army for them to accompany us."

"Oh, I can hardly believe it!" cried Zoe. "Danny, don't you know what this means? It will take weeks to get to Colorado by wagon. *Weeks,* Danny, escorted by the Seventh Cavalry!"

Emmett cast a scornful look at his daughter. "I thought you would find that a pleasant bit of news, Zoe."

"Yes, Father," she saucily replied. "I find it most pleasant indeed. Perhaps even more so, knowing that *you* don't, and there is nothing either of us can do about it." She grabbed Danny by the hand and hurried off to the far end of the room before Emmett could react to her blatant impertinence.

Emmett Fleming sighed and walked to the liquor cabinet where he withdrew a bottle of brandy. He poured two glasses and carried them over to Austin, handing one to his nephew and keeping the other for himself. Swirling the brandy gently in his glass, he glanced at the two young women giggling in the corner. It was several moments before he spoke. "She looks very much like Laura," he said softly. "I had almost forgotten how beautiful Laura was until I saw Danielle. I'll never forget the first time Richard came home with her. They had just come from France where he had met her. Beautiful woman." His words trailed off somewhere with his thoughts, as though he were seeing ghostly images of the past.

"Tell me," he said, shaking himself loose from whatever had taken hold of him, "how is Sophie? Now there's a fine woman for you." Emmett's recollections of Sophie Le Hoult were pleasant ones. He remembered the woman from the one and only time he had met her when he had journeyed to France, bringing Zoe along, to tell Austin and Danielle of their father's death. Being Richard's only brother, Emmett had felt it his duty, but his nervousness at being the bearer of ill news was quickly put at ease by the spirited Sophie.

"Ah, Sophie . . . Yes, Sophie is a fine woman," Austin agreed, reflecting on his grandmother with a strange mixture of fondness and apprehension. He had always felt that way toward her and had never really known why. "She's doing well."

The brandy was beginning to loosen Emmett Fleming up and he talked freely now, visibly more relaxed. Even his suit appeared to sit better on his tall frame. "It's not as though every woman would take in a strange man's son. Yes, she certainly is a rare person, I would say." Emmett was beginning to feel good. "I'll bet you sure were happy when Richard returned to France four years later with his little girl. Must have been lonely over there for a kid, with just Sophie and a bunch of servants in that big house. Yeah, you sure must've been glad to see Danielle. You know, she looks more like Laura than Laura did."

"Emmett, what a foolish thing to say," Jane Fleming

scolded as she approached and took her place on the sofa, followed closely by a servant who placed a serving tray on the small table in front of her.

"You've got to admit, Jane, that Danielle looks amazingly like her mother," Emmett persisted, the effect of the brandy making him just a bit bolder with his wife than he normally would have cared to be.

"I don't deny that, dear, although for the life of me I can't understand why you find it so amazing. They were mother and daughter after all." She glanced up at her husband to see him finishing the last of the brandy, and she could see his face through the fishbowl bottom of the brandy snifter he held up to his mouth. Through the glass he looked all swollen, his eyes and nose blown up to near-comical proportions. But Jane Fleming could not laugh, not when she recognized the familiar signs of increasing inebriation in him. She viewed it all with distaste. After all, she reasoned, how would it look for the chairwoman of the St. Louis Auxiliary Committee to preach against the sins of decadence when she herself lived with a man whose soul was surely headed for hell if he did not curb his abhorrent love for alcohol. She turned away from him with a disdainful look and spoke to her nephew. "Tea, Austin?"

Austin's tone was apologetic. "No, thank you, Aunt Jane. It's late and we should go." He had not missed the animated signals from his sister.

Back in her room Danny did not go to sleep immediately. She was exhausted all right, but her mind was alert and racing with a million thoughts. All this was so new to her—this country—this city—even the dazzling and obvious impact of her own name.

Chapter 3

The Fleming name was steeped in controversy for it carried such power and influence that it had no choice but to pick up flack along the way in its rise to the top of the country's rapidly growing commercial interests. It was known with the subtle impact of a thing that, while never actually before one's eyes, was always imbedded deeply in one's soul. For it carried with it the thought, and the silent hope, that any man could rise from the dregs with nothing but his talents and his keen ambition to carve a name for himself. The Fleming name somehow kept that dream alive in men's hearts, and as the hope continued to grow, so the name of Fleming grew with it, at times slandered for, but at all times, furthered by, its wealth.

Everyone knew the story of how Emmett Fleming had taken a floundering enterprise and slowly brought it back to health, putting its pieces back together again. He had saved it from the madness of his brother, Richard, who had sought to destroy the empire he had built with his own hands, until nothing remained of it . . . until the only proof of one man's intense struggle for something undefined within himself lay locked inside the heart of a madman, and the madman lay locked in the heart of the earth.

Richard could never adjust to his wealth, Emmett had decided about his brother, noting with satisfaction how well he himself seemed suited to it.

Emmett had genuinely grieved when his only brother had died at the age of thirty-eight, ending his seemingly relentless pursuit of endless debauchery. Emmett could never understand why Richard let it all slip through his fingers, choosing to die lonely and impoverished.

Laura's death had been a grievous blow to Richard, but when Emmett had seen him after that, there were no signs of the madness that eventually drove Richard Fleming to take his own life. Twice before that he had tried, and twice before he had failed, and Emmett had stood by helplessly watching his brother destroy himself for a reason Emmett guessed never even existed.

Almost overnight, Richard turned his back on his work, his life, leaving the remains to the poachers and looters who would have succeeded in taking it all had Emmett not stepped in. Richard had worked too hard simply to abandon everything. Something had gone wrong. But what? Even if Richard no longer cared, Emmett did. He would save it from his brother!

And he did. He worked with his bare hands at the Lady Laura, all through those horrible times when Richard stood by laughing at him. But still Emmett worked, and what had once possessed his brother, had somehow taken hold of him, too, in his singular determination to keep the mine alive.

Year after year he worked in that horrible black hole, the flesh ripping from his hands as he tore furiously at jagged stone slabs—deposited by quick lethal avalanches, trapping men alive behind them, slowly sucking the air from them until they suffocated in a slow wailing agony. His ears would pound and nearly burst from the force of the single deadly boulder that would come crashing down upon a startled man from out of nowhere, crushing him, killing him instantly—mercifully.

In time, Emmett was able to raise the production of the mine enough to pay men's salaries again, and to allow him to manage its affairs from a small office in Phoenix, which was easier for business associates to reach than the mine site at Winslow.

When the Apache situation became too heated in Arizona, Emmett, then with a wife and child to care for, wisely moved his office to Bennett. He was one notch above and hundreds of miles away from that wretched site in the side of the mountain that had claimed too many men's lives in its stubborn fight to retain its silvery treasures—too many men, including his own brother. Somehow, Emmett Fleming had always felt that the Lady Laura was directly responsible for

Richard's death, even though Richard had, in actuality, died in the arms of some old French whore in New Orleans.

After Richard's death, Emmett had seriously considered giving up the business and selling his shares for the handsome price offered by some of the big eastern mining interests. But he could never bring himself to do it. The Lady Laura remained his last tangible link to his brother, and besides, he had a family to think of. That, combined with his growing sense of ambition, spurred Emmett Fleming on to increase the mine's output and enhance his own fortune which, as the years slipped by, grew by leaps and bounds.

One day, as Emmett had sat hunched over the ledgers, a man came bursting into the office waving a piece of paper around wildly. "Whooeee!" he yelled, startling Emmett half out of his seat. "Lookit here, Mista Fleming, just lookit here!"

Emmett had grabbed the paper out of his hands and his eyes opened wide as he read the words printed plainly across the telegram. *Mother Lode.* Sweet Jesus, they had struck it rich! Emmett had jumped out of his seat as though a stick of dynamite had suddenly exploded beneath him. "Whooeee!" he cried, slapping the old man on the back. He had run from the office all the way up the hill to the small wooden house on Walnut Street to tell the news to Jane.

A previously unexposed shaft revealed a vein of silver ore equal to, if not greater than, that of the Silver Clip mine of Colorado, already a legend in its time. The prospects were sweet, but even Emmett could not have guessed then how the Lady Laura would surpass the Silver Clip, the Bear Claw and the Old Number Seven all put together.

Several years later when Emmett heard his name mentioned in influential circles, both social and political, and the Lady Laura continued to produce silver, he began to consider the advantages of a political career in the future. By then, one mine had expanded into two, and two mines had grown into a thriving business enterprise with the U.S. Government. It was sponsored by friends in Washington and it grew more lucrative each year as the government's need for silver insured Emmett of a constant source of income.

The profits had been used to build an empire, and ironically, were now dwarfed in relation to the expanse of the Fleming scope. Its reach extended down into Texas where vast herds of longhorn cattle bearing the Fleming brand grazed, growing fat and commanding high prices at the summer cattle markets of El Paso and Abilene. The fingers of the Fleming network even laced their way into the upper regions of the Missouri River where a thriving fur industry had all but depleted the waters of its principal source of income, the beaver. There were several thousand acres of the richest timber country in the world located in Canada. But it was not all glory, and the defeats, when they came, were stunning.

One morning Emmett had been sitting in his barber's chair awaiting his daily compress of steaming towels in preparation for his shave when something caught his eye as he leaned forward to flick some cigar ashes into the ashtray. A partial headline from the *Bennett Herald* leaped out at him. The Lady Laura robbed! Shipments attacked as they left Winslow. What was this? Springing from his chair, he whipped the cloth from his neck and stormed out of the barber shop toward his office.

"What is this about the Lady Laura being robbed!" he had bellowed before he was even in the door. "Why was I not informed of this? Why did I have to read it in *last week's* headlines? Damn it! And how is it that a band of marauding Indians can swoop down out of nowhere and attack those shipments of silver? I thought I had issued strict instructions that every shipment out of Winslow was to be escorted by an armed unit!"

Emmett had stalked about the small office in a rage, puffing savagely on his cigar, trying to think clearly. "Okay, you . . . Wilkens, you get this message to Colonel Chivington. You tell him that unless those shipments are protected, I will hold him personally responsible. I want this thing stopped before it can happen again. If they think they can—"

"It's happened before, Emmett." The voice belonged to Carl Forrester. Although he was one of the few men Fleming really trusted, Emmett glared at him as though the man were a faceless liar. Carl Forrester swallowed hard and faced his boss. "I'm sorry, but it's true. We thought we could take care of it. And for a while we figured we had it licked, but—"

"What on earth! Carl, how long has this been going on?"

Carl Forrester knew he couldn't keep the truth from his

boss any longer, so he took a deep breath and told him how those annoying Indian raids had turned into deadly bouts of armed conflict. "At first they would ride up whooping and yelling and firing their rifles into the air to frighten us. But it never stopped the shipments from going out. Lately . . . well . . . it's gotten worse."

"How much worse, Carl?" Emmett was perturbed that he had to pull the information out of the man.

"We've lost a few men—three. No, four."

Emmett had remained silent for a long time. Then he had expelled a long low breath. "Do me a favor, would you? Get a letter off to my nephew in France. He has to know about this."

Later, alone in his office, Emmett Fleming poured himself a shot of whiskey and drank it down straight and quick. Then he settled himself back in his chair with his feet propped up on the desk, the bottle close at hand. He lit another cigar and stared out the small window at nothing in particular. How ironic it all was. Here he was fretting over this problem with the Lady Laura when the mine had never really belonged to him in the first place. No matter that he had poured his own sweat and blood into it. Somehow, Emmett could not help but feel that Richard had played a final cruel joke on him by willing the ownership of the Lady Laura to his young daughter, Danielle. How strange that he had not willed it to Austin. Why the girl and not the boy? Oh well, just one more mystery to plague Emmett about his brother.

When the boy, Austin, had shown a keen interest in the affairs his father had left behind, Emmett Fleming knew it was merely a matter of time before he would be compelled to cede him control of the Lady Laura over to his nephew. Well, it didn't really matter all that much anymore. There was so much else that he owned, and the Lady Laura had made it all possible. He may have brought the mine back to life after Richard left it to rot, but he did it all knowing that it was never really his. And so, with increasing frequency, he had dispatched regular communications to his nephew in France, informing him as to the progress of their combined interest.

Emmett had wondered that night what Austin's reaction would be when he learned that their silver had been stolen by the Sioux. What the hell were the Sioux doing this far south?

There were too many things left unanswered about this

whole affair. No one knew about those shipments except a
handful of men who, he had thought, could all be trusted. He
had made them all wealthy. What would be the sense
in . . . No, it was too wild to even consider. And yet. . . . His
mind recalled their names: Carl Forrester, Charlie Whittaker,
Frank Merrington, George Hyde . . . his assistants who
would stand to lose everything. Of course, Austin knew about
all this since Emmett had ordered his staff to keep him
informed. It was possible, but highly unlikely, for those
dispatches to have been intercepted. Possible. He'd have his
staff check into it first thing in the morning, however, just in
case.

One key word kept popping into his thoughts, creating an
uneasiness that he would have given anything to do without.
Who? The word burned on his mind. Who else knew about
those shipments except a few select men . . . and all those
damned Indians?

Carl Forrester had been careful to word his letter to Austin
so as not to cause undue alarm, but it was impossible to
disguise the facts even beneath a casual tone and an occasional attempt at humor. The response which arrived forthwith
from France informed them that young Fleming would be
coming soon to look over matters first hand.

Emmett had looked forward to Austin's arrival with a
measure of trepidation, having only met his nephew once,
and that was many years before, when he had gone to France
carrying the news of Richard's death. He had observed that
the twenty-one-year-old Austin did not physically resemble
Richard at all, and at first it disturbed him. The young man
had a sensitive nature, almost feminine, Emmett decided.
But Austin carried it all off so naturally, in such a way as to
eradicate any question whatsoever as to his masculinity,
which was ever present.

Emmett was mildly pleased when Austin had expressed his
eagerness to learn the business, and at the young man's
insistence they had set out immediately for Winslow, Arizona
to visit the mine site. When Emmett returned to St. Louis
several weeks later, he had returned alone, leaving Austin
behind in Winslow at his own insistence. Austin stayed there
for three years, working at the mine as Emmett himself had
done, as Richard had done before him. Austin had shunned
the offer to learn the business from the St. Louis office,
informing his uncle that he preferred to learn from the old

miners, learning the intricacies of the business slowly, irrevocably.

When Austin had eventually returned to St. Louis he had seemed different, harder somehow, and more withdrawn. It was disturbing and had put Emmett ill at ease. Undeniably, the young man's soft edge had hardened like steel, and Emmett could not truthfully say that he had been sorry to see his nephew depart for Europe.

Chapter 4

Emmett Fleming thought that aside from the pleasure it would give him to escort his niece to the party, it would also not hurt his professional image to be seen with such a dazzling beauty on his arm.

When he rapped lightly on her door he was not prepared for the sight that awaited him. There stood Danielle, her shiny, dark auburn hair piled fashionably atop her head in an array of delicate curls, held in place by an exquisite ivory comb. Just a few wispy tendrils escaped the comb to fall softly against her neck.

Emmett blinked several times. Had she come to the door naked? My God! But as his eyes adjusted to the dimmed light inside her room, he breathed a sigh of relief when he realized that it was the color of the dress she was wearing. It was peach, almost flesh-toned, and upon closer scrutiny he did not fail to notice how the sheer fabric clung seductively to her slender body, emphasizing all those sweet young curves. Its elegance was enhanced by its unadornment for its only decoration was a single silk ribbon laced provocatively along the edge of the neckline, which itself plunged daringly low, revealing the contours of her small firm breasts.

When she stepped out into the brightly lit hallway he noticed the necklace about her throat. "A gift from Austin," she said. "Fashioned from silver mined from the Lady Laura." She beamed at Emmett, obviously proud to be wearing such a dazzling piece. It was the only item of jewelry she wore, yet it had more of an impact than an entire roomful of women wearing diamonds and rubies. The simplicity of her gown and locket gave her a look of smoldering innocence, if such a thing were possible. Emmett would have been inclined to think not if he had not seen it for himself.

He escorted her into the ballroom, noticing the stares and wide-mouthed expressions the girl created as she passed through the lobby. He led her to the gentleman whose eye he had caught from across the room. "George, may I introduce my niece, Mademoiselle Danielle Fleming. Danielle has just recently arrived from France."

She smiled demurely, lowering her lashes at the man in the blue uniform of the United States Army. He took her hand in his and pressed his lips firmly against it.

"Danielle, this is my good friend, General George Custer." Emmett completed the introduction, noting with slight disapproval that the general's eyes lingered a trifle too long on his niece.

"Mademoiselle, I would be honored if you would join me in the next waltz," Custer said, unable to take his eyes from her face.

"The pleasure would be mine, Monsieur Custer," she replied in French, smiling with satisfaction at the obviously pleasing effect she had on him. Then, lifting the hem of her gown, she spun off to catch up with her uncle who had managed to disappear within the thickening crowd. He's probably gone after a potential constituent, Danny thought, as she peered through the hazy room. Where was he? She stood on her tiptoes, growing more annoyed by the minute because she could not see above the heads.

It was from that position that Danny suddenly felt herself lifted into the air by a pair of strong hands whose firm grasp about her small waist caused her to gasp out loud from the sudden expulsion of air from her lungs.

"That better, ma'am?" a voice drawled from somewhere down in the crowd. With surprise registered on her face, she looked down into a pair of the most astonishingly bright gray eyes she had ever seen. They were steel gray and seemed to look at her in a contemptuous sort of amusement.

"Monsieur, what are you doing? Put me down at once," she demanded in French. Her surprise was quickly giving way to anger. When he refused to comply, she began to kick about, trying to free herself from his constricting grasp.

"Take it easy there, little wildcat," he laughed, finally letting her slide down in front of him so that now she looked up at him instead of down. But, instead of releasing her, he pulled her closer to him so that she stood pressed against the length of his six-foot frame, held there by his strong arm circled tightly about her waist.

Immediately, she felt his unmistakable rising desire beneath his tightly fitting black chino pants. Her eyes narrowed in irritation becoming slits of amber. She spoke between gritted teeth. "You presume too much, Monsieur."

"Some things are difficult for a man to control, ma'am," he said, his voice low and mocking.

Oh, what an arrogant man he was! How dare he treat her as though she were one of those saloon girls Zoe had told her about. He was holding her so closely, surely everyone must see it, she thought, trying to hide her embarrassment. His eyes raked over her so shamelessly that she felt weakened beneath their glare.

Suddenly, the room filled with music and the people who had been milling about paired off as though on cue, moving across the dance floor to the compelling rhythm of the waltz.

Without the crowd to conceal his actions, Alex Coulter had no choice but to move with it, bringing the reluctant girl along with him. If she didn't put up a fuss, he just might be able to make it to the side door without calling too much attention to himself. Beyond that door lay the patio, opening out onto a garden—displaying an intricate network of footpaths and alcoves where it would be possible to disappear.

"I hope you didn't promise this dance to someone else," he said, tightening his hold and keeping her squirming to a minimum.

"Monsieur, *non*," she gasped against his ear, as she was swept up against him, all too conscious of his tight muscles flexing beneath the blue linen shirt he wore. He glided her across the floor weaving in and out of the other couples.

"Please, you are hurting me," she cried, her voice laced with frustration.

Heedless of her demands, he danced her right out of the crowded room and into the night—past the brightly lit torch lights that framed the stone patio, down the wide steps and onto the lawn—well beyond the building.

The music was close enough to hear, but far enough away so that Danny could not tell, for a moment or two, from which direction it came. It seemed to surround her from all sides and close in over her.

As abruptly as he had whisked her away, he let her go. The

sudden release of the pressure against her lungs caused
Danny to pant for the breath she had been denied in his hold.
They came to a stop beside a tall thicket at a point where a
small footpath ventured out from the larger lane on which
they stood.

She whirled to face him, planting her feet firmly. Mindless
of fear, but speechless with anger, she glared at him, in an
effort to collect herself. She wanted to tell this brute of a
man . . . this rake . . . exactly what she thought of him.

It was then that she noticed his face—all of it, that is, not
just his eyes. She felt herself taken aback by its vivid
handsomeness. For an instant, the anger fell away exposing
something infinitely more difficult for her to deal with . . . if
for no other reason than that she did not know what it was.

Her mind worked frantically to name this new sensation
that crept over her as she studied his face. The black straight
brows only enhanced the brilliance of his eyes . . . so light in
color that they seemed to go right through her . . . to pierce
her very core.

His thick ebony hair, allowed to grow in an unruly crop of
curls, extended down his handsome face in long sideburns
that gave him a rather Spanish look, she decided.

Unexpectedly, she saw his mouth widen into a grin,
exposing flashing white teeth, and it occurred to Danny that
he was laughing at her.

Feeling the fury mount within her, and oblivious to the
unnerving distraction of his good looks, she opened her
mouth to speak—to put him in his place. But no sooner had
the words had a chance to form on her lips, than the sound of
voices caught her attention, causing her to remain with her
lips slightly parted.

One voice sounded vaguely familiar, but before Danny
could turn in its direction, she felt herself once more taken
into strong arms. This time the stranger was pulling her off
into the shrubs, bringing his mouth down upon hers in one
swift, violent motion.

Danny was unable to move from the hold he had on her.
With one arm wrapped securely about her waist and one
around her shoulders, he pressed her to him, crushing her
rigid body against his, bruising her mouth with his savage-
ness.

When she felt his tongue force its way between her parted
lips she grew weak. She fell against him unable to support her

own weight. But when his probing tongue sought out the corners of her mouth she felt his hand slip from her shoulder and fondle her breasts beneath the thin fabric of her gown. Sheer fury allowed her to summon enough strength to beat helplessly against his chest.

What was he doing! What kind of animal was he! she thought frantically, fearing she would faint from the utter horror of his assault. Dimly, amidst the roar of her own mind, and stifled protests, Danny again heard faint voices as they passed somewhere close by. Her mind reeled with confusion and outrage. She was not sure what she heard, or if she even heard anything at all.

Instantly, she was back on her feet again, though feeling wobbly.

"I know what you're thinking, Miss Fleming."

He knew her name! The impudent rake must have . . . somehow . . . known who she was, and still he had treated her in such a shabby way! Oh, it was all too much!

"I don't want you to think that I actually . . . er . . . attacked you . . . I—"

"Your outrageous actions leave little room for dispute," she spat at him, smoothing the wrinkles from her dress absentmindedly. "If that is the type of treatment a woman can expect from you, then it is no wonder, *sir*, that you must pull them off into dark corners to molest them!"

Slipping back and forth from French to English, she stood defiantly before this perfect stranger—her eyes blazing in anger.

"You are the most disgusting and arrogant man I have ever met! How dare you carry me off like a piece of baggage and abuse me in such a manner! Why, I should have you flogged for your insolence . . . arrested . . . thrown into the blackest dungeon to rot where you belong!"

Alex Coulter flicked a contemptuous glance at her, but she kept on, ignoring the abrupt change she saw in his eyes. They had become dark now, cold and distant, but no less penetrating.

"Spare me your tirades." His voice was low and menacing, and she shrank from it, startled. A moment ago, he had seemed almost as though the entire episode were a joke. But he looked menacing now, and inwardly she recoiled from him, not knowing what this man was capable of.

"Your plans for me are quite ambitious, but unfortunately,

they conflict with a few of my own." He allowed his eyes to travel the length of her body, and Danny felt herself flush beneath his impudent stare. At last his eyes returned to her face. "Come to think of it, I just changed my plans."

Her mouth opened wide to protest, but the harshness of his voice froze the words in her throat.

"Before you continue your tantrum, I think you'd better consider that you've been gone a long while and your friends are probably wondering where you are." He gestured with a flick of his head back toward the hotel.

She had forgotten! The party. Uncle Emmett. He must be frantic with worry.

Looking around at the brightly lit hotel in the distance, she heard the orchestra beginning another waltz. Its tune drifted across the stillness of the grounds, invading the trees and shrubs with its dreamy sound.

When she turned back to him, she was alone amidst the shrubbery. She stalked furiously back to the hotel tearing the delicate ribbon of her dress on a bare branch in the process.

When he saw her enter the ballroom, George Custer went to claim his dance. Before Danny had a chance to evade him, he had taken her by the arm, in a profusion of polite apologies.

"I am so sorry, Mademoiselle, that I was unable to take you up on your promise of the first waltz, but I was compelled to step outside with my aide to discuss . . . Well, it's official business, I'm afraid."

Outside! Had he seen her? Did he know what happened?

"I do hope you will allow me this dance," he said, his voice betraying nothing.

Guiding her onto the floor, he noticed the torn ribbon at her neckline, but said nothing about it. Instead, he allowed his eyes to slip past the ribbon to the slight swell appearing just below.

"You look quite lovely, Miss Fleming, and it does an old soldier's heart good to dance with a beautiful woman before he rides out again."

"Oh?" Danny raised her eyebrows, pretending interest, while she continued to smolder inside from her previous encounter. "And what are you riding out for, Mr. Custer?"

"Indians, Miss Fleming," he said simply, as though she would understand exactly what he meant.

"I'm afraid I don't quite—"

"Oh, of course. I had forgotten that you are new to these parts. Indians. That's what it all comes down to, Miss Fleming. Indians and gold. I don't suppose you have any Indians in France now, do you?"

What a foolish thing to say. He was sorry that it had slipped out before he could check it. He wondered whether the beautiful young woman he held in his arms knew that she was the cause of his nervousness. Looking down into her golden eyes he noticed a small glint, and in an effort to conceal the obvious effect she was having on him, he sought small talk.

"I must say, you speak English remarkably well. I can hardly detect any trace of an accent."

"My brother was quite determined that I speak English as fluently as French," she said, leaving it at that. She did not wish to go into any further explanation with this man whom she was not quite sure she liked at all.

There was something about him—she could not tell precisely what it was, but it was unmistakably there. She did not particularly like the look of his shoulder-length reddish-yellow hair, but it was not that. It was, in fact, nothing about his appearance, she decided as she studied his face carefully, unaware for the moment of the disquieting effect it was having on him.

He was holding her much too tightly. Were all American men so forward? Then, dismissing it, determined to salvage what was left of the evening, she said, or rather demanded, "Tell me about Indians and gold."

"That's not a subject for pretty young ladies to worry themselves about," he assured her.

But Danny would not be put off so easily. "I understand that many of them have been forced to live on . . . Oh, what do you call them?"

"Reservations. Yes, well you must understand that this is done in the best interest of both the Indians and the whites," he explained, hoping that she would not pursue the matter any further. Usually, that was sufficient to satisfy even the most active curiosities.

Danny matched his strides across the floor, moving to the music, but not really hearing it. "Surely, General, you can hardly call confining a person to a reservation as being in his best—"

"Miss Fleming," George Custer interrupted, the smile removed from his lips, "it is a sad fact that the Indians are a dying race. They fall prey to the diseases of the whites and their adjustment to the new order is difficult. They will soon vanish with the buffalo."

He spoke so matter-of-factly, and it sent a chill through her, in spite of the heat emanating from her body. She tried to tell herself that it was because of the closeness of the room and the stillness of the night.

George Custer, too, had felt the warmth penetrating from beneath the fabric of her dress, stirring within him old familiar feelings. He had been in the saddle too long, he thought, looking down into her bright eyes. His own Libbie had remained back in Monroe and, well, he had almost forgotten what it was like to hold a woman in his arms . . . and especially one so young and so exquisite.

"You mentioned gold, Mr. Custer," she reminded him. "I'm not quite sure I see the connection."

"You see, Miss Fleming, the Indians—the Sioux, that is—are sitting on a gold mine. *They* call it the Black Hills. *I* call it just a mass of rocks . . . *and* a fortune. Of course the Indians will fight like the devil to keep the area, but this is a young land, Miss Fleming, and you cannot deny the spread of progress just to satisfy the whims of savages."

"But why would they fight to keep the place if it is, as you say, just a mass of rocks?"

"I understand that you are naturally curious about this problem we have here, being a foreigner, of course, but really, you should not concern yourself—"

"I am an American citizen, General, and even though my home has been France since I was a child, I assure you that my curiosity is genuine." Her voice betrayed impatience and an obvious annoyance, and he was instantly sorry he had spoken so rudely to her. But then, softening her tone and looking up at him through her lashes, she added, "And besides, there is *so much* for me to learn here, and I would be so grateful if you were to teach me."

"Well . . . let's see, the Black Hills, yes . . . well, the Indians regard them as some sort of sacred place where they go to pray. Actually, it's about the only time they aren't stirring up trouble for the settlers and miners in the area."

"What kind of trouble?"

She was charming all right, but he wondered whether she knew what she was letting herself in for with a question like that. "I don't think you would care to hear about it, Miss

Fleming, and my duty as a gentleman would be amiss if I were to speak of such things to you." His terseness convinced her not to press the issue.

"Oh, I suppose you are right," Danny said, shuddering, remembering the grizzly stories Zoe had filled her with. Stories about Indians kidnapping white children and torturing them in bizarre ceremonies. Of course! They probably carried those poor little children off into the Black Hills. What a horrible ugly place it must be.

Yes, she supposed it was the only safe thing to do. Keep the Sioux securely confined to an area so they could be watched and kept from harming innocent people. Anyway, it certainly didn't concern her. If this was the kind of country to which she owed her citizenship—for simply having been born here—then she would rather return immediately to France. Indians, indeed! She had never even met one, and in all probability, she never would.

Settling the matter in her mind, Danny turned her gaze upward to meet the general's, shoving aside the uneasy feeling about him that continued to plague her. She smiled prettily and allowed herself to be carried away by the music and the lights and the laughing faces around them.

When the dance ended, she felt her cheeks warm from a sudden flush. "I think perhaps we'd better join the others," she said. "I'm certain Uncle Emmett will be furious with me for staying away."

"Tell me," she heard him say, "did you enjoy the view from the patio?"

Danny looked up at him quickly. Why did he ask her that? How did he know she had been out on the patio?

"I saw you when you came in before," he offered in reply to the question on her face. Then, leaning closer to her he added beneath his breath, "Miss Fleming, if you will pardon my frankness, a woman of your obvious . . . ah, well, that is, you shouldn't go off by yourself. It's not as safe as you may think it is. There's no telling what kind of unseen danger lurks in the dark."

Danny felt his grasp tighten on her arm, but when she turned to protest, she saw that he was not even looking at her. He was staring off somewhere . . . at nothing it seemed, and yet, his eyes flinched as though he definitely saw something. What a strange man, she thought to herself as she watched him, bothered by the unnameable, yet annoying, feeling she had about him. She felt a kind of nervous energy coming from somewhere inside of him. It was obvious to her that he felt ill at ease in the role of the gentleman. Even the officer's uniform he wore seemed to sit poorly on his body, and she guessed he would have been more comfortable dressed in more informal attire. For her part, Danny could not guess what other role he was better suited for. Just another army officer, she sighed. She turned her attention to her Uncle Emmett, whose face lit up into smiles when he spotted her enter the dining room on the arm of General George Armstrong Custer.

Chapter 5

Danny was pleasantly amazed to find that the dining room looked remarkably like the fine Parisian restaurant Austin had taken her to for her twentieth birthday.

The lace-trimmed tablecloth spread beautifully over the length of the massive table and beneath an array of the finest china and exquisite silverware she had seen anywhere. Whoever would have imagined that something this fine would be found here? I wonder just how many other surprises there are to be discovered in this country, she thought.

Before she could dwell on the possibilities, Danny realized she was seated with George Custer to her left and a handsome young man on her right, whose outrageous staring began to make her nervous. So far it had been a rather trying evening, and she really was not much in the mood for any more gawking insolent men.

As she greedily held out her glass to be filled with wine by the maitre d', she noticed immediately the slight disapproving raise of the eyebrows from several of the other ladies present. They probably don't like what I'm wearing either, Danny thought. Then suddenly she remembered the torn ribbon on the silk sheath and as soon as she reached her hand up to it, she heard a stuffy voice pipe up over the others.

"My dear, what have you done to your dress?"

Danny grimaced. "Why, it's just . . . that is, I . . ." She became flustered by the elderly woman's prying attention and found herself at a loss for words.

"Oh, I'm afraid the fault is mine, Mrs. Merrispoon." It was the man seated to her right who spoke in her defense. She turned to look into his face. "She caught it right here on this little old medal—this one here, see—while we were dancing."

Glancing to the spot he was pointing to, Danny saw the small silver medal pinned to the breast of his uniform. He was a soldier and she hadn't even noticed it before. She also had not noticed how handsome he was. Sandy-brown hair framed a face that went at once from sensuous to boyish when he grinned widely. His body was lean and she could tell even from the way he held himself while sitting that he was tall. His eyes seemed almost feminine for a man's—large, hazel—trimmed in lashes long enough to be the cause of envy for any woman.

The sound of his voice was like nothing Danny had ever heard before. It seemed to roll over his lips, spilling from his mouth in a lazy drawl. It sounded almost musical in a twangy sort of way.

"Ma'am? Ma'am, I was saying that I hoped you would allow me to buy you a new dress for my clumsiness."

Why was he doing this? And why was he staring at her so intently? Everyone must see! Reaching for her glass of wine she gazed into his enormous green eyes. "Why, Mr.—?"

"Hawkins, ma'am. Captain Lacy Hawkins." He was a bit too anxious and wasn't very good at hiding it.

"Why, Captain Hawkins, I could not allow you to do any such thing," Danny said, playing along with his game, "and I do not wish to hear another word about it." Her voice was stern but her eyes teased him in the way she was so good at. The wine was beginning to loosen her up. Already she had drained one glass and was sipping on the second and, as usual, and because of it, she was starting to feel a bit playful. She glanced around the table at those seated close to her. There was that strange General Custer, that annoying Mrs. Merrispoon and some gentlemen she did not know. So she decided then and there that Captain Lacy Hawkins would be the target of her attention.

Lacy Hawkins could scarcely believe that the gorgeous woman would be so interested in him. What a stroke of luck! God, she was beautiful, and it was obvious that none of the other women liked her because of it. Jealous fools, he thought, eyeing them with distaste. That old witch, Mrs. Merrispoon, had looked at her dress with blatant disapproval. But from where he sat, it only made her more lovely. The torn ribbon even tended to give her a look of tainted innocence.

He allowed his eyes to roam over her body, noting that the pale peach dress seemed to blend with the hue of her skin, giving the impression that she was wearing nothing at all. And when she moved, the fabric clung to her lean body exposing otherwise hidden contours. His breath stuck in his throat and his mouth became dry when she leaned close to him, brushing his uniform with her bare shoulder. The scent of her perfume wafted up to his nostrils and filled his head with its dizzying fragrance.

"You will pardon my ignorance, Captain Hawkins, but I cannot place your accent," she said, her voice low and husky from the wine.

"Why, South Carolina, Miss Fleming. That's where my daddy's from and his daddy before him. Of course, I haven't been back since the war."

He was strangely uncomfortable and he could not imagine why. He'd never had trouble conversing with women before . . . even the prettiest ones. Why was he suddenly having such difficulty just getting the damned words out?

"Captain Hawkins, surely you don't expect me to believe that you fought in . . . what was it . . . the Civil War?" she asked incredulously. "Why, you hardly seem old enough now, and *that* ended ten years ago."

"Well, the fact of the matter is," he replied, "when I looked out the window of that big old house and saw my two brothers riding off to war, I rode out right after them. Packed me a quick bedroll, slung my hunting rifle over my shoulder and went off to kill some Yankees. It wasn't until we were in the thick of it that they found out I was there, and then there wasn't much anyone could do about it—what with the problem of staying alive and all."

"You certainly took an awful risk, Captain."

"Well, I don't know about that, ma'am, but it sure near broke my mammy's heart when all her boys ran off to war like that."

"I should think so," Danny exclaimed. "Why, your poor mother must have been so worried."

"Oh no, ma'am, not my mother. I mean my mammy." He paused for a moment. "My *mammy*," he said again, this time emphasizing the word so that she would understand. But still she did not respond. "The nigger bitch that looked after us boys while we were growing up." He said it so simply and matter-of-factly, she observed.

"But that did all come to an end with the war, didn't it, Captain?"

"Yes, ma'am, it did, 'cept that some of those old niggers never knew any other life but what they had with us on the plantation. So they stayed on, even after the war."

Did she detect a hardness in his voice? It was difficult to tell behind such pleasant features. And then, too, the wine was fogging her mind. "And you, Captain Hawkins?"

"Oh, after the war I drifted north for a while, headed west after that. One night I got drunk and the next morning there I was in a uniform again."

Danny laughed. "In that case, Captain, it would appear to me that you should refrain from drinking too much. You never know where it will lead you next." She smiled at him sweetly and lowered her voice. "That is not to say, of course, that you don't look exceptionally well in a uniform."

He could feel his pulse quicken. What a tease she was. But that was all right. He would play along with her game if that's what it took to win. Lacy Hawkins blushed politely and smiled broadly at her.

He certainly is a charming man, Danny thought, lowering her eyes, then raising them again to see if he was still looking. He was. Why, he's the first real gentleman I've met in America. Certainly not like that animal . . . Oh! She had almost forgotten all about that! She glanced at Lacy Hawkins from the corner of her eye. He was engaged in conversation with the man across the table and gave no hint that he knew her eyes were upon him. He's so different from that awful man outside. That man who . . . He was so dark and menacing with that black hair that had been allowed to grow much too long. It made him look like such a pirate. And his treatment of her, so shameless and shabby. Obviously a man of limited intelligence; nothing but a brute animal. God, this country must be so full of that kind of man. But Lacy Hawkins was different. He was so clean and neat that Danny was certain she could smell a bare trace of soap on him. It smelled nice—a bit too sweet perhaps, but nice. He did not look like the kind of man who would treat a lady with anything but the highest respect; certainly, a gentleman in every sense of the word. And such a handsome one at that.

Danny found herself wondering, wickedly, what it would feel like to be kissed by Lacy Hawkins and have his arms wound tightly around her. Would his kisses be warm and soft, or would they be harsh and demanding like she had known earlier in the evening?

She saw him laugh and throw his head back. He gave the appearance of being at ease, but there was something about the way he held his head back, a trifle too long, maybe. And the way he laughed out loud sounded a bit forced to her. Oh, but then she had had so much wine. By now, who could tell what was really what?

She leaned back in her chair and twirled the stem of her wine glass between her fingers. She was much more relaxed now than she had been earlier. Even the effect of the episode on the patio . . . and worse, out in the bushes . . . had diminished behind the shady cover of a wine-induced tranquillity.

Lacy Hawkins praised his good luck when that pretty girl he had seen enter the dining room on the arm of his commanding officer had been shown to the seat directly next to his own. What an eyeful she was. A couple of times he had found himself tongue-tied, unable to make any sense of his thoughts, much less his words to her.

He was sure he had said some foolish things, although she had not really reacted as if he had. Funny, he had never had that kind of thing happen before, but then, he had never met a woman quite like Danny Fleming before.

He could not resist the temptation of mentally visualizing the contours of Danny Fleming's figure beneath the silk sheath, although his thoughts would never have betrayed themselves on his face. No, he was quite adept at leaving certain things where only he could know about them. Besides, he was a gentleman—a Southern gentleman, if you will—and a gentleman would never allow his most scandalous thoughts to be observed by anyone, least of all the lady on whom they were focused.

So, Lacy centered his attention on the man seated across the table, all the while his thoughts on the young woman at his side.

Lacy Hawkins had had about as much formal schooling as his daddy would allow. After all, there wasn't much sense in knowing all that book stuff to raise a good crop of tobacco or cotton. But his lack of education did not hinder him, for of all things, Lacy Hawkins had always possessed an abundance of pure unadulterated charm, nurtured to perfection over the years. He had learned at an early age to use his charm and good looks to the utmost. From wrangling pork pies from his mammy's oven to securing favors from the ladies and from his superiors when he served in the Confederate Army.

The cursory history of his war experiences, related for Danny's benefit, had not revealed the fact that he had worked his way up in the ranks of the Confederate Army to the enviable position of fighting side by side with General Lee himself. At war's end there was talk of a commission at West Point, but before it could materialize, he and some reckless young friends had gone on a drunken spree and in the morning found themselves enlisted in the regular army. There, Lacy's prior exploits, fighting with men like Lee and Jackson, carried little weight. In common with hundreds of other former officers, he was suddenly merely another enlisted man.

The snatching away of the limelight depressed him, so he toyed with the idea of becoming a mercenary soldier in Mexico for the handsome salary then being offered. The decision was made for him when Congress increased the size of the standing army in order to deal with the mounting troubles with the Indians out west. Scores of new officers were commissioned and many already holding posts received promotions.

The result of the adding and shifting of commissioned manpower was the organization of the Seventh United States Cavalry. The post of Lieutenant Colonel went to General Sheridan's favorite, George Custer, whose outstanding generalship in the Union Army paved the way for his career as an Indian fighter. That of commander, K Troop, First Squadron went to Lacy Hawkins, whose promotion to captain marked the beginning of his ascent.

Lacy sensed the potential of his superior officer. Beneath Custer's reckless exterior and perennial boyishness lay a well of ambition. The only question was how to use Custer's drive to suit his own needs. Lacy knew that Custer was a man on his way up—some even whispered the Presidency. There was hushed talk of a campaign next spring against the Sioux up north in the Dakotas, and everyone knew that a victory would cinch the Indian fighter's chances of winning a Democratic nomination. Custer was, after all, a hero, and everyone loved a hero.

Lacy Hawkins looked around the table at the assortment of people gathered there. They were all important wealthy people. The kind who could make a man into a monument by merely breathing his name. Lacy had always assumed that he would hitch himself to George Custer's star and ascend along with him. But now there seemed to be another way, and it had presented itself to him on a silver platter. Who would have thought that Emmett Fleming had such a lovely niece? And while Lacy had reacted to the surprise with true delight and a genuine gut desire for her, he was not unaware of the advantages were he to pursue this young woman with serious intentions.

"I understand you will be traveling to California, Miss Fleming," he said, leaning close to her.

"That's right," Danny replied, smiling at him. "My brother and I will be departing in a week. Austin is quite impatient to leave, although from what I've heard, I can't say I share his enthusiasm. You don't suppose we'll have any trouble along the way, do you?"

"Don't you worry about a thing. You'll be in good hands, I assure you."

Danny smiled at his assurance and let him return to his conversation with the gentleman. She glanced down the length of the long banquet table at the faces she knew. Uncle Emmett sat at its head, waving his cigar about in front of him in one hand while frequently raising a glass of wine to his lips with the other. His assistant, Carl Forrester, caught her look and smiled briefly, then returned his reluctant attention back to Emmett Fleming. Politics, Danny huffed. Who cares a fig about that?

Seated several places away was Austin. Too much wine for him, Danny decided, judging him to be much more talkative than usual. If it weren't so noisy in here, I could hear what has him so agitated. Just moments before, everyone had been finishing their last course and sipping on wine, talking quietly. But now the dining room was filled with voices, each talking in a different direction, each growing louder in an effort to be heard over the others. She turned back to Lacy to comment on the sudden eruption of conversation when she heard his voice, loud and angry, at her side.

"Why, he's a desperado! For two bits, I'd—"

"Who is a desperado?" she asked.

"Alex Coulter, that's who, ma'am," replied the red-bearded man across the table.

"Miss Fleming would hardly know about that, Mr. Redmond," George Custer said to the Scotsman. "She's only been here one day."

"And it's just as well," Lacy Hawkins added firmly. "If you don't mind my saying, it's not the kind of thing we should be discussing in front of a lady."

The subject appeared to be closed. But if these men had had their fill of it, she had not. Her curiosity had been stirred, and besides, she felt that Lacy was only bullying poor Mr. Redmond and the others into dropping the conversation.

Reaching for more wine, she raised her glass slowly, purposely to her lips, keeping a steady gaze at the face of the Scotsman. "Mr. Redmond," she purred, "I really would like to hear more about this desperado."

Lacy Hawkins remained silent but she could feel his smoldering presence beside her. She knew he was staring hard at the man, hoping to silence him with his look. She leaned forward, giving the foreigner with the strange accent her most undivided attention, looking up at him through slanted eyes that were the slightest bit hazy from the sweet intoxication of the wine. She smiled at him and waited for him to speak.

Alexander Redmond cleared his throat awkwardly, quite unprepared for the sudden splurge of attention from such a splendid young lassie. Quickly he cast a glance at Lacy, then he spoke. "Well, I canna say I knae tae much aboot him, lass, but I hear he been causing soom trooble the last few years . . . raids on outpoosts, wagon trains, ye know, tha' sort of thin'. Nothin' really serious, I'd say, but—"

"Sir, if you call eight men dead and three seriously wounded as *nothing serious*, then I'd like to know what *you* call a man like that! *I* call him a killer."

Danny stared at Lacy in disbelief. The wrath in his voice was like ice casting a chill over her. Even his face was not as handsome when his mouth was twisted the way it was now. Before she could grasp the full impact of his abrupt transformation, she heard Mr. Redmond clear his throat again.

"Beggin' yer pardon, Captain, but I ken see I donna hae aul the facts. I had nae idea. . . ."

"No, of course not," Lacy replied coolly, staring hard at the man.

George Custer knew the hot temper his captain possessed, and rather than risk further confrontation, he slammed his fist down upon the table, snapping heads in his direction. "Why, I've chased that man and his band of outlaws halfway across this country. Came pretty close to catching him a couple of times too, if only he hadn't slipped across the border like a snake."

Several others joined in the conversation, and Danny listened speechlessly as they spoke, ignoring her presence.

"Lately, he's taken to robbing shipments of silver," Lacy said, "and I can tell you that if we ever do catch him, he'll be sorry he ever caused us so much trouble." He spat out the words with obvious distaste.

"I heard they were having some trouble with him up in the Dakotas this past winter."

Recognizing the voice, Danny looked up to see Austin standing behind her chair.

"Yeah, that's what I heard, too," someone added.

"He certainly gets around," Austin observed, an amused smile on his lips. "But tell me, gentlemen, why is it so difficult to catch him?"

A big man with a shock of gray hair leaned forward. "I hear tell he's lightening quick with a gun—that you'd be hard pressed to find anyone better."

Austin's question was suddenly lost in a flurry of excited conversation.

"Yeah, and I hear he's just as good with a knife."

"Well, that's because he's part Indian."

"I wouldn't know about that, gentlemen," Lacy said, raising his voice above the others. "But I can tell you that he sure acts like one, sneaking around the way he does. I saw what he did to that Army supply post near Laramie last summer and it wasn't a pretty sight. No white man I ever knew would slit a man's throat and take his scalp the way that devil did."

Danny felt the revulsion in her stomach and fought hard to suppress a wave of nausea. Oh my God, do people really do such things in this country? What kind of horrible place was this—where she could be sitting in an expensive hotel restaurant enjoying a good meal and sipping fine French wine, while in another part of the country a killer was ravaging his victims? The man must be a savage!

"Why can't you catch him?" Austin's voice snapped her out of her thoughts.

This time the others fell silent, staring at each other or

down at their feet. It was Alexander Redmond who finally answered him. "Well, this mon, this Alex Coulter, naebody really knaes wha' he looks like. He wears a neckerchief tae hide his face."

"That's right," Custer confirmed. "Half the posses in the West have been out looking for him, and since he took to raiding Army supply posts, it's become a Federal matter also. Only trouble is, we don't know if it's an Indian or a white man we're after. My Indian scouts tell me he's a red devil. But me, I figure anyone who can outsmart us the way he's done has got to be white. Chances are, he's a little of both. But how do you catch a man if you don't even know what he looks like?"

"I saw him once."

They all turned simultaneously to look at the small dark-skinned man who had stood by unobtrusively until then, saying nothing. But now, with the attention focused on him, he took a step forward.

"Well, that is, not really. He was wearing something over his face, and I could only see his eyes. But I'll never forget them as long as I live. They were like steel—cold and hard and as gray and bright as polished silver."

Danielle coughed on her wine, and the glass slipped involuntarily from her hand and crashed to the floor in splinters.

Suddenly, Danny was besieged by polite attention. Austin looked at her quizzically, but before he could react, Lacy Hawkins reached for her, encircling her with his arm. "Miss Fleming, are you all right? Please accept my apologies. I should have known better than to allow this kind of conversation in front of a lady."

"I'm all right, really I am, Captain," Danny protested, catching her breath as she rose to her feet. "I think I would like to take in some fresh air."

But he was reluctant to let her go. "Maybe I should go with you. I mean, just in case—"

"Really, Captain, I'll be fine," she said tersely, pulling away from him firmly. Once extricated from his grasp, she turned to Austin. "I'll just be a while," she said and left.

Austin watched her thread her way through the guests and leave the dining room. Turning back to Lacy, he said, "It looks as though my sister was not prepared to hear about the harsher realities of this land, Captain Hawkins."

"I must apologize for having offended your sister. But

between us, Mr. Fleming, some of those 'harsher realities,' as you call them, are becoming all too true for more and more people. Too many people have already lost their lives trying to pave a way for those who are going to follow."

There was something about the way Austin looked at him that put Lacy Hawkins slightly ill at ease. "And they *are* following, Mr. Fleming, by the droves. The way must be made safe for them. They must be assured that they can go to a new place and raise their families in safety." He licked his lips and reached nervously for his glass, all the while feeling Austin's eyes upon him.

"At the expense of a race?" Austin asked, half to himself.

Lacy seized upon it instantly. "*Indians*, Mr. Fleming. They're *Indians*. They live the crudest form of life, in hovels with all kinds of animals. They're capable of the most sordid crimes and they love to torture their victims in fanatic religious ceremonies." He looked at Austin hard and long, adding slowly, "Especially the young and pretty ones." He cast a slow glance over at the doorway through which Danny had exited, confident he had made his point. "The potentials of this land are enormous, Mr. Fleming," he observed. "They should not be sacrificed for a few thousand savages who do war dances and paint up their bodies like heathens. They remind me exactly of those niggers we had on our place in South Carolina. We all know that the best thing for them is to be working out in the fields. That's all they were ever equipped for—intellectually, of course. Indians are pretty much the same. Instead of being black, they're red, but there's really no difference. Only problem is that some of those Indians don't want to conform to what a civilized society is. You know what I mean? And then, every once in a while we get a renegade like this scoundrel, Coulter, who thinks he can run around the country raising hell and killing good men." Lacy laughed, a short bitter sound in his throat that brought a bad taste to Austin's mouth. "I shouldn't expect much better than that from an Indian if I were you, Mr. Fleming."

Austin did not take his eyes from the Army captain's face. He remained tight-lipped, neither nodding in approval nor giving any hint of his disapproval. But his relentless stare was making Lacy increasingly uncomfortable. "Well after all, when you come right down to it, there's really only one thing we can do . . . if they won't come round, that is."

"Oh? And what is that, Captain?" Austin's question was low, from somewhere deep within his throat.

"I believe you know as well as I do what the final solution to this problem is," Lacy replied. "If the Indians cannot accept the westward expansion of civilization, then they must be removed from the path—forcibly, if necessary." He took a long sip of wine. "I had not expected you to be so sympathetic to the Indian cause."

"I'm not," Austin quickly responded. "Perhaps you forget that it is Fleming silver they are stealing."

"I haven't forgotten," Lacy answered. "And that's why it is so important that we get this over with as quickly as possible. They must be stopped! We must break them down. We must prevent their brutal slaughter of innocent whites. I tell you, they must be broken! They must be!" He turned to each man in succession, as though pleading his case, until his eyes met those of George Custer's, which were smiling in agreement.

It was Austin who finally broke the uneasy silence. "General Custer, I understand your company will be escorting our party to California. Is that correct?"

The general cleared his throat, glad to be relieved of the tense moment. "Well, partially correct, sir. I received new orders this morning. I'm to escort you as far as Bennett, then I'm to head north."

Lacy pulled his eyes away from Danny who had returned and retaken her seat beside him, and addressed his commanding officer. "But, General, sir, I'm sure that whatever is going on up there can be handled by their own men. There hasn't been all that much action there anyway in recent weeks."

"You're forgetting something, Captain, aren't you? Once those mining parties go up into that territory, they'll tear it wide open. We both know the Indians aren't going to like that one bit. No, my boy, it's on to Fort Abe Lincoln for the Seventh. We've got ourselves some Indian chasing to do." He leaned back in his chair and waved away the cigar someone offered him.

I can't stand much more of this, Danny thought miserably, feeling she would go mad with anger. All of a sudden, as though reading her very thoughts, Zoe miraculously appeared at her side. Danny's eyes lit up instantly as Zoe reached out to clutch her hand.

"Danny, won't you be a dear and accompany me back to

my room? I seem to have left my shawl behind." Danny felt a slight squeeze from Zoe's hand as she followed closely behind. "You gentlemen go right on with your little discussion," Zoe called over her shoulder, and winked at Austin, who blushed because of it.

"But how did you know?" Danny asked, once they were outside.

"Know what?" Zoe replied. "I just had to get out of there."

Danny laughed at her cousin's exaggerated expression of boredom, feeling immediately relieved to be outside in the fresh evening air.

"God, it was so dull in there I thought I would die," Zoe said, expelling a long breath of air.

"We really should find ourselves some better forms of amusement than that," Danny suggested, watching Zoe's green eyes suddenly light up.

"Oh, Danny, I have the most splendid idea! Come on!" She ignored Danielle's hesitation, pulling her by the arm into the street and down several long blocks where they turned abruptly into a darkened alley and came to stop in front of a shabby saloon called the Bull's Head Tavern.

my room I seemed to have left something behind," Danny felt a slight squeeze from Zoe's hand on the table out of...

"You just have to put on your nice little dress..."

...who looked beside...

"But how did you know?" Danny asked, once they were outside.

"Know what?" Zoe replied. "I just had to get out of there."

Danny laughed at her equally exaggerated expression of foreboding, feeling immediately relieved to be outside in the fresh evening air.

"God, it was so dull in there I thought I would die," Zoe said, exhaling a long breath of air.

"We really should find somewhere more better there at someplace than this," Danny suggested, watching Zoe's eyes widen—lit up.

"Oh, Danny, I know the most splendid idea! Come on," she grabbed Danny's hand, leading her by the arm...

...the street and down several long blocks where they walked quickly into a darkened alley and came to stop in front of a shabby saloon called the Bull's Head Tavern.

Chapter 6

The tavern was glowing from the yellow-red light of torches placed about its perimeters. Small wooden tables were nestled into alcoves that were filled with men, some noisy and raucous in their merrymaking, others with faces turned downward toward their drinks to escape whatever it was, or whoever it was, that plagued them.

Zoe paused for a moment, deciding the best way to go, and Danny had a chance to survey the surroundings.

Placed intermittently about the rough-hewn walls hung many paintings, each in a simple wooden frame, and all done in the same sepia tones, perhaps by the same hand. One canvas in particular caught Danny's eye and held her attention by some undefined magnetism. It was a lone Indian astride a brown- and white-spotted horse. He sat erect on his pony with a bow lying across the pinto's neck and a quiver of arrows slung over his bare shoulder. He wore his hair in long braids and had a single feather behind his head. He was nude except for a loincloth. His pony wore neither saddle nor halter, only a single rope tied to its lower jaw in place of a bridle.

After staring at it for a long while, Danny noticed that this painting, compared to the others, was different. It, too, was done in muted shades of brown, but it was the only one which displayed a splash of color here and there. The zigzag lightning streaks painted across the pony's body in bright dazzling red and yellow lent a strange cast to the portrait. It was almost as though the brazen colors had invaded the peace of the picture, with a flash of an unrecognizable kind of power. Danny stared fixedly at the warrior in the painting, wondering who he was, or if indeed he had been merely a figment of the creator's imagination.

Her attention was snapped away from the picture by a firm tug on her hand as Zoe finally decided to make her move. They shouldered their way through the crowd, weaving through the scattered bodies, Danny becoming more and more aware of all the men who stood about them. They were different from the ones back at the hotel, and she could not help but notice how much more at ease these men were with themselves than their obviously more wealthy counterparts. Somehow she felt strangely relieved to be away from the scratchy blue uniforms and stiff-collared shirts. She felt freer, more relaxed around the dusty breeches and worn leather boots. Even the buckskin leggings and hide shirts some of these men wore looked softer . . . felt softer too, she thought, when brushed several times by a buckskin sleeve, and certainly more conducive to comfort than starched shirts and tight-fitting waistcoats.

She promised herself she would speak to Austin about getting a pair for her to ride in, but no sooner did she plant the thought than she found herself looking into the face of a young man who was smiling broadly at her. After his eyes took in every feature on her face, they turned to Zoe, and Danny saw her cousin blush as the man's lips brushed her hand.

"Zoe, what a delightful surprise this is," he said. His voice was melodious.

"Why, John Avery, fancy finding you here."

Danny glanced at Zoe in surprise. The name of John Avery had dropped too many times from Zoe's lips to render this the chance meeting she pretended.

Avery's voice had a familiar ring to it, but surely Danny had never met him before. His features were pleasant enough and he had a nice build, lean and tall. But she wondered whether that was sufficient to rate him as high in Zoe's preference as it appeared to, judging from the way Zoe fawned over him. Danny felt a bit embarrassed by Zoe's scandalous behavior, and if Zoe's cheeks lacked a blush for it, then Danny's certainly did not.

But John Avery, on the other hand, seemed almost oblivious to Zoe's attention, and therein, guessed Danny, lay the reason for her cousin's ardor. He was probably the only young man who wasn't courting her, Danny decided. Leave it to Zoe to want the one who doesn't want her. Oh, what did it matter really? Obviously, Zoe was quite mad about him . . . for now, that is. By the time she realized that his affections were not reciprocal, she would surely have forgotten all about him and found herself another object for her shameful flirting.

"Danny, this is John Avery," she heard Zoe say. He reminded Danny of someone else, but she could not bring an image to mind. She searched his face, from his blond, neatly trimmed hair to his gentle eyes, but saw nothing suggestive of another. There was something about the way he stared at her that made her blush involuntarily.

"I'm pleased to make your acquaintance, Miss Fleming," he said, when the introductions were completed. "May I call you Danny?"

She liked the sound of her name the way it rolled off his tongue, and despite the fact that he squeezed her hand a little too tightly and allowed his lips to burn against her hand, she tossed her misgivings aside and flashed him a gay smile. "By all means, John." She was beginning to feel a bit reckless from all the wine she had consumed.

She turned back to Zoe to see whether the exchange had been noticed. But Zoe's attention had already been diverted to the group of men who surrounded her. Oh well, John Avery, Danny laughed to herself, it looks as though you've been replaced already. Leaving caution behind and Zoe to her string of ardent pursuers, she allowed herself to be led away to a corner table and seated by this man who was really a complete stranger to her, and yet, in whose presence she felt at ease. Secretly, Danny knew that if her mind were not so clouded by wine, she would have guessed where she knew him from, but she relaxed beneath the warm seductive spell of the wine and permitted herself to charm, and be charmed by, the likable John Avery.

It was so easy to respond to him, to answer his casual questions, and to laugh at his utterly delightful sense of humor, something she had found sorely lacking in almost everyone else around her. Even when he complimented her by telling her quite candidly, and unashamedly, that she was the prettiest thing he had *ever* seen, she could not help but smile, feeling no embarrassment at hearing it aloud.

She liked his spontaneousness, and he liked the color of her eyes, and the way they shone.

In no time, Danny's foot was tapping to the music's perky rhythm, and she found herself drumming her fingers on the wooden table in time, bobbing her head from side to side. She watched as two men walked out onto the dance floor and entwined themselves comically in each other's arms in an exaggerated embrace. The man with the long gray whiskers placed his hand daintily on the other man's broad shoulders in an awkward resemblance of a waltz, and immediately, everyone who stood around watching, roared with laughter, slapping each other on the back and raising their beer mugs to the pair as they stumbled by.

The music shifted to a sprightly jig and the two figures separated and fanned out across the floor to pick out new partners from the crowd that encircled them. Danny, too, found herself standing in that crowd, clapping to the lively, compelling beat along with everyone else. The entire room seemed to pulsate with the rhythm. Everyone was affected by it—the crusty old miners, the Englishman from New York, the cowboys from Santa Fe, the Army troopers, even those who had preferred to drink alone—all stomping their feet and clapping their hands to the sounds of the fiddles, the snappy strumming of the guitar and the gay tune of the mouth organ.

Her head was swimming with excitement and her body moved of its own volition, keeping in time to the catchy beat. Before she knew what was happening, she felt herself swept into the arms of old whiskers, who half-dragged her about the floor in a merry two-step, before pirouetting away, leaving her behind to dance on her own.

Without a partner, Danny's feet began to move in time to the sound of the guitar strumming and, as the players picked up the tempo, her body moved to accommodate the pace. She strutted around the floor, flicking her head from side to side, gently nudging loose the pins that held her hair atop her head. She swayed to and fro, prancing about, kicking up her feet, with her dress swirling about her ankles. And, as she danced, strands of hair began to work themselves loose . . . a few here and there at first, until in a torrent they all came spilling down over her shoulders, catching the torchlight and sending red sparkles down each shaft.

Not a single pair of eyes could be willed off the young woman who danced with such total abandonment, with her eyes closed to the music and the room, lips parted, arching her slim body in the most wildly seductive movements they had ever seen. It was as if she moved in spite of herself, as though she were not conscious of where she was or what she was doing.

The auburn-haired beauty raised her arms above her head, sweeping up the hair off her neck in a teasing display. Then she stepped lightly away with a flick of her head as though daring anyone there to reach out and try . . . just try . . . to touch her. She held herself there, beckoning, challenging, luring anyone who was man enough to step forward and take the stage with her.

Each man present wanted to, but nobody moved into the circle. None of them would have admitted it, of course, but they were all intimidated by her . . . by her unusual beauty and by her boldness, her raciness . . . and the unapproachable air that inevitably surrounds a woman of such undeniable magnetism. The dance came to an end in a roar of applause, shouts and whistles. Waking to her surroundings, Danny felt a warm crimson flush wash over her cheeks. She followed John Avery back to their table unable to look anyone in the eye.

He pulled the chair out for her and leaned closely over her shoulder. Her perfume was so sweet. The aroma of it had suddenly intensified from the dance and mingled seductively with the delicate scent of the perspiration glistening on her bare shoulders. "You know, Danny, if we had someone like you dancing for us, we just might have won that war," he whispered as he sat down.

"What war was that?" she asked breathlessly, fanning herself with her hand.

"The Civil War, of course."

But the wide grin on his face was lost to her, when her memory was suddenly jarred loose by the association. Of course! Now she knew who he reminded her of. It was Lacy Hawkins, also a southerner. How stupid of her not to have recognized the accent, that strangely musical drawl of his voice. Oh! Suddenly her head was swimming and she longed to lie down. Unwillingly, it all came back to her in one big rush. What an evening it had been. One she would never forget.

She rose unsteadily to her feet, making excuses to leave although feeling sorry at the disappointment that washed

across Avery's face. She had to find Zoe. It was late and they
had stayed far too long. "Perhaps we'll see each other again,
John," she said. "It was so nice meeting you." Turning
quickly, she ran off to find Zoe.

John Avery watched her thread her way through the thick
crowd. What had he said? What did he do wrong? He
watched as she reached the door and let herself out, a small
gust of wind whipping up the ends of her hair—and then she
was gone. But his were not the only eyes watching. From a
recessed alcove along the opposite wall, a lone figure sat for
hours, unnoticed by anyone, hardly discernible from all the
others, but watching all the time.

He was dressed in unobtrusive cowboy attire, black chino
pants that fit tightly over the long lean legs stretched out in
front of him. The muscles beneath his blue linen shirt had
flinched involuntarily as he watched from gaps in the crowd as
that pretty little girl danced her whore's dance. She was no
better than all the others, he thought contemptuously, his
eyes washing over her slim graceful body, reluctantly taking
in every curve, and unconsciously committing them all to
memory. The only difference is that she's a might skinnier
than most, he thought. And when she had suddenly gotten up
from her table, leaving that poor fool behind with his mouth
gaping open, he had not failed to notice the way she moved.
It was as though a hidden well of passion lay somewhere
inside of her, smoldering, purposely kept at a distance.

He felt himself unconsciously harden at the image that
made his loins burn. He had seen women dance before, and
he had admired them. And when the notion came over him,
he had taken those he wanted—easily, without any trouble or
protest. But this woman's dance was different. The way she
strutted around so arrogantly was as if she knew that all the
men in the tavern desired her. The bitch! She was nothing but
a seductive temptress whose dance held a deadly promise for
any man who was fool enough to try. How many men had she
given herself to while sitting protected behind her wealth and
good name? Sure, she could afford to play the sweet demure
heiress by day, and the sultry whore by night. What was she
doing here anyway? Why did she leave her elegant dinner
party of influential people to come here among the common
folk, planting hopeless desires in the hearts of men who could
never in their wildest dreams hope to possess her? The little
bitch should be taught a lesson, Alex Coulter decided angrily,

aroused by the thought that she was not like the others. And it was not just because she was so damned beautiful either.

He raised a bottle of whiskey to his mouth, ignoring the shot glass that stood nearby, letting the fiery liquor pour smoothly down his throat. With his head lowered he looked like any other cowboy, tired and dusty from a long ride from nowhere, having stopped in for a drink before heading out again for nowhere.

He withdrew a carefully rolled cigarette from the pocket of his black leather vest and placed it between his lips, smiling contemptuously to himself. He was *not* just another cowboy. And if the troopers in the tavern this evening knew who sat within their midst, they would have descended upon him in a flurry of gunfire without bothering to ask questions first. He struck a wooden match on the bottom of his boot, then brought it close to his lowered head, cupping the flame in his hands, coaxing small clouds of smoke from the cigarette. Well, that was all right; he liked taking chances. After all, he was used to it. He had even nearly gotten himself hung once or twice, but he had always managed to stay at least one step ahead of his pursuers. And as long as he could help it, that's the way it was going to stay.

A couple of troopers ventured too close and his hand moved instinctively to the place where he wore a gun slung low on his hip. From there, it slid across his leg moving slowly across the taut thigh down the length of his calf to where a knife lay concealed in his boot. He could feel the slight bulge beneath the leather. And then he sat back, confident in his ability to wield a blade as he was in the swiftness of his draw and his deadly accuracy with a gun.

His dark gray eyes turned the color of molten steel as he watched the girl with the long, wild copper-colored hair slip from the tavern. He took another swig of whiskey, but even the burning taste could not erase the taste of her mouth that was still on his lips. Even the hours that had elapsed had not dulled his senses to the feel of her body pressed against his, so soft and yielding, yet so full of fight and wildness. He knew he should leave and head on back, but there was one more stop he had to make first.

He moved silently, almost catlike, through the crowd. His head was bent and dark curls fell over his forehead, helping to conceal his features.

Once out in the night air though, Alex Coulter lifted his

head with a quick toss, flinging the hair from his eyes. He ran his palm quickly through its thick black mass and headed in the direction of the Hotel Pierre.

She was tired. Her body was weary from the evening's activities, but her eyes were wide open and alert. The effect of the wine had dispersed long ago, leaving her feeling a bit sapped of strength. No longer under the dreamy spell of the intoxicating drink she was painfully aware of every ache in her limbs.

When she turned the knob and opened the door, a faint gust of wind washed her face and sent some loose strands of hair scattering. She looked across the room to the open window through which passed the moonlight that bathed the room in hazy luminance. The breeze blew a speck of dust into her eye, and blinking, unable to dislodge the irritating culprit, she crossed the room and lit the oil lamp that sat on her dressing table. One strand of hair had become entangled in her thick lashes, its tip just barely tickling the lid of her eye. With mirror in hand, she gently removed it.

The lamp cast a warm orange glow over her face, and its reflection traveled toward the silver heart at her throat. Its glint caught her eye in the mirror and she moved her gaze downward. Slowly she slid her hand down her cheek and came to rest at the base of her throat where she lightly traced the outline of the heart with her fingertip. Closing her eyes, she moved her hand from her throat to her shoulder feeling the tingling of a million tiny nerve endings along its path. Smooth fingertips eased their way beneath the thin shoulder straps that held up her dress, and each one in turn was gently nudged off her shoulders.

Eyes still closed, she ran her palm delicately over the silkiness of her flesh. The coolness of her hand was sharp and piercing against the heat radiating from her skin. The lamp that flickered close by sent soft shadows washing over her body bathing it in a glow, the color of fading embers. The only sound in the room was that of her own breathing, soft, but deep. Slowly her hand ceased its caressing and came to rest at her own pulsating heart where she could feel its beat beneath her fingertips. For a second she could feel that vibration penetrating into each limb of her body, being absorbed into every fiber. The room became filled with the beating of her heart.

She stood without moving, her mind and body simultaneously absorbed with the reverberations from her breast. She was spellbound by its wild thumping. And as she stood there with her eyes closed and her head thrown back, everything seemed to stand deathly still—everything except the beating of her heart.

"Don't stop on my account, ma'am."

The words were mocking and their harshness was a slap back to reality. With a gasp she whirled around, her hands instinctively clutching for the straps of her gown that rested somewhere on her hips.

"You sure do know how to drive a man to some awful thoughts."

She detested that voice with its drawling insults and taunts. Fumbling with the straps, pulling them up over her shoulders, she glared at him, eyes wide, fists clenched at her sides. "Get out!" she hissed through gritted teeth.

"Well now, is that any way to treat a man who went through an awful lot of trouble to be here tonight?" he asked. "There's a lot of people out there looking for me, baby, and I don't usually go through this kind of trouble unless I've got something on my mind."

His eyes took in all of her at once, moving shamelessly from her face all the way down her body . . . slowly, provocatively. Was the lamp playing tricks on her or did she imagine that his eyes became lighter beneath his heavy lashes as they raked over her?

"If you touch me, I'll scream very loudly," she informed him in the most matter-of-fact voice she could summon.

"And if you do, I'll have to silence you," he warned her in return.

Danny felt frozen to the spot she was on, but his impertinence was boundless, and the anger building up within her came bursting forth in a torrent of words. "You are a detestable, loathsome man," she spat. "You are rude and insulting with your horrendous manners and arrogant airs. How dare you come into this room! You are nothing but a thief . . . and a liar in the bargain. And now you propose to add rape to your list of sordid activities, although it probably would not be the first to your account, I'm sure!"

"Keep your voice down," he warned in a threatening tone. But instantly a little smile crept across his lips. "It does look like you're reading my mind, you know that, Frenchy?"

"Get out of here," she demanded. "I'll not be mauled by a dirty . . . *half-breed!*" She said the words with a sneer that made him narrow his eyes in a cold, unfathomable look that caused Danny to pale in spite of her efforts to appear unafraid. Inside she trembled like a leaf on a windswept day, but the pure rage she felt at his impudent stares had pushed her fear out of the way. That is, until she saw this new look spring into his eyes. Something told her to be careful, to keep her distance. She sensed an unspeakable danger lurking behind the glint in his eyes.

She backed away from him, but in quick strides he covered the distance between them. Reaching past her, he put an arm up sharply against the door as soon as she felt its hardness behind her. "You're beginning to try my patience, Danielle," he said, but the forced annoyance in his tone was evident. It confused her, as did the fact that he had once again called her by name, as if he knew her, almost as though they were not perfect strangers.

The sudden closeness to her produced an unexpected effect on Alex Coulter, catching him off guard for a moment. He could feel her warmth so near to his own. He could almost feel her hair in his hands. And her perfume, that intoxicating scent that drifted from every part of her body, filling him with its heady aroma. He lowered his six-foot frame just enough to look her dangerously in the eye.

"I hate you," she whispered through clenched teeth.

His mouth widened into a grin, a sarcastic smile that she wanted to wipe right off his face. "Is it me you hate, baby, or is it yourself for wanting it as much as I do?"

Oh! His taunting question deserved only one reply. Partly from outrage and partly from the pain of his insult, Danny was blinded to the consequences of her action as she smashed her hand viciously across his face, raising long red welts in its wake.

The sudden flare-up of his eyes, the quickness of his hand as it came upward toward her face, made Danny flinch in anticipation of the blow that never came. Instead, his hand moved rapidly past her face, and in place of the harsh stinging slap she expected, she felt her hair tumble loosely over her shoulders as he deftly and swiftly removed the ivory comb that held it all in place. Then, with a movement as quick and as smooth as a cat's, he produced a crumpled scarf from out of nowhere and stuffed it into her still gaping mouth. The neckerchief he wore about his neck was off with one fast flick; and before Danny could fend off his attack, it was fastened securely over her mouth.

He circled one arm tightly around her waist, effortlessly scooped her up into the air and carried her to the bed. Her eyes screamed the outrage and hate that caught in her throat, unable to escape the confines of the gag. Furiously she beat at him, raking her nails across his face, his neck, arms, wherever she could grab a piece of him, and she felt the blood seep under her fingernails as she clawed at him. But his strength was overpowering and after several frantic minutes of wild struggling and muffled screams, she felt her own strength slip from her limbs. Vainly she tried to move away from him, her fighting growing weaker and weaker until, at last, she lay beneath him, motionless except for the heavy rise and fall of her chest.

When Alex Coulter felt her resistance subside, he slid himself off to one side, throwing a leg across her body to keep her firmly in place. He studied her with a cool calculation that made her wince and instantly brought a flash of anger to her tawny eyes. So, she wasn't through yet, he thought, noting with a strange kind of satisfaction the spark of excitement ignited in him at her resistance beneath him. He could have snapped her wrist any second. He could have sent her into unconsciousness with a single slap. But he did not.

He used his physical strength over her as a taunt to provoke her to further rage. He took the hatred she had for him and used it against her to stimulate his own lustful desires. And he was succeeding all too well.

His mouth burned a trail from her ear to her neck, where it buried itself in the pulsing spot at the base of her throat.

His hands roamed over her body claiming each part he touched. And when the thin silk sheath she wore hindered his progress, he reached up to remove the straps from her shoulders.

But Danny would have none of it. No! He was not going to do this. No. Please!

She came to life again, resisting his efforts to gently remove the gown. But both his arms imprisoned her, stifling her struggles. And when he had her securely in his grasp, he reached up and grabbed the neckline of her silk gown. With one sharp downward thrust, the fabric came ripping away from her, exposing her naked flesh.

Danny tried to heave herself up against him, to throw his weight off of her. But his reflexes were lightning fast, and he shifted his body over hers again, bringing his mouth down heavily to the hollow of her throat, kissing her neck, shoulders, breasts, consuming her wildly, despite her silent screams of protest and her desperate thrashings.

"Danny . . . Danny . . ."

His words, breathlessly whispered against her skin, sounded like a groan, and she trembled in apprehension of what he would do next.

His knees were between her thighs, holding them apart, while his hands reached up to hold her own hands above her head. She felt his body pause momentarily above hers before it moved further . . . deeper, into the space created between her legs.

His penetration was sharp and quick, taking her breath with its initial thrust, and then sending a terrible pain, sharp as a knife, right through her, making her body heave upward in agony. But her screams were lost behind the gag and only muffled sobs escaped.

If only she could faint. If only she had a blade to plunge into his black heart. She was so beside herself with humiliation and rage that she had not even noticed that the searing pain had subsided and left in its place a warm sticky sensation. Gradually, the pain lessened and finally disappeared. He now lay inside of her, motionless, their bodies as one, locked together.

Then he began to move inside of her—slow, rocking motions that brought no pain, but terrified her nevertheless. She lay beneath him in silent distress, feeling his movements growing steadier and faster, harder and more demanding, until she gasped for air behind the gag as he drove himself further and further into her in what seemed to her frantic mind like some awful frenzy.

Afterward, she was so tired and weak, with so little energy left in her limbs, that she barely had the strength to fight him off when he reached up—while still deeply embedded within her—and fastened her wrists to the bedposts with leather strips that had come out of nowhere, much the same as the neckerchief had appeared before.

What was he going to do to her now? Hadn't he done enough, she thought frantically? She would never let him know the humiliation she felt, laying naked under him. He had remained fully clothed throughout, having loosened his pants just enough to accommodate the act.

Danny tilted her face up to his and narrowed her eyes at him as he attached her wrists to the bedposts.

"Just to keep you set long enough for me to get the hell out of here," he said.

When the ties were secure, he lifted himself from her sweating body and stood by the side of the bed looking down at her stretched out form.

"You should be able to work yourself loose in a while. That is, if you struggle with those knots as hard as you did with me."

Oh! That horrible, mocking voice. Why did he have to look at her as though he had not just had his fill of her? Why did the color of his eyes change to steely gray when they passed over her body . . . that same startlingly bright color that flashed out at her when she had called him a half-breed?

Yes, she would struggle against the knots that held her, as fiercely as she had against him twice this evening. And if she ever saw his face again, she would rip it to shreds for doing this to her. She would fight this man until she had not an ounce of strength left in her. She vowed she would never allow him to forget for a moment exactly what he was. She would fling it at him again if she ever got the chance!

Danny tugged furiously at the leather strips that bound her wrists, all the while watching him steadily with frightened eyes as he made his way to the window with long catlike strides.

"I always like to finish what I start," he said brazenly, as he swung one lean leg over the wrought-iron railing and turned to look back at her.

"Next time, we'll spend more time together. Sorry, but I really must run."

For a brief moment, seeing her there, feeling her frustration and agony keenly from across the room, Alex Coulter was half-tempted to go back to her—to untie her hands, to free her mouth, to bury his face in her hair and to tell her that he was sorry for having hurt her, for making her first experience of love such a harsh one. Damn it! How was he to know she was a virgin?

Danny stared back at him, her tawny eyes piercing the

darkness like shards of glass. The gag he had hastily tied around her mouth had become dislodged during his kisses, and with a few tosses of her head from side to side, it fell beneath her chin. She coughed, then spat out the crumbled cloth that filled her mouth.

When she spoke, her voice was low and husky, penetrating the stillness of the room. Her panting was heavy as she gulped in the air she had been denied.

"If I had a knife, I would plunge it to the depths of your heathen's heart!"

The sound of her voice excited him, but the words struck bitterly and sharply, like the lashes of a whip whose sting he would never forget.

Alex Coulter tossed his head back, whipping the black curls from his forehead. He laughed contemptuously, flicking aside whatever tenderness had lain in his heart a moment before.

"Yes, I believe you would do precisely that, Danny. Just as I would not hesitate to break your pretty little neck if you ever decided to try it." With that, he was gone.

Danielle felt the rawhide knots give way from her persistent pulling and tugging at them. When they began to give slightly, she worked even harder, a renewed frenzy rising in her. Just thinking about him made her nearly mindless with fury. But it was an unsettled fury. Oh yes, she hated him, all right, but for some inexplicable reason, the initial outrage she had felt at his hands slipped away into something else.

It was something that made her vastly uncomfortable, even though she could not place it. It was without shape, lacking definition.

Danny squirmed under the uneasiness it thrust upon her. He was gone, but the room was saturated with his presence. The sheets beside her were laden with the scent of his musky male odor. It drifted to her nostrils, swirling about in her head, filling her lungs with each deep breath she took.

She remembered his look, those eyes watching her. Just now, before he disappeared into the night as quickly and as quietly as he had appeared, the way he had stood there glaring at her, but not seeing her . . . seeing past her, inside her . . . was unsettling to her.

He had left, but still she was not free from him, from his pirate's face with its long black sideburns that raked down his cheeks to the tip of his jawbone, from the cruel drawling voice that had taunted her, from those incredible eyes that seemed to be shrouded behind a curtain of smoke one moment, hard and piercing the next.

All of a sudden, Danny felt ill, and a growing wave of nausea began to creep its way into her throat. A thought had just taken hold of her numbed mind. How long had he been there in the shadows watching her?

In all her anger and hurt she had forgotten. The window. Of course, she remembered now that it was open when she came in.

And then . . . something else began to take hold. With sickening certainty, one horrible thought pierced her mind.

Oh, my God . . . she would not think of it . . . she *could* not think of it!

Desperately she fought to avert this new thought that kept pushing its way into her mind, burning its path into her consciousness with its undeniable presence.

No, it wasn't possible, she screamed inwardly. Hot tears began to spill from her eyes. She flung herself onto her stomach and sobbed breathlessly into her pillow. No! It can't be true! It just can't be!

But it would not retreat. It would not go away as she demanded, pleaded, for it to. It was the same image that had filled her mind earlier when she stood mesmerized beneath the warm caress of the oil lamp across her bare breasts . . . as she stood on the edge of eternity listening to her heartbeat.

His image . . . his image. No, it could not be!

Chapter 7

In the days that followed, Danielle Fleming found more things to dislike about her new home. Well, perhaps that was not the right word to use. She had not really found her home yet, although she surely had been jostled about from place to place.

Austin had promised that this would be the final leg of their journey, and also hinted that it would probably be the toughest.

They had thousands of miles to cross to reach the West Coast, but, thank God, once they reached Bennett, they could ride the rest of the way by rail. Danny hardly thought she would ever be so eager to see the railroad again, but in comparison to the wagon, it was sheer heaven.

First New York. Then St. Louis, although she would prefer not to think about that place. And now they were on their way to Bennett, Colorado, a place she knew even less about, and somehow did not much wish to find out. At least they would not be staying there too long. San Francisco was to be their ultimate destination, hers and Austin's that is. That was where they would eventually make their home.

Day after restless day spent aboard the train that had carried them from New York to St. Louis had given her the first hint of the vastness of this country. And now, just two days out of St. Louis, she was obliged to admit that it certainly looked to be true. The country sprawled out endlessly in all directions. It was flat and dry and dusty, with the heat shimmering above the ground and playing tricks on her eyes.

It did not at all resemble the neat, manicured fields of the

French countryside she had always loved so passionately. Instead, the ground was spiked here and there with low growing bushes, thick and spiney, which dislodged themselves from their roots and rolled about the land, skipping the surface on a gust of wind, tumbling this way and that and eventually disappearing behind the curtain of dust raised by the wagon wheels. Dismally, Danny wondered how anything could live out here.

Their party was comprised of six wagons pulled by teams of six horses each, a chuck wagon drawn by a team of very ornery mules and two wagons laden with supplies and provisions. They had been instructed to bring as little with them as possible to make the trip less cumbersome with unnecessary wagons. All their fine things would be sent for later. Meanwhile, they had to suffice with what there was.

She and Dossie shared a wagon, while Zoe was tucked away in one further ahead with her mother, and Austin and Emmett shared another. During the daylight hours, both men preferred to ride horseback rather than at the reins of the team. That particular task was delegated to members of their armed escort who, taking turns during the course of the day, would slide from their mounts over to the hard wooden seat perched high on the wagon. It was hard work keeping a team of horses in check, the drivers were jerked and jostled all over the place as the wagons passed over rocks and ruts.

The ride was boring and tiring. They made three stops each day, one at about noon to rest the horses and change drivers, one later in the afternoon, and finally at the end of the day as the sun's rays disappeared over the flat horizon, to make camp for the night. When the monotony of the ride lulled her into a semi-trance, she would crawl from the seat and disappear into the shady recesses of the wagon where she could sleep for an hour or two, if for no other reason than to pass the time. It was dark within the wagon, and dank from lack of circulating air, but at least it provided shelter from the burning rays of the ever-constant sun.

Closing her eyes to the uncomfortable stickiness covering her body like a sheen, she pushed back the nausea that crept over her. Danny tried to keep her mind riveted on cooler things, like refreshing pools and soothing breezes—like the ones that would wash gently over her face and through her hair whenever she sat astride Destiny back at her beloved Chateaudun. It all seemed a million miles behind her now.

Around noon on the fifth day out, Lacy Hawkins reined his big bay horse close to the rear of Danny's wagon and peeked inside at the sleeping girl. His gaze lingered over her partially clad body, her bare arms and legs shiny from perspiration, her auburn hair strewn about her face and her thin cotton petticoat matted to her body. Involuntarily the muscles tightened at his crotch and he shifted position in the saddle to accommodate the uncomfortable bulge in his pants. He wondered what it would feel like to touch her, to stroke her skin and to kiss her full moist lips which were partly open and teasing. He wanted her and he found it hard to keep his mind off how much. Ever since meeting her he had thought of nothing else. Lacy Hawkins could no longer imagine the rest of his life without Danielle Fleming. It was only fitting for a man on his way up to be graced by a beautiful woman on his arm.

He cursed under his breath that she had been sleeping, but then thought better of it. This was something he could not rush, he reminded himself. He had to be careful and plan his moves accordingly. After all, Danielle Fleming was not merely *any* woman, and there were certain things to take into consideration. One was Austin Fleming.

At this point it was hard to tell what kind of plans Austin had for his sister. A soldier probably wasn't included, Lacy thought bitterly, for the first time in his life cursing his lack of education and, more important, his family name which, compared to the Flemings', was about as insignificant as a speck of dust on this prairie.

Well, it didn't matter. He wouldn't be a soldier forever. Things were going to be happening very soon, and then he'd see whether Mr. Austin Fleming had any doubts as to whether he was good enough for his sister!

About an hour after sunup each day, with the teams hitched up, horses stepping lightly and mules balking as usual, the train moved out to the crack of whips in the air. Slowly the big rimmed wheels churned forward. Almost grudgingly they creaked their way laboriously across the arid terrain, straight into the heat of the day.

Just before sunset the cumbersome wagons would circle one another forming a crescent, with the chuck wagon at its center. By the time the sun had sunk from the sky and the nighttime closed in around them, their little stronghold was aglow with warm burning fires.

After this evening's meal, the men went off—some in groups for a few hands of poker, others by themselves—and a lull came over the camp over which only an occasional whisper or cough could be heard. Danny sat at the fire's rim, her knees pulled up to her chest, her arms wrapped around them, talking quietly with Zoe and Dossie. After a while she scrambled to her feet. "I'm going to look for my brother," she said. "Seems I never see him lately. I wonder where he's gone to."

"I think you'll find him over there." Dossie gestured toward Custer's tent. "I saw him go in a while back."

Several minutes later Danny returned with a frown on her face.

"Did you find him?" Zoe asked.

"Yes I found him," Danny replied sourly. "But as usual he's busy." She stood with her hands on her hips for a moment, then turned away.

"Hey, where are you going now?" Zoe called out.

"I'm just going to stretch my legs a bit. I've been cramped inside that wagon for too long and my muscles ache. I'll be back in a while."

"But, Danny, wait!" Dossie jumped up and ran to her. "They said not to leave camp, you heard them say so." She spoke in a scolding tone.

"Oh, I know," Danny whined. "But I'll be right back. *Really*. Go on back to Zoe and keep an eye on her, or there's no telling what kind of mischief she'll get herself into."

"Lord, if that ain't the truth," Dossie exclaimed. "All right, but you be careful, you hear. And don't go straying outside the wagons."

Danielle strolled over to where the horses were tethered for the night. The animals watched her from the corners of their eyes while they munched silently from their feedbags. Moving quietly among them, she noticed a small patch of trees about forty yards off which seemed to beckon her with feathery fingertips, hinting of the coolness that waited beneath them. The perfect stillness beneath the pines lured her into the grove where the ground was moist and rich, not dry and gritty like the dirt the wagon wheels traversed. And the air here was like a whisper against her flesh, so soothing and refreshing after the stifling heat of the day.

Somewhere above the moon shone down through a

cloud-streaked sky, its silvery face obscured by the thick growth of branches overhead. It was so peaceful here, so quiet and serene, where only darkness stretched out before her, marred here and there by the big shadow of a tree. Still, an eerie feeling began to creep over her, and she had the awful sensation of being watched.

Suddenly, a sound like a branch snapping beneath a footstep. A gasp stuck in Danny's throat. There was no mistaking the unmistakable sound of shuffling leaves on the ground as someone came toward her.

Her hand flew up to her mouth in an instinctive gesture, and she waited, frozen with fear, as a figure came closer.

"Here, I thought you might need this."

A familiar voice spoke out of the darkness, but she was still too frightened to speak, even when she held out her hands mechanically to accept the shawl he plunked into them.

"Sorry if I frightened you, but you shouldn't be out here by yourself. You were told not to leave camp."

"Lacy, I . . ." She bit her lip nervously, and slowly her heart eased its rapid thumping. "You startled me."

"Yeah, it looks that way, doesn't it? You know, you could get lost out here and never find your way back without a trail to guide you." He sounded plainly annoyed.

"Oh, Lacy, the camp is just over there," she laughed, pointing over her shoulder.

"Really? Can you see it from here?"

"Of course I can. It's right over—" She looked through the dense trees to the place where she thought it was, but saw nothing.

"You can't see it from here," he said. "If I hadn't come out here, you might have met up with . . . Oh well, what does that matter now? I'm here. You're safe now."

Danny trembled to think of what might have awaited her beyond the pine trees. Surely there were wild animals lurking about in hidden places . . . wolves maybe. It was something she had never even considered. She swallowed hard and wrapped the shawl tightly around her shoulders. Her flesh was a mass of goosebumps, not so much from the cool nighttime air as from the chill of the unknown.

Lacy wrapped his arm around her tentatively. "Come on, let's sit here for a while." He led her to an isolated flat-topped rock that allowed them to sit side by side.

Danny was not interested in dallying, especially now that she had been alerted to their possible danger.

"Hey, what's the matter?" he asked, feeling her tenseness. "Don't worry, it's all right."

How did he know that? Didn't he just say that there were things to fear out here?

He leaned over and brushed her temple with a kiss that took Danny by surprise. He whispered her name close to her ear, and when she turned to look at him, she saw a strange look on his face. "Lacy, I think we'd better—"

His mouth came down on hers almost desperately. The hardness of his kiss bit into her. His lips were soft, but wet, and they slid over hers in a slippery kind of way. She tried to ease herself away from him, but his arms circled her shoulders even tighter, pulling her against him so that he could feel the soft swell of her young body against his.

His breathing decreased in pitch, becoming labored. Her body was crushed against his and desire raged inside of him. He could not believe that he had her at last; that she was really his, and all he had to do was take her. Here she was as he dreamed it would be, in his arms, so willing. Her lips tasted so delicious beneath his. Whatever restraints he had planned on exercising rapidly diminished to nothing.

"No, Lacy, please don't," she whispered.

"Oh, Danny, come on, it's all right," he mumbled against her ear.

"Lacy!" Her voice was stern, and she pushed against his chest to free herself from his grasp.

"We'll go back in a minute, honey."

She felt the sickening tickle of his tongue swirling at her ear, taking little nips at her lobe, and she shivered from it. Somehow, it did not please her, nor make her tingle. "Lacy! Stop it, please."

"God, Danny! Please let me do this. I won't hurt you, I promise. But you're driving me crazy—"

"Lacy—Lacy, we've got to go back now. I—"

"Danny, I love you. Please, I love you," he said hoarsely, still clinging to her.

"*I said, no!*" Her words were harsh and loud and forced him to break away abruptly. His face bore an unfathomable look as he eyed her closely. She grew anxious, and without knowing why, heard herself offering a weak excuse. "It's just that . . . well, it's so dark out here . . . it makes me nervous." She lied, hoping he would understand and ease his pursuit.

"It's all right, I told you," he said, with a hint of impatience in his voice. "Nothing will happen with me here." He patted the gun holstered at his hip. "Just one more kiss, huh— please, Danny? Honey?" He had not meant to plead with her but that's how the words came out. He simply couldn't help himself.

His mouth closed over hers again, and she sat in his tight embrace forced to endure his soggy kiss and hot moist breath at her throat. His tongue pushed its way into her mouth and searched it thoroughly, pushing her to anger. This was enough! Quite enough! She pushed sharply against him and squirmed away. "I'm sorry, Lacy," she said angrily, "but I'm going back *now*." She gathered her skirt and stalked away.

All right, Lacy told himself, control yourself. You almost blew the whole thing, fella. His ragged breathing gradually lessened and resumed its normal pace as he watched her disappear into the darkness. Okay, I've got to remember that she's not that kind of woman. Next time I won't come on so strong. But there's *going* to be a next time, you can bet on that.

The darkness concealed the thin smile that grew on his lips. That's right, Miss Danielle Fleming, play hard to get. What the hell, I can play along. The prize is worth it. Trouble is, you've probably never been with a real man before. Where you come from, I'll bet they're all like that brother of yours, so refined and proper. Well, out here it's different. . . .

Chapter 8

She lay in bed with the covers thrown back and her nightdress twisted around her hips, feeling the heat of the night gradually fading away to the cool of dawn.

Longingly she recalled similar daybreaks when she would steal from the big stone house and sneak past Sophie's watchful eye and race across the lawn to the stable where Johnny would have Destiny waiting for her. A pang of loneliness pierced her tranquillity as she reflected back on the green French countryside, to the sprawling fields and vineyards scattered checkerboard across the land over which she galloped her spirited mare, to the neat little towns and hamlets that graced the countryside of the Rhone River Valley with their peaceful presence. And Paris. Who could not look but with love and utter enchantment on the quaintness, the color, the contrasts of the charismatic city, with its tree-shaded avenues and by-lanes? Who could resist the excitement of the fashionable salons where she had spent so many gay hours enraptured in conversation with friends and acquaintances?

She missed it all. Even Austin was not here to poke his harmless fun at her. She missed his company and his easy laugh, even if he had been ignoring her lately.

Oh, it wasn't that she didn't like it here at Uncle Emmett's ranch. It was just that . . . well, she felt homesick, and her nerves were still on edge from all that traveling to get here. Since leaving beloved France, they had hardly spent a week in one place. A stay in St. Louis and then that dreadful wagon ride to Bennett. From there, the hot, dusty coach ride to the Fleming ranch had her thinking she would go mad if it did not end soon.

When Austin had insisted that they leave immediately for California, Danny had finally put her foot down. In no uncertain terms Austin had been hotly informed that she was not going to take another ship, train, wagon, coach or horse one step further than the one-hundred-and-eighty-mile radius of the ranch, not for a whole month! After several unsuccessful attempts at persuading her to change her mind, Austin had resigned himself to making the last leg of the trip by himself. One month, and then she was to follow him to San Francisco, like it or not. Meanwhile, he would go on ahead and make arrangements.

Who did he think he was, ordering her about? She'd show him. She still had three more weeks left and who knew what could happen.

She rose from the bed and sauntered to the window to check on the progress of the day. It was getting lighter and she bit her lip in apprehension.

She reached deeply into her dresser drawer to the spot that hid her trousers and riding blouse. She had not brought the linen shirt Austin had given her, but she would never have left behind the pants. The light tweed trousers slipped easily past her hips. It felt so good to have them stretched over her skin again. Judging from the fit, Danny could tell she had lost a pound or two. In spite of it, though, her body had managed to retain its perfectly slender lines, and the rather hectic pace she had become almost accustomed to had not taken as much of a toll as she had thought it would.

The corners of her mouth turned up into an unconscious little smile when she slipped her arms into the sleeves of an apricot-colored silk blouse and felt the slippery fabric slide over her bare skin. Meticulously, she buttoned each row of tiny covered buttons at each cuff, and slipped each pastel button into its little slot up the front of the blouse. Then she took the long ends of silk that hung from the collar and fashioned them into a loose bow. Flopping down onto the unmade bed she pulled on a pair of knee-length kid boots and from the pocket of the trousers she took out the cloth-visored cap that kept her hair out of her eyes when she rode.

She could barely wait to get her legs straddled around the girth of that big black gelding. She would really give him a ride today.

An enormous reservoir of nervous energy flooded through her veins, waiting to be put to use. She had felt it growing stronger ever since her arrival at the ranch a week ago, although she could find no reason for it. Why, if ever there was a place conducive to rest and relaxation, it was the *Hacienda de Agua Azul*, House of Blue Water. Emmett Fleming had been right in choosing the name, for nowhere else in the dry wind-swept state of Colorado was there a place so marvelously lush as this.

Danny was nostalgic—a pang of longing—for her beloved France when she spotted the graceful cypress trees imported from Europe pressing against her bedroom window. It was a paradise here, a carefully planned and executed eden. And, while it was peaceful here, she was somehow struck with a feeling of contrivance. Despite the ranch's overwhelming beauty, its unnaturalness hung in the air as a stiff reminder of what money could buy.

She slipped easily out of the house and made her way to the stable. Each of over forty animals in the stable had been carefully handpicked and bred to produce one of the most valuable lines of Arabians in the world.

The horses were magnificent with their sleek lines and flowing manes. Bred for grace and intelligence, they were large animals, and one felt almost awed in their presence. When one of the mighty beasts reared, striking out with dangerously sharp hooves, or when the wind whipped its mane about its perfectly formed head, then one could appreciate being permitted on the animal's back. Of them all, it was a black gelding that Danny favored, perhaps because it made her think of Destiny.

But Leyland Peets, the stableman, had opinions of his own. "If it's a ride ya want, Miss, then you'd be wanting that brown mare in the corner," he had told her, pointing into the corral.

Danny had been surprised by his choice. "That little thing? Why, she hardly looks like she could carry a child."

"No, Miss. I'm tellin' ya, that's an Indian pony there and she can give ya a run for ya money. Why, that little critter would run her heart out for ya, she's—" But Danny would not listen and chose the gelding anyway.

She could hear him pawing the ground as she approached the barn. She was smiling to herself as she rounded the corner of the barn, but what she saw made her stop short and frown. The horse that stood waiting was not the Arabian. Instead, Leyland Peets had thrown the saddle over the little brown mare.

The animal looked at Danny with lively black eyes as she approached it. She walked around the mare, hands on her hips, looking over the animal. She'd settle this matter with Mr. Peets later, she decided, placing her boot into the stirrup and lifting herself easily onto the horse's back. With a jolt, the mare took off at a brisk trot as soon as she felt Danny's knees tighten around her girth. Danny soon discovered, to her utter delight, that old Mr. Peets was right; the little horse just loved to run. Danny leaned low as she effortlessly guided the mare over the countryside.

The fence posts bobbed along the perimeters of the *Hacienda de Agua Azul* in either direction for as far as the eye could see, following the land's gentle rises and slopes. There was one spot, just to the west, where there was an opening in the barrier.

Sensing the closeness of the flatlands, the mare's strides became quicker and perkier as she cantered along the fence pulling at her bit. Danny felt her excitement and knew that all that was necessary was to give the barest hint, and they would be over that fence in a flash, racing toward the foothills of the Rocky Mountains. The animal made no attempt to resist when Danny turned her head and led her away, nor did she balk when her reins were pulled up sharply and a quick snap to the right spun her around so that suddenly she found herself facing the fence again.

The mare waited, muscles flinching, for the signal. And then, all of a sudden, she felt the quick kick of bootheels against her flanks. Sprinting instantly, she leaped forward, stretching her neck with each stride that grew longer and faster until the fence stood but a few feet away. Then she sailed up into the air and over the wooden boundary, landing lightly and smoothly on the other side without breaking stride. She bounded across the land with the wind racing past her ears whipping her coarse mane around her eyes, and the laughter of her rider was close to her ear. Small hooves thundered across the dry Colorado land.

After a while the pony slowed to a trot, and then to a slow even walk. The race across the flatlands had parched her throat and she sensed that a cool wet relief lay ahead, somewhere in the hills. Feeling no restraints from Danny, she began to climb, carefully picking her way around boulders and across rocky paths until she felt the ground becoming softer beneath her step. As they climbed higher, Danny could

feel the welcomed change in the air. It was noticeably cooler
and the numerous trees helped block out the burning rays of
the afternoon sun which had risen high into the sky, scorching
the land further below.

When they came to the top of a large grassy slope, down
the center of which ran a delightfully sparkling stream of
water, Danny dismounted and they both quenched their
thirst.

After drinking her fill from cupped hands, Danny flipped
onto her back and gazed up at the perfectly blue sky, one arm
bent crookedly behind her head. It was so beautiful here, so
placid. She could stay in this spot forever. How different it
was out here with no streets cluttered with pedestrians and
carriages. She was slowly beginning to relax in her surroundings, to feel a part of them. The sky is so blue, maybe even
bluer than it is in France, she imagined. She felt the warmth
of the sun seeping into her, turning the color of her
complexion from its usual fashionable white to a glowing
brown, but she didn't mind.

The sound of a nervous whinny invaded the serenity of her
thoughts, but she willed herself to ignore it, not wishing to
break the spell of the moment. A second whinny, this time
louder, forced Danny to open her eyes and tear herself away
from her daydreams. She leaned on her elbows and glanced at
the mare, wondering whether the animal had already had her
fill of grazing and was eager to be off again. A sharp crack
caught her attention, and then another whinny. But it wasn't
the mare!

She whirled her head around to look up the slope—
nothing—then searched across the stream—still nothing.
Suddenly she was gripped by a sickening feeling. Slowly, she
forced herself to sit up and then, with every ounce of
willpower she possessed, she forced herself to look behind
her.

Two men sat astride horses not more than twenty yards
away. She sucked in her breath and rose to her feet, all the
time painfully aware of what the men in this country were
capable of. Her amber eyes grew large and her pulse
quickened when she saw the subtle movement of one man's
hand sliding from the reins to his hip removing the gun from
its holster. She stared with growing horror as he held it
loosely in his lap, but pointed right at her.

They were so close, but their hats threw shadows across

their faces. For what seemed like an agonizing eternity she
stood frozen to the ground with terror racing wildly through
her blood, unable to peel her eyes from the menacing figures.

As if on cue, both horses advanced toward her in unison.
She saw them take a couple of wary steps before her
adrenaline forced her into action.

Danny turned in a flash and ran, stumbling over her feet in
an effort to get away. She didn't know where she was running
to, or how far she'd get. All she knew was that she must run
as fast as she could to get away from them. She had to make it
to her horse!

Running breathlessly she looked back over her shoulder
and screamed at the sight of a large black horse bearing down
on her rapidly. She could feel its thundering hooves pounding
behind her, and could see its flaring nostrils. She was frantic
with fear, involuntary sobs tearing at her throat as she saw the
rider lean forward in the saddle, then out far to the side.

In one fleeting instant the horse swept by. The force of the
man's tackle knocked her to the ground, and the momentum
of the attack carried them tumbling over each other for
several yards before finally coming to a halt with Danny
pinned beneath him, struggling furiously to escape. In the
midst of the struggle, she heard him shouting at her in
Spanish. She fought her attacker with all of her strength, but
eventually even that failed her. She lay helplessly drained
beneath him with her arms trapped above her head and her
legs spread-eagled on either side of his body. Glaring into his
face she noticed for the first time how young he was, and it
surprised her that at a time like this she had enough of her
wits about her to notice anything at all. He was dark-skinned,
with large black eyes and an unruly crop of black hair that had
fallen loosely into his face when he lost his hat in bringing her
down. She wanted to beg him not to hurt her, but her words
stuck in her throat and the only sounds that escaped were the
choking sounds she made as she gasped for air.

She felt her heart stop dead in her chest when she flicked
her head sharply to the side to escape the tart smell of garlic
on his breath. She saw the hooves of the other man's horse
draw up just inches from her face. One step closer and she
would have been crushed beneath them! She was trapped!
There was nothing she could do . . . no way of escape. The
gun was still pointed at her as she lay on the ground, and even
when she felt the man lift his weight off of her, she stayed
there, terrified that at any minute a bullet could rip through

her skull if she dared move. She watched with wordless fright as the man who had attacked her brushed the dust from his pants, all the while muttering under his breath and casting angry glances her way. The one on the horse raised the point of his gun in a couple of short jerky motions, gesturing for her to get up and to be quick about it. Instantly, she obeyed, scrambling to her feet.

She stood before them like a frightened animal, her eyes flicking nervously from one to the other. When the man on the horse slung a leg over the saddle and dropped to the ground, she felt dread leap into her heart and retreated instinctively. They stood before her menacingly, eyeing her up and down calculatingly. She could see their faces clearly now. The other man was fair-skinned, and she noticed tufts of sandy brown hair beneath his hat. She guessed him to be an American.

While she bore up under their scrutiny, she vowed that if they wanted her, she would make them pay for it, for she would not die easily.

They exchanged a look between themselves, then without a word, the dark-skinned man came toward her. She shrank back from him closing her eyes tightly, ready to lash out as soon as he touched her.

But he did not. Instead, he quickly reached up and pulled the cap from her head. The swiftness of his movement took Danny by surprise, but it was not nearly equal to theirs when they saw the mass of auburn hair tumble down, spilling over her shoulders and down her back. The one with the black eyes gasped, but it was the American who finally spoke, breaking the silence. "Well, I'll be. Would you look at that, Tomas."

Danny blinked hard at him. She had expected to hear a bellow, a curse, a roar . . . the type of sound that would naturally come out of a man who was about to commit rape, or worse. But his voice provided no threats. It was . . . it was actually pleasant, as though he were genuinely pleased by the unexpected development.

"Ay, *caramba*," uttered Tomas. "*Señorita*, we think you a boy. What you doing here?"

Danny felt an instant rush of relief surge into her limbs, but something in the back of her mind told her to remain guarded. She spoke haltingly, the words coming out with difficulty from her scratchy throat. "I . . . I . . . was riding, and I . . ."

Tomas turned quickly and spoke something to his friend. The other man shrugged and said nothing, studying her long and deliberately.

"What we going to do with her?" Tomas asked, running a hand through his hair.

At last Danny stepped forward in her own behalf. "Why don't you just . . . let me go?" The question sounded more like a plea.

"What you think, Matt? Should we do that?"

She turned pleading eyes on the American.

"I don't know, Tomas. But I'll tell you what I do know. Old Jake ain't gonna like this . . . no, sir, not one bit."

"Please, please, I swear to you, if you'll let me go, I won't tell a soul. I could never even find this place again if I wanted to. Oh, *please* let me go!"

Matt was sorely tempted to give in to her. On the other hand, if they brought her back to camp, Jake might see his way clear to letting him keep the woman. Jesus! He had *never* had himself a woman like this before. Fancy finding her out here. Even the clothes she wore could not hide the plain fact that she was a magnificent woman. He felt his mouth go dry at the thoughts running in his head.

Tomas saw his friend wavering and stepped in before they made a mistake that could prove costly. "No, Matt, we cannot let her go. She find this place, others they could find it too. I say we bring her with us and let my father decide what to do."

"No! No, please!" But her appeals were lost amidst the flurry of movement as Matt mounted his horse again and Tomas pulled her roughly along to where the brown mare was waiting. He picked her up in his arms when she tried to resist, and forcibly placed her in the saddle. He led the mare to where his own horse stood, mounted quickly, then turned to Matt, signaling with a nod of his head for them to move out.

Danny found herself being led away from the grassy slope by the strangers, one on either side of her. Making any attempt at escape would be impossible.

They rode in stony silence for about half an hour, slipping through several dark canyons and wound their way single file cautiously down a narrow path. It was so steep that Danny had to close her eyes to its treacherous angle and put her trust in the sure-footedness of the Indian pony.

At last the ground leveled beneath the horses' hooves, but Danny found herself once again held in close check by the men riding on either side of her. Tomas had grabbed the reins from her hands and had complete control of her mount.

They were riding through a long corridor of steep rocky walls that rose up ominously beside them. Stretched ahead lay an expanse of land, as far as the eye could see. Hot, arid and, above all else, flat. There was nothing of note to be seen out there, and the mere fact that they were headed in that direction did little to quell Danielle's fears.

She opened her mouth to protest, when, without warning, Tomas jerked his horse's head sharply to the right. He must be mad, Danny thought. The wall behind those bushes is solid rock!

Her hands flew up to protect her face from the sharp branches as they entered the brush. Thorny twigs scratched at her trousers, catching the fabric and tearing away little bits. She winced at the sting caused by a thorn that raked across the back of her hand, drawing a droplet of blood.

When they emerged from the dense under-growth and she opened her eyes, she could not believe what she saw.

Before them was a lush grassy slope, half-shaded by the mountain in whose shadow it lay nestled. At the base of the slope, she could make out four cabins, each of good distance from its neighbor and separated by patches of thick green trees. Behind the furthest cabin was a small corral peeking out where several horses roamed. Two others were hitched loosely outside of what Danny judged to be the main cabin due to its larger size.

She gulped hard as they approached within yards of it, and Tomas brought their horses to a halt. She did not fail to notice, with a sickening feeling, the foreboding look Tomas threw at Matt as he dismounted and went inside, leaving Danny alone with the American.

She was just about to turn to him to say something, when a roar from inside the cabin instantly stopped her. A shudder swept through her body and she cringed unintentionally in the saddle.

Rapidly, Matt was in motion. He dismounted and was standing beside her, arms outstretched toward her, telling her to get down.

"Be quick about it," he warned. "Come on, he'll be coming out in a minute."

Danny was stuck to the saddle. She willed her legs to move, but they disobeyed her.

Matt glanced nervously back toward the cabin, then impatiently at her. He could not wait for her all day to make up her mind, damn it. He reached up and jerked her, unceremoniously, from the horse's back, depositing her on the ground in front of him.

He could see the fright stamped on her face and felt kind of sorry for her now. "Look," he offered, "don't say anything. Here, put this on."

When he couldn't think of anything else to do, he shoved her cap at her. But when she did not move, he sighed and took matters into his own hands.

Shooting a quick glance over his shoulder, he grabbed handfuls of her hair and began furiously tucking them beneath the cap. Without even realizing it, no longer cognizant of her own actions, Danny helped him in his efforts to get the cap on her head. She sensed that he was trying to help her, and that was enough for her, but she began to feel his anxiety with increasing dread.

They worked like demons, and no sooner did Danny sweep the last few strands hurriedly away from her face than the cabin door flew open with a tremendous bang. Three figures emerged.

As they passed from the darkness of the cabin into the brilliance of the day, Danny noticed instantly that Tomas was not among them. Suddenly, an unnerving tremble seized her, and she watched with eyes growing wider as the men drew closer.

The oldest of the group walked slightly ahead of the others. She felt a sickening fear clutch her throat beneath his hard penetrating stare.

Jake Alvarez was an imposing figure. Though not a tall man, nor particularly broad in the shoulders, everything about him suggested that he was a man who lived dangerously.

His face was a mass of intricate lines, each deeply etched into the olive flesh that stretched tautly over high cheekbones and a long straight nose. He had a thick black mustache that extended in all directions over his upper lip and down the sides of his mouth, where it grew into a ragged unkempt beard.

As he stalked toward Danny, squinting from the blistering glare of the sun, he looked as though his face had been carved out of granite. The only mobile portions of its craggy surface were his small, round black eyes that flashed from beneath bushy brows.

He was slightly below medium height, his frame thin and wiry. He walked with a brisk gait almost as though there were a spring wound tight somewhere inside of him.

Danny could not take her eyes off him, terrified of what he would do when he reached her.

Unconsciously, she slipped behind Matt. As she did, she let her gaze slip momentarily from Alvarez's face down to his feet, unable to bear looking in his approaching eyes any longer lest she faint. It was then that she noticed he was not wearing any boots.

Jake Alvarez had been lying on his cot in the dark coolness of the cabin with his son, Francisco, Tomas's older brother, and one of his other men, Pierce Morgan. With a bottle of tequila dangling limply from his hand, he was doing absolutely nothing except escaping the heat of the day.

Then, from out of the blue, his idiot son, Tomas, had barged in uninvited, disturbing his peace and stammering like a nervous fool about bringing a stranger into camp. Jake felt the blood rush to his head.

"What!" He had exploded like a loaded cartridge.

He had jumped to his feet, throwing the bottle behind him. It landed in the spot he had just occupied on the cot, spilling its colorless liquid into a pool that quickly seeped into the thin mattress, creating a wet stain.

He had stormed over to his youngest son and stood within inches of his face, daring Tomas with his look to repeat what Jake *thought* he had heard. It was unbelievable that his own son would be fool enough to bring someone into the camp. In his mounting anger, he was hard pressed to keep his arm at his side instead of planting his fist squarely in Tomas' face.

Shoving past Tomas disgustedly, and with a sharp jerk of his head toward Cisco and Pierce, he stalked out of the cabin slamming the wooden door open with the forceful slap of his open palm.

The sun's glare was so strong that he could barely make out the shapes standing several yards away. He recognized the tall lanky build of Matt Turner, but he could not distinguish the other figure. "What the hell is going on here," he muttered when he noticed the other person cowering behind Matt.

He signaled with a shifting of his eyes for Matt to step aside. It was then that Alvarez saw the boy Tomas and Matt had brought with them.

Instantly, he diverted his attention to Matt Turner and showered a barrage of harsh language on him, switching back and forth from English to Spanish.

It was apparent to Danny that these men, some of them anyway, were Mexicans. Ha, she had even thought it would be fun to take a trip into Mexico once she and Austin had settled in San Francisco!

Jake lashed out with caustic words at Matt. Danny was at once relieved that the man's fearful attention was not directed at her, but was also suddenly apprehensive for Matt Turner's questionable safety.

"Wait, Jake, wait!" Matt cried, throwing up his hands in protest of the verbal assault. "I think you should see this." As he spoke, he reached past Jake, toward Danny, and snatched the cap from her head.

Once again her hair spilled about her face and shoulders. Under the blazing sun, it shone brilliantly with coppery streaks running along each tousled strand.

"*Por Dios!*" Jake exclaimed, his eyes wide in disbelief.

She shuddered as his beady eyes left the spectacle of her hair and traveled the length of her body, raking shamelessly over each contour, then back up to her face where they lingered a few moments more. He turned sharply to face Turner.

"Go get Nando," he ordered harshly.

Matt seemed reluctant to obey and shuffled around in his spot nervously. "Where is he?" he asked, hoping to stall for some time.

"Where is he!" Jake echoed, his voice growing louder again, brimming with venomous impatience. "Where do you *think* he is, you idiot? He's with Bianca. Now go!"

This time Matt did not dare disobey. But before he could put his legs into action, Cisco Alvarez stepped forward, risking the old man's wrath by doing so.

"Nando is not going to like being bothered now. Maybe we should—"

"I said go!" Jake bellowed at Matt, purposely ignoring

Cisco's warning. He would never tolerate any insubordination—least of all from his own sons!

Turner gathered his strength and walked off in the direction of the cabin which lay at the furthest end of the clearing. He returned minutes later, ashen and alone.

"He's coming," was all he said, keeping his gaze steadily on the red-haired woman.

Jake Alvarez was eyeing Danny also, although for different reasons. Yes, this little *gringa* was beautiful, but her unexpected presence here spelled nothing but trouble. Trouble among his men if he allowed her to stay, and trouble for him if anyone should come looking for her.

If what Tomas had said were true and she *had* found her way here on her own, then it would be possible for others to find their way into the sanctuary. He also knew that if he let her go, she would probably be able to easily lead others here now that the hideout had been revealed to her. The fools had not even thought to blindfold her!

His eyes raked coldly over her, assessing her value, but unable to determine its true worth from the way she was dressed. Then he saw the silver necklace clasped around her neck.

Jake Alvarez smiled wickedly behind his shaggy mustache. Now *that* would certainly bring a pretty price across the border, he thought to himself, and it would be such an easy matter to take it from her. He reached for the treasure at her throat.

Danny guessed instantly what it was he wanted when she saw him eyeing her throat with a strange hungry look in his black eyes. She backed away from him slowly, shaking her head.

"No!" she cried. "No, I won't let you have it!"

"Don't try to stop me, *señorita*, or it will be the very last thing you do," he said, his eyes threatening.

His tone forced a cry from her lips. "Please . . . take anything I have . . . take my horse . . . but not this . . ."

The *gringa* stood there blatantly defying him and Alvarez was suddenly taken somewhat aback by her fiery resistance. But his astonishment vanished quickly and was replaced by anger. He was rapidly growing tired of playing games with her, as she would soon learn.

He grabbed her roughly by the arm and pulled her close to him. She could smell the tobacco and the liquor on his breath and thought it would make her retch in his face. Danny fought against his painful grip, but he only tightened his hold, causing her to cry out. Still, she defied him.

"You'll have to kill me first!" she shrieked.

"That can be arranged, little spitfire," he said, laughing contemptuously. "But it would be such a shame to put a bullet through such a pretty head, eh, *señorita?*"

He ran a gnarled hand over her shoulder and stopped at her neck. Danny saw his boney fingers bend to snatch the necklace away.

"No, you bully!" she cried. "Leave it!"

The crisp order from somewhere behind her caused Alvarez to halt in midair, fingers within inches of the prize.

"*Leave it.*"

This time the words were purposely stressed and there was no mistaking the force behind them.

Jake Alvarez was many things. He was a greedy man, willing to kill to obtain what he wanted. More than once his hot temper had gotten him into irreconcilable trouble—once landing him behind bars for two years. But unlike his son, Tomas, he was no idiot.

His hand dropped to his side and he released Danny with an angry shove, sending her stumbling backward, off balance. When she regained her footing, she spun around to see who had spoken to Jake in that way.

A tall figure broke out of the shadows of the trees and made its way toward the group. The only sound breaking the stillness that had befallen them was the tinkling of the spurs on his black boots with each step he took. The other men parted to let him pass and he stepped out into the open.

He was dressed entirely in black. The legs of his chino trousers were tucked into his boots and he wore a gunbelt slung low on his hips. His thick black hair extended down the sides of his face, meeting at a point beneath his chin, and the thin black mustache he wore made him look Spanish.

In spite of the fact that part of his face was concealed beneath the curls falling over his forehead, Danny felt something strangely familiar about him as he approached. She watched suspiciously the way he moved, with long easy strides and lean muscles tensing beneath the fabric of his clothing.

His shirt was open nearly to the waist as though he had

dressed in a hurry, and around his neck was a loosely knotted light-colored scarf that emphasized his suntanned skin and enhanced the brilliance of his eyes.

His eyes! She had seen those eyes before!

The recognition seared her mind like a branding iron. It was him! That dirty brutal savage who had—

She charged at him, taking them all by surprise, and the impact of her blow as she drove her clenched fist directly into his stomach was enough to knock the wind out of him and send him staggering backward.

Before he could regain his balance, she fell upon him, flailing viciously, using all her exploding anger in a burst of frenzy—clawing, beating, grabbing at him with every ounce of strength she could muster.

She wanted to kill him! She wanted to rake her nails over his arrogant face and tear pieces of flesh from him.

So blind was she to everything else that she did not even hear the shouts of the men, who had formed a circle around the scuffling figures, cheering and stamping their feet.

"Brute! Savage! I hate you! I hate you!"

Jake Alvarez cheered the loudest. "Ho, Nando, look out, *amigo,* she's behind you! Would you look at that little demon. She fights like a wildcat! *Dios!* I have never seen a woman like this one. Hey, Nando, look out!"

He laughed raucously with the others as Nando swerved to deflect her blows and twisted sideways to avoid her sharp teeth and nails.

Danielle had managed to land some powerful blows despite her size, and he was rapidly tiring of this game. Reaching out, he restrained her swinging arms and managed to get hold of her.

Feeling herself in his grasp, Danny whirled around and came up on the other side, kicking violently at his knee, bringing a growl of outrage from his throat.

He had had enough! With one swift jerk, he wrenched her around to face him while twisting her arm up behind her back in an excruciating thrust. Danny screamed when the pain shot to her shoulder, but she continued to fight, yelling at him through the tears.

"You pig! You dirty rotten pig . . . I hate you and your half-breed heart. You bastard!"

"That's enough out of you, lady," he said harshly, pulling

her roughly toward him and up against his chest. He brought his other arm around her waist, pinning her to him, restricting her movements by his powerful strength.

Her hair lay matted about her face and she could feel the sweat pouring down her body. Her breath rasped in her chest and she sobbed helplessly against him.

"Hey, *amigo,* you know this one, eh?" Jake called out.

"Well, it sure looks like she knows him," Pierce Morgan laughed.

"Ay, that Nando. He sure has a way with the *señoritas,* eh?"

The men howled with laughter, and Danny felt her cheeks flush scarlet from the embarrassment.

Chapter 9

Crouching on the dusty cabin floor, her wrists tied tightly behind her, Danny heard heated voices through the small window above her head.

Her dilated seeking eyes moved quickly about the small dank room she'd been shoved into by a pair of rough hands. It was sparsely furnished with two rickety cots, a wash basin and a table in the center with no chairs. Whose room was this? Was it *his*? That animal's?

Danny's mouth drooped in a frown as she contemplated her state of affairs. Closing her eyes, her head fell back against the wall and she felt everything evaporate into the hot stale air of the cabin—all hope, panic, hatred—leaving her weak with utter despair.

The snap of Jake Alvarez's staccato voice outside jolted her to her senses. She heard someone shuffling around on the other side of the door, and a moment later it swung open. Before her was someone who looked very much like Tomas Alvarez, with the same black hair, dark complexion and ebony eyes. But it was not Tomas, nor was it his brother Cisco. It was a woman. There was no mistaking that even in the darkness of the heavily shaded cabin.

She was dressed in a bright red skirt that swirled about her ankles in a tier of ruffles from beneath which peeked bare brown feet. The thin, white cotton blouse she wore dipped dangerously low over one shoulder, exposing smooth dark flesh and pendulous breasts. She was beautiful, with full red lips emphasizing a jet black mane and gleaming dark eyes. There seemed to be a primitive earthy quality about her that immediately filled the room.

97

The girl stepped forward leaving the door open. Sauntering by, hands on hips, she eyed Danny suspiciously with a raised eyebrow. Thick black lashes fanned across her cheeks as she cast a downward gaze at the girl crouching on the floor.

They sized each other up for several long tense moments in which Danny felt the girl's resentment by the glare from her dark eyes. Suddenly they both heard heavy footsteps at the door.

He walked straight into the room and stood next to Bianca with his thumbs hooked over his gunbelt.

"I told you I didn't want you in here." He directed the words to the floor, then flicked a steely look at the black-haired girl.

"Oh, Nando," she complained, "I just wanted to see what all those idiots are drooling over, that is all." She shot a contemptuous look at Danny. "But I see it is nothing but a boy . . . a *gringo* at that." She flicked her head away, tossing her black mane about and gave a haughty laugh. "What you think, Nando? Do *you* think she is beautiful?" she challenged him, running a hand through her hair.

He shifted nervously from foot to foot, doing his best to ignore the question while his gray eyes raked over Danielle.

"Eh, Nando?" Bianca persisted.

Finally he tore his eyes away. "Yeah," he relented. "Yeah, I think she's beautiful. Now I want you out of here, and I want you to stay out."

Bianca Alvarez laughed as she turned on her heels and walked out, her black hair brushing about her shoulders. "I see you later, *caballero.*"

The rusty springs of the cot creaked when he sat down, gingerly clutching his abdomen. He gave a short laugh when he noticed Danny's eyes on him. "You landed some pretty good blows. But then, I guess I had it coming."

The admission of guilt went right past her. Throwing her head back to shake the hair from her face, she glared back at him with eyes glassy and wide.

"You don't think you're going to get away with this, do you?" she hissed at him. "There are men combing these hills for me right now and you know it!"

His look turned pensive before he rose. "You're right about that." He walked to the place where she sat and cast an icy glare at her that made her shrink unconsciously despite her resolve to appear unafraid. Inside, she trembled like a frightened rabbit at the door of the wolf.

"That's why it's time we broke camp and headed out," he was saying. "And don't get any ideas because you're coming with us."

A look of pained shock sprang into her eyes, and in answer to it, he turned and abruptly stalked away, saying, "Well, damn it, I've got no choice. Don't you see that? I can't leave you here. And if I let you go, you'd have them down on us in no time."

Had she detected a note of apology in his tone? It was gone the moment he turned back to her with cold gray eyes.

"You're coming with us, and that's all there is to it. I can't let you go until we're out of here . . . until I've got no further need of you."

He strode to the door with long purposeful strides, muttering under his breath. "Man, you sure did upset things around here." Then, over his shoulder he ordered curtly, "Get some rest, we'll be riding out at dusk." The door slammed shut and she heard his heavy footsteps as he retreated, leaving her alone with her misery and fear.

She had no idea how long she remained in that cramped position on the dirty floor, but judged it to be quite a while by the ache in her joints when she finally rose. Danielle trudged to the cot, lay down on the thread-thin mattress and slipped into a dark dream.

It was hard to tell if she'd been asleep for minutes or hours, but all of a sudden she felt herself being shaken awake by a rough hand on her shoulder. She opened her mouth to scream, and immediately a hand came down across her mouth, forcing her voice back down her throat. The voice that was by now a familiar one sent a new terror racing through her blood.

"Quiet now," he whispered, a thin smile touching the corners of his mouth. "You don't want to bring the others, do you?" Cautiously he removed his hand from her mouth to test her reaction, ready to silence her again if need be.

"What do you want?" Danny demanded as she scrambled to her knees.

Without answering he reached behind her and sliced off the leather strips about her wrists, his gray eyes raking over her as he worked. Even in the dim, fading light he could see the way her breasts heaved beneath the clingy silk of her blouse. He remembered them as soft and firm and burning with a fire that even she did not know she possessed. His look told her everything that was going on in his mind, and she recoiled from him, her eyes narrowed into slanted bits of amber glass.

"No! I won't let you touch me again! I'd die first! I won't let—"

He reached for her quickly and in her desperate attempt to elude his grasp, she lost the rest of her protest. She struggled against him, but his strength prevailed and she found herself on the cot again, locked in his arms with his body poised over hers making escape impossible.

"When are you going to learn that it's useless to fight me, Danny?"

His mocking voice made her cringe with humiliation and seethe with rage.

"No!" she cried as she twisted and turned, frantically trying to avoid his hands as they sought to undress her.

"Hold still, damn it," he muttered between his teeth as he fumbled with her buttons.

"Oh, I hate you! You're a dirty animal and I can't bear to have your hands on me, can't you see that!"

When her garments lay in a crumpled heap on the floor, he rose from the cot, and eyeing her calmly, undressed himself. The sight of her kneeling among the rumpled covers, clutching one desperately to hide herself from his eyes, her tangled hair all over the place and her golden eyes bright and wild, Alex Coulter could not have denied himself what he wanted if he had tried. A smile of grim amusement stretched across his lips.

"See, I told you the next time we'd spend more time together."

Danny tried to cry out but swiftly his body came down on hers making her immobile, the sudden weight taking her breath away all at once.

His mouth came down on hers in a hard angry kiss, and Danny felt the panic leap into her heart. She recalled too vividly the way he'd taken her the first time, harsh and quick, without any regard for her feelings. There had been no gentleness in him then. He was an animal, and she felt herself about to be consumed by him once again.

He held her pinned in his arms pressed up against the length of his lean muscular body as he kissed her strongly, almost brutally, his tongue ravaging her mouth, sending her reeling.

A sharp pounding erupted in her temples that slowly worked its way down into her limbs, across her abdomen and lay at the pit of her loins like a raw burning. Without knowing what she was doing, or why . . . with every thought, instinct and nerve ending concentrated on the strange fire racing through her body . . . Danny's arms slowly worked their way around his neck where they stayed wrapped.

In response, his hand released its painful grip and slid to her neck where it entangled itself in a thick handful of hair, while the fingers of his other hand traced lightly across her breasts. Holding her firmly against him, with the heat of his hand now at the bare flesh of her back, his mouth slipped from her lips and burned a trail to her throat where it buried itself at the pulsing hollow there.

Danny felt herself go weak and a tremble spread across her flesh drawing her closer to him. Her head fell back and she began to moan in spite of herself. Everything seemed to be slipping from her grasp . . . all will, all thought . . . everything except this pounding sensation surging through her veins that seemed to make her blood boil. She struggled against him weakly, halfheartedly, and when his arms closed over her again, she closed her eyes and let him have his way.

She pressed her slender body hard against his, confused, half-crying, not yet aware of this nameless new feeling that had invaded her body . . . indeed, her very soul.

Her unexpected yielding seemed to bring a new tenderness to his lovemaking, as though her surrender had erased in him all trace of the hardness she already knew him capable of. And with her eyes closed, it was difficult to imagine that it was the same man. His touch was soft, gentle, playful, and she felt herself responding in a way she had not known before.

Somewhere deep within her a small voice spoke. So this is it; this is what it is like. A burning pitch that starts from somewhere in the recesses of the mind and spreads like a wildfire through the body, its fever washing through the loins, making you incapable of acting against it, and not really wanting to. Not really understanding what it is, but knowing that somehow nothing else in the world matters.

His lips moved from her throat to her breasts where his tongue tickled and teased her taut pink nipples to erection and his mouth engulfed them. Gently, slowly, his fingers weaved across her belly to the soft mound demurely hidden between her white thighs.

No, he mustn't . . . no . . . But her mind's feeble protests were drowned out by the surging roar of her own passion.

"Danny—Danny—"

His voice against her naked flesh deafened the world to all else. Half-sobbing with shame, and yet aching from the hunger that flooded over her, it was impossible for Danny to ignore the feel of his body against hers—his legs, long and taut with muscles—the warmth of his bare chest against her own naked breasts—the thickness of his hair in her grasping fingers.

She had expected a quick brutal rape. This was something she was not prepared for, and against her will, she responded to his searing caresses as her hungry young body took possession of her senses.

"No, please don't . . . ," she murmured when he spread her thighs apart with his knees. But he just laughed softly and kissed her gently on the lips, letting the slow easy movement of his body erase her misgivings.

Just when the world stood still—just as he rose above her, his maleness hard and ready, the thin thread to which Danny clung so tenuously snapped in two and sent her spiraling backward into an abyss.

Instantly, Alex's body suspended above hers in midair. All muscles tensed stilling all motion as if they'd both been frozen in space.

The sharp raps at the door brought Danny crashing back to reality and elicited a series of harsh curses from low under Alex Coulter's breath. Releasing her, he sprang from the bed.

"All right, all right!" he shouted disgustedly when the rapping was followed by a voice calling from the outside.

Danny scrambled to her feet, clutching her blouse and trousers, fumbling with the buttons and feeling the flush of shame scorch her cheeks.

"Christ, I forgot," Alex said. Impatient with himself for getting caught with his guard down, he grabbed for his clothes. "Hurry up and get dressed." All traces of softness had vanished into thin air.

He was still breathing hard from the sudden interruption. With the blood surging through his veins and his passions yet soaring, he dressed quickly and efficiently, strapping on the gunbelt. He shot a look over at Danny as she fumbled with her buttons, trying desperately to fight down the shame that swept over her.

"Well, come on," he said brusquely. "We don't have all day." And brushing her hands aside, he finished buttoning her blouse, noting with amusement the way she kept her golden eyes averted.

"There's no need to feel that way," he said quietly as he worked. "You were born for it, if you don't mind my saying."

The compliment only provoked her to flare up at him. She pushed his helping hands aside and brushed past him. "I presume *now* you will let me go," she said, forcing a bit of arrogance into her voice.

"What? Let you go?" He let out a laugh. Then, as if suddenly reminded of something, the laughter was gone. "So that's it!" He whirled to face her, a dark menacing expression shadowing his features. "I should have known. Man, you sure do learn fast, don't you? The last time we met you were just a virgin, weren't you, Danny? Here you are now making up for lost time. And I thought you were actually enjoying yourself." His expression turned into a sneer. "I guess I didn't figure you to be such a good actress."

For a moment it looked as though he was going to pounce on her. Finally he tore his eyes away, releasing Danny from the terror of their metallic brilliance. He coldly informed her, "I'm not letting you go. Not as long as I can use you. Right now you're my ticket out of these hills. After that, we'll see. Now come on. Let's go." Reaching out, he grabbed her by the arm and yanked her along with him.

Outside, the sunset showered its beauty on the earth, dazzling all of nature's creatures with the fire of its orange skies.

Danny tried hard to remain with her feet firmly planted on the ground when Alex attempted to get her into the saddle. Embarrassment washed crimson over her cheeks when she heard the laughter from the others who stood watching the furious little scene. Eventually her strength gave way to his, which seemed never to end, and in a single overwhelming move, he hoisted her up into the air and plunked her down onto the Indian pony with a thud that jolted her senses. With her head reeling, she was oblivious, until it was too late, to the strips of rawhide he tied tightly about her wrists, attaching her firmly to the saddle pommel . . . a cruel and acute reminder that she was going nowhere . . . that she was his prisoner and that she was, more and more, at his mercy.

Danny fought hard to keep back the tears, but as they rode slowly and silently out of the hidden valley a while later, the hot sting of tears pinched her eyes and the taste of salt was on her lips.

The half-light of the moon cast a hazy luminance on the darkened earth through a smoky streak of cloud. Alex Coulter's eyes swept the rocky ground as he led the way out of the hills and onto the flatlands, noting with their usual alertness the way the filtered light glinted off the surfaces of their guns. Nor did he miss the way the moonlight spread over the face of the girl riding wordlessly beside him, enhancing her perfect white complexion, making it seem almost of alabaster. But most of all, as he looked at her from the corner of his eye, he could see the way the light trickled down her cheeks as it floated along the tiny tears that spilled silently from the most beautiful eyes he had ever seen.

Chapter 10

It seemed to Danny as though they'd been riding for an eternity. Oh, her body ached so. Every muscle cried out in sheer agony and every bone felt the hardness of the saddle as they plodded on through several nights without stopping for rest. Sitting astride her horse in a half-dazed state, she nodded out every now and then nearly toppling out of the saddle. All she could feel was the raw red flesh burning beneath the leather Alex Coulter had fastened tightly around her wrists.

She had no idea of where they were or why on earth they had to travel, even at night, with hardly any light to guide them. Her trousers were soaked from splashing through countless streams, and the nighttime air chilled her with its crispness, sending shivers through her aching weary body.

She had spoken very little to anyone, and even when one of them spoke to her, she turned her head away to avoid conversation, despite the consequences of possibly antagonizing them. She decided that these strange men she was riding with were some kind of bandits, but could only shudder at the extent of their devilry. My God, they were probably killers!

She could barely keep her wits about her whenever Alex dropped back from his spot up ahead with Alvarez to ride beside her. Oh, she hated him—everything about him.

She sat slumped in the saddle, watching the black hard ground pass beneath her eyes. Soft moans began to escape through her lips and silent sobs racked her chest. Hot stinging tears spilled from her eyes. God, would they ever stop?

Danny was sure she'd been in the same position for days

and when they eventually did make camp, she could barely straighten up.

As though mesmerized she watched the others unpack their saddle rolls and ready things for the night. When everything was taken care of, and only after he'd spoken briefly with Jake, Alex appeared at her side to help her off the horse.

"Just untie my wrists," she snapped, suddenly springing to life. "I can get down by myself!"

"Why, ma'am, I couldn't allow a lady to do that. I'd be neglecting my duty if I did. But I will free your hands."

His voice crept through her with its slippery sarcasm, but before she could retort with something particularly caustic, he yanked her down so quickly that her head flew back and her hair whipped about her face wildly before settling in a frazzled mass.

As she hit the ground, her legs went weak and rubbery, unprepared for the unexpected weight put on them after so many days in the saddle. Her arms flew out to steady herself for the fall, but Alex reached out and caught her just in time. He didn't pick her up. Instead, he dragged her across the ground for several yards and propped her against a tree. She slid to the craggy ground, mindless of the tiny tears in her blouse. From her seated position, she watched dazedly as the others gathered around the camp fire like hazy figures. She was tired . . . so tired . . . that she could not even run away if she wanted to. Miserably aware of her own vulnerability, Danny hated herself for her helplessness. But more than that, she hated Alex Coulter for forcing her into such a dreadful situation. Who did he think he was anyway? Damn him!

The horses were munching at the feed in their nose bags, and while the others ate directly out of tin pans, Alex Coulter's figure stood silhouetted by the fire, long lean legs placed slightly apart. Bianca Alvarez also stood by the flames, poking the crackling branches with a long stick, throwing glances at Alex and inching closer to him. Flexing her fingers, she ran them slowly across his back, calling for his attention.

Alex looked at the dark-eyed woman and smiled. Then, leaning toward her, he whispered something into her ear that made her laugh out loud. Winding a strong arm around her waist, he drew her close; and lowering his head to her upturned face, he kissed her long and passionately on her full red lips.

Danny watched until she began to shiver uncontrollably and her teeth started to clatter. From where she sat she could not feel the soothing warmth of the fire, and she vainly wrapped her arms around herself as protection from the moist ground and brisk night air.

She was still trembling when Alex appeared in front of her, a blanket dangling from his hand. Kneeling, he placed the scratchy woolen blanket around her and tucked it tightly beneath her chin. Then, through the blanket he began to rub her arms vigorously; next, her hands and her legs until she felt the blood beginning to surge once again through her numbed limbs. When the shivering subsided he held a bottle up to her mouth.

"Here, drink this. It'll make you warm."

What was it? Whiskey? She wasn't going to touch that sickening stuff, and certainly not straight from the bottle! With the blanket restricting her movements and her arms trapped at her sides, Danny twisted her head sharply to one side.

"Look, don't give me a hard time," he snapped. "I said drink this!"

With that he grabbed her hair and yanked her head back, shoving the tip of the bottle to her mouth. He pushed it between her lips. It clanked hard against her clenched teeth, and she had no choice but to drink, half-choking on the foul tasting liquid.

The liquor started taking effect even before Alex lowered the bottle from her bruised mouth. Danny winced at the raw sensation that spilled into her throat, but when it reached her stomach, she felt its burn turn to warmth . . . smooth and silky . . . and soon her muscles began to relax and her nerves started to unwind. At last, the sleep she'd been craving for days overtook her like a giant black wave, sucking her into its watery depths.

It was a temporary respite, for at dawn, they were on the move again. By noon they were surrounded by nothing but huge blistering boulders and massive granite walls that rose sharply all around them. Except for those times when they passed through the shadow of one of the monolithic slabs, the sun shone down on them without mercy. As they rode on into the heat of the day, Danny began to grow weaker and had trouble keeping in the saddle. From out of nowhere Alex appeared at her side, drawing his big Appaloosa stallion close to her small brown mare. From his vest he pulled out a familiar cloth cap.

"Here, put this on."

But the throb in Danny's temples left little room for anything this day, much less a gesture of kindness from this despicable man. She flicked her head away with an upward tilt of her chin.

"Okay, suit yourself," he said, with a disarming smile. "But if this hat doesn't sit on your head soon, you're going to fry under this sun quicker than a strip of pork fat."

He sounded playful, as though he were poking harmless fun at her. Ha! She knew damn well just how harmless he really was! She refused to look at him, and if he insisted on pushing that cap at her, she'd tear it from his hands and throw it beneath her pony's hooves.

Alex had no trouble reading her thoughts, and with a sigh of exasperation, made one swift move of his body to come down softly behind her on the pony, while his stallion, now riderless, dropped back where its reins were caught by one of the men riding the rear.

Danny whirled this way and that trying to get a piece of him, but he was too quick. Realizing that it was useless to fight him, she sat rigid in the saddle while his hands gathered her hair. He swept it off her shoulders gently picking loose strands from her face and tucked it all beneath the cap.

He was close, so horribly close that she could smell his sweat and the faint odor of liquor on his breath.

They rode in silence, he, seemingly at ease and moving to the gait of the horse, while Danny sat stiffly in front of him, flinching whenever his hand left the reins to fondle her shoulder. It was hot, very hot, and she'd begun to perspire heavily beneath her trousers. The apricot blouse clung mercilessly to her flesh and her swollen feet felt like they would burst inside her boots. Alex leaned close over her shoulder and she felt his warm breath at her ear.

"I thought we'd make a little detour on the way," he whispered, knowing to tighten his hold on her.

"I hate you," she whispered back through clenched teeth. "God, how I hate you!"

"I'm glad to see you're in a pleasant mood today, Danny," he laughed mockingly. "I was beginning to think you'd quieted down."

"You didn't think I'd ever let you touch me again, did you?

You're nothing but a miserable dog! A dirty half-breed dog! And I'd die rather than have you touch me! I hate you!"

"Yeah, well, one of these days I'd like to see just how much you do hate me, but not now."

With that, he reached forward and snapped off the restraining rawhide with a single lash. He brought the pony to a halt, and sliding off its rump he took one long stride to its side and jerked Danny down to the ground. When he'd half-dragged her to a clump of cottonwood trees, he stood back with his hands on his hips.

"Take your clothes off," he demanded. "And be quick about it, we don't have all day."

"I won't do it!" she hissed. Her fists were clenched at her sides, nails digging into the flesh of her palms.

"Damn it, Danny, I told you we haven't got all day. For one thing, if you don't get out of those clothes yourself, I'll take them off for you. And another thing, as long as we're riding together, you'd better learn to do as you're told." His voice held a chilling warning.

"I won't let you touch me again. Not after what you did."

"Well now, if I remember correctly, you sure didn't act like you were a virgin."

She was horrified by the caustic remark. "What? What do you mean by that?"

"A woman doesn't dance the way you do, baby, unless she's got a fire in her blood. Yeah, baby, that's right. I was at the Bull's Head that night, and I saw you dancing. I just did what every one of those other men wanted to do. And I must say, my love, in spite of your protests and, shall we say, your inexperience, you were quite a little hellcat. I rather enjoyed myself."

The rage that mounted in her turned her face white. "You dare speak to me like that after what you've put me through? You're the most selfish, the most narrow-minded egotistical man I have ever—"

"That's enough!"

His bellow silenced her on the spot. "I didn't come out here to argue with you *or* to rape you!" He stalked back to the pony and pulled something from behind the saddle. When he came back to her, he flung it at her feet. "Pick them up and put them on, and if you don't, I'll do it for you."

A rumpled red skirt and white blouse lay on the ground. She recognized them instantly as Bianca's. "I won't wear anything of hers! Get those things away from me! Do you think for one minute that I would put on the same clothes—''

Alex was at her side in a flash, scooping up the garments with a sweep of his arm and tearing the apricot blouse from her body.

Danny screamed and flung her hands up to her suddenly exposed chest. "No!"

"Then put those on!" he yelled back. "And be quick about it unless you want to ride barebreasted the rest of the way!"

Grudgingly, she slipped into the skirt and blouse and tossed her own garments away. She was still too furious to notice the soft breeze rustling the hem of the skirt as she walked back to where he waited by the horse.

"Isn't that better?" Alex asked when they were both remounted. Then, he urged the pony into a canter.

She would not acknowledge him with a reply.

Gradually, Danny began to relax as the cool wind blew on her cheeks and neck. Without warning, Alex slipped the blouse off her right shoulder, then the left. She tensed immediately, ready to take another swipe at him. However, as his hand retreated to the reins, she started to calm down again.

Truthfully, she had to admit, this attire did free her from the constricting heat of her own heavy garments. She continued to ride with her legs wrapped around the mare, which caused the skirt hem to rise above her knees. The air felt so good against the skin of her slender legs.

When they caught up with the others, she did not miss the wide grins on the faces of the men or Bianca's gypsy eyes that traveled bitingly over her as the band resumed its slow steady pace. With a shrill whistle, Alex called his stallion to his side and slid from the pony's back into his own saddle. The big horse lurched forward, prancing in high-stepping strides, his magnificent neck arched and his snowy mane whipping all about his beautiful white head. His splotched rump disappeared up ahead where he took his place beside the unimpressive brown horse ridden by Jake Alvarez. Danny could see the two men laughing as the stallion settled into the same dull pace as the others. They're probably laughing at me, she thought bitterly. Damn him!

As the day progressed, Danny lost all concept of time and direction. She tried to pay attention to the way they were heading. If she could have seen the sun, she might have been able to get her bearings. But as they wound their way higher and higher into the mountains, the sun would sometimes disappear behind a jagged peak only to reappear some minutes later in another position.

Slowly, as the hours dragged by, she began to realize that there was a method to their seemingly aimless meandering. It finally occurred to her that these people were running away, although from what she had no idea. In their flight, they were simply covering their tracks, leaving a trail that would be nearly impossible to follow.

Dear God, Danny thought despairingly, no one will ever find me! Where are they taking me? What are they going to do with me?

Sometime during the late afternoon, Alex once again pulled up close beside her. Without speaking, he pulled from his saddle pack a strip of dried meat that he called jerky. It had seemed rancid to Danny the first time she'd bitten into it, and she could barely choke down a couple of bites. But once she realized that it was all she would get, she'd taken to nibbling at the pieces he gave her, picking at them at first, then wolfing down the meat hungrily, despite the foul taste that, strangely, she was becoming, if not accustomed to, then at least tolerant of. She accepted the food, but only when he'd ride off would she eat it. For in her scorn of him, she did not even wish him to see her in a moment of weakness, not even in a moment of hunger.

"I'll show him I can take it," she grumbled to herself. "I'll not let him destroy me."

Pierce Morgan, riding at her side, turned to look at her. "You say something, miss?"

He was glad for the company. If they had to ride together, he'd just as soon pass the time chatting with the lady. All this silence made him jittery, and Lord knows, he wasn't the type of man to sit still for very long.

Danny did not fail to notice the way he turned to her, almost too quickly, too eager. Don't be fooled by his face, she warned herself, glancing quickly at his smiling features and easy brown eyes. Unsure of whom she could trust, she averted her eyes to the ground, and with a shrug, Pierce Morgan shifted in the saddle and focused his own eyes on the monotonous horizon ahead.

Later that night, after they had eaten and the fire had grown dim, Danny turned to Alex who was sitting a few feet away. There was just the red glow of his cigarette visible through the midnight darkness. Her voice, soft and innocent, drifted toward him.

"Why do these men call you Nando?" She was like a child whose curiosity had gotten the better of her at last. She couldn't see his face but she could hear him deeply draw a breath into his lungs as though he had not expected the question. Then she saw the tip of his cigarette glow brighter as he inhaled a final time before flicking it away and sending red sparks leaping into the air.

When she'd spoken, his thoughts had been miles away from this place . . . from this time, and he needed a moment to collect himself. "Most of these men are Mexican," he answered at length in a low voice. "You know how they are, they like giving everyone a Mexican name. Makes them feel like one big family, I guess."

Danny considered it for a moment. "Well, then why don't Matt and Pierce have Mexican names also?"

Of course, thought Alex, why not? It was the most logical question in the world, but it irritated him. "How should I know," he replied, shifting uncomfortably in his spot. She could sense his uneasiness without seeing it.

"You'd better get some sleep," he said, rising to his feet. "We'll be breaking camp at dawn."

She did not see him leave, but she knew he was gone. And after several minutes of fighting her weariness, she fell asleep. When she awoke in the morning, reluctantly giving up the safety of her dreams, she opened her eyes to an alarming sight.

The camp was gone! The men were gone! The horses! Everything—gone!

Crawling out from beneath her blanket, her eyes still sleepy to the brand-new day, she spotted Alex working silently to the side where both horses stood saddled and waiting. With a nod of his head, he stood back and waited wordlessly while Danny rose groggily and trudged across the open land to take her place yet again in the saddle.

Chapter 11

Danny had lost all idea of how many weeks had passed. She could not even be sure which summer month it was, although somehow, it didn't seem to matter much.

The Colorado Rockies rose all around them like massive pyramids, some scattered randomly, others bunched together in vast precision against the startling blue sky. The snow-capped peaks contrasted against the rich browns, reds and greens of the mountains. The spring thaw had melted the snow from all but the highest summit, sending silvery rivulets of water into the valleys. The little streams still continued to work their way downward, finding paths into rivers that cut sharply into the crust of the earth.

Danny would gaze in speechless awe at the majesty around her. Everywhere there were things to be seen as she and Alex traveled through the range of twisted and carved formations. She could hardly believe that one moment they would be clattering over the rocky terrain of a dried riverbed and the next moment they would be climbing higher and higher until they would come to stop in the middle of a grassy knoll. The constant sound of water accompanied them, sometimes in murmuring trickles, other times in a deafening roar.

In the stillness late one morning they came across a great blister of a hollow rock with a spring of turquoise water riffling over boulders below, and opened above to the sky. Deep beneath its concave jagged edge, where it seemed impossible for any man to descend, stood a single lance with a lone hawk's feather staked at its head.

Alex explained that the Indians believed man first emerged on earth from the underworld through its crystal clear stream, rising up the forbidding walls, and out into the light of day.

113

Someone, sometime, had placed deep within the rock the symbol of his belief, the proof of his existence, acknowledging the validity of the myth with a mortal proclamation.

How dark and mysterious it all seemed, this place that was so sacred to others. Looking down into the immense cavern, Danny felt a tremor race through her body. Out here, where there was nothing but the earth and the sky to fear, standing hardly noticed among the raw rocks, she knew it was the land, and not man, that was master. And she knew this was Alex Coulter's land. And that he, like it, was as harsh and as fearsome.

She watched him riding silently beside her, his hands motionless on the reins, directing his horse with subtle pressures from his knees. He looked at ease, his handsome face relaxed and a faint smile on his full lips. His eyes were drinking in the sights as though he'd seen them all before and was remembering them fondly.

After following a river for some days, they entered the Lodore Canyon and Danny wondered aloud whether she'd ever seen anything quite so beautiful. Lichen grew in places of perpetual shade, weaving its crusty fingers over boulders and up hollowed tree trunks. Small, dark furry shapes scampered among the boulders to disappear into the ice cold water. Alex pointed to the muskrat and mink that lived along the river, sharing the territory grudgingly, but peaceably, with the beaver whose construction work was everywhere. After watching for a while, they rode out of the grotto.

Somewhere overhead they heard the cry of a golden eagle. Raising her hand to her eyes to shield the sun's glare, Danny saw the solitary bird circling the sky, its massive wings fanning across the blue panorama, gliding on currents of air. Alex too watched in fascination as the big bird soared high into the sky, pushing down columns of air with each stroke of its seven-foot wingspan. When it flew to a distance where they could scarcely see it against the sunlight, the eagle folded its wings, drawing them close to its body, and like a daredevil diver, spiraled toward the earth and disappeared behind a nearby peak.

What they did not see was the tiny dot on the ground below that twitted about unaware of its rapidly approaching fate. The bird plummeted toward its prey, the finger-like feathers on its wings spread to adjust its rapid descent, its powerful talons outstretched. Without interrupting its sweep, it snatched its prey into the air, holding the small creature lifelessly in its claws.

The captor flew to a protruding ledge where a pair of quickly growing eaglets waited. Opening its razor-sharp talons, it dropped its catch into the nest and soared off into the sky. While the eaglets tore at the prey she'd left for them, the mother bird watched from her pine-tree perch, sweeping the land with eyes that could see for miles, marshal of the air, master of its environment.

The two people moved slowly out of the canyon unaware of the eyes that followed them from the treetops.

"Jacaronda," Alex commented, pointing to a spot in the distance that looked vaguely like a town. "But don't get too excited about it," he added dryly. "We're not even passing through."

"What? Why not?" Danny was shocked and her voice held a note of annoyance that he did not fail to notice.

"Not now," he replied firmly. "Maybe on the way back . . . We'll see."

"The way back?" she echoed angrily. "The way back from *where?*"

In a flash, all the pent-up anger she'd been restraining sprang forth. It had been weeks since she'd even seen a town. She wanted to rest, to sleep in a real bed and have a real bath, with soap and lots of steaming hot water. Unable to believe that he had no intention of stopping, she daringly suggested, "You could leave me here, and I could find my way to that town."

"What the hell are you talking about? You'd never make it out of these mountains alive. I said we're not going and that's it." He regretted even mentioning it to her in the first place. For some absurd reason he hadn't expected her to react that way. Well, what the hell did he expect anyway? he harshly questioned himself.

"You could ride down there with me then, only part of the way, of course, and when we get close, you could simply let me go."

"Let you go? What the hell do you mean, let you go?" He seemed truly amazed that she had suggested such a thing, and his own anger was quick to surface.

"Just how long do you plan on keeping me with you like this? All you want from me is a body to keep you warm at

night up here in the mountains! You can't continue
to . . . Oh! You're a horrible man, Alex Coulter, and I hate
you for this! You're a miserable bastard and I curse the day I
ever set eyes on your liar's face! You told me it was
temporary—until you could get away. Well, you're away
now, and you *still* won't let me go! You're a liar, God damn
you, a liar!"

Alex was out of his saddle instantly, and in two long strides
reached the pony and pulled Danny from its back. His eyes
narrowed, piercing her like daggers.

"I've had about as much of your cursing and insults as I'm
going to take. If you don't stop it *now* . . ." He left the
ominous threat hanging dangerously in the air. But his grip on
her arm was painfully tight, and Danny had to grit her teeth
against crying out.

In the past few weeks she'd learned to curse as well as any
man he knew. So, he thought, she had picked up something
after all, spending those nights with Jake and the boys. What
other things did she pick up? What else had she overheard?
He'd probably find out sooner or later when she used it
against him.

"I told you *maybe* I'd let you go when I had no further use
for you," he reminded her. "And that time hasn't come yet.
And don't suppose it's only your body I'm after."

"Well, what then?" She would not let up now that she was
as angry as he.

"It's simple, baby," he said with a contemptuous chuckle.
"You're my security out of here. We were being followed
until a few nights ago."

Golden eyes looked suspiciously at him. "Followed? By
whom?"

"There were four of them. Two were Indians—probably
Crow. Your uncle is a smart man, he knows only an Indian
could find his way around out here. The other two were
white. What's the matter, don't you believe me?"

"No, I don't," Danny defiantly declared. "You're just
saying that to frighten me."

"Oh really? They picked up our trail right after we split
from Jake. It's you they're after," Alex told her. "I'd say your
uncle hired himself the best trackers he could find, but he
didn't count on me."

"So that's it," she accused. "My uncle! Of course! I should
have known. What do you have against him? Do you really

hate him so much that you had to kidnap me to prove it? You're a low creature, you know that?"

Alex's gray eyes flashed brilliantly. "Is *that* what you think? Come on, mount up, we're getting out of here." The order emerged as a snarl and he didn't even wait to see that it was carried out before mounting the Appaloosa, turning its head away from her.

Danny climbed on top of the brown mare and followed sullenly behind him, tears stinging her eyes, believing she would never be rescued.

Hours later, Alex reined up the stallion. "I thought we'd make camp here for the night," he said, breaking the enforced silence that had accompanied them all morning.

Danny glanced around, complaining, "But there's nothing up here. It's wide open. What if there are Indians around?"

"There are," he replied, simply, dismounting. "But you can relax. Indians don't like it up this high. There's not much reason for them to come up here, except maybe to gather their lodge poles. They pretty much stay down on the plains where their food supply is. Look."

She followed his pointing finger with her eyes to a spot on the earth below. From where they stood several thousand feet above the surrounding country, she saw a remarkable sight.

Buffalo. Darkening the earth with their numbers, a huge wave was moving across the land as one great mass in aimless pursuit over the grasslands. It was difficult to determine the size of the herd, but surely it had to be a hundred miles long and at least that wide.

"That's one of the last of the great herds," Alex remarked. "You'll never find them in numbers like that anywhere again."

"Why not?" she asked, her eyes glued to the shaggy beasts.

"Because they've been systematically hunted and shot by white hunters. The carcasses have been robbed of their heads and their hides, or sometimes only their horns, and left to rot in the sun."

"Don't the Indians kill the buffalo too?" she called over her shoulder. She knew they did; she'd heard it before.

"Yeah," he replied as he worked at unsaddling the horses, "but out of need, not sport."

The sudden reminder of nearby Indians brought her to his side in a hurry. "The Indians . . . what if some of them *do* come this high?"

"Don't worry about the Indians in these parts. They're Sioux. Oglala most likely. Maybe some Brulé or some Cheyenne. They're friends of mine."

He removed his Winchester from its leather holster on his saddle and laid it carefully down beside the other things, then set about unpacking the blankets.

"Is that what you are?" Danny asked.

Without pausing from his work, Alex looked up briefly and nodded.

"What else?"

"What else what?"

"What else are you besides Sioux Indian?"

He glanced at her from the corner of his eye, just the barest hint of a smile turning up the corners of his mouth. "What makes you think I'm anything else?"

"I heard some men talking once. They said you were part Indian and part white. I was wondering what the other part was."

"My mother was an Oglala Sioux. I never knew my father, so I don't know what else I am."

There was something in his voice the way the words bristled in the afternoon heat with an electricity of their own. Even though Danny had no reason not to believe him, she felt the uncomfortable sting of a lie.

"We'd better stick close together tonight," he said, tossing her blanket down next to his. And then taunting, "I know how much that must excite you, Danny." Gray eyes flicked over her, while unconsciously he ran his tongue slowly over his lips.

Danny did her best to ignore his rakish stare. Oh, he was forever reminding her how impertinent he was. Just when she'd forgotten what a selfish rake he was, with his hungry stares and roving eyes, he would say or do something once again to remind her. And above all, he never let her forget exactly how much of a prisoner she really was.

She was his prisoner, yes, but she was also a prisoner of her own body, and he repeatedly proved to her, mercilessly at times, the extent to which she was a slave to her own passions.

She continued to fight against the stirrings he awakened in her. He had no right to make her so shamelessly aware of her own body . . . of his body . . . of what his body had the power to do to hers. He was a devil, teasing and tempting her in the most wicked and scandalous ways, as though it were he, and not she, who had control over her own body.

"Here, fill this up over there." He tossed a half-empty canteen at her and gestured to the water that ran off a nearby ledge.

When she returned she found him standing dangerously close to the edge of the bluff whose walls dropped vertically away at his feet. He looked to be deep in thought, with black brows furrowed. Other than that, his features remained unreadable, and in profile Danny studied the straight line of his nose, his full lips just slightly parted and the strength of his jaw.

Just that morning, he'd shaved off the beard he'd grown on the trail, and Danny was glad of it. He looked too much like a pirate with only his silver eyes sparkling from behind the dark covering of his black beard, mustache and hair. And although she never would have admitted it to him, she liked him much better this way, for it was easier now to see how handsome he was. He had not, however, trimmed the length of his hair which had grown to his shoulders and hung in loose thick curls about his face and neck.

The fading sunlight played across the beads of perspiration dotting his brow. One tiny glistening drop fell from his brow to his cheek and finally off his chin onto the front of his shirt.

A shiver ran through her body for a moment which even the lingering heat of the day could not dispel. Alex Coulter was a Sioux Indian. At times he struck her as almost savage. But at other times, like this, he was so quiet, so wrapped up in private thought. What kind of problems were running around in this man's mind? He shared so little of them with her that she could not help but wonder.

"It's beautiful up here," Danny commented, interrupting the silence and snapping Alex out of his trance.

"Huh?"

"I said it's beautiful up here, away from everything else."

The sun was inching its way behind a craggy tor and the spectacle of light that shot out over the raw peak dazzled her with its stunning array of red, pink and orange streaks. Directly above, the sky was turning a velvety midnight blue.

"What are you doing?" Alex inquired when he saw her up on her toes, head thrown back, arms raised above her head and fingers outstretched as though she were reaching for something.

Quickly she pulled her hand back to her side and gave him a sheepish look, ashamed at having been caught doing something stupid. "I . . . I just thought . . ." She groped for the words, sure he would never understand. "Up here it looks so close . . . the sky I mean. For a minute I almost thought I could . . . touch it." She looked away, embarrassed. "It's silly, I know."

"Not so. The mountains have a way of doing that to you."

Was she mistaken or did she detect a note of tenderness in his tone? In the next instant, it was gone when he gave a contemptuous laugh and said, "But you'd better hope you never can touch the sky, baby, because if you do, it will all come crashing down on you."

"How do you know?" she asked timidly.

"How do you think I know?"

His question in answer to hers silenced Danny and for several long minutes neither of them spoke. At length Alex's low voice drifted through the air. It sounded dull and lifeless as though the words coming from his lips had been meant only for the furthest recesses of his own mind.

"It's so beautiful," he said quietly, echoing Danny's feelings. "Like a woman. But any man who doesn't know it like the back of his own hand is doomed. It's a gorgeous place, but it's also frightening in its beauty. And it's where I live."

Danny looked out over the country that sprawled thousands of feet below them filling her senses with its staggering beauty. The aura of snowcapped peaks rising like sawtoothed spikes through the transparent cloud layers—the crystal clearness of the air that played with cool fingertips across her sun-browned flesh—the soothing serenity of a clear blue mountain stream trickling gently over the soft green ground. It was a calm place on earth, an ethereal world that seemed to have been created with an almost poetic imagination, and she was struck speechless by the contrast of its raw wildness and delicate perfection.

Alex's last comment floated through her mind: "It's where I live."

"Where?" she questioned, thinking he meant a place far from this heavenly spot.

"Out there," he replied mechanically, with a nod of his head to the paradise below.

He seemed a thousand miles away, oblivious to her presence. Small hard lines etched the corners of his silver eyes in deep grooves, emphasized by the bronze of his suntanned skin. His mouth was set in a tight line and his eyes blazed downward with a fiery brilliance that told Danny there was much going on inside of him.

"Out there," he repeated quietly. "In that grotesque dreamworld where we all play our sordid little parts."

She looked at him with a puzzled expression troubling her delicate features. "Dreamworld?" she repeated, not sure she understood his meaning. "The dream is peaceful, Alex. Reality is the nightmare."

She watched him intently for a sign of response, but she did not expect it with such stinging force.

"Maybe *your* dreams are peaceful," he shot back. "Maybe they're filled with nothing but music and love where everyone lives happily ever after." He snorted contemptuously. "It looks like I came along and shot your pretty fantasy full of holes."

Danny was too stunned by his harsh attack to reply to the taunting sarcasm. The hot sting of tears pinched her eyes, but she willed them to stay hidden. "No," she said weakly, her voice cracking from the pressure of keeping it under control. "No, that's not what I think dreams are. I think they are, well, transparent, and that if we look through them, I mean *really* look through them, we'll see what makes them so beautiful, or so awful. That is, if we have the courage to look through them. Dreams are simply mirrors of our lives, and if we can't look at them, then we aren't really able to face ourselves, I suppose."

She sighed deeply and a thought that was meant only for her own mind slipped out. "You're a hard man, Alex Coulter, but I guess you've got your reasons."

Her remark shocked him. For God's sake, Alex warned himself, don't go and do something stupid. Don't say something you might regret later on.

"Sometimes," Danny continued, "we see things in our dreams that bear no resemblance to what we are, or what we think we are. But I think—"

His words, sharp and biting, cut right through her. "Tell me, madam, do *you* have the courage to believe in things you've never seen?"

"I don't know," she admitted.

"Yeah, well, sometimes I wonder whether we can stay sane after what we've seen, in and out of our dreams."

Danny took a step closer to him. "We must not let our dreams control us, nor believe everything they tell us, or they will devour us. You'll still be here tomorrow, Alex, but your dreams may not."

He didn't even hear her. He spoke through gritted teeth as if addressing a silent invisible figure. "Can't they see the world is on fire? Can't they see it?"

She wanted to touch him, to place her hand ever so lightly on his arm, but something made her hold back. Something told her to wait.

"Dreams are what we are," he said. "That's all. Nothing more, nothing less. Just what we are. The ironic part is that all they ever really do is remind us that we never really know who we are or where we've been or what we've done."

"Or why." Her whisper, barely audible, floated into the space between them.

Smoke-gray eyes turned on her and searched her face in a strangely questioning way, and inwardly Danny sensed that something had slipped out—something not meant for her to see. There it was, written all over his features, the one thing she'd never expected to see on Alex Coulter's face. Fear. Unmistakable for the brief instant it showed itself, washing over him like a cold dark cloud before retreating quickly behind a hard forceful exterior.

The air was suddenly laden with tension, but for some reason she was not frightened by it. Instead, something else was in the air, something that captured her attention as soon as she realized that Alex could not look her in the eye. She also saw his vulnerability. It confused her for she'd never seen him like this, and she did not quite know how to approach him. Carefully, oh, so carefully. Maybe, just maybe, he was reachable now.

Easing closer to his side she could hear his breath, deep and steady, matching the rise and fall of his chest. "What can a man see in his dreams that makes them so hideous to him? What do you see in your dreams, Alex?"

He turned to her, almost with a snarl, lips curled back over his teeth, eyes blazing and shrinking her with their heated glare.

"I keep my visions to myself," he said, slashing the words

across her face as though he'd used his blade instead. The impact was as great. The result as sure.

Danny retreated, barely able to get the words out from between trembling lips. "I . . . I . . . the fire . . . I'd better see to the fire. It's getting cold, and I—"

She turned and ran, leaving him in his vicious mood to vent his rage upon the empty space he faced rather than at her. Not when she had tried, really tried, to reach him. Damn him! Damn him to hell!

In an explosion of tears she stumbled blindly back to where Alex had tossed some sticks and branches for the fire. Dropping to her knees she tried to gather them into a pile, but in her frustration, she succeeded only in shuffling them about. Her futile efforts only added to her pain and anger, and with a choking lump in her throat and the harsh stinging tears falling from her eyes, she lost her self-control. With a cry, she flung the branches to the ground and jumped up to run away from this place that had suddenly turned so ugly.

Alex's strong hand on her shoulder stopped her flight. His grip was tight, but not painful, and she could feel his eyes on her. With firm but gentle pressure he turned her around and raised her chin, bringing her eyes to his. With just the tip of his thumb, he wiped her wet cheek dry.

"I'll make the fire," he told her. "Stick around, huh?"

He took a step backward and studied her apprehensively. When he was confident that she did not mean to run again, he dropped to his knees and set to work at getting the fire going.

The flames danced brightly once started, sending yellow pitches of light into the night. Millions of tiny sparkling sequins graced the evening sky. Alex sat without speaking, watching the fire playing soft games on the face of the young woman who lay on her back in the grass across from him. The reflection of the flames spiked her auburn tresses, casting coppery streaks streaming down each silken shaft, and her eyes, open wide to the sky, gleamed like small pieces of raw amber stones.

She hadn't spoken to him anymore, and Alex regretted his harshness with her. He hadn't meant to make her cry. But damn it, why did she always have to ask so many questions? Why did she want to know anything at all about him when she never, for a minute, let him forget precisely how much she hated him?

He watched the slow rise and fall of her breasts, and

suddenly his mind was filled with her—her body, those breasts, small and firm, pressed against his chest, her smooth golden thighs parted beneath him, the taste of her full sensual lips, sweet and yielding, against his own. He rose silently from his cross-legged position at the fire and went to her side without so much of a sound as to rustle a single blade of moist grass.

She looked to be asleep, and for several long minutes he stood looking down at her. She's probably playing possum, Alex thought, smiling to himself. She's hoping I'll go away. His gray eyes traveled the length of her young slender body, and as they did, his mouth went dry and his voice, when he spoke, emerged as a husky whisper.

"No woman has a right to be as beautiful as you are."

Danny's eyes snapped open and her body grew rigid.

"I want you to come with me," he whispered. "Over there where the grass is high. I want to lay you down in the tall grass and make love to you. Come on, it's the right time of the night for making love." He reached down to take her hand, but she pulled away.

No! She would not let him have his way! Not after what he'd done earlier, cruelly shutting her out and making her feel like the world's biggest fool for her efforts. She'd had many long hours to think about it, and she still hurt with humiliation. She'd never give anything to this man willingly!

"Oh I see," Alex drawled above her. "Make him pay, is that it, little lady? All right, if that's the way you want it."

He slapped her hand aside and yanked her to her feet. "After all," he said, dragging her away, "who ever expects to get something for nothing in this world? Not me, that's for sure."

Wrapping his arms tightly around her like two steel bands, he drew her to him and brought his mouth down upon hers. He kissed her savagely. The force of his lips on hers told her that he'd had enough of her struggling. He wanted her and if she would not give in willingly, then he was perfectly ready to take what he wanted.

Without easing the pressure of his embrace, Alex pulled Danny down into the tall grass where cool green fingers gently folded over them. Very soon her strength was expended from her fruitless struggling and she laid nude beneath him, her skin jumping from the torrid touch of his hand as it worked its way over her body.

Softly he slid down her body, kissing the flesh at her pulsing throat, running his tongue lazily and teasingly over her breasts, brushing her erect tingling nipples and kissing them fully, before gliding past them to tease the smooth skin at her inner thighs.

She squirmed beneath his touch, but could not get away from him. No, she could not have done that if she tried. It was as though her body had once again turned against her, and while her mind cried its silent protests, her body proved its supremacy, taking her over rolling waves of passion—raw animal passion—passion she was powerless to withstand and which, to her dismay and confusion, she had no desire to stop at all.

"No . . ." she whispered, her voice breathless and quick, when his head drew closer to the spot between her legs where he had lain so many nights before, growing hard inside of her. This was something new—something frightening, and she meekly tried to close her legs to him, to deny him that which she was really too weak to resist.

"Don't," he moaned, pushing her thighs further apart with his hands. "I want to kiss you here, too, Danny. I want to kiss you everywhere. Please, let me do this . . ." And ignoring her denials, the rest of his words were lost within her as he drove her nearly to madness with his probing tongue and deep kisses.

When Danny felt she could endure no more of his maddening caresses, when she was sure she would succumb to this deliciously shameful torture, he left her writhing on the ground while he quickly tore the clothes off his own heated body.

When he was as naked as she was, he dropped again to the ground, this time placing himself gently between her parted legs. Easing forward he met her waiting body with his and entered her, slowly at first, setting all of their nerves tingling at once with the breathless anticipation of the moment and the easy rhythm of their joined bodies.

His breathing had grown rapid, accelerating to the beat of the increasing pitch of their lovemaking. And bringing his mouth down on hers with an urgency that seemed to explode from him all at once, he penetrated her fully and quickly.

Danny moaned softly, meeting each thrust with her arched body until the pattern formed by their two figures grew in intensity and the fever of their passion rose, tossing them over the edge together, where in each other's arms, they tumbled about, drowning in their own private ecstasies.

Later, when the night in all its starry beauty stretched above them, they laid side by side with the hush of gentle mountain breezes blowing coolness across their heated bodies. From that spot, with the earth spread thousands of feet below and the sky reaching into infinity, they were alone in the world, each lost in private thought, but each feeling the undeniable presence of the other through the darkness.

Just two people—a man and a woman—alone in the entire world, with nothing more to testify to their solitary existence than a million reflections sparkling like diamonds across the endless night.

Chapter 12

Opening his eyes to the stark blue sky stretched endlessly above him, Alex Coulter stretched lazily and rose to his feet. He stood for a few minutes, naked in the morning sunlight, feeling a trace of the heat that would descend upon them in a few hours. Right now, though, the weather was cool, clean and refreshing.

Still undressed, he pulled from his saddle pack the garments he had kept hidden during the trip into the mountains. He stuffed into the empty pack his linen shirt and chino pants and slipped comfortably into buckskin leggings and beaded moccasins. He didn't bother putting on the deerskin shirt he'd also brought along. Too hot today, he decided, content merely with tying a scarf around his forehead to absorb the perspiration and keep the hair from his eyes. Naked to the waist, with his thick shoulder-length hair flowing beneath the makeshift headband, he startled Danny who was already up and sitting, daydreaming.

My God, she thought, golden eyes racing over him, he looks so much like an Indian, from his bronzed chest right down to the way he dresses. And yet, there were those sparkling bright eyes that no Indian could attest to.

When the horses were saddled he offered a hand to help her mount, but she turned her head with an upward tilt of her chin, scoffing the gesture. Alex Coulter smiled to himself at her defiance that had become so familiar to him by now. With a shrug, he climbed into his saddle.

"We're headed out, and we've got a lot of plain to cross before we reach shelter, so don't give me any trouble."

Why did he have to speak to her as though she were a

child? And what did he mean that they were headed out? Did that mean they'd finally reached wherever it was they were going? Danny's mind raced with countless questions, but she knew asking would only annoy him. He never told her anything, damn it! She wanted to know what was happening, where he was taking her, and if he would ever let her go. Maybe he'd release her once they reached this place. Maybe . . . Oh, what was the use?

It was mid-afternoon when they emerged from the shadows of the mountains. Before them stretched hundreds of miles of land—flat, brown and dull, with sporadic mounds of sand and rock spiking the hot dry air.

Over the next few days subtle movements caught their attention and the seemingly barren ground came alive with perky inquisitive creatures whose burrows were scattered about the ground by the thousands as though flicked there by an unseen hand.

Some days later the land changed again, shedding its monochromatic hues to reveal a lush paradise, resplendent in a rich fertile carpet of green grass that grew so high and thick that Danny could not see her calves as they rode through it.

Prairie grass, Alex told her, grown to such luxurious lengths by years upon years of fertilization by passing herds of buffalo.

"What is this place?" Danny asked, unable to contain her curiosity about the green eden.

"Powder River country. But if you think this is something, wait until we get to the Hills. Just north of them stands Bear Butte, and right in between runs the Belle Fourche—sweetest little river I ever did see."

"What's there?" She was almost afraid to ask.

"I have friends in these parts. I'm guessing that's where they'll be because they usually are around this time of year." He yawned and stretched his arms over his head, and she could see the taut muscles rippling across his bare back. "If not, we'll keep on going until we find them. But they're in the area, I know it."

"And how do you know?" she challenged him, golden eyes flashing.

"I've been speaking to them, that's how I know."

Danny rolled her eyes in exasperation. "I should have known better than to expect a straight answer out of *you.*"

His face remained as impassive as an Indian's, but inside he secretly acknowledged that Danny had grown far too head-strong. She sure was a difficult woman to tame—always fighting him, every God damn inch of the way.

"You always have to be shown everything, don't you? All right, watch." And cupping his hands to his mouth, he let out a whistle that sounded remarkably like the call of a mountain sparrow. Then, an answer could be heard in the distance, and soon the air was filled with the call of the songbirds, although the winged creatures were nowhere to be seen.

Alex shrugged in an I-told-you-so manner and sat back in the saddle with an obnoxious grin on his lips.

"Your friends, I presume?"

"That's right, ma'am," he drawled. "Hunting party. Passed another yesterday. I'd say we're getting real close now."

Who were they? And where was he taking her? And when they got there, then what? Danny sighed and resumed her sullen watch over the paradise of the Powder River Valley.

Days later they spotted Bear Butte in the distance, casting its powerful shadow protectively over the Black Hills.

The air bristled with static energy, creating shimmering shadows of deception before their eyes. In spite of it, Alex pressed on, urging his stallion into a brisk canter. The animal's big chest swelled with each stride and in no time his dappled coat was splotched with sweat and froth. Danny's mare eagerly picked up the pace, coming alive in the heat of the day, matching the Appaloosa stride for stride.

In no time the horses were engaged in a furious gallop, neck and neck, straining forward with each stride. But bit by bit the stallion began to pull away with massive strides that flew over the ground. Danny's mare struggled valiantly to keep pace. With a surge of strength she pitched forward, her short, quick strides furiously covering ground, her nostrils flared and burned from the sharp intake of air. Her tangled mane whipped up behind her, stinging Danny in the face.

The terrain slipped by in a blur, and the earth's echo grew louder the closer they got to the hills. Crouching forward in the saddle and tightly clutching the pony's wildly tossed mane in her fists, Danny held on for dear life. Then she heard a snapping sound pass beneath them, followed almost simul-taneously by an awful high-pitched squeal.

The screech sent shudders through her, but no sooner had she heard it than she was jerked with a sharp whiplash that tore the muscles at her back and neck and sent her flying over the pony's head toward the ground that came up swiftly before her terrified eyes.

She somersaulted in midair and hit the ground with a bone-shattering jolt that bounced her eyes around in her head.

She sat there dazed, feeling nothing but the shock of finding herself still alive.

Alex had seen it happen in the split second when he'd glanced over his shoulder. Instantly, he had pulled the stallion's head around sharply and galloped back to her, flinging himself out of the saddle and racing up to her on foot. Still panting heavily from his frantic ride, he glared down at her while she sat giggling helplessly.

She just might have laughed all day had she not felt so stupid. I wasn't paying attention, Danny scolded herself, as she rose shakily to her feet and began to brush the dirt from her legs. Mr. Peets told me that little mare loved to run. He told me she would—

But a noise from behind swept her thoughts out of her mind. It was a groan—deep and throaty. Biting her lip hard to keep it from trembling, Danny turned slowly around.

The brown mare was laying in the dust, her brown eyes peering wildly ahead, her right foreleg bent at an awkward angle. The sesamoid bone protruded from an open gash in the skin.

She ran to the animal and flung herself down beside it, cradling its head in her arms and stroking the pink fleshy muzzle. "He was right—Mr. Peets was right about you," she sobbed. "He knew, didn't he? And you knew, too. And you showed me. God, you showed me. I love you for it, you crazy little animal—for your spirit and your heart and—"

Alex placed a hand on her shoulder and drew her to her feet. It was then she saw the rifle he held in his hand, and crying hysterically, she turned away from what was about to happen—from what she knew in her heart had to be. She stood with her back to the drama, hands clasped tightly over her ears and tears flowed from her amber eyes. The explosion, when it came, rocked her senses.

Alex worked quickly and quietly to remove the saddle from the dead horse. He left the bridle where it was, though, preferring not to get too close to the bloody bullet-shattered skull. Then, hoisting Danny up into his own saddle and climbing on behind her, he gave his stallion a couple of quick kicks and turned the big white head in the direction of the Black Hills.

Already vultures were circling overhead, leaving their treetop perches as soon as the figures below had left the scene. They converged upon the carcass, tearing their fill of flesh from the bones. They left the rest for the coyotes that would follow sometime during the night when the moon was high and the night owl screeched its lonely song.

Chapter 13

Long before the land was called America, small children sitting snugly around warm lodge fires learned through the stories the old ones told of how their world had come to be. They were taught how each man and creature, every blade of grass and whispering of the wind was a product of one great undertaking—a single working so immense in scope, so boundless in breadth, that the passing of a man's life proved nothing more than an incomprehensible instant across its massive face. A person's life was but a single brush-stroke across a cosmic canvas, and yet, as much a part of the total concept as anything else that had ever been created.

The Great Plains was a spot on earth that no one else seemed to want, except perhaps the dusty buffalo, the deadly scorpion and the rattlesnake that slithered across the broken ground. There, among the rough hills and blistering flatlands, the people—called the Sioux—had come to settle, and there they adapted their life-style to become the nomads of the prairies, moving across the land in their ever-constant trail of the buffalo.

They were the Teton Sioux, whose numbers exceeded that of the Crow, Shoshone and Arapaho nations combined.

The summer season, hot lazy times when nothing much mattered except lolling around in the shade, found the people camped by the Powder River or the Rosebud, or along the banks of the Tongue where soothing mountain breezes whispered over their lodges. Alongside each conical dwelling stood a staked travois where strips of buffalo meat hung drying in the sun, proving too much temptation for the summer flies that swarmed over it, competing furiously with the snatching hands of mischievous youngsters who ran by naked to and from the river.

During the winter moons, when the frozen snow and bitter winds whipped across the plains with deadly ferocity, they camped within the protective arms of a hidden lea, with tipis rising rakishly to the winter sky like tilted cones. Smoke-browned tops and painted flanks were the only splashes of color against the ground that lay covered with a light snowfall.

In spring and autumn the people took off for the *wani-sapa*, the annual buffalo hunts around Bear Butte where they could gather enough meat and enjoy a little congenial visiting with friends and relatives. Amidst the feasting, dancing and playing, the men went out to hunt the buffalo, slaying the huge beasts with stunning arrays of marksmanship and daredevil riding, letting loose their arrows with remarkable precision and collecting much food for the winter. When the hunt was over, they dressed the meat, slung it over the backs of their horses and returned to camp where the women waited.

Skilled hands worked over the carcasses quickly. The hides were stripped from the bones and steeped in a bath of tanbark from the hemlock tree. Once tanned, they would be used to cover the lodge poles or replace a hide worn thin by too many winters. With a stiff needle made from a sliver of bone, some hides were fashioned into shirts and leggings and then bedecked with colorful beads or brightly stained porcupine quills for decoration.

Over raging fires the hooves were melted down for glue, and the tallow was simmered into candles to illuminate moonless nights. Everything had its purpose. The bones were diligently reshaped to serve as utensils or implements of war. The bladders were filled with the juice of herbs and berries and used as nursing bottles for infants. The stomachs were suspended over tripods of sticks into which were dropped hot rocks to make the water boil.

The women worked hard stopping only to pass a bit of raw liver on the tip of a knife to a waiting child who savored the delicacy. Nothing was thrown to the dogs except perhaps some fatty tissue or hard grizzle that wasn't much good anyway.

When the hunts were over, the camp dismantled, some returning hundreds of miles to their favorite places, others a

mere mile or two upstream. Moving camp was always a time
of fun and visiting, of horse-racing and trick-playing, singing
songs and trading laughter. At the front of the reckless
column rode the chiefs, the ones who would select the places
where they would rest. Behind them came the people—the
old men, the women, the children and babies, followed by the
helpless ones and all the travois. In the rear came the pony
herds and then the warriors, war clubs at their sides, bows
within easy reach.

The younger warriors galloped up and down the column
performing daring maneuvers on their ponies, showing off for
their friends and hoping to catch the eye of a pretty girl with a
fancy stunt. The girls, with their faces vermilion as a sign of
one greatly in love, rode in their fringed saddle trappings and
whitened deerskin dresses, chatting gaily and casting shy
glances at their favorites.

Even though they allowed their campsites to be chosen for
them, or followed the leadership of a particular man or group
during the hunt or in battle, each individual retained sole
authority over his life, with each one's inner voice directing
his movements on the earth. Nothing could interfere with the
right and will of any man to roam the plains freely or live in
any village he desired. Even their trusted allies, the faithful
and spirited Cheyennes, held their lodges open to the Sioux.
Often in return, young Cheyenne men spent many months
with their Sioux brothers, and Cheyenne girls married into
Sioux families and bore the children of Sioux men.

The happy practice of intermarriage led to even stronger
ties among the Sioux and Cheyenne people who shared not
only the plains, but many similar customs and beliefs and an
intermingling of the blood. Together they raided the camps of
their enemy, the Crow. Side by side they hunted the buffalo
on exciting forays that sometimes took them deep into the
regions around the Great Yellowstone.

But over the harsh years of sun-parched summers and
bitter ice-encrusted winters, many of the tales and legends
died with the old ones and now lay buried and forgotten,
locked within time-eroded graves.

For more than a half-century the people had felt subtle
changes brushing over them, altering to the slightest degree a
life-style that had been centuries in the making, jeopardizing
a heritage that traced its beginnings back to a time when
white men knew not of the existence of this continent, and

threatening the freedom and dignity upon which Sioux lives depended. Soon the passing of white travelers through their lands, which had begun many years ago as a harmless trickle, had grown to a raging flood, with no end in sight.

The Sioux had always accepted their white brothers' peaceful intrusions into their country, allowing them ready access in their journey across it. But not all kept going. Some stayed. And then some more, until the people felt their lands were being snatched up from right under their noses, as more of the earth's riches were revealed to the white man's greedy eyes and hungry hands. Truly, the whites were a strange people.

For as long as they could remember, the people had been making war on their enemies: the Crow, the Shoshone, the deadly Pawnees. So it was right, therefore, that they should fight the white men who came into their valleys cutting down the trees, robbing the streams of the beaver and clearing the plains of buffalo. It was right that they should rid their country of those pale-skinned men who had no regard for the earth and who sought to destroy everything that lived or grew upon it.

Sporadic outbursts of anger soon turned into deadly skirmishes, and there followed the wars of the 1860s, largely the result of white encroachment on their lands. Soldiers and miners blatantly ignored legal treaties, violated the sanctity of the land and the sovereign right accorded the Sioux by the Great Father in Washington to maintain what was theirs by written law.

Their fierce persistence had not proved entirely fruitless, for in an unprecedented move, the U.S. Army had dismantled its outposts and marched its troops out of the Powder River Valley forever, relinquishing its hold on the territory to the red men who had fought so desperately to keep it.

The peace, however, was short-lived, as slowly, year after year, the miners and homesteaders returned, driving the Indians back once again by their sheer numbers. This time a new greed, gold, obsessed the white men. Day after day, while the people watched calmly from the surrounding hills, secure in the trust of their last treaty, column after column of mounted horsemen passed below—an endless procession led by the man the whites called Custer. To the Indians he was known as the Long Hair.

He and his government-appointed expedition had cut their

way right through the heart of the Sioux lands, invading the sacred places where they had buried their dead.

So began a slow parade of tears. The year was 1875 and it was a time of conflict. Small children bore witness to scenes which many men, in their entire lifetimes, never had to see; burning villages, trampled dogs and babies, bodies of young mothers strewn across the festering land—all victims of random, surprise attacks on their villages by armed forces of blue-coated soldiers.

In their anger and frustration, the people retaliated. Their hearts were bad from the pain of lost loved ones; their blood ran hot from the wanton destruction of their homes and villages. And in their desperation, they descended upon their molesters with vicious determination. Often they swarmed over their victims, outnumbering small mining parties, even larger army regiments, killing until there remained not a single foe left alive in the settling dust.

The slaughter grew in its awful destruction as each side sought to avenge the brutalities of the other, losing many lives in the process and gaining not much in return, least of all an understanding of how it had started, why it was happening or where it would lead.

Into the turmoil rode two figures astride a single horse. It was one of their own who rode out of the mountains and across the plains. One of their warriors was coming home after a long journey to the Southwest. They knew he wouldn't stay long; he never did. But they also knew he never failed to return to them. This time he brought with him a woman.

Tasunke-Witko looked at the riders who passed by his lodge, a wide grin on his usually laconic face. So, he brings a white woman into camp, the Indian thought. He watched the man slide off the horse's rump, then walk around its side to lift the woman out of the saddle. And when Tasunke-Witko saw those sparkling gray eyes focused strongly on his own black ones, he stepped forward and stretched out his hand.

The other man grasped it firmly, his bright metallic gaze searching the Indian's somber face.

Tasunke-Witko cast shy eyes down at his moccasined feet. "My heart rejoices that you have returned to the camp of our people," he said softly. "Many suns have risen on your journey and I can see you are tired. I see too that you have not returned alone. Come, you must rest. Then we will talk."

Chapter 14

It was deep in the heart of the August moon when the drowsy days were hot enough for the children to swim naked in the melted snows of the Belle Fourche, and the women, dressed in their elkskin and calico work dresses, dug wild prairie turnips or gathered berries on the hillside.

As the shadows of evening lengthened across the hide walls of the lodges, the women returned to camp to resume work on moccasins and leggings with awl and sinew, and to prepare the evening meal, pausing now and then to gently brush the summer flies from the faces of sleeping babies.

In the twilight of the evenings the men found little to do. Some sat cross-legged in the shade of their lodges with the flaps curled up to coax the dry breezes inside, while others loafed under lofty pine shelters fixing arrows or drawing pictures in the dust. The headmen sat in select circles passing their eagle-wing fans slowly before their faces. The pale blue smoke from their pipes spiraled into the air and filled it with the sweet fragrance of red willow bark.

From large round kettles suspended over the fires came onion soup, boiled buffalo meat, peas and wild turnips. Methodically, the women spooned out the food, while the hot coals glowed red on the bare chests of the fathers, husbands and sons who called themselves the holy men, hunters and warriors. Taking a spoon of meat from the kettle, a bit was offered first to the sky, a bit then to Mother Earth and a bit for each of the four great directions. And then they commenced to eat heartily and noisily.

Sometimes in the evening one of the circles that comprised the tribal crescent would hold a feast and everyone would gather around a single fire fed with enough kindling to keep it burning well into the night. To the steady driving beat of the drums they would dance. The women would form a ring inside of which the proud warriors strutted, resplendent in their war regalia. Elaborately beaded and fringed shirts and leggings swayed to and fro. Feathered war bonnets bobbed up and down to the rhythm of the drums, some trailing behind the dancers like stately mantels. Each feather, be it hawk or eagle, signified a particularly brave feat.

On the surface what appeared to be a most ostentatious display was nothing more than a show of sincere reverence to the Great Spirit, for what better way was there to show one's thanks and respect than to dress in one's very finest and proclaim for all the world to hear that 'I am the embodiment of my creator'?

Peering through the meat racks, obscured by the shroud of night, Danny watched the spectacle. Her eyes were wide at the sight of the women dancing with scalps dangling from the ends of long poles and the near-naked bodies of the men, glowing red from the reflection of flames. They strutted like proud peacocks, kicking up their heels, whipping their long black braids over their bare shoulders in boastful displays of male egotism that were as much a part of their culture as the air they breathed.

Several times she saw them push one man into the center of the circle to dance, but each time he backed out, embarrassed. She recognized him as the same Indian who had met them the day they rode into camp—the one Alex had embraced and called Tasunke-Witko.

The first thing that struck her about him was his unusual appearance. For an Indian his complexion was light, lighter even than hers which, by now, had grown to a deep bronze. And his hair, too, was light, almost sandy brown, and soft and fine. Only his eyes were like the others, black and brilliant.

But it was not only his unusual physical features that singled out this particular man from all the others. It was his manner. Where the others were boastful, he was shy. Where the others were loud, he was quiet, almost sullen at times. Where the others were friendly, he was aloof. Danny could scarcely believe Alex when he told her that Tasunke-Witko was one of the bravest, most influential and revered among the Oglalas . . . indeed among the entire Sioux Nation.

"What!" she exclaimed. "That slender unassuming man? A hero? Then surely he must be a chief."

"No, he's not a chief," Alex corrected, "not like Smoke or Bull Bear were chiefs. But he used to be a shirt wearer."

In answer to the confusion written on her face, he went on to explain that it was an old Sioux custom to appoint several men as joint chiefs, or shirt wearers, so called from the ceremonial shirt worn by the men as their insignia of office.

"But they took it away from him," Alex muttered. "The shirt. They wouldn't let him keep it."

"Why not?" she questioned, unable to tear her eyes from the dancers.

"The others kept the oaths they had made then," Alex answered. "But he had not."

She wanted to learn more about Tasunke-Witko's broken vow, but dared not ask, not when she heard the spark of anger rifling Alex's hushed voice.

While Danny watched the dancers, Alex watched Danny, a frown shadowing his features. She had become much too independent lately, balking at his orders to remain inside the lodge and not to sashay around the camp where there was no telling what kind of trouble she'd get herself into. She knew precious little about these people or the effect she was having on them.

Many of the men in camp, especially some of the younger, more hot-blooded of them, had already approached Alex with offers of many fine war ponies for the white woman with the long, dark red hair and golden eyes. She was a rarity to them. Even the white women who rode the wagons with their pioneer husbands, or the wives of the army officers at Fort Laramie could not compare with this one whose body was as slender as a boy's and yet who was so obviously a woman. A man did not have to be white to see it, and her attraction held no less magnetism to a red man. To them she was a very different woman—one certainly worth possessing. Each man in camp knew that he would be perfectly within his right to lure Danielle away from the man she belonged to, if not by offering ponies for her, then by stealing her from under his nose.

Of course, it was an Oglala woman's right to stay with her new man or return to her old one, as the whim took her. But Danny was ignorant of the complex social workings and even less aware of her own rights within them. And besides, Alex doubted whether any man who eyed her so possessively would, or even could, give her up if he had to.

The entire situation reeked of impending trouble, and Alex knew he could not avert a direct confrontation and serious disruption within the tribe without relinquishing his woman. He decided to speak of the matter to his friend, Tasunke-Witko, after the dance. Perhaps in the Indian's own experience lay the answer.

Tasunke-Witko had once himself attempted to take another man's wife. It was something he seldom spoke of, partly because it was not his nature to speak much at all, partly because to speak of this one thing caused him much pain.

The scar he bore below his left nostril, where a once irate husband had aimed his gun, was memory enough of the single great mistake of his life. He had disgraced himself in his people's eyes, abandoning the vows he'd taken as shirt wearer when he took the woman and brought disruption into the tribe. In the confusion, the woman fled leaving Tasunke-Witko to bear alone the humiliation and disgrace of being stripped of his ceremonial garment.

In time he'd won back the admiration of the people and the elders had given him another kind of chieftainship—War Chief of all the Oglalas. It was a rare honor. Only men such as Sitting Bull of the Hunkpapas had received it. But it did little to erase the memory, and the former disgrace remained like a blot on his soul. Whether it was his resulting shame over his broken vows or the bitter pain of a rejected lover, it was sufficient to render him incapable of reliving the experience out loud although, no doubt, its presence plagued him each and every day of his life.

Like Alex Coulter, Tasunke-Witko was an extremely reticent man, even morose at times. And also like Alex, he always appeared to have a lot on his mind.

Often he would go into the hills where he would sit alone, finding in his solitude some of the answers he needed to keep his people's memory alive within himself and to seek solace in order to live with his personal tragedies.

A gentle and unassuming man, he was nevertheless a pillar among his tribe, having attained at the age of thirty-three a reputation among his people and his enemies as a brave man, a fearless warrior and a fanatical observer of the ways of the Sioux. Rather than rule, he led the Tetons in their determined struggle to keep what was theirs by heritage and to preserve what little was left of it. He was not a boastful man, but he was immensely proud of what he had accomplished for their sake. Just as he was proud that it was *he* who had brought down the most buffalo during the tribal hunts and that it was *his* coup stick that had touched the most enemies in battle.

His life was governed by a series of patterns that had been formed a millennium ago. The concept of power and the definition of ambition were unknown to him. He sought to be no different than he already was, nor any better. In his timeless struggle with life on the plains, he merely wished to be.

Yet that wish was being threatened with frightening certainty, and if it were not for this reserved man who got excited only when his warriors were in formation behind him, if it were not for the unswerving loyalty he retained only for himself and his people, if he were not idolized by the warriors of the Sioux and Cheyenne, whose numbers reached into the thousands, then surely the people would have perished long ago for lack of a more determined leader.

Tasunke-Witko listened quietly to Alex voice his concern over Danny. He spoke in the language of the Sioux, for the few words of English he knew he refused to speak.

"Tell me, friend, did the woman come willingly?"

"No, she didn't," Alex grudgingly admitted.

The Indian's face broke into a smile. "And you question whether another man should take her as you did?" He didn't expect a reply and didn't receive one.

Alex knew he was right. Besides, why worry about something that might not happen? Changing the subject he said, "I heard they sent some whites up here a few months back. What did they want?"

Tasunke-Witko tossed a twig into the fire and watched it crackle. "They sent presents and made a big feast and invited me, but I did not go. I do not want to talk with them. No good would come of it."

"You haven't spoken to them yet. Perhaps if you did—"

"I have no need to speak to them. Others have spoken before me. Red Cloud spoke to them and Red Cloud now lives on their reservation, unable to hunt his own food, carry his own bow. My uncle, Spotted Tail, has spoken to them, and he now lives on their reservation, following the orders of the whites who will tell him when he can sit and when he can stand and where he may go. If my speaking to them will mean the confinement of my people, then I will speak no words with the whites."

It was one of the longest speeches Alex had ever heard the usually reticent man make. "Sitting Bull has spoken to them many times and he still remains free," Alex reminded him.

"Sitting Bull is a great medicine man," Tasunke-Witko replied. "But his medicine is no good to us. He has told me of his wish to take his Hunkpapas north to Canada to the home of the Grandmother where the redcoats will protect them and give them arms to hunt with. I say Sitting Bull is a fool to think the soldiers here will not track him down and make him come back."

The Indian was unusually talkative this evening, but then he had much on his mind . . . much that even a quiet man could not contain to himself.

"Everywhere they are around us," he went on, anger smoldering beneath his calm surface. "The bluecoats hunt us until there is no place for us to go—no room for us to hide, to live. We must fight them, and to do this we need guns."

There it was, the one thing that placed this Indian apart from the others, for he recognized that in order to defeat the white man you had to fight him at his own kind of war, with his own kind of weapons. He knew that as adept as his Sioux warriors were with their familiar instruments of war, bows and arrows were simply no match against live bullets and the Army's big Gatling guns.

He looked at Alex from the corners of his black eyes and popped a berry into his mouth. "They are closely watched at the reservation. It is hard for them to get guns to us. The last time my men went there they came back empty-handed . . . not a single rifle."

Alex responded without hesitation. "There's a shipment of silver due from Winslow in about two weeks that you should be able to turn over for arms. They'll be taking the northern route to Fort Defiance where they'll pick up an army regiment for protection, then across the Divide and northeast to Bennett. They seem to think there's no immediate threat from the Apaches."

He noticed the Indian's raised eyebrow and shrugged. "They're fools if they think they can expect no trouble from the Chiricahuas, especially since the death of Cochise and the split into factions like they are now. I hear there's been a lot of raiding going on down there lately."

News traveled fast on the plains and it was common knowledge that the warring Apaches were wreaking havoc in the Southwest, with the Chiricahua reservation serving as a way station for Apache raiding parties moving freely in and out of the Arizona territory into Mexico. It was a dangerous place to be if a man was not an Apache, but no less dangerous than his own part of the country, Tasunke-Witko knew, particularly in its present state of siege and the increasing struggle for survival.

Alex stretched his legs out in front of him and leaned back on his elbows. "If your braves set out tomorrow, they could meet that shipment of silver in time before it crosses the Divide when the Army will be least expecting it. There's a small outpost there where they plan on changing guard, and I figure if you can hit that, they'll just walk right in without suspecting a thing. Instead of a fresh guard waiting, they'll find you."

Tasunke-Witko worked the plan over in his mind, nodding as he listened.

"But you'll have to be quick about it," Alex warned. "You'll have to get down there, cut those telegraph wires, hit the shipment and get out fast, 'cause as soon as they know what's happening, they'll have another company out of Fort Wingate in a hurry."

Tasunke-Witko looked at Alex with a question stamped on his face. "Wingate? I thought you said it was Defiance. My friend, how many of the white man's forts are in the area?"

Alex looked away sheepishly. "Well, two. The replacements will come out of Wingate which is on the other side of the Divide in New Mexico. That's why you'll have to work fast. You'll have just enough time to get the Lady Laura's shipment and whatever guns you can carry, and hightail it out of there. In the confusion, they'll think it was the Apaches. Tell your braves to wear their hair long and loose so they'll pass easily for Apaches."

The Indian let out a hearty laugh and slapped his slender thigh.

"I'm sorry," Alex snapped, mistaking the laughter. "That's the best plan I could come up with."

"Your idea places us within the midst of our Apache enemies and right between two of the white man's forts. I only laugh because for always you have been testing me with impossible feats. Ever since you and I were boys together, always you throw the impossible before me."

"And always you have proved that my plans were no match for your own bravery, my friend."

Tasunke-Witko blushed and cast his black eyes down at the ground, embarrassed by the praise.

Rising fluidly to his feet and placing a hand on Tasunke-Witko's bare shoulder, Alex said softly, "My friend, a man must know his dreams are true even if they live in another's heart. If I did not place the impossible before you, then you could not show me that even *that* is possible." He turned to go, but the voice of the Indian stopped him.

"*Kola washtay,*" he whispered, "your woman will be safe while I am here."

Chapter 15

They had been in the Oglala village now three weeks and Danny was quickly learning how easy it was to adjust to something when you weren't left with much of a choice.

By now she'd learned how to prepare the food for the kettles by hacking the flesh away from the bones of the dead animals the hunters brought in. She would then soften it over a fire and mix it with melted fat and marrow into a rather rancid tasting concoction the Indians called *wasna,* or pemmican. She'd even gotten used to handling the dried buffalo chips that the women gathered from the prairie to feed the camp fires. But it was more than just growing accustomed to something unpleasant and bearing it all with a stiff grin.

Gradually she began to acquire a feel for the movements of life around her, and even though it was so contrasting and contradictory to anything she'd ever known, she felt drawn to it.

She could no longer deny that she'd come to love standing on the flat land, feeling the dry wind whipping her hair across her face, and the warmth of the sun, huge and yellow in the sky, penetrating her flesh, massaging her muscles. She'd come to crave the sight of the Black Hills, lush with growth displayed in a dozen shades of green. And on a cloudless day, stretching out forever under an infinity of bright blue sky, the plains, an enormity of land traveling the distance as far as the eye could see.

She felt the freedom of the people and the wildness of this place flowing through her limbs, standing her nerves on end. Each day it grew stronger, stimulated by all she saw around her, and she settled at last into the slow easy life of the Oglala

camp. And like the others, her nerves also would spring to
life whenever she watched the warriors ride out for the hunt,
whooping and yelling, shaking their lances high over their
heads.

It was impossible to deny it. She liked it out here!

But she knew she must never let Alex know, for it would do
his arrogant ego little good, she decided, to see her running
around acting like his squaw. Often she had to remind herself
that he was a callous man, wicked in his treachery and always
luring her into a false sense of caring just to catch her off
guard so that he could humiliate her again.

Alex Coulter was reluctant to deal with her strange moods,
but he was also unable to take his eyes off of her in spite of
himself. She was even more beautiful with her skin all
browned. Lately, she'd taken to wearing the deerskin dress
she'd been given by one of the women, with her hair in two
long braids over her shoulders. At night, she would loosen
the braids, carefully running her fingers through the auburn
tresses to work out the pattern of the plaits, and with a final
shake of her head, the mass of dark hair would cascade down
her shoulders and back. Sometimes when she moved, the
coppery tendrils would part to reveal hidden contours of her
firm young body, and Alex found it impossible not to stare at
the gentle swells and curves in all the right places.

These warm summer days he was spending less and less time
with her, though, returning to the lodge at night, only to eat
and then to sleep. In the morning he would rise early while it
was still dark and the rest of the village slept. Silently slipping
into a breechcloth, moccasins and nothing more, and tip-
toeing out of the tipi on cat feet, he would slip out of camp
with Tasunke-Witko at his side.

The two men spent much time together, and often Danny
would catch sight of Alex's Appaloosa stallion and the
Indian's favorite yellow pinto disappearing into the hills.
They came and went as they chose, sometimes bringing back
rabbits or an elk slung across their horses' backs; sometimes
with nothing at all to show for the many hours spent away. No
one questioned their movements nor seemed even aware of
the time they spent together. No one, that is, except Danielle,
who was quick to notice anything out of the ordinary—out
here most things were.

On this particular morning, with the summer sun's rays

drenching the hillside, Danny was picking chokecherries with the other women, tossing them into the hollow she had made with her dress, every now and then popping one into her mouth to feast on its succulent sweetness. From where she stood, Danny watched a party of eight Indians gallop into camp and dismount at the lodge of Tasunke-Witko.

Returning to camp from the hillside shrubs, she went to her lodge where a staked travois stood with its meat drying in the sun. Pulling some strips from the rack, she set to work, only mildly interested in the newcomers who had spread their blankets on the hard ground, taken up cross-legged positions and waited for the light-skinned Oglala to come out.

As she mechanically pounded the dried meat with a heavy stone-headed maul, she wondered what the commotion was all about. It was evident that this was no friendly get-together, nor were they here to reminisce about last week's victory over the Snakes, nor tomorrow's hunt that would take them clear to the White Horn Mountains. She could tell by their voices that they were angry, and it seemed that the elder headmen were attempting to soothe some of the younger, more hot-blooded men with calm words. One in particular, the one they called Worm, the Oglala holy man and father of Tasunke-Witko, spoke soothingly, but he was not at all successful.

Danny shrugged fatalistically and resumed work on the pemmican, crushing berries into the flat white paste with her bare hands, then licking her fingers clean. What she did not know was that the Indians who rode in that afternoon had come from places far away. They were called Hunkpapas, Brulés, Minniconjous, Sans Arcs, Blackfeet and Two Kettles. Like the Oglalas, they were Sioux.

One leader from each band had been chosen to council with the Oglalas about the latest development in their tenuous and uneasy relationship with the United States Government. It seemed the white men were calling for a big council in order to discuss certain matters of importance which, predictably, they had neglected to define. And it was on some vague notion that the Indians were expected to travel hundreds of miles on horseback to attend this council which had been personally handpicked by the Great Father in Washington. So each band sent its most skilled orator, its most honored warrior—the one man they felt would best put

into words the feelings that ran in their hearts. The Hunkpapas had sent Tatanka Yatanka, the man the whites called
Sitting Bull.

"Do they think we are so stupid that we do not know the
real reason for this council they call for?" Sitting Bull was
furious. He knew what the white men wanted, and he was not
willing to give it to them.

Pa Sapa, the Black Hills, was the very core of their world.
It was where the warriors went to speak with the Great Spirit,
where they buried the bones of their dead, where came the
lodge poles for their tipis. It was their link with the spirits of
all those who had passed this way before, and it was the place
where each of them would eventually find his place. The
Black Hills were the last refuge . . . the final peace. They
belonged to the Sioux!

Sitting Bull reminded them that six short winters ago the
white fathers in Washington had given these lands to the
Sioux forever, by treaty, considering there to be little value in
the mass of hills and bluffs. But the white man's clamor for
the yellow metal called gold grew so loud and demanding that
the bluecoats had launched an armed invasion on Pa Sapa,
penetrating the sanctity of the place without asking the
people's permission. Perhaps Worm had to be reminded of
how the soldiers, numbering over a thousand, had marched
out of the big, wooden soldier fort raising a trail of dust to Pa
Sapa, led by the soldier chief called the Long Hair . . . the
one the whites called Custer.

Worm's memory might be short, but Sitting Bull's was not,
and he recalled for them all that it was on the Long Hair's
claim of gold that the whites had descended upon the land
like locusts. And now the Great Father was sending a
commission to negotiate with the Sioux for the gold-rich
Black Hills, and he did not even have the courage to say so!

Sitting Bull's memory needed no prodding. Bending forward from his cross-legged position, he scooped up a handful
of arid dirt, cupping it tightly in his palm. Slowly he let the
dust trickle from his clenched fist, watching it scatter in the
wind.

"I will not sell *any* land to the whites. Not even this much."
Opening his hand fully, he released the pinch of dust trapped
there. In a moment, that too was swept away by the constant
summer wind.

The other Indians began to murmur amongst themselves at

Sitting Bull's gesture, nodding their heads in stoic agreement, some stirring nervously, shifting positions. The mood around the circle was tense, and a suppressed fury could be detected on their broad brown faces. One warrior rose to his feet and immediately a hush fell over them.

When Tasunke-Witko stood up, he seemed to tower over the others even though he was slightly below medium height. His lithe sinewy limbs and his fair complexion were in striking contrast to his companions, as was his light brown hair that hung below his belt, worn that day in two braids covered in buffalo hide. He was naked except for a breechcloth and deerskin moccasins.

He had remained silent until then, listening to the others speak, but deciding for himself what he would do regardless of the outcome of their council.

He, Tasunke-Witko, was opposed to selling any Sioux lands, especially the Black Hills!

With controlled rage he stood in the middle of the circle of men, looking down into their faces. He would *not* attend the white man's council, he hotly declared, adding with emotion, "One does not sell the earth upon which the people walk!" His voice was smoldering and the others trembled inwardly. If need be, he vowed, he would go to war to protect their lands. It was the only way!

He was not afraid of the white man's big guns or the soldier chief with the hair like red gold. He would make war on the whites to keep what was theirs!

Tasunke-Witko was prepared to carry his name—the name that in the white man's tongue meant Crazy Horse—over the plains to the hearts of the people, into the hills to the ears of the Great Spirit and into the lives of the whites!

The others watched apprehensively as Crazy Horse strode angrily out of the circle straight for the herd of ponies. Leading a brown and white pinto from the cluster, he grasped its mane in a strong hand and flung himself into the air in a swift graceful motion, landing silently astride the horse's bare back. A quick tensing of his leg muscles and they were off at a gallop.

As horse and rider disappeared into a cloud of rising dust, a second rider jumped onto his horse, and the ground trembled and shook from the pounding of hooves as the Appaloosa stallion thundered out of camp across the open plains in hot pursuit.

Alex returned to the lodge hours later, long after the sun had disappeared behind the tallest peak and the only light that remained was that of the opaline moon peeking through the clouds that streaked the evening sky.

His mood was black and he spoke little except to tell Danny in a harsh voice that they'd be leaving in the morning.

"Be ready," he ordered. Then, in silence, he stripped off his buckskin shirt and leggings and lay down beside her.

He made no move to pull her close to him as he usually did. Instead, he lay with one arm bent behind his head, staring up at the smoke-browned opening above him, waiting for the sleep that would not come.

Sleep evaded him as it was often so good at doing, playing torturous games of hide and seek. The simmering fire in the center of the tipi cast a shadow upon the hide wall, and every once in a while an imperceptible breath of wind would find its way in through a spot on the hide worn thin, stoking the dimming embers and causing the shadow to undulate hypnotically.

Alex Coulter's face looked like a monument of indecision, his muscles flinching involuntarily at the wrenching pain of being torn in two—standing with each foot in a different world and knowing that only one of those worlds could endure.

Visions leapt through his mind—of the Black Hills, of his people. But who were his people? Was it the whites to which he owed his undivided loyalty? Or was it the reds? The ever increasing pressure weighing heavily on him made it more and more certain that he could not live in both. The pressure was becoming too great as each side moved further away from the other and from any hopeful bridge of understanding, leaving a man like Alex divided down the middle—outside both worlds and yet undeniably committed to each. In which world did he belong? The question never ceased to consume his mind.

Was this his place? With his mother's people? Beautiful sorrowful-eyed Wind Song. It was a recollection that sent fearful tremors racing through his flesh.

There would be no sleep for Alex tonight, for too many memories sprang from the past to play cruel games with him. But more than the sharp stabs of old wounds, there was this persistent ache, dull and throbbing, that at times lay harbored deep within him, smoldering in silence, yet dictating his every movement. At other times it exploded from within in an implosion of hate and anger directed at himself but catching too many others in its deadening way.

All the while the shadow continued to dance on the wall. Blinking his magnetic gray eyes, he traced its outline. It was *her* shadow . . . this woman asleep beside him.

He watched hypnotically, unable to deny its power over him, and hated her all the more for it. Damn you, Danielle Fleming! Damn you! He cursed to himself, his mind raging against her, but wanting her—always wanting her—and ever hating himself for it.

Danny stirred in her sleep and nestled closer to Alex. Without thinking, he removed his arm from behind his head and placed it tenderly around her shoulders, drawing her near to his own naked body. And it was when she lay in his embrace that he realized how much he'd grown used to holding her like this.

That was the way sleep found him when it spread its lacy fingers across his eyelids and sent him tumbling backward into a dark dream. A dream of a time that no longer existed except in his mind and in his heart, and to two people whose existence in his past was as painfully certain then as their absence was now. It took him back along invisible threads to the most loving memory of his life . . . now only a vision, but then, a beautiful Indian woman. Wind Song.

Wind Song's aunts and cousins had teased her mercilessly when the French trapper offered Black Crow many presents for his lovely young daughter. Had Black Crow's greed for more presents angered Jacques, he might have withdrawn the offer for the girl, but so determined was the Frenchman to win the fragrantly delicate fifteen-year-old Wind Song that he granted her father's demand and threw in several personal items of obvious value to him, preferring to part with them rather than risk losing the Indian maiden whose soft brown flesh he craved so thoroughly. It worked. Black Crow was pleased, Wind Song was pleased, and Jacques had the wife he wanted.

Less than a year later Wind Song grew large with child. It would be a boy, she told Jacques, and she would name the infant Fernando, a name she had learned from one of Jacques' books. When her time came they were camped away from the village, trailing the banks of the upper Tongue, emptying the traps Jacques had set the previous spring. The birth had been difficult, coming at dawn when the call of the night owl could still be heard in the mountain stillness.

Wind Song laid in a heap, grasping her contracting stomach with clenched fists as the pains grew steadier and stronger. Breathing heavily, pulling herself up along the length of stake Jacques had driven firmly into the ground, feeling the wooden splinters piercing her palms, she felt a constricting spasm explode within her womb. But just when she thought she would pass over the edge to the other side of the world, another convulsion of pain snapped her back to reality, driving her wild with its searing intensity. Then, everything went dark. With her moist cheek against the soft earth, she drifted in and out of a dream, hazy one moment, crystal clear the next.

Gradually she became aware of Jacques' presence. He was speaking to her gently and stroking her cheek, gently brushing back her matted hair. She looked down at the tiny doeskin bundle he placed at her breast, into the eyes of her son. And she knew he was special.

They continued living with Black Crow's Oglalas until Jacques felt the child was strong enough to make the journey north. During the summer the village camped in the fertile valley of the Rosebud, pitching their tipis amidst groves of cottonwood, box elder and juniper trees. In the winter they remained in a protective valley sheltered from the harsh winds. But as the ninth winter approached, a noticeable change came over Jacques. He knew how much Wind Song loved being with her people and how much young Nando loved to race his pony with the other boys. But he could no longer deny the longing he had to return to the north country and its stark isolation.

Wind Song sensed it, and so, sometime during the moon of the Falling Leaves, with winter approaching, Jacques returned one day from hunting to find their belongings packed into neat bundles and strapped to the travois that would pull them across the miles of frozen snow and ice. When the others left for the Powder River country where they hoped to find antelope and buffalo, Jacques, Wind Song and eight-year-old Nando turned toward the upper regions of the Missouri River in search of beaver pelts.

That winter would remain indelibly imprinted on Nando's mind forever. The sheer beauty of the nights, crystal clear, overwhelmingly silent—so still you could almost hear a snowflake flutter to the earth—the awesome mountains with jagged peaks and delicately carved fissures through which shot vast streaks of color into the evening sky, the smell of freshly cleaned pelts his father would sling off his shoulder onto the dirt floor of their lodge, his mother's face, always laughing, always kind, always there.

Suddenly . . . gone.

Chapter 16

When the first slivers of light pierced the sky, they left the Indian camp, Danny using a pony the Indians had given her. When they had ridden a mile or so, Alex gestured back toward it with a flick of his head.

"Crazy Horse said to say farewell to the woman whose hair is the color of the setting sun. He's named you Falling Sun, and he hoped that as my wife you'd be pleased with it."

"Your what! *Wife?*" Tawny eyes grew wide at his impertinence. "Just what did you tell those people, Alex Coulter?"

"I didn't tell them anything, baby," he laughed.

"Then why did he say that? You must have said something!"

"If you'll just shut up for a minute, I'll explain. That's better. You actually look sweet when your mouth isn't open, Danny. Now, according to Sioux custom, all a man and a woman have to do to marry is simply take up together. It's sort of official when the man, shall we say, fulfills his husbandly obligations." He paused, watching with a gleam in his devil gray eyes as Danny's mouth dropped open, then added with a mocking drawl, "So it looks like you and I got married . . . Oglala style, that is."

Oh! What a horrible man he was! Again he had tricked her! Was there no end to his treachery?

Alex was no longer smiling when he saw the look on her face. "Well, what the hell did you expect? A march down the aisle?" With two quick jabs of his bootheels into the stallion's flanks, he was off at a gallop, leaving Danielle coughing in his dust.

In the days that followed Alex became withdrawn to the

157

point where he would not even bother to answer her taunts and jeers. During the nights he took her without mercy, tearing into her without regard for her feelings, physical or otherwise. He bruised her arms with his grasp and ravaged her mouth with his, claiming every part of her over and over again as though each time were the first. And still she continued to fight him, flinging her head from side to side to escape his kisses, until he was forced to still her by pulling her head back sharply by her hair and holding it there while his mouth closed over hers, forcing his tongue between her lips, searching all corners of her mouth, filling her and leaving her breathless.

When they rode, Alex would watch from his saddle the way Danny raced her horse across the prairie, long slender legs wrapped tightly about the animal just as they were at times wrapped about him. Seeing her like that during the day, and feeling her beneath him at night, he knew there lay within her a passion that had yet to be realized, whose depths he felt himself drowning in, unable to save himself. He'd never known a woman like her, so thoroughly provocative and untamed, like the spirited Indian pony she rode. But where the pony had reluctantly compromised its freedom, he sensed that a part of her would always remain out of his grasp, teasing him with its promise, challenging him with its defiance.

Some days later their routine changed at Alex's insistence, and they rode by night with just the light of the stars to guide them. During the day they slept in the shadows of the bluffs, but only in shifts. Alex seemed tense, more alert, always searching the distance.

The heat was stifling even for this time of year, so late in the summer. And with a stab of homesickness, Danny sadly recalled her beloved France and the way it would be now, so fresh and vibrant. Not like this, she thought angrily, throwing a contemptuous glance over the surrounding country. With a pang of despair she reflected on how she and Austin would ride along the delicately landscaped paths and park lanes, and how handsome he looked in his tailored riding coat and fine Italian boots. He was such an excellent horseman. She had always been so proud to have her brother riding beside her.

From the corner of her eye she looked at Alex Coulter and frowned. He was so different. His edges were rough where Austin's were smooth. At least Alex had seen fit to leave behind the buckskin leggings and quilled shirt in favor of a burgundy linen shirt and black, tightly fitting breeches that he tucked into the tops of his leather boots.

His silence was beginning to grate on her nerves, and with the increased tension in the air, thick and heavy, Danny began to think again of escape, until she could think of nothing else. She longed to be free of him, and the heat and dust and grime, and the endless hours and days in the saddle. She was a mess to look at, with her hair hanging loose and unkempt and the dirt streaked across her cheeks, her skin browned almost as deeply as his. Alex caught her stooped over her reflection in a small creek, her face one big frown.

"What's the matter, love?" he asked in that awful drawl she hated.

"I'll tell you what the matter is!" she snapped.

But he cut her short with a low warning. "In case you don't know it, we happen to be in the heart of Snake country, so if I were you, I wouldn't be making too much noise."

The bastard! Was it just a trick to shut her up, or was this really hostile Shoshone country? Was that why he'd been so edgy lately? She shot him a look of hatred anyway, and keeping her voice down to a whisper, said, "You've turned me into an Indian. I haven't had a decent bath in weeks, nor a good night's sleep, nor a decent dress to wear! Just *look* at me!"

"I am, my love, believe me, I am," Alex drawled, his lips curling into a smile. "But don't worry. Until we get out from under the noses of the Snakes, you're safe from me. I wouldn't want your cries of ecstasy to give our location away."

She didn't even bother answering his gibe, but swished past him in icy disdain.

"Do you remember that town we passed a few weeks back?"

Yes, she remembered it all right. She had nearly begged him to take her there but he wouldn't do it. Oh, she hated him for that.

"What about it?" Danny asked, suspicion in her golden eyes.

"If you want, we'll stop there for the night. If we ride hard, we could make it by sundown."

For a stunned moment Danny just stared hard at him in disbelief. "If I *want*? You know very well—!"

"Keep your voice down, God damn it," he ordered. "I wasn't kidding about those Indians."

"You miserable bastard," she sneered at him. "What do you want me to do, beg you to take me there just so you can have the pleasure of turning me down flat? Not on your life, you dirty rotten weasel . . . you lowdown savage . . . you . . . !" She cursed at him in hushed tones, her cheeks flushed with anger and her eyes blazing brightly. "Oh, damn your miserable soul to eternal hell!"

Instead of lashing back at her, Alex merely chuckled. "I've got to admit I've been called a lot worse than that. Remind me to teach you some real good words sometime, Danny."

She flung her head away so she would not have to look at his scoundrel's face, but she could not escape the sound of his voice.

"Don't get too excited about this town. We'll only be staying the night, and in the morning we'll be riding out *together.*"

He said it with finality as if she had nothing to say about it, and no matter what she said or did, it was impossible to induce him to tell her more, least of all to make her any promises.

The town of Jacaronda sat between two mountains. It was a good town, as far as they go, but of course, there was always the chance that he'd be recognized. Just one night wouldn't hurt, Alex thought, and besides, she wanted a bath. What the hell, he decided, he could use one too. He just hoped she didn't throw a tantrum when she found out that he was taking her to Unity's place. It was the only place that was safe in Jacaronda, because he knew its proprietress, Unity McKeever, for more years than he could remember.

Before Unity's place down in Amarillo had become too hot, he'd spent much of his time there, along with men like Pierce Morgan and Ernesto Ortega. "Nothin' lasts forever," Unity had told him with a dispassionate shrug when he paid his last visit there. She knew it had gotten too dangerous for him. Of all the people in the world, Unity McKeever was one of the very few who really knew Alex Coulter. She knew he ran around with that bandit, Jake Alvarez, and his band of no-accounts, and that he traipsed across the plains with the Indians. She knew all the horrid little embarrassments of his life, all the mistakes and the things he suffered for in retrospect. She knew because he had told her.

She was older than he was, but in those days she still had feminine allure, enough to appear, to his young eyes, as an extremely attractive woman. She was old enough to be his mother and she had been his lover. In a remote sort of way, Alex loved her as nearly as he could love any woman. She had proven herself to be a carefully guarded vault for some of his innermost thoughts and fears, and Alex knew he could trust her with some, though certainly not all, of his blackest nightmares. It had been many years ago, when Alex was first beginning to awaken to the pain of his particular stigma of being part white and part Indian, and the toll of Unity's profession had only just begun to dull the sparkle in her eyes and erase the glow from her cheeks. Whatever glow was there now was put there by a splotch of red rouge, and sometimes it was difficult for Alex to believe that she was the same woman in whose arms he had learned the finer details of love.

They reached Jacaronda just as the sun was descending in the western sky. Alex pulled up and dismounted when the town was not even a quarter of a mile away.

"What are we stopping for?" Danny demanded, instantly suspicious.

"Look, I told you we're going to Jacaronda, and we are. But not until I'm damned good and ready. We'll wait here a few more hours until I'm sure most of the town is asleep. If I walked in there now, you can bet somebody'd recognize me. Or have you forgotten that I'm a wanted man?"

"I haven't forgotten," she sneered as she swung her leg over her horse's neck and jumped down. "Believe me, I haven't forgotten. Particularly since you've added kidnapping to your list of crimes. You certainly do pick strange pastimes for yourself, Alex Coulter. Why, I'll bet—"

"Shut up, Danielle, I'm not in the mood," he said dryly. "But I'll tell you what I *am* in the mood for." Bright gray eyes raked over her shamelessly, and Danny turned crimson beneath his lustful glare. She turned to storm away, but with a quick graceful movement, he reached out to grab her and pulled her to the ground, rolling on top of her and smothering her mouth with his.

When he was finished, he wouldn't let her put her dress

back on, but held her beside him, her breasts pressed against his chest, until it was time to go. When they were both dressed, he said, "All right, mount up. And remember, no funny tricks. I'll have enough to worry about without wondering what kind of mischief you're up to."

He paused for a deep breath, then added, "Look, there's something else. Just in case there's any trouble down there . . . Well, I mean, not that I'm expecting any . . ."

A tremor of fear sprang into Danny's heart.

"Here, hold on to this," he said, pushing a small pearl-handled dagger into her hands. "There's no reason for me to think you won't use it on me, but I'm hoping you won't. Tie it to your thigh with a piece of rawhide, and if anything happens, don't hesitate to use it. Don't look so shocked, my love, I *know* you can use it. Or did you think I wouldn't find out that those young boys taught you back at Crazy Horse's camp?"

"Whose is it?" she asked, examining it closely.

"It belonged to someone I used to know. Doesn't matter who."

"Was it a woman?"

"Yeah."

"An Indian?"

"Yeah."

"Was her name Wind Song?"

Alex Coulter's eyes flashed with deadly intensity at the sound of the name, and inwardly Danny shrank from the terror of them.

His expression turned abruptly from pure rage, fiery and bright, to feigned confusion. "What the hell are you talking about?" he asked, annoyed.

Danny shrugged with indifference and sighed. "Sometimes you talk in your sleep. Wind Song is one of the names I've heard you muttering, that's all."

"Well, you must have heard wrong. Now, remember what I said, baby, no tricks."

Avoiding the main street, they traveled through the back alleys until they came to the rear exit of one of the buildings. "Wait here," Alex said curtly. Dismounting, he walked in long, catlike strides to the door where he rapped on the glass pane.

The door opened and revealed a woman silhouetted against

the interior light. Several words passed between them before Alex returned to fetch Danny.

Once inside she glanced suspiciously about. The sound of voices coming from behind closed doors confirmed her fears.

"What's the matter, honey, ain't you never seen a whore-house before?" Unity McKeever asked, a wide grin on her face. Without waiting for a reply, she switched her attention on Alex.

"Alex Coulter, what the hell are you doing in these parts? I've been hearing some nasty things about you, you devil." She flung her flabby arms around his neck, and Danny watched with growing revulsion as Alex wrapped his own arms tightly around the woman's waist and pulled her close. She was old enough to be his mother, and Danny was sickened at the sight of Alex kissing that garish female fully on the lips.

"It sure is good to see you again," Alex said. "I've brought you something." He reached behind him and drew Danny forward.

Unity's eyes traveled over Danny, quickly appraising her worth. "Honey, you always did know how to pick 'em, I've got to hand it to you. She'll really bring the money in!"

The color drained from Danny's face. My God, what was he, her recruiter?

"That's not quite what I meant," Alex chuckled. "No, Unity, this one's mine. What I meant was that maybe you could turn her into a woman again. You know, a bath, and a dress or something."

"Oh sure, honey. Tell you what, she can use my room, how's that? I'll have someone come up to fill the tub. And as for you, you rogue, you can come with me. I ain't seen you for such a long time, and we've got us some reacquainting to do." She laughed wickedly as she led the way upstairs.

They deposited Danny in one of the rooms at the end of the hall, locking the door at Alex's insistence, and continuing off together, laughing loudly down the hall.

Danny stared at the door for several minutes before she could move. Did he prefer that old woman . . . that cheap painted whore . . . to her? Was he coming back? Damn it, why didn't he ever tell her anything? How dare he treat her like this!

She flung herself down on the bed, oblivious to the smooth

texture of satin sheets and lace trimmings. Warm tears spilled
onto her cheeks which she made no attempt to hide when,
several minutes later, an elderly man entered with a bucket of
steaming water. He walked stoop-shouldered to the scroll-
footed porcelain bathtub that was in front of a simmering fire,
and wordlessly emptied the bucket. He returned several more
times until the tub was full, then left her permanently.

Afterward, she lay on the bed with her hair in damp curls
casting a sneer over the room. Not even a discriminating
whore, she thought disdainfully, eyes flicking over the ornate
furnishings and garish decor. And that smell, that ever-
constant, nauseating smell of Unity's lilac perfume wafting
from every corner. The chamber bore a look of total
decadence, from the shocking paintings on the walls to the
mirror suspended directly over the massive four-posted bed.

From downstairs could be heard the cheap tinkle of a
saloon piano, intermingled with girlish giggles and an occasional grunt or bellow from one of the neighboring rooms.
Embarrassment surged through her when she bitterly remembered that she had every reason to be here. After all, she was
a whore too, wasn't she? She was *his* whore. How could he
have the nerve to do this to her? He had no right . . . no right
at all!

Her mind raced with a million thoughts, all converging on a
single point. Escape! She could not bear to be locked up in
this sickening place a minute longer! Jumping from the bed,
she began to pace nervously like a caged lioness stalking its
freedom. There had to be a way out!

Across the room, behind a writing table, stood another
door. Racing to it, Danny tried the crystal knob. Carefully,
she eased the door open so that she could barely peek
through the slit. She pushed it wider and stared into what was
obviously an adjoining bedroom.

Wetting her lips, she stepped inside and ran on tiptoes to
what she knew was the hall door. She pressed her ear against
its smooth oak surface straining to hear if anyone was on the
other side. Hearing nothing, she reached out a trembling
hand and tested the knob. It wasn't locked!

She quickly scanned the hallway, and seeing nothing,
sprang into action, her feet fairly flying down the corridor to
the stairs and then swiftly down the steps. Somewhere in her
jumbled mind she heard men's voices, loud and boisterous,
some thick and slurred, from the adjoining saloon, but there

was no time to think about it. At the end of the stairs she spotted what was probably a rear exit, one hardly used judging by the grime that had been allowed to build on the window panes. But even the coating of grease and dust could not obscure what lay on the outside. Freedom!

Tearing the door open, she burst into the night.

She ran fast and hard, the echo of her own footsteps resounding in her brain like plangent waves against a shore. When she felt she could go no further, her legs barely sustaining her weight, she collapsed in a heap, gasping for breath.

Although exhausted, and suffering from a splitting headache, she noticed something that sent a cold wave of stark fear right through her.

Alex! He'd come after her!

He pulled her unceremoniously to her feet.

"If you wanted my company, why didn't you ask for it instead of trying a damned fool stunt like this? Or was it just a stroll in the moonlight you wanted?"

His awful mocking voice made her cringe.

"Why can't you let me go?"

"Let you go? I can't do that, baby. Sorry, but you're my ace in the hole. Which reminds me, you got me away from a good hand of poker to come after you. Look at you! You're a mess! And you just had a bath! You're going to have them thinking I've been beating you."

As he spoke he brushed the dirt from her dress. "Listen to me, Danny. We're going back in there, and I want you to behave yourself!"

His grip tightened like a vice around her arm just above the elbow, and flinging her around, he pushed her back in the direction of Unity's place.

"Where are you taking me?" she asked weakly, stumbling along as he shoved her through the door.

"Back to your room. And if you ever try to run away again, I'm going to—"

"Run away? Well now, whoth that runnin' away?"

They both turned simultaneously. "It's nothing, mister," Alex told the man who staggered toward them. "Really, it's nothing. Go back to your whiskey."

"Young fella," he said, pulling himself up to full height, then falling back into a slouch, "don't you worry 'bout a thing. No, thuh, I won't tell a thoul." He smiled at them with a mouth of rotting teeth, most of which had already fallen out leaving large gaping holes through which he sputtered a spray of saliva at them.

"Well, that's just fine," Alex said, nudging Danny along, hoping to get away before the fool called too much attention to them.

"No, thuree, why iffen you two wanna go runnin' off to git married up, then no, thur, I ain't gonna tell a damned thoul, not old Willard Thpree." He slapped his thigh and cackled loudly. "Hey, I know! Oh boy, ain't thith gonna be thomthin'!" Without warning he let out a holler that made Danny's head ache more and made the hair at the back of Alex Coulter's neck stand on end.

"Hey, Judge," he yelled into the crowded saloon, forgetting his promise as easily as he'd made it. "Judge, you got yourthelf thom cuthomerth. Come on over!"

Alex cursed beneath his breath, then turned quickly to the girl at his side, leaning so close she could almost taste the whiskey on his breath. "No tricks now, baby, or I'll break your pretty little neck."

"Ain't thith thomthin?" Willard Spree exclaimed. "Theth two wanna git hitched. Heard 'em thay tho mythelf."

Unity pushed her way through the throng. "Honey, I gotta hand it to you," she said to Danny. "I always did say that the woman who lands this handsome devil has got to be something special."

"Oh, but there's been some kind of mis—" Danny began, but stopped when she felt Alex's fingers dig into her waist.

What was he doing? Surely he wasn't going through with this charade? Did he really expect her to marry him simply to satisfy the whim of some drunk? Had Alex gone completely mad?

While Judge Decker led the others into the saloon, Unity turned to Alex, her face bearing a grave expression. "Alex, honey, I got me a gut feeling that this ain't something you two planned on doing. Not tonight leastways. But I think for your sake you'd better go through with it. Those people in there are getting ready for a wedding, and if they don't get one, there's gonna be trouble."

Alex cast a fearful look into the crowded saloon, then looked down at the girl at his side, whose complexion had gone white. Tightening his hold around her waist to keep her on her feet, he asked, "Is there anyone here tonight I should know about?"

"Don't think so, hon, but I'll keep my eyes open."

Alex drew an uncertain breath. "Okay, look, buy me a few minutes, would you?"

"Sure thing," said Unity, and turning away, she called loudly to the man behind the bar. "Sam, set up a round for everyone on the house." As she suspected, everyone moved in unison to the bar to claim their free shot of whiskey.

Alex led Danny into the hallway out of sight from the others and placed her with her back against the wall. He braced a hand next to her head and hooked the other in his gunbelt.

"I know what you're thinking," he said softly, recognizing the suspicion in her golden eyes. "And I want you to know that I didn't concoct any of this. I never planned on getting married myself, least of all like this." He felt strangely uncomfortable looking at her. "Well, you can see the kind of life I live. How could I expect any woman to . . . Well look, we don't seem to have any choice . . ." His words trailed off awkwardly, but it was just as well, because Danny decided she'd heard enough.

"Is that supposed to be a *proposal?*" she demanded, her eyes wide in disbelief. "Because if it is, then I do *not* accept! I would never marry you willingly if you were the last man on earth! If I'm to become your wife now, then it's only because I've been deprived of any choice in the matter! To even think otherwise is insane!"

She held her voice down to an angry whisper, but her face flushed scarlet and her amber eyes blazed her hatred and indignation. With fists clenched at her sides, she vented her outrage, fearing she would burst from keeping it under her breath. She wished she could scream at him, but even she knew it would serve no purpose to call more attention to them.

"And furthermore, I have never in my life heard a proposal like that, if indeed that's what it was! And you can be sure I've heard many!" She saw the almost imperceptible twitch at the corner of his mouth.

"What the hell do you want me to do, get down on my knees and beg you to marry me?" He was furious and his own face became crimson beneath the tan.

"The only time I ever wish to see you on your knees, Alex

Coulter, is when you are forced by them—when you are finally caught and have to beg for your miserable life!"

Almost instantly Danny regretted the stab of pain she saw in his eyes. But in the next second, it passed, and he glared at her with eyes like molten steel, melting away the strength she had gathered.

"Not on your life, baby," he sneered back. "Not on your life."

Reaching for her roughly, he clasped a strong grip around her arm and yanked her along with him into the saloon where the others waited.

In the confusion, Danny tried to focus her attention on Judge Decker, taking in everything that was visible about the man, and wondering what had taken him for such a cruel ride. Tiny moisture-laden beads of sweat dripped off his stubbly chin onto the front of his shirt. The jacket he wore looked like it might have fit him once, but now hung loosely about his shoulders, one sleeve longer than the other, the collar frayed and stained yellow. While he downed his final shot of bourbon, Danny watched with revulsion as the pathetic man of the law tried to lift the glass to his lips without shaking the whiskey from it. She felt almost sorry for the wretched man, although why she should feel sorry for anyone else was beyond her.

Alex fidgeted nervously at her side, his eyes darting across the nameless faces, looking for a sign of recognition. He found Danny's hand and grasped it tightly while his other hand brushed lightly over his pistol. Just in case, he thought, just in case.

What a damned fool spot to be in, he cursed bitterly to himself. Exactly what he didn't need. If his name rang a familiar bell to just one person, there'd be a lot of trouble. Any one of them could be a bounty hunter, U.S. marshal or some fool kid hoping to try his gun against the fabled lightening quick draw that was synonymous with Alex Coulter's name.

The ceremony was a mockery. Danny saw the judge's lips moving, but barely heard the words. "Power invested in me . . . Territory of Colorado . . . man and wife."

A rousing cheer went up and several people rushed forward. Danny threw up her hands and a little cry escaped her lips when a burly man pulled her into his great hairy arms and smothered her mouth with a disgusting kiss.

"Me next, me next!" someone shouted.

Panic gripped her as hands snatched at her from all directions. Suddenly, she felt herself swept into the air. She flung her head around to fight off her attacker, only to find herself looking with wild frightened eyes into familiar silver ones.

"That's it, fellas," Alex said, forcing a strained laugh, ready to blow the head off the next man who touched her. "I think the lady's a little tired from all the excitement, so I'm just going to take her on upstairs, and—"

Shrill whistles split the air and Danielle saw some of their crude gestures before turning her face away, sickened. All the more reason to hate Alex Coulter, she swore.

Only when they were in Unity's room with the door bolted behind them did he let her down. "We'll be leaving at sunrise," Alex said as he unbuckled his gunbelt and slung it over the chair. "We'll have some hard riding ahead so I want to get an early start."

He came up behind her and placed his hands on her breasts. Automatically, she tensed. Then she felt him brush her hair aside to expose her neck and press his lips warmly against her skin.

Only he had the power to make her feel as though he were possessing her merely by his touch . . . with just the burn of his lips against her fevered flesh. She closed her eyes as his mouth moved to her earlobe, then to her cheek and finally to rest upon her lips.

He kissed her thoroughly, invading her mouth with his tongue and calling up in her all the old feelings of desire and rapture . . . of being carried off to another realm where nothing else mattered except the passion of the moment. Grasping a handful of her hair, crushing its silken mass in his fingers and pulling her head back, Alex smothered her mouth with his telling her with his lips how much he wanted her, and proving it by the way his hands tore at her dress.

Danny felt herself on fire, her flesh scorched wherever his lips touched it. She was being consumed by him and she was powerless to prevent it. She was helplessly tumbling into the pit of his demands, dissolving into boiling liquid from the intense heat of her own urges. The last thing she remembered was Alex's handsome face above hers and the smell of fresh-cut lilacs.

No sooner, it seemed, had her head fallen onto the satin-covered pillow, than she was being nudged awake.

Instead of a moon-streaked sky and the angry face of Alex Coulter leaning over her, she awakened to the pastel shades of Unity's room and a pair of startlingly gray eyes that held only contentment.

"You want some breakfast?" he asked.

With the memory of last night to deal with and her temples pounding, Danny pulled herself up and half-stumbled to the wash basin to splash cold water on her face. At the dressing table she sat down to brush her hair, but lifting her arms merely made her head ache more and she winced from the pain.

Alex came up silently behind her, his nakedness all too obvious, and taking the brush from her hand, said, "Here, let me."

With long gentle strokes he ran the brush through her auburn hair, gently working out all the tangles. Danny's temples continued to throb anyway. Moaning, she pushed his hands away and rose, slightly wobbly. The smell of lilacs was beginning to nauseate her and she knew if she didn't escape it soon, she'd be sick. Alex guessed it only because he had to admit that the sweet smell was a bit too much for him also. "Here, put this on," he said, handing her the beaded buckskin dress.

"I'll just have coffee and eggs, Manuelito," Alex told the white-haired man in the kitchen as they sat down at the table. "And the lady will have some eggs, maybe some bacon, and tea." He ordered without bothering to ask whether his choice suited her.

Danny cast a scornful look at Alex, then addressed the old man. "I'll have coffee, too, if you don't mind."

Hunched over her plate, wolfing down the food and sipping greedily on the black coffee, Danny kept a suspicious eye on Alex and Manuelito as they spoke. She heard Alex thank the man, then send him off laughing.

Sitting back in his chair, Alex stretched his long hard-muscled legs out in front of him. "I see your tastes have changed," he remarked with a grin, recalling the time when Danny turned her nose up at the bitter taste of coffee. He added mischievously, "You'd be surprised at the things you can acquire a taste for."

"I can assure you there are some things I'll never acquire a taste for!"

"What's the matter with you?" he asked, surprised at her harshness. "Can't you ever be nice?"

"Ha! That's a strange question coming from you. If you don't like it, you've no one but yourself to blame for it."

Alex gave her a long measured look. "There are some other things you seem to have learned from me. You were delightful last night, my love. You'd never know that just a few months ago you were an innocent little virgin."

Suddenly she'd lost her appetite. Pushing her plate away, she slapped the linen napkin down on the table and got up to leave.

"Sit down!"

His command was uttered with force, and Danny knew if she did not comply on her own, he'd be beside her in a flash, using physical strength to carry out his demand. Biting back the epithets she wanted desperately to hurl at him, she sat back down.

"I thought you were hungry," he said, annoyed.

She ignored him.

"In that case, let's go."

Chapter 17

The country they rode over had the look of creation still in progress. An awful silence followed them like a shadow, and Alex did not have to tell Danny that they had entered hostile Indian territory, for she felt his apprehension keenly.

Crouching at the bank of a stream, Alex stretched out on his stomach, drinking the clear water from cupped hands while his eyes darted back and forth across the horizon.

"Who are they?" Danny asked, unable to contain her curiosity.

"Utes," he said, brushing the dust from his pants. "A war party."

"How long have they been following us?"

"A couple of days. They probably—" He stopped abruptly, focusing his attention on something Danny could not detect. "Mount up. We're getting out of here."

She obeyed instantly, a growing terror building within her.

"Here, take this," Alex said as he thrust a small derringer into her hand. "Be careful, it's loaded. Remember, anyone who carries a gun should be prepared to use it."

As the sun rose in the sky, Danny's anxiety reached a feverish pitch. The air was electric, sizzling with tension so thick she was sure she could shoot a hole right through it.

Alex reined up the stallion and glanced around hurriedly. The big horse pawed the ground, snorting through flared nostrils, sensing danger. "Over this way," Alex said. He grasped the reins out of Danny's hands and galloped toward a cluster of boulders.

There was no time for explanations. With a slap on its

rump, he sent the Appaloosa off at a gallop with the pony chasing behind. He'd worry about them later. Right now there was a war party of Utes hot on their trail and something told Alex they'd played cat and mouse long enough. They were ready to strike. He sensed it—knew it. He waited anxiously behind the barricade for the moment of impact.

When it came, it was as though a storm had suddenly erupted in violent flashes of lightening and roaring clashes of thunder. Danny screamed when an arrow whizzed by her head.

"Get down!" Alex shouted, pushing her to the ground with a vehement shove. But not before she'd seen the painted faces of their attackers and heard the spine-chilling yells above the stampede of hooves and the explosive volley of fire from Alex's gun.

Through the choking cloud of dust and smoke, it was impossible to tell how many Utes there were, but it seemed as though they were being attacked by an army. As the Indians passed, the air above the fugitives' heads was littered with a spray of arrows, one just missing Alex by an inch before it cracked against the rock wall behind them.

"One of those bastards has a rifle," Alex cursed aloud when deadly bullets ricocheted off the granite boulders with a deafening squeal that set Danny's nerves screaming. Then, all was quiet. Out of nowhere a curtain of eerie silence fell over the land.

"Are you all right?" Alex asked as he reloaded his gun and glanced quickly at Danny to see her trembling on the dusty ground, clutching the side of a boulder as if clinging to life itself. She could barely nod her head. "They'll be back. Only this time *we've* got to end it. If we don't, they could hold us here for days and we'd never last." He leaned over and gripped her shoulder tightly. "This time you've got to help me, Danny. Can you do it?"

Kill? Oh my God, she couldn't do it! Involuntary little wimpers came from her as Alex tightened his hold.

"Can you do it?" he demanded, shaking her harshly, and forcing her to the rude realization that if she wanted to survive, she had no choice. "Damn it, answer me!"

Her voice emerged scratchy and barely audible. "Yes . . . yes . . ."

"Good. Use the pistol I gave you. And remember, you don't get much distance with that thing, so you'll have to wait until you can get off a good shot. Don't worry about missing, just shoot at anything that gets too close. Okay, baby, this is it." He took his position again over a low boulder just as the sound of hooves filled the air.

This time the brown-skinned warriors rode right into Alex's line of fire, shrieking their hideous war cries and lashing a string of arrows at them. Vaguely, she heard Alex shouting to her.

"Fire! Now!"

Mechanically, as if moving outside of herself, Danny raised the pistol. She heard a man scream as one of Alex's bullets ripped through his heart, its force propelling the Ute backward clear off his horse in a burst of power and blood. But before Danny could react, a savage cry tore over her head, and she found herself looking up into a painted mask of terror. The glint of a knife caught her eye as the sun sparkled off the razor-sharp blade, and Danny knew with cold stark certainty that the man intended to plunge it deep into her.

Without thinking, she raised the pistol and fired.

The expression on the Indian's face as the bullet burst through his throat was a strange mixture of pain and surprise. Danny screamed as his body tumbled forward and landed at her feet.

She whirled toward the land beyond the rocks, expecting to see more Utes advancing, but there was nothing except the dense curtain of dust and the sound of Alex's gunfire still exploding all around them, echoing from the surrounding hills. Beyond the dust came the sounds of moaning—of men dying—and when the air cleared, five bodies were strewn across the dirt.

Danny gazed upon the ghastly scene, her face blanched with fear. Then she looked at the man at her feet who lay with his head twisted to one side, streaks of war paint mingling garishly with dust, eyes staring fixedly into space. He was young, no more than sixteen or seventeen years old. It was perhaps that which increased Danny's horror the most.

Turning away from the scene of her crime she leaned her back against the rock, knees pulled to her chest, arms wrapped tightly around them, the gun still dangling from her hand, feeling strangely void of emotion, as though some unseen hand had reached deep within her and wrenched it all out with one violent twist. She had nearly lost her life, but at this moment, it failed to frighten her. She had just killed a man, and yet, she could only marvel at the speed at which her remorse over it fell, leaving in its place nothing except indifference.

Her head fell against the rock and she scanned the sky for a sign of something pleasant amidst all this death and misery. But what she saw made her scream instead. The noise jolted Alex around, but he was not quick enough. The arrow entered with a pain that was sharp and hot, and a low animal growl escaped from his throat. In the next instant, he fired his gun at the lone Indian who had crept up on them from behind and was perched on a ledge overhead. Even with the arrow imbedded in Alex's shoulder, his reflexes had been lightning quick, and Danny saw the body fall to the ground even before she heard the crack of Alex's pistol. When she turned horror-stricken eyes to Alex, the gun was still smoking in his hand and a grimace distorted his features. She went to him automatically.

"Pull it out," he gasped, gritting his teeth.

"I can't!"

"Damn it," he snapped, "you've got to!"

The arrow had penetrated his shirt and leather vest, and it lay imbedded in bone and muscle.

"How far in is the shaft?" His voice was taut and she could tell he was holding himself in check. She forced her eyes to look at it.

"I can't tell . . . I can't see it . . . I—"

"Help me off with this," he ordered. "They'll be back soon to collect their dead, and if we don't get out of here, we'll be sitting ducks."

She helped him slip out of his vest and shirt which was already soaked with blood. "All right," he said, "take a look."

Her gasp told him what he needed to know. The arrow had pierced his right shoulder just beneath the blade. There was no way it could be pulled out. Taking firm hold of her hand he demanded her full attention.

"All right now, Danny, listen to me. You're going to have to cut it out. There's no other way. I want you to do exactly as I tell you and it'll be all right. Are you listening to me, Danny?"

She nodded dumbly, and simply because there was no choice to be made, she found herself following his instructions like a string puppet moving according to someone else's will. She made a small fire with dried twigs, then thrust the blade of his hunting knife into it. Alex leaned against the rock for support, fingers clutching its craggy surface, knuckles whitening under the pressure. "All right," Alex groaned, "do it . . . now."

Blind to everything else, Danny plunged the knife into his flesh with cuts deep enough to expose the arrowhead. Alex moaned. The barb was exposed now, but how was she supposed to get it out? With the point of the blade she tried to dislodge the shaft, and a cry broke from her throat when she felt it stubbornly holding ground. She drew the blade from the wound, her mind working furiously.

Alex raised his head. "Go in after it," he gasped.

Without hesitation, Danny jabbed her fingers into the bloody wound, caught the flint by one of its barbs. "Hold on!" she shouted, gave it one quick twist and tore the arrow loose.

Staring down at the bloody mess in her hand, Danny came close to fainting, but the sound of Alex's voice kept her from losing consciousness.

"Help me with this." Already he was back on his feet, but his breathing was sharp and ragged. He tore a strip from his shirt and tried to wrap it around the open wound to stop the flow of blood.

Flinging the bloody flint to the ground, Danny hastily wrapped a makeshift bandage about his shoulder, then helped him on with his vest. The pain was plainly written on his face.

"Remind me to give you a big kiss for this, baby," he said breathlessly. "Now, let's get the hell out of here." Grabbing Danny by the hand they scrambled over the rocks, leaving the safety of their barricade behind. Running across the open land, he put his fingers to his lips and emitted a shrill whistle. It was answered in seconds by the sound of a nervous whinny, and from out of the hills the big Appaloosa stallion came galloping with Danny's new Indian pony at its heels.

They rode at breakneck speed for what seemed like hours. It was only when Danielle's pony started to give way and fall behind that Alex relented and slowed the pace enough to allow them to catch their breath. When Danny caught up to him she gasped. His brow was drenched with sweat and his color was ashen, despite his bronzed skin. He swayed in the saddle, looking about to fall over any second.

The sudden thought of his passing out in the middle of hostile Indian country scared Danny tremendously. She had to do something, and quick! Reaching forward, she snatched the reins from his hands, knowing instinctively that they had to get out of sight. Her eyes scanned the horizon for a clue—a mass of rocks, a patch of trees—anything. Then she saw it—halfway up the hill, a big black orifice like a huge mouth open wide to them. Without knowing what she would find there, she turned the pony's head sharply in the direction of the cave and started the uphill climb. Looking back over her shoulder every now and then, she was worried about Alex's precarious position in the saddle.

When they were within twenty feet of the cave she jumped down quickly. Alex could barely help himself out of the saddle, and Danny had all she could do to keep on her own feet beneath his weight when she pulled him to the ground. His flesh was aflame and she knew immediately that his body was wracked with fever. It was a sultry afternoon, but as Alex stumbled along, leaning heavily against Danny, he clamped his teeth together tightly to keep them from chattering. He staggered a couple of times as she half-dragged him up the hill toward the cave opening. Feeling the fever begin to consume him, he slipped into momentary lapses of semi-consciousness.

Miraculously, he remained on his feet, and a small voice from somewhere in the back of his mind kept commanding him to stay awake. He had to remain conscious as long as he could, for he knew it was only a matter of time before the fever's pitch made him mindless. "Danny," he gasped, trying desperately to focus his attention, ". . . cover . . . entrance . . ." With a lifeless motion he flopped toward the shrubs that surrounded the mouth of the cave.

"Yes, yes," she hastily assured him, doing her best to hurry him along, while he grew weaker in her arms.

He continued to walk forward, lifting each leg as though it were made of solid lead, each stride taking more and more of his strength away until there was none left. Then, staggering for several feet, he fell face forward onto the ground.

Faintly he heard Danny scream, but he couldn't see her. His vision was blurred, and while he still had the capacity to know what was happening, it was quite another thing to will his body to obey his commands. Get up! his mind challenged his body. But already weakened, the most he could summon was enough strength to crawl on his belly toward the cave. He was too heavy for Danny to lift to his feet, so all she could do was urge him on, tugging him by his arm each time he collapsed.

The chill that had wracked his body had evaporated, leaving him unbearably hot, burning up inside and flushing his cheeks to a deep crimson. His throat was so dry he could hardly breathe. As he inched his way torturously up the hill on his stomach, he had the feeling that he was trapped somewhere out on the treacherous desert sands, with the intense glare of the sun turning his flesh to blisters. Unconsciously he tried to speak, but all that emerged from his parched throat was a scratchy moan, a sound that made Danny tug at him even harder to get him to the safety of the cave.

His mind was beginning to wander and he could barely focus his thoughts in a single place. The fever had risen to such a degree that he was scarcely conscious, incapable of coherent thought. He felt himself pass from brightness into darkness and he felt the ground beneath his moist cheek and palms become cold. In his delirium he did not know that he had at last made it to the cave.

"Jacques . . . "

Through the mist that enveloped him the name emerged like a shrill, piercing call that welled up from the depths of his delirious mind. It came spilling forth from his parched lips, bouncing off the walls of the cave and back at him, penetrating his subconscious and resounding in his head with a deafening roar. And with it pain exploded in his head with such violent force that it plunged him into unconsciousness.

He opened his eyes and saw Danny's hazy image above him. "How long have I been out?" he asked in a weak whisper.

"Three days."

He raised his head and tried to sit up but he was still much too weak. Danny reached out to help him, pulling a saddle up so he could lean against it. "Is that better?"

"Yeah," he answered. "Please . . . some water."

She held the canteen to his lips and he drank until his thirst was quenched. Even in the dimness of the cave he could see how pale she looked and the dark circles beneath her eyes. Poor thing, he thought as he gulped down the water, she must have had precious little sleep these past three days. "Was I out of my mind?" he asked, when she pulled the canteen away.

"I'm ashamed to tell you some of the things I heard coming from you."

"I'll bet." He frowned, his black brows drawn across his face in a scowl. "I kept having dreams . . . They were so strange, like being locked away in a prison, only there were no bars . . . no doors. There was nothing keeping me there and yet there was no way out."

"Who's Jacques?"

Alex looked up at her, the expression on his face a strange mixture of surprise and confusion. "I . . . I don't know. If that's what I said, then . . . ah . . . I . . . I just don't know."

She saw a glimmer of pain sweep across his face as he stammered. "Well, you're awake now," she said. "The dreams are behind you."

"I must have given you a rough time." God only knew what he had said when he was half out of his mind with fever. He dared not ask her to repeat any of it for him, thankful that she did not force the matter.

"I'd rather tangle with a wounded grizzly bear, than nurse *you* back to health again."

"I've got to admit I feel a hell of a lot better." A sudden thought occurred to him. "Where are the horses?" he asked quickly.

"Don't worry, I've got them tethered outside. I built a wall out of shrubs and they're hiding behind it."

"Very clever," he conceded. "Where did you learn to do that?"

Danny looked at him, hands on her hips. "I'll have you know there are some things I am quite capable of doing on my own, without your help."

"All right, all right." He shifted position, and a stab of pain in his shoulder reminded him of what they were doing here in the first place. "Any sign of our friends?" he asked as he rubbed the stiffness out of his shoulder.

"Here, I'll do that." Dropping to her knees behind him, she began to knead the muscles in his shoulder which had become stiff over the preceding days from remaining unused. "If you want this shoulder to heal, you're going to have to use it," she said. Bearing down on him she heard him grunt.

"I know," Alex said, grimacing, "but what about our friends, any sign of them?"

"Day before yesterday I saw a party of six passing. Other than that, nothing."

"Which way were they headed—Hey, not so rough!"

"Sorry," she grumbled. "East."

"Good."

"What's so good about that?" she demanded, digging her fingers into his flesh making him wince.

"They're headed back to camp, so they must've stopped searching for us. They probably think we're out of the territory by now, but all the same, when we leave in the morning, we'll have to be careful."

"What are you talking about?" she exclaimed, jumping to her feet and running around to face him. "We can't leave here in the morning, you're not strong enough yet. It'll be days before you can even—"

"I know, I know," he interrupted with an impatient wave of his hand. "But we only had enough food in our packs to last a couple of days and you've probably eaten most of it. If we fire one shot for game, they'll be down on us so quick you won't know what happened. That means it's got to be done without a gun, and as much as you'd like to think you can handle it, I think it's safe to assume that I can handle a bow and arrow better than you can. So, first thing in the morning, before sunup, we'll ride out of here. When we've covered a good enough distance, then I'll get us something to eat. I don't want any arguments."

The next morning, with the hazy translucence of dawn still an hour away, they prepared to leave. "Give me a hand with this, would you?" He drew a fresh shirt from his parfleche, one that was not torn to shreds and soaked with blood. She helped him put it on, and then his leather vest over it. Standing back, she watched him rise shakily to his feet, his gunbelt dangling from his hand. "Just one more favor," he said, holding it out to her.

Taking the belt, Danny fastened it around his hips as he himself would have done. Then she knelt down and tied the holster to his thigh, noting with disapproval the way the muscles beneath his pants twitched involuntarily at her touch. She glanced up at him, a scowl on her face that he could think of such a thing even now. He smiled at her sheepishly, as surprised as she was at the feelings he could not hide.

He surveyed the cave quickly before they left, grinding the heel of his boot firmly into the ashes of last evening's fire.

The stallion neighed when Alex approached and placed a firm hand on its fleshy muzzle. "Yeah, I know, boy, it's good to see you again, too." He rubbed the horse's forehead, adding, "You've got that lady over there to thank."

The remark did not go unnoticed by Danny, but she chose all the same to ignore it. She guessed that it was probably his way of thanking her, but decided stubbornly that if he could not say it to her face instead of that horse's, then she did not feel the slightest obligation to acknowledge it.

By the time the sun began to send its streamers across the sky, they were miles away from the craggy mountains of Utah.

Chapter 18

Alex leaned over in the saddle, his eyes bright and menacing, the warning in them no less chilling than the one in his voice. "Don't do anything foolish, or I'll break your arm."

Looking past him, Danny saw the reason for the threat. In the middle of the desert was a small town, as bleak and drab as the surrounding country. Turning back to Alex, she saw an unreadable look on his face, with something unsettling tugging at the corners of his mouth and hiding behind his eyes.

"What is it?"

"I don't know," he said in a low, uncertain voice. "But I've got a gut feeling about this place."

"Then why are we stopping?"

"There's someone I have to meet here," he answered. "A friend."

It would be good to see Chalako again, Alex thought, after . . . how long had it been this time? Two years? Three? But whatever excitement he may have felt over the impending reunion was drowned out by the foreboding feeling in his mind. Be careful, he cautioned himself.

Alex knew there was nothing in that town he couldn't handle. After all, he'd fought his way out of tight spots before. But it wasn't just the town that set his nerves on edge. It was almost as if the place were in some way a turning point—a point of no return.

At one time the town of Caliente, Nevada, had been a thriving community on the brink of a boom whose only potential lay in the caverns of its untapped silver mine. But years of work and prayer proved it to be nothing more than a shallow vein, a shattered dream for all those men who poured their lives and souls into it. Dejectedly, they had packed up their belongings, slung their parfleches across the shoulders of haggard mules and ridden out of town.

A few men, those who had no particular place to go, lingered on, keeping the town barely alive. Drifters passing through on their way to California's gold fields found themselves still there years later, and desperadoes fleeing the law took advantage of Caliente's sanctuary. Little by little the town built itself up again, its meager population consisting of the worst assortment of outcasts and misfits who found in Caliente an opportunity to be nothing more than what they were. The town had become a stronghold, a refuge for all those seeking escape from more than just the desert sun.

Danny's spirits sunk to a new low when she saw that it wasn't much of a town at all, merely some dilapidated wooden structures. They dismounted in front of a rundown building, barely a shell of a structure, with a dangling sign atop its doorway proclaiming 'Hotel' in cracked and peeling letters. Across the road stood another shaky building whose walls looked as though they'd collapse with the first strong wind. The sign across its doorway read 'Saloon'. No visible sign of life could be seen other than a single swayback mule tethered to the hitching post in front of the saloon. Absorbing the sun's scorching rays, the pitiful creature was nervously switching its tail to flick away the flies that landed on its salty sweat-covered hide.

At the hotel desk, Alex brought his fist crashing down on the counter, rudely awakening the clerk from his afternoon nap, sending the man's eyelids snapping open like shutters. The man grumbled a few words and handed Alex one of the keys that hung from a nail on the wall. Once inside the room, Alex tossed it onto the bed and closed the door.

"Now what?" Danny made no attempt to disguise her annoyance.

Unbuckling his gunbelt and placing it carefully over the back of a chair, Alex walked to the window, drew the flimsy curtain aside and cast a scornful look over the lonely stretch of road. "Now we wait."

"That hardly answers my question," she complained, adding with a hint of scorn, "But then, that's your specialty, isn't it? Or is it killing? Somehow, I never can decide what it is you're best at."

Alex heaved an impatient sigh. She was in one of her bitchy moods today, damn it. Well, he didn't like being here any more than she did, and if Chalako weren't here, he would have passed this godforsaken place right by. He never did like ghost towns, especially the ones that never really died. God, he hated this place!

"We'll wait here until nightfall. I'm betting Chalako will be in the saloon tonight."

"What's so important about seeing this Chalako?"

"He's an old friend."

But guessing there was more to it than that, Danny persisted.

"You seem to be risking an awful lot simply to see an old friend." She recalled all too well how reluctant he'd been to show his face in Jacaronda. Why was he willing to do it now? If this meeting was so important, why didn't he have the man come up to the room?

"In a town like this nothing goes unnoticed," he explained when she asked. "If I have anyone up here, chances are the whole damned place will know about it. But if I meet him in the open, no one will suspect that either of us are any different from any of them."

"But what if you're recognized? Don't you think people will suspect something when they see us walk into that saloon tonight?"

"Ah now, wait a minute. *We* aren't going anywhere. *I'm* going out and *you're* staying here. If you think for one minute that I'm going to bring you into a room full of the meanest lowlife this West has ever seen, you'd better think again."

"Your chivalry at this late date hardly merits any thanks from me, Alex Coulter," she informed him in disdain. "Why the sudden concern over my welfare?"

"Let's just say I was always real careful of my possessions," came the low mocking reply.

"I won't have it!" Danny stormed. "I won't have it! The last time you locked me in a room I thought I'd go insane. You can't do that to me again!"

Alex turned abruptly and snatched up his gunbelt. "Don't tell me what I can't do!" he shouted back at her.

She watched with eyes growing wider as he buckled the belt around his hips. "Where are you going? Damn you, don't you dare leave this room without me! You miserable cur . . . you bastard, you come back here!"

He ignored her protests and locked the door behind him.

His name was Chalako. No one knew whether it was his first name or his last because he went by no other. He had appeared one day at the village of Black Crow, the Oglala medicine man whose preference for the white man's bangles made him a favorite of the territorial traders.

Chalako was a big man, towering well over six feet, who dressed like an Indian and spoke like an Indian which was why men claimed that he had Indian blood in him. Probably Nez Perce, they concluded, seeing as how he'd first been seen trading his treasures over in the Wallowa Valley.

He was a solitary trader, not even wishing to burden himself with the company of any of his Indian wives, although he never failed to love each of them with a devotion uncommon to his type of man. He moved quickly along the rivers and over the plains, through the forests and across the mountains, always on the move. In his parfleches he carried glass beads from Vienna, cloth from Germany and silver from the Southwest which he shrewdly traded for pelts and buffalo robes. He turned his items over rapidly, rarely holding on to anything of real value any longer than it took to trade it for something else. The only things he kept for himself were the things he could fit into one small pack that he slung over his back as he paddled his birchbark canoe along the waterways of the West. Never keep more than you can carry on your back, he always said.

That's what he had told Jacques, the young Frenchman he'd taken under his wing that year . . . It must have been sometime around 1843. Jesus, that was a long time ago.

The big man, stoop-shouldered and now old beyond the age where a man could roam about the wild country alone, remembered a time when he thought he'd live forever, without need of anything other than a knife, a gun, an axe and a few trinkets to trade to the Indians. It was when he first met that stubborn Frenchman and saw too much of himself in the young man's eyes. Jacques' almost reckless determination made Chalako become aware of his own mortality. He had realized that he could not remain a free man forever. That is, not unless he chose to die with only the icy chill of a winter blizzard to chase the fear from his dying bones.

Chalako had decided a long time ago that he would not die

alone, and for the past few years, with the season of his life fast approaching, it was not only the infirmities of old age that kept him close to civilization. Oh, he still got around all right, but what the hell, there wasn't much sense in running about the damned country anymore. Most of the Indians were staked up like flapjacks on the reservations, the rivers were nearly depleted of small game, the plains almost cleared of the buffalo, and the saddle sure was a sore place for his aching bones to be. Besides, that rascal Nando was racing around the country like a wild Indian. Chalako was certain he'd never catch up with Nando if he himself didn't stay in one spot long enough for Nando to catch up with him.

The old man chuckled to himself. That boy sure takes after his daddy, he mused. But suddenly the smile melted from the craggy face and a frown tugged at the corners of his mouth. It was a good thing Jacques was not alive to see some of the things his son had been up to. He wouldn't be pleased, not at all.

"Why the frown, old man?"

The voice seemed to come from out of the past. It was Jacques' voice that pierced Chalako's thoughts, but looking up, he saw it was Jacques' son.

"So you've finally decided to come see your friend," Chalako remarked, ignoring the question.

"Two years is a long time," observed Alex as he pulled up a chair and sat down.

"Three," Chalako replied.

"Huh?"

"It's been three years, not two."

Alex shrugged. "It's hard to tell sometimes." Placing a bottle and two glasses on the table, Alex filled both and slid one across to Chalako. "Why do you stay in this hellhole?" he asked. His disgust for the town was evident on his handsome face.

"I don't. Spent the summer up north with the Blackfeet." As he spoke, Chalako studied the younger man's face searching for any visible signs of change. A lot could happen to a man in three years, and one look told Chalako that much had happened to Alex Coulter. It only served to confirm the stories he'd heard. "I've been hearing things about you."

"Yeah? Well, you shouldn't believe everything you hear," came the casual reply.

"I don't. I usually cut it down by half. But even then, Nando, what's left amazes me—shocks me. How long do you think you can keep this up?"

"As long as I have to," Alex answered, his expression turning sour.

Chalako shook his head in dismay. "I think about what your father would have said to all of this."

"To hell with that! When are you going to learn that I'm not him? Do you think I care if he would have found what I'm doing offensive? Suppose I find some of the things *he* did offensive?"

"Like what?" demanded Chalako. "Like sending you away at a time when—"

"Yes, like that, okay!" He slammed a clenched fist onto the table, causing the bottle and glasses to clatter from the impact. "Look, what does any of that matter now, Chalako? It's foolish to talk about what would have been. The man's dead, so let's leave it at that." He took a quick swallow of whiskey and turned his steely eyes away. "It's always the same whenever we meet. We always wind up arguing about him."

"And we always will, my young friend," remarked Chalako dryly, "until you learn to live with your past."

Alex shot him a sidelong look. "Has it ever occurred to you that maybe it's *you* who can't live with it . . . with my not being him, or like him? Never mind, don't answer that, I'm sure it has."

He poured another shot and downed it quickly, feeling the burning liquid hit the back of his throat and simmer down in his gut.

"There's one thing in particular I heard," said Chalako, "and I've been wondering whether it's true." He hesitated, unsure as to whether he should ask. Always, just when he thought he knew Nando best, the young man deceived him, exposing himself to be a complete stranger in so many ways. Proceeding cautiously, testing each word, Chalako said, "I keep hearing these stories about how these silver shipments are falling into the hands of the Sioux."

He paused to await the reaction. But there was no explosion of anger, no denial, and so he continued. "And how the mastermind behind it all is a man who rides with the Indians. Part Indian himself they say. Now, assuming such a ridiculous thing were true, I got to wondering how such a man would know exactly when and where to strike. Would seem impossible, unless of course, he's getting his information from the inside."

Alex's features were implacable, except for a spark of brilliance ignited in his silver eyes, telling Chalako he'd struck a nerve.

"There are some things, my friend, that are best for you not to know," Alex said. Chalako knew him well enough to know that the reply had been gauged so as to neither deny nor confirm the suspicions.

Nando was such an unpredictable man, Chalako thought, so foolishly reckless and irresponsible that it was highly possible he had had his hand in all of this. But then, it was also possible that he had nothing to do with it at all. For twenty-seven years Chalako had been trying to unravel the mystery of this enigmatic man and fit all the pieces of the puzzle together.

"Most men are reluctant to part with their secrets," Chalako said, "and I'm not asking you to do that now. All I'm asking is for you to be careful 'cause I've been hearing a lot of other things too. I'm telling you, these plains are gonna bust wide open, and it's coming real soon. Those whites are itching for it and the Indians ain't gonna let it go so easy. I don't want to see you get caught up in something you ain't prepared to handle, seeing as how your daddy was a white man and your mama was a Sioux." He reached forward suddenly, grasping Alex's wrist, and even at the age of sixty-three, his strength was formidable. Pulling the younger man closer, forcing him to look into his aging blue eyes, Chalako said, "I know you're going through some bad things, boy. Believe me I know it, right down to the stinking shit of my guts. But you and me, we're alike, and we've got to get through this thing in spite of all them sons-of-bitches who'd cut our hearts out in a second if there was a price for them. But I ask you, who's gonna pay piss for the heart of a half-breed?"

He watched his words sink into Alex's brain, searing their impressions into his mind and casting a fiery reflection in those silver eyes. "Those smart asses got only one life to lose, but you and me, we've got two—one white and one red. That's a double death, sonny boy, and I don't know hardly a man who could face up to even one." He released Alex's wrist and sat back. "But that's all right. Yes, sir, that's all right with me, 'cause after it's all over and those idiots are through shooting holes into each other, I'm still gonna be here with my skin and my scalp intact. Before I put my life on the line for anything, I've got to be ready to give up breathing. And boy, I ain't ready to do that. Not on account of nothing. My life may be filled with the kind of indecision that splits a man apart when he's a part of two different worlds, but I wouldn't trade it in for all the glory in heaven. No, sir."

Alex could feel no anger toward the weathered man, only a kind of grudging affection. "You always were a philosophical old fool," he said, smiling.

"Ah, but that's the key word," Chalako said, raising a finger into the air. "Old. I'm an *old* fool, and I admit it. But you, Nando, at the rate you're going, you'll never live to be my age. That makes you a bigger fool."

The tone of his voice changed abruptly, catching Alex by surprise. "I heard you weren't traveling alone this summer."

Alex sighed heavily, and grudgingly revealed to Chalako his activities over the preceding months, carefully avoiding what he felt the old man should not hear, but not failing to include the part about Danny, since that's what Chalako had referred to.

The trader's eyes widened as the tale progressed. "My God, Nando, this is too much! Even for you! Jesus Christ, have you gone clear out of your mind? Kidnapping that girl and forcing her to marry you? How the hell did you think you could get away with something like that?"

It was useless for Alex to explain that he really hadn't planned any of it. Yes, he knew how stupid that sounded, damn it, but that's the way it was. And he didn't *force* her to marry him either. That just kind of happened too.

"Okay, so I made some mistakes," he relented. "But what the hell difference does it make? All I have to do is get her to San Francisco where her brother is waiting for her, and she'll take care of everything. She's always telling me how much she hates me. I'm sure between the two of them they'll have the marriage annulled without my consent or my presence. Money can buy anything, my man, or haven't you heard?"

Chalako shot him a stern look. "Nando, this is no joking matter. You're playing dangerous games. Christ, I can't believe it! She's a Fleming! Does she know anything about the Lady Laura? The truth, I mean?"

"Sure. She must. Her brother must've told her. She's a

tricky one, always keeping me on my toes. She's a wildcat too. All fight."

"That's a switch, isn't it?"

"What do you mean?"

"I didn't think the ladies ever resisted your advances, Nando. Makes me wonder about this one if she's got the guts, and the brains, to fight you."

Alex Coulter's handsome face had always made him a prime target for women, but to Chalako's memory he'd never even remotely considered marrying any of them. He wondered what kind of woman this Danielle Fleming was if she'd done what none of the others could do, albeit unwillingly. Yes, sir, if what Nando had said about her was true, the little lady had to be a fighter.

Glancing beyond the swinging doors of the saloon, Chalako saw the fading light of early evening. "What do you say we take what's left of this bottle and go outside for a while? And on the way out, take a good look at the man at the end of the bar. In particular, look at the gun."

Alex felt a surge of excitement race through his veins, and as he turned to leave the saloon, he allowed his gaze to steal a quick but thorough look at the man Chalako had singled out, noting the pearl-handled Colt revolver holstered at his side.

"What'd you think?" Chalako asked when they were outside.

Alex shook his head thoughtfully and ran a hand through his thick black hair. "I don't know. But this goddamned town gives me some uneasy feelings. It makes me think every stranger I see is after my hide."

"But that's just it," exclaimed Chalako. "If he's the law, he would've nabbed you by now. And if he's a bounty hunter, he'd probably stay hidden in some dark corner like a rat and get you somewhere out in the open when you leave town. I don't know, Nando, maybe it's not you he's after."

"Then we shouldn't worry about it. Besides, you know better than to ask too many questions in a town like this. Come on, there's a corral down at the end of the street behind the stables. Let's go over there. I always did feel more comfortable around the horses." And slinging an arm around Chalako's shoulders, the two men walked off into the night.

Chapter 19

Danny sat for hours on a chair next to the window—hoping to catch sight of Alex emerging from the saloon—until the monotony of her vigil cast its power over her and she fell asleep with her head on the sill.

Eventually the sound of voices in the hallway awakened her. Wearily, she tiptoed to the door and pressed her ear against it. What she heard made her shake her head hard to be sure she wasn't still dreaming.

Some men were grumbling, obviously angry and obviously planning a cruel fate for none other than Alex Coulter. Apparently, Alex's luck had run out, for someone had recognized him. Danny was horrified. She strained to find out why these people wanted to kill Alex and who they were, but she had no luck. It seemed almost pointless to try to determine their reasons when she realized that there were a great many men, with a variety of reasons, who wished to put Alex Coulter into his grave.

After the voices disappeared down the corridor, Danny was burdened with a sense of panic and helplessness. She had to find Alex and tell him! But what could she do, the door was locked? She surveyed the room with frantic eyes, tears of frustration beginning to spill over her cheeks. In desperation she went to the window and threw it open.

A dark figure lurked in the shadows below, his face concealed by the moonless night. Without thinking, Danny thrust her head out and called to him.

"Mister, Mister!"

She saw him tilt his head up, then take a step back to get a better view.

"Up here," she called, growing bolder. "Say, um . . ." She

193

didn't know what to say to him. She had to get him up here so he could open the door for her. Just get that door open! her mind screamed.

"Would you . . . ah . . . come up here for a minute?" Oh Lord, that sounded ridiculous. No, she'd better change it. "I mean, would you like to come on up?"

Her own voice asking the absurd question sounded foreign to her. My God, she must be insane to think she could get away with something like this, but she had to try.

"Come on, honey," she forced herself to beckon in her most sultry voice. "Come on, I'm waiting for you. It's the third door on the left. Knock three times . . . I'll be waiting." She pulled her head in when she saw him leave the hotel entrance. She didn't know how she would explain the locked door, but would get him to retrieve the key from the desk clerk.

She'd also have to think of some way to stop his advances once they were together. Hastily scanning the room, she spotted the oil lamp. That'll do, she thought. When he comes in, I'll lead him over to the bed and then I'll come up behind him with—

Her heart leapt into her throat when she heard three sharp raps at the door. All right now, I must be calm and do everything as I rehearsed it, she told herself.

The darkness of her room clashed with the bright white light from the hall, creating a startling silhouette in the doorway. Fleetingly, she wondered how he had known to get the key. But the question disappeared instantly as the man advanced, backing her into the room. He kicked the door shut behind him with a thunderous bang.

When her eyes readjusted to the dimness, Danny gasped. Alex! He reached out sharply and grasped her by the wrist, yanking her forward with such force she thought her arm would snap out of its socket. She found herself crushed against him, her already aching arm twisted behind her back, the pain making her dizzy.

Savagely he brought his mouth down on hers, choking back the cries that rose from her throat. At once his tongue forced its way between her lips and ravaged her mouth without mercy. Brutally, he bit into her lips and she winced at the taste of blood in her mouth.

When he was through, he pushed her away with a violent shove that sent her spinning across the room like a top.

"You like playing the little whore when it suits you, don't you, Danny?" His eyes were so intolerably cold that she recoiled at the piercing stare. "Well, let's see just what a good little whore you really are."

"Alex, no!" The words broke from her throat in a scream, as he pushed her roughly toward the door. And throwing it open with an angry slap of his open palm, he shoved her through.

Moments later they were standing outside the saloon. "Do exactly as I tell you. There's a man in there standing at the end of the bar by himself. You'll know him by the pearl-handled gun in his holster. I want you to go over and be real nice to him, do you hear me?" He tightened his unbearable grip on her arm. "Get him to buy you a drink. Dance with him if you have to. Do your best to make him happy."

He was a madman! He was actually demanding that she go in there and flirt with that man as if she were nothing but a common whore. If he wanted his revenge on her, surely he didn't have to resort to this!

"It doesn't matter for you to know who he is," Alex said. "I don't know that myself. You just find out who he is and what he's doing here. Do whatever you have to do to get me that information. And I mean *whatever* you have to do."

"Alex, please . . ." she cried. "I don't know what to do!"

"Don't lie to me, you little bitch," he hissed, his face white with suppressed fury. "You knew what to do back there when you wanted to run away again, didn't you?"

"But Alex, you don't understand, I wasn't going to—"

"That's enough! What kind of fool do you take me for?" And with that, one strong shove thrust her through the swinging doors and into the garishly lit saloon.

The man at the end of the bar had short squat hands and Danny noticed with instant distaste the dirt he'd allowed to cake under his fingernails. The thought of those hands on her body sent revulsion coursing through her. She cut the thought immediately from her mind. Involuntarily her eyes traveled across his body, pausing at the flaccid middle that hung much too far over his belt and the flabby muscles beneath his shirt.

He reached out and slung a heavy arm around her shoulders, pulling her so close she could smell the dirty sweat that soaked through his shirt and mingled with the stale odor of whiskey. She had no idea how many hours she was forced to endure his disgusting embrace as he plied himself with whiskey and she asked nonchalant questions, cringing each time he pressed his mouth to her ear and whispered obscenities into it. He bought her one drink after another and Danny drank them down quickly, trying not to notice the effect they were having on her. By the time he wound his arm around her waist and led her back to the hotel, she was so tired, and half-drunk in the bargain, that she could barely think straight, much less walk.

"You and me got some business to tend to," he said when they were in her room. "What's the matter, honey? Don't tell me you're a shy one. You sure didn't act like it back there. Come on, we both know what it is we both want." He moved for her slowly, keeping his eyes fixed on her body. "Come on, I ain't gonna wait all night."

"Stop that!" Danny burst out, snapping her arm from his grip.

Even through the darkness she could see his face turn white and she cringed at the sound of his angry voice. "I don't know what kinda games you're playing, but after leading me on the way you did, I ain't leaving without getting what I came up here for." His arms came around her and he pulled her against him. "You didn't struggle like this when I kissed you before, what's the matter with you now?" He ran a stubby hand roughly through her hair, forcing her head back so that she had to look at his disgusting face and smell his foul breath. "You're as hot for me as I am for you, don't think I don't know it. I sensed from the beginning the kinda fire you got burning in you. Come on now, let's see what we can do about that."

He chuckled greedily and thrust a hand into her dress to grab at her breast, and without further warning, he was all over her, pawing her, grinding himself against her, trying to pull the dress off her body.

Danny cried out, and pushing both hands with all of her might against his pudgy body, she sent him staggering backward. Quickly he regained his balance and came at her, his glassy eyes driving a bolt of terror right through her. She tried to leap out of his way, but he snatched her by the arm with enough force to fling her around and send her tumbling to the floor.

Danny looked up with eyes wild with fright as he placed his boot heavily on top of her and fumbled with the opening of his trousers.

"Since you're already down there, s'pose we start by seeing what you can do with that gorgeous mouth of yours."

"No, please . . ." Her hands flew up to her face to ward off the disgusting attack. Just as he came toward her and brushed his male hardness against her lips, she heard him grunt, jerk convulsively and fall beside her with a look of utter shock on his face. He landed with a tremendous crash. Out of his back protruded the handle of a knife. He was dead!

Danny felt sick and in a wave of terror opened her mouth to scream. But from the shadows a hand reached out and clamped itself firmly over her mouth. It took some minutes before she recognized the touch and could once again think coherently.

Alex loosened his grip and strode to the window. Peering out and seeing nothing but the moonlit town sleeping below, he turned quickly back to the room. Jesus Christ, he hadn't anticipated any of this!

"You killed him," Danny said, her voice a mixture of shock and accusation. "You killed him!"

"I can see that, thank you," Alex sneered, shooting a contemptuous glance down at the body. "I wouldn't have had to do it if you weren't so damned good at your teasing. Shit, you must have driven him half mad. I only did the poor fool a favor."

"I can't believe I'm hearing this!" she exclaimed incredulously, her shock rapidly giving way to anger. "Don't forget, Alex, it was *you* who started this thing, not me. *You* forced me into this horrible situation. You can't blame his death on me! You miserable scoundrel, how dare you abuse me like this! You wouldn't think he was such a poor fool if you knew what he was after."

He was at her side in a flash, spinning her around to face him squarely. "If you're playing tricks on me, Danny, I'll—"

"You'll what? Break my pretty little neck? Well, go on and do it then, but be quick about it, because I'm getting damned tired of listening to your threats!"

She wrenched herself free from him and stood her ground, knowing that in her defiance of him lay her only strength. Her hair hung loosely to her waist and her cheeks bore a faint flush. And her eyes, which a moment before had been dark and murky, glistened like polished stones.

"What are you trying to prove, Alex, that you're stronger than me? Only physically, you know." Her narrowed eyes flared wide at the way he stood there, thumbs hooked into his gunbelt in that casual arrogance she hated so much. "You disgust me!"

"Is that so?" he drawled. "If I recall, I didn't always disgust you, did I, my love? Particularly when you were so eager to spread your legs for me. Makes me wonder how many other men have disgusted you as much as I have."

His derisive words and taunting smile drove Danny out of her mind with fury. "After what you've put me through, you dare say that, as though you'd come along and whisked me out of some dirty brothel? Am I supposed to thank you for all of this? For ruining my life, for pulling me away from the people I love, from forcing the worst degradations on me, for making me your wife regardless of the consequences? Simply because I've had nothing to do with your sordid activities, don't think a lot of people wouldn't like to see a noose around my neck just because I'm *Mrs.* Alex Coulter. Let me assure you right now, I'll get away from you if it's the last thing I do. And you'd better hope I die trying, because while I live you'll never be a free man!"

A look of uncertainty lay in his eyes, and Danny was pleased to see she'd succeeded in wiping the smile from his face. "I'm not as foolish as you think I am, *my love*," she went on heatedly. "You're probably assuming that I'll eventually have this sham of a marriage annulled. Well, surprise, Alex, but an annulment is *not* in my plans. Did you think I could ever forgive you for the shabby way you've treated me? Did you really imagine that I wouldn't have my revenge? Ha! I'm surprised at you!" With a backward toss of her head she sent her hair whipping about her face, but as soon as the last coppery strands settled back on her shoulders, she shot him a cold look, her eyes narrowed and gleaming like a cat's.

"No, my love, I'll never have our marriage annulled. I'll continue to bear your name and be your wife for as long as I live. And for once *you'll* know what it's like to be forced into something you don't want. Sooner or later you're bound to grow tired of me and you'll probably let me go. But I can wait, and when it happens, I'll *still* be your wife. With *your* name I'll go my own way and do exactly as I please, when I please, and with whom I please. It will make me ecstatic to know that somewhere you exist with a little bit of me hanging around your neck. No, Alex, I'll never have this marriage annulled, never! I've stood a lot of other things, I can stand being your wife. Even if it makes me sick, I *will* bear your name!"

When she was finished, she was breathless, eyes glinting brightly, cheeks fired to a scarlet flush.

For a moment she thought she'd gone too far when she saw the muscles in his jaw tighten and the anger flare in his eyes. He looked like any second he'd leap at her and tear her into small pieces. But instead of pouncing on her, he dropped his eyes to the floor and turned his face away. "Man, we sure do bring out the worst in each other. You know, you're really beautiful when you're all fired up like that."

Danny threw her hands up and shook her head. "You are the most infuriating man I have ever known! And you needn't feign compliments for my sake when we both know you hate my guts."

"Don't be too sure about that," he replied, lightly brushing a strand of hair from her cheek. "When you're angry like that and your hair is wild and your eyes blaze like gold, you remind me of a wild animal. As a matter of fact, I find you most desirable when you're like that." He leaned forward to kiss her, but she drew away sharply.

"Yeah, well, I guess maybe now isn't the time for that," he muttered, glancing at the body on the floor. "All right, what did you find out?"

She answered his questions mechanically and when he was through cross-examining her, he exclaimed, "So, that's it!"

The man had never told Danny his name, but she did learn that he was a professional killer—a bounty hunter—and that his next stop was El Paso and his next victim was the Mexican *bandido*, Jake Alvarez. In seconds Alex was all motion.

"We've got to move fast. If Jake is down in El Paso, it means only one thing—he's heading for Mexico. I'll have to go after him." He saw her eyes widen and her mouth drop open. "Don't argue with me, Danny, I've *got* to. Don't you see? Jake wouldn't be anywhere near El Paso unless he was thinking of crossing the border. He always said he'd go back one day for good, and if he does, I'll never see him again."

"And if you ride out of here after him, you may not *live* long enough to see him again," Danny remarked sourly.

Alex smiled. "Is that a note of concern I hear in your voice? I didn't think you cared that much."

"I don't," she snapped. "I'm just wondering what I'm

supposed to do while you chase all over the country looking
for that greedy Mexican outlaw." She wasn't surprised that
Alex felt the compunction to race out after the man. But was
it merely for a final goodbye, or was it to satisfy the strangely
morbid urge he had to tempt danger? He seemed to almost
enjoy placing his life on the line, as though the fear of it
somehow strengthened him.

"I've got it," Alex said, "Chalako will take you to San
Francisco."

"San Fran— What are you talking about?" Surely he was
drunk or insane, or both!

"He'll take you there," Alex said. "Back to Austin."

The room began to whirl like a kaleidoscope in a flurry of
words and phrases that made no sense to her. "That's where I
was taking you. But it looks like you'll have to get there
without me. There's no need to worry, Chalako's a good
man, you can trust him."

His recommendation of the man did little to stem Danny's
anxiety. "I don't believe it. I just don't believe it."

Alex looked at her, puzzled. "I would have thought you'd
be glad to be rid of me. How come you aren't laughing? Jesus
Christ, what are you crying about now?"

"Nothing," Danny replied, sniffing back tears.

"All right, look, I've got to ride out now, but I'll see to it
that Chalako comes for you and takes you to your brother. I
guess it's the least I can do." Coming up close to her, he
placed a hand softly against her cheek. "Your skin is hot like
you've got a fever." Then, forcing the tenderness away, he
wound an arm tightly . . . arrogantly . . . around her waist
and pulled her against him. His kiss was firm, lingering longer
than he had intended.

"You'd better stop that crying, Danny, or I'm likely to
think those tears are for me," he said over his shoulder as he
strode to the door.

The last thing she heard was the sound of his laughter as he
disappeared down the hall.

Chapter 20

Nightfall found Chalako and Danielle sitting around a small crackling fire, its embers tinting their cheeks with a warm glow. Their comfortable solitude was broken by a wolf howl, its mournful call evocative of a lonesome lover. Soon it was joined by the howls of an entire pack and became both incredible and terrifying. Some yowled, some yipped, others whined and barked, and the air resounded with wild chords and an undercurrent of shrill wordless lamentations.

"Never heard of a healthy wolf attacking a man. They howl in harmony. Makes them sound like they're more than they really are," Chalako said, reading the fears that were visible on Danny's face. She smiled at him weakly.

It was as if an unspoken agreement existed between them not to discuss Alex Coulter, although occasionally Chalako slipped. At first Danny thought his references to Alex, or Nando, were mere slips of the tongue, but she soon realized otherwise. She wondered bitterly whether he was not trying to turn her feelings for Alex into something other than resentment.

"Ha!" she exclaimed. "Why should you sing his praises when it's on his account that you're involved in this?"

"I know," he sighed. "But there's things about that man that you don't know. Sometimes I wonder myself whether he ain't got reason to feel the way he does about things."

"And how is that?" she queried harshly. "With a hatred and bitterness for everything that lives?"

"Oh, no, Danny," he said, shaking his head at her. "Not the man I know. Maybe that's why it's so hard for him to control those things you accuse him of. Maybe he cares too much."

Danny turned her gaze away, muttering under her breath, "You'd be hard pressed to convince me of that."

But her anger failed to convince Chalako that it was only distaste she felt for Alex, and he wondered if, in spite of herself, she was not really in love. Chalako hoped that for her sake she was not. It was so much easier to understand a man like Alex when you didn't love him.

"I'll bet you'll be glad to get back to your brother," he said to break the uneasy silence that had developed.

Danny looked away wistfully. "I haven't seen Austin in so long."

"What's he like?" Chalako was curious about the man whose name he'd heard over the years.

Danny's expression turned pensive. "You know, in some ways they're alike—Austin and Alex, that is. It's nothing I can put my finger on, though, just a feeling. Austin hardly ever loses his temper and when he does, it's usually brief. He keeps such a tight rein on his emotions most of the time. I really wish he would learn to loosen up. He wasn't always like that, of course. Before he became involved in the business he used to laugh easily and we had such grand times together. But he's changed in the past few years, ever since he returned that first time from America. He tries to hide things from me, but he doesn't do a very good job of it. Sometimes it lays there between us like a huge canyon. Oh, I don't know, Chalako, it's all so strange. The way I've been living these past months, it's a wonder I can think at all. I know it's insane to even imagine that the two of them are alike. Why, it's incomprehensible! To think that Austin is in any way like that devil is sheer madness. Ha! Alex should be so lucky. It certainly wouldn't hurt him to have some of Austin's manners, or his charm, or his self-control. Although I dare say the only reason he married me was to get his hands on Austin's money. To hear that scoundrel talk, you'd almost believe he didn't plan the whole thing. What kind of fool does he think I am? Not fool enough to let him get his hands on my brother's money, I can tell you that! Not when Austin worked so hard for it. Did you know that he actually spent three years in this country working in that dirty hole until his hands were raw?"

She was beside herself, and Chalako knew it was best to let her get it all out of her system.

"That's when he changed," she went on. "When he

returned to France he was like a stranger to me. Impenetrable . . . just like Alex."

"This country does strange things to a man," Chalako offered. She made no response, but her look told him she didn't buy that.

"That's a pretty necklace you're wearing," he said, attempting to change the subject.

Danny's hand went up to her neck to tenderly caress the silver heart. "A gift from Austin. Fashioned from silver mined from the Lady Laura. Perhaps you've heard of it. I believe it's in Arizona somewhere, about thirty miles south of . . . of . . ." She searched her memory for the name of the town.

"Winslow," he said.

"Yes, that's it. So you have heard of it then?"

He shrugged. "Who hasn't? But I didn't know they were selling silver from the Lady Laura in France."

"They aren't. The necklace was made here, especially for me."

Chalako sensed need for caution. He should change the subject again before he said something he might be sorry for later. There was a quality about the way she spoke of the Lady Laura . . . almost as if she didn't know.

"Austin thought it appropriate that I should have a piece of his mine close to my heart, I suppose."

"*His* mine?" Chalako tried to keep his voice casual. So she didn't know! Nando was wrong. She didn't know!

"Actually, it belongs to me. But I've never done anything for it. Austin is the one who's done all the work."

My God! His mind swirled in a flurry of shock and dismay. He cleared his throat nervously and steered the subject away from the silver mine.

As the evening hours slipped by and the fire gradually died out, Danny felt herself warming to the leathery old man as though he were already a dear friend in whose presence she felt safe. She crawled over to him, dragging her blanket along the ground, and laying it out at his side, said softly, "I'm glad you're here with me."

It had been a long time since Danny had met anyone so unassuming and genuine as this man who spoke with kindness in his eyes. He was an example—living proof that you could survive out here and still retain a part of yourself that was decent and good.

To the seasoned veteran of the plains a woman like

Danielle Fleming was a rare thing, and he even entertained the thought that maybe she was exactly the thing Nando needed. Someone to match his tantrums, shout him down, stand up to him and force him to look into himself. Someone to understand him, and maybe even love him. He had to admire her guts when it would be so easy for her to give up. But knock her down and she'd get right back up. He sensed it in her, even in the way she moved, all grace and determination, but with a sureness and confidence that was rare in a woman. He didn't know what would happen when she next met her husband—if indeed they ever did meet again—but he suspected it would be quite a confrontation.

At daybreak they were back in the saddle, each lost somewhere in private thought. But Danny's shouts yanked Chalako back to the present. Squinting, his gaze followed her pointing finger to where a spot grew on the horizon.

"Dust cloud," he said as he watched it.

"It's moving fast," Danny observed, adding under her breath, "and it's no dust cloud."

Chalako flashed her a worried look. "Come on, let's get to those hills up ahead."

They stopped at the foot of the hills and dismounted, quickly leading their horses up the steep rocky path. They were breathless when they reached the top, but gasped at what they saw. There was nothing there except some gentle swells in the otherwise flat terrain. Nothing to hide behind, and a frantic glance below revealed riders approaching at a gallop—four faceless nameless pursuers.

Chalako began to shove bullets into the chamber of his gun.

"What are you doing?" Danny cried, running to him and grabbing his sleeve. "You can't fight them off out here in the open! It's suicide! We'll never make it! We can't do it!"

"You're not staying," he said as he worked. He didn't know who it was who seemed so intent on running them into the ground, but at this point, it hardly mattered. "Look," he said, grasping Danny firmly by the shoulders, "we can't both make it out, and since I'm probably the better shot, then I stay."

"We'll both stay!" she declared hotly.

The elderly man stood his ground, the fury whipping up in his blue eyes at her defiance. How could he convince her that it was senseless for both of them to die?

"Danny, you're no quitter, damn it. You're a fighter. I knew that the minute I saw you. Listen to me, don't stay behind for me. You've got too much living ahead of you, don't waste it!"

Tears burst forth from her amber eyes. How could she leave him? It tore her heart apart to think that whether she stayed or not, she'd never see him again.

Reading the thoughts in her frightened eyes, he said, "Danny, listen to me, he needs you." Then he recalled the other man in her life—the one who waited in San Francisco. "They *both* need you."

"But you!" she cried. "Why should it be you?" The salty tears streaked her dusty cheeks, leaving crooked little paths.

"I told you why," he said impatiently.

"Oh, no," she sobbed, dispelling his claim of being the better shot. Of course he was, but what did it matter? He'd be outnumbered four to one. Without cover what chance did he have?

"God damn it!" he roared. "I'm an old man, Danny! I've lived my life the way I've wanted to, and I'll be damned if I ain't gonna die when I want to die!"

He waited until he was sure he'd made his point. Then, as if the wind had carried it away, the anger fled from his eyes and he released his grip on her arm. "Ah, what the hell," he muttered with a shrug of his big shoulders. "I never did want to be an old man anyway. Always said I'd rather go out fighting than just sitting around waiting for it to come in my sleep."

He picked up her horse's reins and placed them in her trembling hand.

"Chalako—"

"You ride hard, you hear? Head west, and in a couple of days you'll make it to a small town where you can get some help. You'll make it, I know you will." He paused to look deeply into her golden eyes, then he shook his head free of her lovely vision. "I gotta tell you, that Nando's got himself one helluva woman. Now go on, get out of here. *Yeeaaa!*"

With a high-pitched yell he brought his open palm down sharply across her horse's rump and sent him flying across the flat-topped hill, with Danny clutching tightly to his mane, her eyes clamped shut to hold back the tears that were on the verge of bursting forth like a river surging through a shattered dam.

With fear clutching at her, Danny huddled close over the horse's neck. But even the thunderous pounding of her horse's hooves could not drown out the distant crackle of gunfire.

She screamed at the explosive volley that rose into the air and echoed sharply throughout the surrounding hills. Then there was silence, with only the quick beating of the pinto's fleet hooves to break the death-like calm.

She rode until she could go no further. Pulling the pinto up, she scrambled down, dropped onto her knees and retched violently. Her slender body wracked with bone-shaking heaves that made her feel like she would die. She rose, exhausted, and stumbling to her mount, led it over to a small thicket at the base of a nearby ledge. With the curtain of dusk rapidly descending, she had to think of resting for the night. Her horse was tired and she couldn't ask it to go on. Wasn't that something Alex told her once? Searching her memory she even came up with the sound of his voice. "Lose your horse and you're as good as dead, unless of course you're an Indian."

Yawning, she curled up into a tight little ball and soon fell asleep.

"See, I told you there was another one."

A voice pierced her dreams and she was roughly yanked to her feet. One terrified glance revealed four men hovering around her like hungry vultures.

The man who pulled her up reached forward to touch her, and in a movement that was pure reflex, Danny leapt for him, baring her nails like a cornered cat. But he was fast enough to avoid her scratches and swing her around so forcefully that her shoulder nearly wrenched out of its socket, bringing curses to her lips as she hurled a string of invectives at him.

"Hey, Will, looks like you got yourself a wild she-cat!" one of the others laughed.

Will twirled her around and pulled her up against him, and Danny felt the breath go out of her lungs. She fought with squirms and vicious vituperations until he reached a hand into the front of her dress and squeezed her tender nipple so tightly between his fingers that she cried out in pain.

"Well, shut the hell up then," he warned through clenched teeth. And even when she obeyed, she felt a wave of embarrassment flood over her as she was forced to stand by in silent humiliation as he continued to grope around inside her dress to the amusement of the other three men.

"Hey, Will," one of them with an ugly pitted face called. "She put up more of a fight than the man did."

The sudden vilification of Chalako's sweet memory brought a surge of blind fury to Danny, and with a burst of strength she didn't know she had, she tore herself loose from her captor and sprang at the miserable bastard who had spoken so lightly. With a shriek she slashed at his face, raking her nails across it and raising red welts from his eye to his chin.

Before he could react, Will grabbed her from behind, swung her around and slapped her across the face with the impact of a locomotive. She staggered backward and fell to the ground, and for a moment everything went black. When her vision cleared, she was somehow back on her feet, her cheek throbbing violently, looking in speechless terror from one face to another. Why were they doing this to her? Dear God, why?

Will Garvey shoved a foul smelling cloth into her mouth and then fastened a dirty neckerchief over it. "That should keep you quiet. You'll have time later to show me your stuff."

He was so close she reeled from the sour smell of liquor and tobacco on his fetid breath. She thought if she had to look into his horrible glassy eyes, she'd faint. His voice was low and menacing and she shrank from the feel of his words, hot and smelly, on her cheek.

"Most men don't never get to have a woman like you. Looks like I'm a lucky man."

"Hey, wait a minute!"

They both turned simultaneously to look into the face of the boy, who looked to Danny to be no more than seventeen or eighteen at the most.

"I seen this lady before," he said, opening his mouth to reveal several missing teeth. The stench of stale alcohol seeped from his young pores and seemed to have turned them old before their appointed time. "Sure, sure," he said excitedly. "I ain't likely to forget a face like that. Was in Jacaronda a few weeks back. You sure do get around, little lady, don't you?"

The other men looked at her with blank expressions on their hideous faces, apparently not sharing in his good memory.

"We got usselves invited to a wedding one night, remember, Wesley?"

Wesley Stiles stepped forward at the sound of his name, his

stupidity ringing from ear to ear in a telling grin. "Well, Lonny, I don't remember much 'bout that night. See, I had me here this bottle of whiskey and this little whore, and—"

"Ah, shut the hell up, Wesley," the youth snapped. Then, turning his attention to the others, he crooked a thumb at Danny and said, "Know who this pretty lady is, boys? This here is *Mrs.* Alex Coulter."

Garvey recognized the name and knew instantly what their unexpected prize was worth. But when the other two failed to make the connection, his bellow shot through Danny like a bolt. "Don't stand there like you was gunshot, you idiots!"

Lonny Garvey knew the kind of anger his brother possessed, and before they were all forced to suffer at its hand, he spoke up quickly, addressing the others. "Coulter," he repeated, watching for a sign of recognition on their blank faces. "The guy half the U.S. Army is looking for." Still no reaction from Wesley Stiles or Del Grass.

Will couldn't believe it was taking them this long to make the connection. "The *half-breed,*" he snarled.

Finally the information sank in and Wesley and Del grinned.

"You know, Will, this Coulter might just be willing to part with some of that silver he's been robbing in exchange for this pretty little lady, you think?" Lonny suggested.

"Yeah. But it wasn't only silver I was thinking about. I'm thinking maybe we can get even more."

"More? Shit, Will, what could be worth more than a shipment of silver? Man, I can just about taste it already."

Garvey gave his younger brother a crooked smile and drew the boy close. "I was thinking about the price on his head. I hear it's up to five thousand now—alive."

Lonny whistled through his teeth. "Must be pretty important if the Army wants to do the killing themselves."

"That's what I figure," Will confided, adding, "All we gotta do is get him here."

"How you gonna do that?" Del Grass asked. "You gonna send him a formal invite?" It was a stupid thing to say and he regretted it as soon as he spied Will's hand reaching for his gun. "What I meant was . . . well, he's not likely to—"

"Stop your stuttering, you goddamned idiot! I know what you meant, and that's why *I'm* boss around here and you ain't!" He turned back to his brother, knowing that only Lonny had enough brains to understand what he was getting at. "Maybe we'll send him something that's sure to catch his eye. Let's see . . ." He ran a liquid glance over Danny. "I think this'll do," he said, and in one sharp snap he tore the silver necklace from around her neck, drawing beads of blood where the chain bit into her flesh.

No! No! He couldn't take her necklace! Not the one Austin gave her! No, please, don't! But it was useless. Her mouth was gagged and she could not even plead with him. She watched as the pendant was tossed to Wesley, and through her numbed mind she heard Garvey's curt orders issued in a staccato voice.

"I want you to take this back to Jacaronda. At Unity McKeever's place look for a man named Morgan, Pierce Morgan. He used to ride with Coulter. He'll deny it, but he should know where to find him. You give him that necklace and tell him we'll be waiting for Coulter to show, *alone,* back at the hideout. Then I want you to ride north to Fort Laramie and tell the officer in charge to be waiting for us in Caliente where we'll deliver the prize." His look grew fearsome. "And, Wes," he added, when the man was mounted and stuffing the necklace into his pocket, "if I find out that you got drunk and blew this thing, I'm gonna come looking for you to shoot your belly full of lead."

Wesley Stiles gulped hard. He'd sooner have a pack of hungry wolves after him than a single Will Garvey.

When Wesley was out of sight, Will gestured with a jerk of his head to mount up. He shoved Danny over at Lonny and said gruffly, "She rides with you, up front. I don't trust the bitch."

As they rode, a single, indisputable impulse worked its way into Danny's mind. This was obviously a vicious game in which only the strongest would survive, and *she* was going to be one of them. She would not let this break her! She was prepared to do whatever it took to stay alive, even if it meant letting a disgusting creature like Garvey have his way with her. If he wanted her body, he could have it, but she'd never let him have her spirit! To that he'd never even come close!

Suddenly, Alex's image loomed before her blurred eyes. Knowing now what it meant to survive, she felt she knew him in a way she never had before, or thought she ever could. She cried inwardly at the countless ways she had tortured him with her cruel taunts when he'd only been trying to do what she was trying to do now. Until this moment he'd been a stranger to her, a reckless forceful man whose chief aim seemed to be to bend her to his will. He had forced his way into her life despite her objections and yet, when you came right down to it, they weren't so different after all, both clinging desperately to life.

Alex had told her once that a single thin line separated love from hate, and Danny felt herself crossing over to his side. If only there was some way she could tell him how she felt, and warn him of the impending trap. But . . . would he come?

With a chilling shudder she recalled her last words to him, and how she had so brutally reminded him that she'd always be an unseen weight around his neck. This was his chance to be rid of her. All he had to do was ignore her predicament, an easy enough thing for him to do. It was difficult to tell what a man like Alex Coulter would do, and while a little part of her prayed desperately for him to come to her rescue, a voice from out of her memory warned her not to expect him. She knew that his unpredictability and sheer recklessness had been the downfall of many others, and now she wondered fearfully whether it was her turn.

When they reached the hideout Lonny wasted no time in getting a bottle of whiskey uncorked and in circulation. Danny crouched in a corner of the room, blinking back the tears and choking on the stale acrid air of the cabin that seeped into her nostrils.

"Give me some of that," growled Will, snatching the bottle out of Lonny's hands.

The boy let it go, but the irritation that sprang into his eyes spoke of the resentment he felt toward his brother's ruthless audacity. He remained tight-lipped about it, though, guzzling the whiskey when the bottle came back to him, until eventually the sneer on his face turned into a drunken grin.

The Garvey brothers and Del Grass sat around the table growing disgustingly drunk and devising ways to spend the reward money that they could already smell.

"Scum like that shouldn't oughta be allowed to run free," Will bellowed, smashing his fist on the table and making the bottle jump.

Lonny mumbled something in agreement and cast a hazy look at Danny. The sight of her suddenly reminded him of the things that he'd thought about on the ride back to the hideout when she sat in front of him with her slender legs parted wide to accommodate the girth of his horse. Several times he had allowed his hand to fondle her breasts, but for the most part, he'd restricted his impulses until he could take her proper-like.

The other men chuckled greedily as Lonny staggered toward her and then set about taming the creature who fought him with every bit of strength she had. In the end he succeeded in tearing off her dress. The yells and jeers that ensued tore at her very sanity, driving her mindless with fury, fear and degradation.

The bottle passed quickly back and forth between Will and Del, while their eyes remained glued to the scene in the corner, each bursting at his chance to have some fun with her. Watching Lonny only increased the pitch of their lust. And furthered by the effect of the whiskey they became mean and dangerous men, capable of anything.

"Shit, man," Del drawled, "she's no better'n any whore. She'd have to be a whore to marry a breed. Why shouldn't we have our turn too?"

Danny whimpered, her screams reduced to nothing behind the grubby gag. Her cheek bore a livid blue bruise from Will's forceful slap earlier and everywhere on her body rose rude red welts and scratches where Lonny's brutal lust left its toll. Moaning like a wounded animal, she continued to struggle.

"Hey, boy, looks like you could use some help!" Will sprang to his feet. "Come on, Del!"

It took the three of them to hold her down while each man raped her, not once, not twice, but repeatedly, finally cursing themselves when they could no longer keep their erections.

It wasn't so much the actual act that wounded her the most, nor the bruises her body bore at their hands, nor the way they slapped her face to still her or laughed at her in an awful mixture of excitement and drunken lust. What hurt most was the cruel way they'd taken her pride and trampled it into a million pieces. Her body would heal in time, but what of her soul? Would that ever mend? Could it ever hope to escape the permanent scarring of this, the most vile moment of her life? The taste of blood in her mouth and the wet sticky semen drying between her legs were the last things Danny remembered.

"Consider yourself lucky," Will said the following morning, staring at the half-demented girl who lay on the cot, regaining consciousness. "If we hadn't come along, you'd have died out in that desert. Here, get yourself dressed and then fix us something to eat, damn it, we're hungry." He tossed a rumpled garment at her and left.

Danny's brain pounded as sharply as if she were standing in the hallowed center of an erupting volcano. Fighting down the nausea, groaning from the pain of strained muscles, she rose weakly and slipped on the calico dress he'd thrown at her. Where it came from she didn't know. It smelled of mildew and must, and along its neckline she detected the almost imperceptible trace of cheap perfume.

When the three men came in, their breakfast was on the table and so began a regiment of nightmares.

In the days that followed she cooked their meals, fetched their whiskey when they snapped their fingers and somehow endured their lustful advances. Of the three, it was obvious that Lonny Garvey had taken a fancy to her, and when he wasn't drunk or hiding behind his brother's irrational anger, he was almost civil. Will Garvey watched it all with a half-smile on his thin lips.

Shit, man, he thought, spitting at the floor, women ain't nothing but trouble nohow, and the thought of Lonny finding out the hard way brought him a strange kind of pleasure. Lonny fell all over her, trying pitifully to please her in his own crude ways, while in her eyes laid enough disgust and hatred for any man to see plainly, except one who was acting like a lovesick calf.

For Danny the days, and especially the nights, passed in a blur. In time her body would heal, but she trembled inwardly to think what would happen if she ever lost her sanity. It was her spirit that was keeping her alive. That alone made it possible to restrain the impulse to reach for one of their pistols and put a bullet through her own head.

Wesley Stiles had been gone just over two weeks when nervousness seeped into Will Garvey's awful black countenance. His lean angular body paced back and forth on the porch of the cabin, and in a loud, angry voice he called for Lonny and Del.

"Okay, today we move," he told them.

"Whadda ya mean, Will?" Del asked, his dull wits showing.

"Whadda ya mean, Will," Garvey echoed in bitter sarcasm, glassy eyes blazing daggers at Del, reducing the man to liquid. In disgust he turned away and addressed his brother.

"I was gonna have this idiot take the woman back to Caliente," he said, jerking a thumb over at Del, "but I guess you'll have to do it, Lon." Clamping a strong hand on Lonny's shoulder, he pulled the boy close, increasing the pressure as he spoke. "I know how you feel about that little whore, boy, but there's gonna be no mistakes, right?"

Lonny flinched beneath Will's vice-like grip, holding at his side the clenched fist any other man would have received in the mouth for daring to treat him like this.

"I'm asking you something, boy!" Will's voice grew louder. "There's gonna be no mistakes, is there?"

"No, Will," Lonny answered stiffly. "I don't know what kinda mistakes you think there'd be, but nothing'll happen if I'm there."

"Good. Take the woman to Caliente, get a room at the hotel and wait for me and Del to show up with the breed."

Lonny cast an uneasy glance at his brother and spoke cautiously. "Ah, Will, whadda you plan on doin' with . . ." His look strayed to the far end of the porch where Danny sat.

Will scratched his stubbly chin. "Well now, Lon, you know we ain't got no use for her once we hand that breed over to the Army. Don't make no sense riding with a woman hanging 'round our necks, now does it?"

Lonny shook his head.

"And we can't trust her to stay put and wait for us to come back, can we?"

Lonny swallowed hard, feeling suddenly sick at whatever Will was getting at. He gave another half-hearted shake of his head in reply.

Will shrugged fatalistically. "You know what you're gonna have to do then, don't you, boy?"

Lonny's mouth dropped open and his eyes bulged in disbelief. "Will, whadda ya talking about?"

Forcing a sympathetic tone into his voice, Will said, "I know you've taken a fancy to her, Lonny, but Christ, she's just another whore. There's plenty more where she came from. Once we hit Abilene with that reward money, you're gonna forget—"

"No, Will! There ain't none like her! None, and you know it too!"

Will turned and cast a sidelong look at Danny who sat with her bare legs stretched out in front of her, all golden brown and smooth-skinned, rich auburn hair falling over her shoulders. He knew what the boy meant, and he sure was pissed that he had to let this one go. But she knew too much. By the time they found her body, the breed would have been handed over to the Army and he and the boys would have hightailed it out of Caliente with the reward money. And he wasn't about to let Lonny's damned fool feelings get in the way!

Lonny's whining was beginning to get to him, and dropping his fulsome smile, Will reminded his brother with one dangerous look of the harsh penalties for disobeying his orders. "You gonna do as I say, boy, or you ain't never gonna do another thing in your life," he hissed.

The youth looked at him with pleading eyes. "I can't do it, Will . . . please, I can't."

"You *what*, boy?" Will narrowed his watery eyes, chilling Lonny to the core with the ice-cold stare.

Lonny swallowed hard and licked his lips nervously, expecting to feel the blow of Will's fist at any moment. "Please, Will."

"Never did like a man who begs," Will sneered, and Lonny knew there was no talking to him.

He knew it all by heart. Time and time again he'd watched in silent horror at his brother's hideous metamorphosis into a scheming demon, leaving all trace of humanness behind and emerging as the devil himself. Over the years Lonny had paid dearly in flesh and blood for this dark side that existed in Will. The seeds of hatred had been planted long ago and were kept alive by the very man who had sown them deep within Lonny's heart. There was not a day of his life that went by that Lonny Garvey did not wish fervently for his brother's death, in one form or another, to relieve him of the awful hold that was like a strangling hand at his throat. But along with the hatred and contempt came the one thing that inevitably kept Lonny from putting a bullet in Will's back—fear. Lonny had learned early in life that the only way to keep his own throat from being slit in the night was to become like the man he despised the most. If Will could not easily find a reason to hate him, Lonny reasoned, he'd turn his sadistic attention elsewhere and Lonny would be assured of living to see another day.

The following morning when they rode out together, Danny wondered what had happened to bring about such a fearsome change in Lonny who seemed unwilling, or unable, to look into her eyes. They fell into an uneasy silence as the day wore on.

Soon it would be autumn, the season of shadows. Then what? What lay beyond this summer? The question lingered in her mind without an answer.

These days millions of questions danced through her mind, so very few of them finding the right answers. And always the biggest, most perplexing and distressing question of all was the man who had caused it all to happen . . . the one whose silver eyes burned upon her memory and into her dreams.

Oh, Alex, Danny cried inwardly, why do you shut me out? What is it that frightens you so much that you won't let anyone look at it? For an inexplicable reason, she'd always felt that it was not merely his mixed breeding that drove him to such extreme bitterness, although the real source of it remained as much a mystery as the man himself. The sad irony of it was that in all probability, she'd never find out, for chances were, she'd never see Alex Coulter again.

It brought a pang of regret to her heart. But what was there to regret? Hadn't she prayed to be rid of him and his damned arrogance ever since the day she set eyes on him? She told herself it was for the best, yet a part of her refused to believe it. From somewhere deep inside a small voice cried out in silent agony for the one person . . . the *only* person she needed now above all others to spare her from her misery.

"Oh, Alex," she cried. "Where are you?"

Chapter 21

"Nando, how could you do this to me? You know I wait for you, and instead of hurrying back to me, you went and married that . . . that French *puta!*"

Bianca Alvarez was steaming, pacing back and forth, stopping every once in a while to shake a fist at him as he laid stretched out lazily on the bed, one arm propped behind his head, watching her with mild amusement. She stamped her foot angrily and turned her back to him, skirts swirling about her ankles. He'd almost forgotten what a fiery temper she had, but his voice was soft, remembering also the best way to calm her down.

"Bianca, come here," he said, holding a hand out to her. "Come on now, I'm not going to ask nicely again." But when his coaxing failed to bring a response, he forced sternness into his tone and ordered, "Get yourself over here beside me." This time he got a response, but not the one he expected.

The girl turned to look at him just quick enough to spit at the floor and turn away again, arms folded petulantly across her breasts.

With a sigh he rose and went to her, coming up close behind, letting his mere presence crawl over her flesh before he even touched her. When he heard the faint quickness of her breath and felt the tension beginning to melt, he wrapped his arms around her and nestled his face in her thick, jet black hair.

"*Chica,*" he whispered, "please, it's been a long ride and I want you."

Gently turning her around to face him, he kissed her long

and passionately, making her forget her annoyance and instead want his caress, his mouth, his body over hers, the way it had always been between them. Without removing his lips from hers, he lifted her into his arms and carried her to the bed. Placing her on the thin mattress, he lowered himself over her. He was smiling, the mischief stirring in his gray eyes.

"You mustn't pretend to be so hurt, Bianca. I seem to recall that the last time we saw each other you told me you hated me."

She gazed up at him with big black eyes framed in mink-like lashes, a pout on her lips. "Oh, Nando, that was only because you are always running off and leaving me. You know I wait only for you." Her slender brown fingers cupped his face and guided his mouth toward hers, which was waiting, lips moist and parted.

He kissed her lightly on the eyelids, feeling the brush of her lashes across his lips. Ever since that summer when he had returned from spending the winter months with the Oglalas, and discovered that she had turned into an erotic creature almost overnight, his desire for her had never waned. That was when she'd first acquired the habit of running her hand up under her hair, sweeping it above her head seductively while flashing her big eyes at him, and brushing his arm with her full pendulous breasts. She was a tease and she knew it.

Jake smoldered whenever his beautiful daughter attempted to seduce the men in camp, but he never tried to stop her. She was free to turn her wiles on any of them, and she did so constantly. It wasn't that a man wasn't sorely tempted to reach out and stroke the soft full body that she held out to him so blatantly, it was simply that Jake would have shot the gut out of any man who tried. Besides, it was pretty much acknowledged that she was Nando's girl, and no one wanted to mess with Nando.

Back then Jake had encouraged Bianca's growing relationship with Nando; the young man had merely taken what was so generously offered to him. He never claimed to love her. At times when they had lain in each other's arms, panting from their lovemaking, she would turn her face up to his and ask if he loved her. He would say, "Isn't it enough that I love making love to you?"

He had never loved any woman, but if he had, it could well

have been Bianca Alvarez, for she'd brought him so much unselfish unrestricted pleasure. He'd taught her how to make love and she'd been an avid pupil, greedy to learn. In no time she'd even created her own amazing techniques that drove him crazy.

She knew exactly how to please him, and set about it this evening with an ardor he'd never noticed before, as if she was making a concentrated effort, calculating each move, directing every caress with flawless precision. Her body slid over his with the graceful movements of a lioness, and while the sensation drove him half-mad with anticipation, he felt mildly ill at ease when he realized with a start the cause of her behavior.

Bianca's pride was hurt over Danny, and she was trying to make him forget her.

The name appeared in his mind like an angry flash, chasing away all thought of anything else, even the delicious olive-skinned girl he was with. He shut his eyes tightly to block out Danielle's image, but he could not shake it from his mind. Her eyes remained to haunt him, bright, glowing amber lights, upturned just slightly at the corners, the same eyes that had flashed at him in anger and hatred, the same golden eyes he'd damned so many times.

Bianca worked over his body slowly, moist red lips tracing little patterns lightly across his flesh, turning it hot with her teasing touch. Softly she brushed past his chest, gently nipping at the taut skin of his stomach, and lower, running her tongue across his thighs, gently at first, then bolder. She took him into her mouth, kissing his throbbing manhood fully. And with rocking motions that grew faster and stronger, she brought him to a peak of frenzy.

Great spasms gripped his body and he arched his back above the mattress, grasping her head in both hands while husky moans escaped from his throat. Those eyes, that hair! God, he wanted her—had to have her! *Danny! Danny!* The name resounded through his brain, sending uncontrolled shudders through his limbs.

The maddening kisses grew softer until at last his trembling ceased and he lay still, eyes closed, breathing heavily. When Bianca slid her body back up the length of his and kissed him deeply, he could taste himself on her lips. She nestled close to him, her voice a bare whisper at his ear.

"I pleased you tonight, Nando, no?"

Wrapping an arm around her naked shoulders, he drew her close to him. "Yes, you pleased me very much."

How could he tell her the truth? How could he tell her that while he had writhed in passion it had been another woman's image in his fevered mind? He could not hurt her with a truth like that.

"You can spend the night with me, Nando, no?"

"No, I've got business to talk over with the boys. I'll see you in the morning." And slipping off the bed, he quickly dressed and strode for the door.

"Oh, by the way," he said, looking over his shoulder at the girl who lay still nude on the bed, her full, round body glistening in the moonlight that filtered in through the open window, "Tell Ernesto I said hello."

Bianca sat up with a jolt. "What? But, Nando, you know Ernesto does not ride with us anymore."

"Yeah, I know," he replied with a teasing smile. "But I figure the next time he sneaks into camp to spend the night with you, you can tell him I said hello."

He never for a minute believed her story about waiting only for him, and while it may have been true that she waited, she sure as hell didn't wait alone. He was able to get out the door just in the nick of time to miss the water pitcher that came hurling through the air to smash against the door.

Silent footsteps led him to the cabin where the others were engaged in a heated game of five card stud. Pulling up a chair and taking a long hard swallow from the bottle of tequila that sat on the table as community property, he motioned with a flick of his head to be dealt in. It took only one hand to learn all he had to know.

It was true, they were leaving for Mexico in the morning. Jake had decided suddenly one night, informing them that whoever didn't like it could leave.

Tomas Alvarez raised a dark eyebrow when Nando pushed himself from the table. "What's the matter, *amigo*, leaving so soon?"

"Sorry, pal," Nando replied, "I've got some things to talk over with Jake. Tell me, what kind of mood has he been in lately?"

"You know him, Nando. Always he pretends to be so mad all the time. But I think since he decided to go back to Mexico, he has, how you say, cool out a bit."

"*Sí*," Cisco Alvarez agreed with a laugh, "I think it is a good thing we go back. I hear that unmarked longhorns bring a pretty price across the border."

Matt Turner looked up from a good hand and said, "Did you seriously think Jake had any other reason for going back? That old rattlesnake can smell a profit a mile off."

"No, I guess not," Nando replied as he let himself out of the room.

He entered Jake's cabin without knocking, his smile evaporating when he saw Bianca there. From the looks on their faces, it was obvious they'd been arguing.

Bianca plainly did not want Nando to leave again, and after he'd left her cabin, she'd thrown a shawl over her shoulders and stormed off to her father in the hope that there was something Jake could do to persuade him to ride with them to Mexico. For over an hour they argued. She had cried, cajoled and teased, but to no avail. She'd even threatened to run away, and forgetting her place, had called her father some horrible names, only to be harshly reminded that she would do as she was told until she found herself a husband. Bianca had always thought Nando would be that man. Jake had known all along that he would not.

"Let him go, Bianca," he'd said to her. "Don't you see you can't keep him here? Besides," he added, softened by the sight of the tears in her dark eyes, "there are many fine *hombres* in Mexico, and you will meet others to take your mind off this one."

"No! I won't have any others! Papa, please, you know he is not like the others. Nando is different. He's—"

"That's enough, Bianca, my word is final. We leave for Mexico in the morning with or without Nando."

Jake had grown impatient with her whining and outbursts and if it were not for the tears staining her cheeks, he would have sent her flying with the back of his hand. "Tell you what, *niña*, when Nando comes to me later, I will speak to him."

Her eyes widened into great black orbs and she flashed him a smile that made him melt. "Oh, Papa, please try. It means so much to me."

Peering out the window at the hazy crescent moon that filtered through streaky clouds, Jake sighed heavily. "*Sí, quierda,* I know it does."

Maybe it was time to loosen his control on her, Jake

thought. Maybe he should even allow one of the other men to court her, now that Nando was leaving them. Nando. Ah, yes, he must speak to that young devil about this.

Ah, Nando, my friend, thought Jake sadly, there is too much hatred inside of you, too much anger. Perhaps it is best that my little girl gets her heart broken now while it is young and strong and can easily mend. But what of an old man's heart? Will I live long enough to feel the scars grow over an old wound? I think not. I think there are not days enough left for me to ease the pain of losing you.

Turning from the window, he found himself looking into those familiar gray eyes that were the cause of Bianca's tears. Shuffling to the table, he sat down in one of the rickety chairs with the front legs pushed up off the floor and spoke in a fatherly tone to the man who'd been like another son to him.

"Nando, always I have offered you a refuge, a place to hide from your enemies, white and red alike. My home has been your home since you were a boy. I have denied you *nothing*." He shot a purposeful look at Bianca who stood with her back pressed against the wall, a pout on her full red lips. "And always," Jake continued, "it is to us you return after running all over the country robbing silver and chasing after some wild dream of yours, and angering so many men in high places that you are a wanted man. For me, it is a part of my life to keep forever one step ahead of the law. But you, Nando, you are playing a dangerous game. Even the Army has put a price on your head."

"A very generous price, too, Papa," Bianca chimed in. "Maybe we sell him to the soldiers, eh?"

Jake gave her a threatening look. "Shut up, Bianca, I'm not talking to you."

Nando's face broadened into a wide grin. "I think I can keep out of the Army's way, Jake. I've done it often enough. Besides, I've had good teachers."

"*Sí*, Nando, but there comes a time when a man must stop running. Maybe your time is now, eh? We move out in a couple of hours when it gets light. Come with us, Nando. There is room for you here."

"Jake, you know I can't do that. I can't follow you to Mexico and leave behind the thing I've sworn to fight for."

Bianca stormed forward, black eyes blazing. "Oh, pah! What have you sworn to fight for anyway?"

Knowing what a bitch she could be when she was not

getting her way, Jake put an end to it before it got out of hand. "Shut up, Bianca," he yelled, silencing her instantly.

The air in the room grew tense, and Nando moved nervously to the window, leaving a stony silence in his wake. Jake dropped the legs of his chair onto the floor with a loud clap and shuffled over to him, the clank of his spurs shattering the predawn stillness.

"This thing you chase after . . . this thing that has eluded you for so long . . . do you think you will ever find it? Do you think it even exists?" He placed his hand on the younger man's broad shoulder and felt the muscles stiffen beneath his touch.

"I can't stop until I know that it does not," Nando said softly.

"And then?"

"And then perhaps I'll join you in Mexico, if you're still there."

"And if *you* are still alive," remarked Jake sourly.

"Ah, my old friend, do you doubt that I can take care of myself?"

"No, *amigo*, I know you too well. And you forget that I knew your father, too." He shook his head thoughtfully. "No, Nando, it is not your enemies I fear for you. It is yourself. I wonder sometimes whether you know who your enemies really are."

Jake turned away and took his seat again, fingers toying absentmindedly with the half-empty bottle of tequila on the table. "Bianca, leave us alone."

"But, Papa—"

"Damn it. I said, leave us alone!"

Tears welled in Bianca's dark eyes, clouding her vision so that she could barely find her way to the door through the watery veil. Flinging it open, she fled from the place.

"Let her go," ordered Jake when Nando started after her. "Why must you make it harder than it already is? Here, have a drink. Then I think it is time you and me said some of the things we have left unsaid for too long."

The two men stared at each other for many long moments, much longer than a man would dare look another in the eye. But the look that passed between them was not a calling out nor an ultimate invitation to death. It was an exchange of mutual respect and an unspoken understanding of what the other was all about. The single look held with it the unconscious memory of many years spent together, learning from and teaching one another.

As a young boy, Nando had absorbed all of the wily old Mexican's knowledge, all of the instincts, intuitions and cunning that were essential for a life on the run. Jake had poured into the boy a bit of himself, reluctantly sharing him with the Oglala Sioux, to whom the boy invariably returned. And although Jake found it difficult reckoning with the wildness that raged inside the boy, he nevertheless felt himself irresistibly drawn toward it.

That first time Nando had returned with Crow scalps dangling from his saddle, Jake had to fight down the nausea. But he could never hate him for it. In fact, the more repulsive he found some of Nando's exploits, the more he realized, and understood, that the boy was merely fulfilling a custom that had been passed on to him by the Sioux. And Jake loved the boy the more for it—for his total abandonment to a culture that was as much a part of him as the heart that beat in his breast.

The figure standing before Jake now was no longer a boy, but the same wildness still raced unchecked through his blood. Jake felt it keenly and suppressed a smile.

"We've led many lawmen on a merry chase, have we not, *amigo?*"

"Don't forget the bounty hunters," laughed Nando.

"There's a strange breed for you," remarked Jake with a sour expression. "Hunting a man for the rope is one thing, but hunting him down for the price on his head, there's something about that that gives me a bad feeling down in here." He placed a hand on his belly. Deciding the subject was too unpleasant, he changed it abruptly. "We spent many nights in this cabin, eh? For years we have been right under their noses and still they could not find us. If your own hiding places are as good as this one, then it is no wonder they have not caught up with you. I hear even the one they call Custer is after you. He is a man much to be feared, *amigo*. You must never let that one get too close. They say he can smell an Indian from two miles."

Nando recalled the night that seemed so long ago when he found himself with a ravishing girl in his arms and George Custer nearly breathing down his neck while the music drifted across the lawn of the Hotel Pierre. "Don't worry, Jake, my white friends have taught me well."

Jake shrugged with feigned modesty. "Pah, if you have learned anything from me, it is that too many women are bad for a man's soul, not to mention his stomach."

They laughed loudly together, Nando slapping Jake on the back as the Mexican walked past him to the window. The first faint slivers of dawn were beginning to streak the sky and a halo of pale light hovered over the distant mountains to the east. Jake looked out a long while, wrapped in thought. At length he spoke. "She is a beautiful woman," he said, half to himself. "Maybe she is the most beautiful woman I have ever seen."

Nando came up behind him. "Bianca? Listen, I want you to know that—"

"No, not Bianca. I meant the Fleming woman. The little French *señorita* with the red hair who has my daughter so upset. It took me two days to calm her down when we heard the news of your . . . er . . . marriage. It is a good thing you were not here then, she would have plunged a knife into your heart."

Nando's eyes swept the floor and a wave of guilt washed over his handsome face. "Jake, about Bianca, I—"

"There is nothing to say, Nando. She is a woman, and has a woman's foolish notions. You have been good to her. But now she will come with me to Mexico. There is nothing for her here, especially since her *hombre* has himself a wife."

"Ah yes, my wife. I'd almost forgotten."

"Nando, a face like that is hard to forget. Tell me, where is she now, your wife?"

"I left her back in Caliente with Chalako who'll see that she gets to California where her brother is. When I heard you were leaving, I rode like the devil to get here. Maybe I'll see her again one of these days."

"Ah, I see," commented Jake dryly. "It is so simple. You kidnap a beautiful woman, then you drag her across the country with you, and then you marry her. And after going through all that trouble, you leave her with a friend." He eyed Nando suspiciously. "Tell me, how could you bring yourself to part with such a lovely creature?"

Nando laughed contemptuously. "That lovely creature would just as soon put a knife in my back."

Jake came up close to him then, his tone growing serious. "You listen to me, Nando. This woman has friends in high places, and if you are not careful, you could find yourself with a rope around your neck and the French *señorita* not far off, if you know what I mean."

"Don't worry about Danny," Nando replied. "I can take care of her."

"Does she know everything?"

"No, I haven't told her."

"I see. So, tell me, how does it go with your friends up North? I hear the situation is getting hot for them. Do you think there will be much fighting?"

Both men remembered the campaign the Sioux had launched some years back to rid the Powder River country of the whites. It had been at the expense of many lives, white and red alike. The blood was all the same color and whether it sizzled under the blistering plains' sun, or caked and dried on the sides of rocks, no one could tell from whom it had spilled. Seven years ago—a timeless eternity and a fleeting instant. So much had happened in between, and yet, so little progress had been made.

"It doesn't look good," Nando said, his head bent, black hair falling into his eyes. "The Government's putting pressure on the Sioux to sell the Black Hills. Nobody really knows what's happening. Even the Sioux are split over it."

"And your friend? What does he think?"

"Crazy Horse? He's opposed to selling *anything* to the whites, and he's determined to fight to keep the Hills. Most of the hostiles share his feeling and are ready to follow him into battle."

"How are they fixed for weapons?" asked Jake. "Bows and arrows are no match for the Army's guns."

"Yeah, well, Crazy Horse keeps in touch with the agency Indians who get him arms whenever they can. And I've done what I can to . . . well . . . to see that they get what they need."

Jake sighed impatiently and shook his head. "So you continue to rob from your own silver mine to provide them with guns, is that it, Nando?"

"Guns and food! Those people are practically starving!" His voice rose, but before he let it grow louder, he put up his hand. "Let's not get into that again. You know how I feel about it, and there's no use trying to talk me out of it."

"Hold on, *amigo*. Don't you think I know that? No, Nando, even if you stopped now, you are too involved. The whites would never forgive you for causing them so much misery. To them you are just another Indian to chase down."

Nando began to pace the room in long, panther-like strides, and Jake, hoping to avoid the inevitable outburst, once again switched the subject. "How does it look for us to move out?" It seemed to work.

"You could waltz out of here in broad daylight and nobody'd notice except the buzzards. The Government's sent a commission from Washington to the Red Cloud Agency to negotiate the sale of the Hills. Even the hostiles are supposed to attend, though I doubt that Crazy Horse will have any part of it. With all eyes turned on those talks, you'll have no trouble getting across the border."

"That should be some sight, eh, Nando? All those Indians? Do you think they'll make much trouble?"

A worried look flashed across the sun-bronzed face. "For their sakes, I hope not."

"*Sí,*" muttered Jake. "The wrath of the soldiers can be deadly when directed at their red enemies. We have seen it so in the past."

Nando came forward, fists clenched at his sides, his voice cold. "Yes! And we've seen women and children brutally murdered and their bodies mutilated and left in the sun to rot! We've seen the white soldiers thunder through peaceful villages, shooting everything that moves, and we've seen gold-hungry miners carving roads through the sacred places and digging up the earth!"

His voice pierced the room with a reverberating echo. Gray eyes blazed brightly from his tanned face, and his mouth formed a hard, almost ugly line. He stormed around the room like an angry wounded animal, his boots stomping heavily on the wooden floorboards.

Jake knew the explosion was inevitable. There was nothing they could speak about that would not have led to something like this. He stood by silently as Nando vented his rage against the white world—and mostly, Jake knew, against himself for being a part of it.

In a torrent of vicious accusations and bitter truths, Nando described for Jake the scenes he'd witnessed ever since he was a child—scenes of his people dying in pain, the blood oozing out of their broken bodies, the life washing from their broken hearts, the culture wrenched from their souls.

Over the years Jake had heard it all many times. What had started as little skirmishes had turned into a war—white against red—with both sides taking their frustrations and anger out on the innocent people who got in the way. Jake knew that the man who stood before him now would one day have to make his choice, and that with the increasing hatred between the two sides, Nando's choice would have to come soon.

"Nando," he said quietly, "there is something I must know. You have always been more Indian than white. At a time like this, it would be so easy for you to go completely over to their side, and yet, you do not. A part of you remains behind holding tightly on to your white heritage. What is it that keeps you here, when they need you so desperately?"

It was the one question Nando dared not ask himself for fear the answer would betray his one fatal weakness. It was the one thing he had not the power to resist, nor the will to live without.

It was a golden-eyed woman who had entered his blood like a poison.

Averting his eyes, feeling suddenly tired, his voice emerged as a husky groan. "It's her," he said, and turned away sharply, ashamed of the truth.

Jake closed his eyes and ran a hand through his hair. So, Nando had gotten more than he bargained for.

"The men are getting restless," he said. "I give Pierce one more hour and if he is not here by then, we leave without him."

It took all of Nando's strength to force composure back into his voice. "Where is he?"

"Jacaronda. He went to fetch that little whore he's so *loco* over. Wants to bring her along. Between you and me, *amigo*, I don't think she'll come. Women don't like this kind of life, running from the law, living out of one rotten hellhole after another. Pah, even *I* don't like it."

"Who are you kidding? You wouldn't have it any other way."

"Ah, *amigo*," Jake smiled, "you begin to know this old man too well. Maybe it is best that we part before you are able to see into my brain, eh?"

Suddenly, there it was, the reason Nando had ridden hundreds of miles to see him. And looking up, Jake saw those silver eyes upon him and a strong browned hand outstretched toward him. Grasping it in his own, Jake wrapped his boney fingers around it and drew Nando close in a telling embrace.

"I am going to miss you, Nando," he said, when they released each other.

"So will I, Jake, so will I."

There was so much more to say, but both men knew if they tried, the words would just get in the way. Jake took a deep breath and let it out slowly.

"It has been hard on her, you know, tagging along after her no-good papa all these years. But she is a good girl, my little *niña*. Nando, maybe you go to her now, eh?" Turning away, he shuffled to his cot.

"And here I thought you were up here crying your eyes out over me." He stood with his feet braced apart, thumbs hooked in his pockets, smiling down at her.

Bianca sat up and brushed the remainder of her tears away. "An *hombre* like you is not worth crying over," she sniffed.

He dropped to the ground at her side and put a strong arm around her shoulder drawing her near and feeling her tremble at his touch.

"You know, *amigo*," she whispered, "just because you have a wife does not mean you cannot come to Mexico to visit your Bianca, does it?" In her heart she knew as well as Jake did that they'd never see him again, but she asked anyway.

"Do you think I could stay away from that gorgeous mouth?" he asked, brushing a finger lightly across her parted lips. "Or that fantastic mane?" He ran a hand gently across her cheek to grasp a handful of jet black hair. "Or those beautiful breasts?" Slipping his arm from her, he gently cupped her full breast in his warm hand and brought his hungry mouth down upon hers.

Bianca responded by melting against him and meeting his tongue with her own. But just as her head was beginning to swim as it always did when he was this close to her, he pulled away abruptly, flipping over onto his stomach and pressing his ear to the ground.

"What are you doing?" she demanded, annoyed that he'd broken the spell of their moment together.

The reverberating sounds told him that a rider was approaching fast. "Someone's coming, let's go," he said, taking her hand.

As they made their way down the hill, a horse came

thundering into the valley below. Seeing Pierce Morgan fling himself from the saddle and race into Jake's cabin, he left Bianca where she was and raced down the hill. Something was up, he could feel it. He could see the sweat lathering Pierce's horse.

The men were huddled around the table when Nando flung the door open with a loud burst. He walked in, eyes flicking from man to man, seeing only fear in their startled eyes. Then, a glint from the table caught his eye, and squinting at its brightness, his gray eyes widened at the sight of the silver necklace whose broken links indicated it had been snapped by force.

"Where did you get this?" His voice was razor sharp and accusing.

Pierce Morgan stepped forward. He'd ridden for days without stopping and his face plainly showed the strain of it. His eyes were set deeply into their sockets, framed by black circles that gave him an almost comical look. His lips were cracked and swollen from the rigorous ride under the blazing sun, and his throat was raw and scratchy from gulping down the dry air as his horse had sped southward. His voice was a hoarse whisper.

"Nando . . . I got here as quick as I could."

"Where did you get this!" This time the full force of Nando's anger lay behind the question, and sweeping the broken necklace off the table he held it clenched in his fist as he shook it threateningly in Pierce Morgan's face. His voice was like the roar of a wounded animal. *"It's hers!"*

He listened incredulously to the man's story while the rage built inside of him, pounding in his temples and blinding him with red fury. Whirling around, eyes frantically searching the room, he spotted what he was looking for, and in two long strides reached the gunbelt that lay across the back of the chair. Snatching it viciously, he buckled it around his hips while the others watched in silence.

At that moment Bianca burst her way forward and threw herself at him, her eyes wild with fear. "You cannot go back there!" she cried. "I won't let you!"

He pushed her aside with a powerful sweep of his arm, but she quickly regained her footing and placed herself in his way. "Nando, they will kill you! This is a trap, don't you see? Are you so stupid that you would risk your life for *her?* Please,

Nando, don't do it!" She turned excitedly to the others. "Damn it, can't any of you stop him? Don't you see what he's walking into?" Running to her father, she pulled at his sleeve. "Papa, *please!*"

Jake caught his daughter by the arm and held her as Nando stalked from the cabin. "Let him go!" he ordered, knowing it was no use to stop him.

"You call yourselves his friends?" she shrieked. "Stop him!"

Nando threw the saddle forcefully onto the Appaloosa. Vaguely, he heard Bianca screaming and sobbing, but he could no longer tell what she was saying. He was totally unaware, as he slipped the bridle over the horse's head, that she had wrestled free of her father's grasp, and in the confusion that followed as they all piled out of the cabin, had grabbed the pistol from Jake's holster and had it pointed at his back.

"If you put one foot in that stirrup, I will shoot you." Her voice was hard and cutting, but there was no mistaking the tremble behind it.

Nando lowered his hands and turned to face her. She looked so outraged and at the same time so pitiful that he smiled tenderly at her and went to her. "Would you shoot a man in the back, Bianca?"

The tears spilled from her ebony eyes, and removing the scarf from around his neck, he lightly dabbed them away. When the gun was dropped to her side, he drew her close and kissed her half-open quivering mouth.

"You are a fool, Nando," she cried when he released her and climbed into the saddle. "You go for that yellow-eyed woman who is not worthy of you. You are so eager to die, but I am not the one to do it."

He left her standing with the others, the gun still cocked, dangling from her hand. Digging his heels savagely into his horse's flanks, he rode out at a gallop, turning the animal's head northwest toward his woman.

Danny—she'd become an obsession to him, and he could no longer fight her presence in his soul. For all her moods she was the most exciting woman he'd ever known, and by far the most beautiful, so delicate and yet so passionate. The thought of seeing her again somehow made the impending danger worthwhile.

As he urged his horse out over the flatlands, putting no restraints on its pace, he knew suddenly that he loved her . . . that he had loved her from the beginning. When he saw her again and felt her smooth naked flesh so close to his and tasted those sensual sweet lips, he knew he would *have* to tell her that he loved her.

Chapter 22

For Danny, entering Caliente again was like stepping back into a nightmare.

Lonny had been purposely harsh with her since they left the hideout, keeping his brother's harsh commands in mind. Can't slip up, he reminded himself repeatedly. Gotta do this just like Will said.

Following him to a dingy room with a window that overlooked the street, Danny sat on the edge of the bed and watched him pace back and forth. What was he so afraid of? she wondered. What had him so edgy and tense? "How long do you think we'll have to wait before Will shows?" she asked timidly.

A small twitch pulled at the corner of his mouth, and Danny realized she'd struck a nerve.

"You're afraid of him, aren't you?" she said, testing him.

He whirled to face her, glassy eyes narrowed. "I don't know what you're talking about."

"Oh, I think you do."

"Shut the hell up!" he snapped, his face contorting into an ugly mass of rising anger. "I don't need to hear no shit from you, you hear?"

"So, it's true!" she declared, daring him to refute it.

Lonny glared hard at her, his eyes watery and seething hatred at her. "You're only making it easier for me to do what I have to do."

"What is that? What did Will tell you to do? Kill me?"

Until now, she figured it would be Will who would send the bullet through her brain, but the picture was suddenly crystal

233

clear. What a monster! What kind of man could force his own brother to kill the one thing the boy seemed to want so much?

"So that's it! It's *you* who's going to kill me! Not him, you!" She fought back a sob at the hopelessness of her predicament, for when Will Garvey arrived in Caliente, she'd already be dead.

"Lonny, don't you see what he's doing? Don't you see?" Her voice bordered on hysteria, for she was fighting for her very life, and knowing the type of fear Will instilled in Lonny made her task seem impossible. She felt sick inside as the blood drained from her face, leaving her pale and trembling. "He's a monster! Please, you can't do this! You can't!"

"What are you to me anyway?" he sneered. "Nothing but a whore, that's all. Don't you think I seen the way you was making up to them back there?"

"B-but Lonny, I only did it so they wouldn't hurt me. They're cruel, horrible men. Will hurt me, you know he did! My God, are you so inhuman that you'd do his dirty work for him now? Don't you see it's you he wants to hurt, because he knows how you feel about me? He knows that—!"

"Shut up, dammit!" His voice bellowed over hers. "What do you know about it anyway? He's my brother and he knows what's best, so you best mind your own goddamned business!"

Danny's fury came spilling forth in a torrent of vicious words and harsh accusations. "You're a monster!" she shrieked, racing to him and beating him with clenched fists. "You disgust me! I hate you! Do you hear me? I hate you!"

With one sweep of his hand he sent her spiraling to the floor. Her face was a white blaze of terror in the center of a mass of tangled hair as she continued to hurl invectives at him between choked sobs.

He came for her then, both hands outstretched, aimed for her throat. *"I told you to shut up!"* He brought his open palm slashing across her cheek in a powerful slap, followed by another and another, until her head reeled and she could hear nothing above the roar of her own mind.

"Shut up! Shut up!" He continued to hit her, whipping her head from side to side with such force she was sure it would fly off her shoulders.

The room began to spin and she knew that at any second the blow would come that would end it all. Without any forewarning the beating stopped and, opening her eyes, she saw Lonny standing above her with his hand frozen in midair, a horrible look on his face. Danny held her breath, and it was then she heard the sound of horses in the street below.

Lonny drew himself up and started for the window. Mindless of her actions, and driven by an unthinkable desperation, she did what she knew she had to do. She sprang for him, catching him by surprise, and in an instant she had his gun out of his holster and pointed at him.

"If you're wondering how far I'll go," she hissed, "you should know that I've already killed a man, and he deserved to live more than you."

"Give me that gun," Lonny ordered through gritted teeth.

Danny backed away from him, the pistol never wavering from its target. "Don't come near me," she warned, "I'll kill you. I swear I will."

"You think I believe that story about your killing another man? Give me that gun, you bitch." He edged closer, ready to pounce.

"Never!"

Lonny licked his lips nervously. Miserable lying bitch! When he got it away from her, he'd beat her silly. Anger made him make his move, but the explosion that ripped through the room was the last thing he heard. With the shock plainly imprinted on his face, he staggered forward, small gurgling noises coming from his throat, hands clutching at the hole in his chest. He fell forward, dead.

Danny stared dumbstruck until a noise in the hallway forced her eyes from his body. Bootheels, brisk and sharp, followed by the pounding on the door, paralyzed her, driving a spike of new terror through her.

"Open up in there!" a voice commanded, and when she failed to respond, the man issued a dreaded order. "Break down the door."

Bit by bit the door shattered from the incessant battering, splinters of wood spraying the room. One final burst threw it wide open.

A soldier entered and looked at her in amazement. Only the voice from behind snapped his eyes away.

"Sergeant, what's going on in here? We're not here to investigate shootings." Another uniformed figure brushed past him, flicking splinters of wood from his sleeve with disdain.

"Lacy! Oh, God, Lacy! Help me! Please, help me!"

He stared dumbfounded at the scantily clad woman who ran to him.

"Danny! Is it you? My God, what's happened to you?" He wound his arms tightly around her slender body to calm her hysterical sobbing. "It's all right, honey, it's all right. You're safe now."

The room began to fill with troopers and confusion soon reigned, with everyone talking at once and no one quite sure what had happened.

"All right, Sergeant," Lacy said brusquely, "get rid of *that.*" With a contemptuous flick of his head, he gestured to the body on the floor. "It's obvious what happened here." Then, turning to the girl in his arms, he stroked her hair tenderly and spoke soothingly. "We'll have you out of here in no time, honey. Sergeant!" The man marched up briskly. "I want you to take six good men and escort this young lady back to Fort Defiance."

"But, Captain, I thought we were here to—"

Lacy flashed him an irritable look. "I gave you an order, soldier."

"Yes, sir," the sergeant responded, snapping to attention.

Lacy turned back to Danny. "You go with them, Danny. I have some business here, but I'll be following in a day or two."

He watched until the sobbing girl was led out of the hotel, lifted onto a horse and led out of Caliente by an armed escort. "And now," he said, his voice steely, "let's take up our positions. Lieutenant, take two men and cover that rooftop. Place two more on the roof of that saloon and two more by the stables. The rest of you men spread out. I want this whole damned place covered."

His eyes scanned the dusty little town of Caliente with contempt. "There's no way Coulter's going to walk out of this," he muttered under his breath. "No way."

Danny settled back in the wooden tub, leaning her head wearily against its side, feeling the steamy water drip off her shoulders and down her breasts. Closing her eyes to its gentle ministrations, she basked in the languid aroma of pleasantly scented vapors and bathed slowly, washing every inch of her body with hypnotic precision.

It would have been so easy to drift off into sleep and let her dreams take her to a time and place thousands of miles away in the past when there was never anything more to cause pain and sorrow than what she read in colorful romance novels. What happened to turn the dreams into such stark reality?

She emerged from the tub dripping wet, teeth chattering, and with a brisk rubdown, brought a resurgence of blood into circulation. Without a previous thought, she picked up the torn remnants of the calico dress and tossed it into the fire.

On the bed sat the plain brown box that had been brought to her earlier by an awkward young soldier who explained that it was a gift from Captain Hawkins. Only now did she lift the lid and open the folds of white paper to reveal a dress folded neatly inside.

It was a white dress showing not much style, but pretty in a simple sort of way. Well, white would look nice against her sun-browned skin and dark hair, she thought, neither pleased nor displeased by the gift, as she slipped her slender arms into the long sleeves and adjusted the buttons at the fitted bodice.

She sat down at the dressing table to brush her hair which had grown so long over the past months it fell in silken ripples below her waist. She brushed in rhythmic strokes, wondering whether Austin would notice how long it had grown. She knew he would.

Austin—the name floated like vapors through her mind. She knew he was waiting for her, but still she took her time, running the brush through the shafts of hair working up a rich luster that caught the light in red sparkles. He'd come all the way from San Francisco to be with her, so she had to look her best.

Involuntarily, her thoughts pivoted sharply to another man whose arrival a few short hours ago had set her emotions into a spiral. She had watched from her window with tear-filled eyes as the company rode into the fort and the prisoner was led away under armed guard, chained hand and foot. Peeking her head out the door, she had managed to catch the attention of one of the troopers and draw him aside to ask what was happening.

"We picked up that desperado in Caliente," he'd explained. "Gave us a real fight too. Killed one of the men; knifed him. Captain Hawkins said to lock him up."

Danny had tried to maintain her composure. "I see. Can you tell me what they will do with him?" She was fearful of his reply.

"From what I hear," he confided, "this character's been

wanted a long time. Now that they got him, they'll probably execute him."

She had gasped. "Do you think they'd really do it?"

He had just shrugged and replied, "Seeing as how he killed a man in front of so many witnesses, I don't see how he's gonna live past sunrise."

Hours later she could still hear those awful words ringing in her numbed mind. They were going to execute Alex, and in her dazed state, with her thoughts whirling about like a cyclone, Danny realized the only hope for Alex's salvation had to lie somewhere with Austin. She regretted drawing her brother into this for the sake of a man he did not even know, but there seemed to be no other way. They couldn't execute Alex! They just couldn't!

It was well past lights-out when she threw a shawl over her shoulders, crossed the parade ground and knocked softly on Austin's door. It opened quickly, throwing a warm glow into the darkness.

He took her by the hand and drew her into the room, taking the radiance of his oil lamp with them and leaving the parade ground to the luminance of the moon.

Austin sat on the sofa, one arm dangling over the side, looking at nothing in particular, but seeing a million things flash before his eyes. He wondered how objective he was being—how fair to her. Damn her! He was tired of being fair to her, always thinking of her and denying himself! At times he resented her for the unintentional hold she had on him, and always he hated himself for being prisoner to his own damnable emotions. Yet, he was still thinking of her tonight when he heard himself saying things he never thought he'd have the courage to say. Like how he had always wanted her, and how, if he could have, he would have bought her love . . . with words, presents, whatever it would have taken. God, hadn't he tried over the years?

Now he was losing her and he was powerless to stop it. She was asking him to be objective and to have all the right answers when she herself had none.

No, objectivity was not in abundance this evening as he listened to her excuses, laughing at her explanations and cursing her stubbornness to see things for what they really were. And all the while he loved her even more.

Was it out of revenge that he heard himself arguing with

her when he felt he had heard enough and would not, or could not, hear anymore?

"You must see this thing for what it is, Danielle," he implored. "What kind of relationship could you have with a man like that? You are everything he is not. What would you get out of it? I know you, Danny, and I know this thing cannot work for you, only for him. He's not for you and you know it!" He sounded like he was pleading with her, despite the force behind his assumptions. "You need things he can never give you. In the end you will only wind up hating him for what he cannot help being. And by God, you'll hate me even more for knowing it from the beginning! This is not fair of you! You have no right to do this to me—to play around with my life as though I were a temporary object of your fancy—to cast me out of your life for the sake of a man who can never be good enough for you! Not when it is I who have given you so much!"

The words poured forth as though washing from an open wound, his voice growing louder and uncontrolled. "You took everything I had to give you until there was nothing left except my very being . . . and you took that too! Dear God, Danielle, how many years do you think I have waited, holding it all inside? How many nights do you think I laid in bed dreaming of nothing else! How many times do you think I have looked at you and wanted to—"

Blinking as though a blinding light had just passed before his face, Austin gasped sharply when he recognized the person staring back at him with wild eyes. It was his own reflection in the mirror above the mantle. When had he started to scream?

Frozen like a statue, tiny beads of moisture broke out on his brow, despite the coolness of the room that was no longer warmed by the fire. The sight of his own contorted features turned his thoughts away from everything else and toward the sickening truth of what he had become.

The energy flooding his veins seconds before disappeared abruptly, leaving him exhausted. Eyes sweeping the floor, his voice scratchy and low, he barely managed to get the words out.

"You are the only woman I know who can drive me into a rage. I should take you up severely on it. But for now, I'll settle for a brandy." He forced a strained laugh. "From the look on your face, I'd say you can use one as well."

It wasn't often that Austin lost his self-control, but when he did, it frightened Danny, for she would see him as the one thing he always tried to disguise—the man behind the brother, with a man's hungers and emotions.

Refusing the drink, she walked out onto the porch, shocked by his confession, not knowing what to say to him, knowing only that Alex had to be saved. She did not have to hear Austin come up behind her to know he was there. Facing him, she said, her voice barely a whisper, "Austin, if you want, I'll beg you. I'll throw myself at your mercy."

He turned away, an expression of sharp annoyance on his face. "Danielle, please, at least spare me the dramatics."

Damn him, she thought angrily. Why was he making it so difficult? Undaunted, she stuck to her resolve. She placed a hand lightly on his sleeve and felt his muscles stiffen beneath her fingertips. "Austin . . . Austin—"

"Danny, please." For Austin Fleming there was no choice to be made. He saw the fear written in her eyes. Even that did not mar her perfect beauty, and his eyes drank their fill of her exquisite features that seemed to have grown even more ravishing than he remembered. The amber eyes in whose depths he'd found himself languishing from the very day she came into his life. Those lips, so soft and ripe, and so easily within reach now. He could even see the faint quiver on her full bottom lip. He ached to taste her mouth on his.

Danny stared at him blankly.

His breath ragged, he said, "What do you want me to do?"

"I . . . I—"

"Come on, Danielle, this is not something that can take all night to decide. He's to be executed at dawn, you know."

The harsh reminder forced all other thoughts from her mind. "I thought you could intervene with General Sherman or President Grant—use your influence to get a stay of execution or clemency. Anything! Austin, please, there must be something you can do!"

"As a matter of fact, there is."

He said it as though he'd known all along he would help. Why had he tortured her by trying to talk her out of it? "You seem to have it all worked out," she remarked bitterly. "Perhaps you'll let me in on your little scheme."

"Before I do, there's one thing to be, shall we say, gotten out of the way."

"What is it?"

"You, sister. I want you to return to France immediately. And I want this marriage annulled at once."

Her mouth dropped open. "Austin! No! I will not return to France and there's nothing you can do about it!"

Of course, it all fit together now. If he couldn't have her, then he'd see to it that Alex Coulter couldn't either. Oh, but he was so clever.

That old defiance sprang back into her eyes and her chin tilted up at him in familiar resistance, and the sight of it brought a rush of familiar feelings. No longer were they strangers, but brother and sister once again. Danielle, as usual, was stubbornly refusing to comply with his wishes, and Austin, as usual, was letting her have her way. In the end it was decided that she would not return to France and that he would do what he could to help Alex, although how he would go about it he felt compelled to keep to himself.

"Austin, if I could just see him—talk to him. If you could arrange to have him brought here. Oh please, Austin," she begged.

Could he ever refuse the plea in those golden eyes? "I'll do what I can," he muttered. "Go back to your room and wait there. Oh, and stop by General Trench's office on your way and ask him to join me here, would you?"

She turned to leave, but his hand reached out for hers just as she opened the door. For a moment his face looked like a paradox of conflicting emotions before settling into an expression she found impossible to read. He stood so close she felt the warmth of his breath on her cheek, and when she heard his voice, she knew how hard it was for him to say the words.

"I have loved you so much. At times I thought I would die if I could not have you," he whispered. "When you married Alex, I felt I had lost you forever. But still I feel closer to you than any other creature on this earth. I'll never stop loving you."

As painful as it was, Danny owed him the truth. "I love him, Austin."

"I know you do, Danielle."

Then she was gone and he was alone again, her final words echoing in his mind.

Austin Fleming knew that with Danielle's reckless ways she had to be protected. But how could he protect her from the one thing he himself had no control over—her own husband?

Alex Coulter's name raced through Austin's mind in a strange mixture of emotions, all of them black and white and contradicting. A searing rivalry existed between the men over the one thing each wished, above all else, to possess. But unknown to anyone else, it was hardly an innocent rivalry between two complete strangers vying for the same prize. The simple truth of the matter was that Austin Fleming and Alex Coulter were not strangers at all. They were, in fact, the best of friends.

The circumstances of the unlikely relationship had begun at a time when Austin had come to America the first time to work at the mine and had emerged from the black sooty hole one day to hear his name called behind him. Turning, he'd found himself looking into the most brilliant eyes he'd ever seen. They belonged to the man who was to change the rest of his life.

Austin's feelings for Alex Coulter ran the gamut of human emotion, from anger and outrage at Alex's abusive treatment of Danny, to an unspoken, almost grudging respect for him. And now Alex was his rival for Danny's love. How ironic, Austin thought, that it should be the only man in the world he trusted who would take Danny from him.

How could he blame her for loving Alex? Hadn't he too fallen victim to Alex Coulter's disarming character? Hadn't he too been trapped by Alex's wild sense of freedom and unmercifully attracted to the raw vitality of the man? In the end it was not Austin's feelings for Danny that compelled him to help Alex. For once in his life, Austin would do something for himself, because he could not, underneath it all, allow his best . . . his only . . . friend to die before the firing squad at dawn.

His mind began to work frantically, devising the plan that would eventually save Alex Coulter's life. He went over it again and again until he had it memorized, rehearsing anticipated dialogue, covering every minute detail, every possibility. If it failed, it would make no difference to Alex, he thought. They'd execute him anyway. But the thought of his own death loomed before Austin. If his plan failed, it would mean his life, too.

Would it be worth it? It was hard to tell these days how anything would be resolved. He'd seen Danny again after so many long agonizing months, and their meeting had not gone well at all. He wondered bitterly how much she would love Alex if she knew the truth about the Lady Laura and the secret friendship. How much had Alex told her? What went on all those weeks they'd spent together in the wilderness while he waited in San Francisco sick out of his mind? The absurdity of the whole situation stunned him. Danny with Alex—it was simply too insane! Was it just a crazy coincidence? He was beginning to wonder more and more.

The sharp rapping at the door snapped Austin out of his dark thoughts. A light layer of perspiration soaked through his shirt making it stick uncomfortably to his back. He rose wearily and went to the door. Taking a deep breath, he steeled himself.

"Good evening, General Trench. I'm glad you could join me. There are some important matters I'd like to discuss with you."

Chapter 23

One hour was all the time she could have alone with Alex. When she entered the room, she found him standing with his back to the door, looking at the starry night out of the window. After what seemed like a breathless eternity, he turned to her, and without speaking, walked slowly forward, gray eyes sweeping over her thoroughly.

The sound of his voice finally broke the silence. "I've got something for you," he said as he reached into his vest pocket.

Danny's eyes dropped to where the fabric of his trousers stretched taut over his lean legs, emphasizing the contours of sinewy muscles beneath. His tight pants outlined parts of his body only too well, and the bulge she saw between his legs left little doubt what was on his mind.

Alex glanced down sheepishly. "Did you think I could be in the same room with you for more than five minutes and *not* want you?"

"What do you have there?" she asked, pointing to his clenched fist to change the subject.

"Oh, I nearly forgot. Here, I believe this belongs to you." He opened his palm to reveal the necklace she thought she'd never see again. She gasped at the sight of it, and from out of nowhere sprang unwanted images, set into motion by the silver links laying in a small heap in his hand. She hesitated, unable by the impact of those memories to respond.

"What's the matter," he asked. "Don't you want it?"

Danny swallowed hard. She couldn't tell him. He must never know what that necklace had come to mean to her. Gingerly, she lifted it from his hand. "It's nothing, Alex, nothing. I just . . . well, I thought I would never see this again, that's all." She smiled for his benefit. "It seems to be broken. I'll have it repaired at once. For now, I'll put it in here." Opening the dresser drawer, she dropped the necklace in, shutting the awful memories away, for a while at least. When she looked at him again, a smile touched her lips. "I'm glad to see you're still alive."

Alex laughed. "Yes, but not for long."

He reached for her, but she retreated, shaking her head at him as though he were a naughty boy. "Alex, please, there's no time for that."

"There doesn't seem to be much time for anything else," he commented.

She shot him an annoyed look. "Must you be so . . . so . . . at a time like this?"

"What the hell do you expect me to do!" His bellow exploded all at once, telling her how upset he really was. Grabbing her by the arm he pulled her to him before she could resist. Crushing her against his chest, he held her tightly, his mouth covering hers in a demanding kiss, taking her breath away. When he released her at last, she was limp from the force of his passion, but she knew that if she didn't stop it now, it would soon be too late. She had to tell him that all was not hopeless.

"Alex, wait," she insisted. "Wait until you hear what I have to tell you."

"It better be pretty damned important," he snapped. He was beginning to tire of her protests. He wanted her, but he wasn't going to eat dirt to prove it. Nor was he about to accept any phony excuses at a time like this—no postponements and no denials, not when he had laid his life on the line for her.

"There's something you must know. I've spoken to Austin this evening and he has agreed to help you."

He eyed her cautiously, gray eyes narrowed into slits, his full attention focused on her words rather than her body.

"I've asked him to use his influence to . . . Well, he knows people in high places, and I thought maybe he could—"

"Forget it. It won't work," he said sharply.

"It's your only chance, you'd better hope it works. He knows people in Washington, and I'm certain there must be something—"

"I said forget it! Just forget it! I don't need his help!"

"What are you saying?" Danny asked incredulously. "You need all the help you can get!"

"Let's put it this way, I don't *want* his help."

His reaction confused her. Perhaps he hadn't heard her correctly. "You don't understand. Austin can get you a pardon. Of course, he could make no promises, but I know he can."

The sound of his voice exploded in her brain, sending her thoughts scattering from the impact. "I told you I don't want his help!"

She stared at him disbelievingly. It was so against his survival instincts to refuse help. It didn't make sense. It was not like Alex Coulter to allow himself to be led off to slaughter like a meek little lamb without a final struggle to proclaim the injustice of it. Why had the wolf suddenly turned into a lamb?

"Alex, are you mad? He's the only one who can save you!" His look was not that of a man who wished to be saved. It was the same implacable look she'd come to know so well. "Why, Alex? Why?" was all she could ask. His cruel reply only threw more mystery on his strange behavior.

"You mean you don't know why? Come on, are you really up to your old tricks?"

Know what? What could she know when he'd always done his best to shut her out? Whenever she questioned him, he had always turned on her, accusing her of knowing more than she let on and of only asking stupid questions to bring more torment into his life. Damn him! What about the torment he brought into her life? Hadn't she suffered enough torment and humiliation because of him? She had a right to know what he was talking about!

She felt the chill of his stare like a polished mirror in which was reflected her own rush of emotions. The mocking smile on his mouth hardened into a thin, taut line as he shoved past her and walked to the window. He stood there with his head bent, hands resting high on the panes, his breathing growing labored as though he were holding himself in strict control.

He knew he had no right to keep her out of his life, but he asked himself over and over how he could tell her the things she wanted to know. How could he make her understand the reasons for his failings, the causes of his bitterness? Surely she'd hate him more if she knew, and how could he stand that?

He felt fury mounting within him, against him, tearing at his brain with vicious claws, blinding him to the consequences of his actions. Drawing his clenched fist back, he sent it smashing through the window with a thrust that was lightning quick.

Danny shut her eyes to the sound of shattering glass, and when she opened them again, Alex stood before her, blood dripping from the deep cuts on his hand. She moved toward him, but he put his hand up to stop her from coming any further. The swiftness of the movement caused the droplets of blood at his fingertips to go flying into the air, blotting her white dress with splotches of red. His eyes were dark and distant, and she could read nothing of what he felt in them. But never in the world did she expect to hear what he said next.

"You want to know why I won't let your brother come so nobly to my rescue, is that it, my love?"

She waited, tense and speechless.

"Don't you think I know that he's in love with you?"

She looked at him blankly. "B-but, that's just . . . he's my brother, of course he loves me."

"That's not what I meant and you know it!"

He knew! My God. He said it as though he had *always* known.

Danny's mind reeled. How could Alex possibly know about this? Tonight for the very first time the words had been uttered out loud from Austin's own lips, but there'd been no one else present to hear them, and as far as she knew, the dark secret remained forever hidden in her heart and Austin's. Her mind scrambled to make some sense out of this. The only person Alex could possibly have learned it from could only have been—Austin!

Suddenly, Danny felt sick. The color drained from her face, her extremities numbed and the light rapidly turned into black blotches as she fainted.

She awakened in Alex's arms and felt herself being placed on the bed. A film of perspiration covered her flesh, leaving it moist and clammy. He was stroking her hair, pushing the damp strands from her face while he whispered to her tenderly. "I'm sorry, baby, I'm sorry."

She didn't even realize that she was crying until he dabbed the tears from her eyes with his thumb. Bending forward, he placed his lips gently against hers, tasting the salt of her tears.

When her arms went around his neck he felt the pressure of her mouth seeking his and was able to forget everything else—the pain in his heart, the pain he had caused her, the dull throbbing in his torn hand. All he knew was the frightening intensity of his desire for her.

"Your hand—" she whispered against his shoulder.

"Not now. I want to make love to you first."

She moved her body up to meet his, feeling the sticky, drying blood of his wound against her skin as he caressed her breasts. He entered her quickly, his desire having mounted to the point where he could contain it no longer.

Arching her slender body upward to meet each thrust, she called to him in a raspy voice. He responded by driving himself deeper into her, sending wild tremors through her limbs and a fierce burning through her loins. She accepted him greedily, hungrily, desperately, giving every inch of herself to him, allowing him free access to her passion, denying him nothing.

They clung to each other, filling each other's senses to the ultimate peak where nothing else mattered in the entire world except one man and one woman, whose need for each other was paramount to their very existence and reason for being.

Later, as Danny wrapped a strip of torn sheet carefully around Alex's hand, she had no idea whether they had three minutes left or thirty. She spoke as if in a dream. "How long have you and Austin known each other?"

Alex sighed and shrugged. "Four years I guess."

"Four years! I thought a few months perhaps, since we arrived in this country, but four years?"

"Yeah, well, he's been here before, remember?"

Danny ran a hand through her hair, her face a mass of confusion and doubt. "I wonder why he never told me," she muttered to herself.

"Maybe you'd better ask him that."

Yes, she would do that. She'd find out later from Austin what kind of game he was playing, and why he had purposely kept his friendship with Alex a carefully guarded secret. But right now there were other things to think about. Eyes ablaze with determination, she said, "Alex, you *must* let him help you. His love for me has nothing to do with you, don't you see that? If he's your friend, why won't you let him do what he can?"

The question was never meant to receive a reply, for the

rapping at the door invaded their privacy and chased it away. The brusque voice reminded them, all too harshly, that their time together was up.

Several uniformed men entered the room and took Alex Coulter out with them. Forming a tight compact garrison around him, the tips of their bayonets pointed directly at him, they led him back to the guardhouse.

The thought of impending death failed to frighten Alex. He had been close to it so many times before, and had tempted it, daringly throwing his life in its path. It was the rash aspect of his nature that made him do it, and secretly he had to admit that he craved the excitement and exhilaration derived from courting danger and narrowly escaping with his life. It was a game—a very dangerous game—but so far he'd managed to win every round. This time, though, his luck was running out. At dawn it would all come to an end.

In a way, he could not wait for the morning to arrive, and he found himself looking for a glimpse of the hazy streaks that would grow across the eastern sky heralding a brand new day. It would be his last, but at least it was better than this. His confinement within the dank abode walls of a prison cell, locked behind iron bars, was a death surely worse than any that awaited him at the hands of a firing squad. Sadly, he'd always hoped his death would have been one more befitting an Indian brave. Hell, there was no honor in dying this way.

If only he hadn't killed that damned trooper he wouldn't be in this jam now. Oh sure, there were lots of things they could have gotten him for. While the morality of some of his acts might have been questioned, the evidence against him was nil. What else besides killing that soldier? Robbing from his own mine? Ha, wouldn't that be something? Yeah, they'd scrutinize the deed to the Lady Laura from here to the Mississippi, but they'd never find anything wrong with it. It was as valid as the noses on their faces. Of course, if they did that, it would put an immediate end to the charade he and Austin Fleming had been playing all these years.

At the sound of the guardhouse door being unlocked, his thoughts scattered, leaving only a stony hardness to his features.

Captain Lacy Hawkins found him lying on his cot, motionless. He was dressed as he'd been the day he was apprehended in Caliente, in a short, black leather vest over a light blue shirt, and black breeches tucked into knee-length leather boots. The only thing missing was the gunbelt he usually wore around his hips. After sending the guard to wait outside, Lacy approached the cell cautiously and stood for several minutes observing the prisoner.

Then the man on the cot rose and approached the iron bars to stand with his thumbs hooked arrogantly in his pockets, a mocking smile on his lips. His presence was imposing and Lacy Hawkins hated him for it.

"Any last requests?" he drawled.

"Only one," replied Alex, silver eyes glaring. "Get out."

A thin smile spread over Lacy's lips as he reached into his pocket and withdrew a small pouch and two sheets of paper. Pouring a line of tobacco into the folds of paper, he rolled them into cylinders, twisted the ends closed and passed one to Coulter. Alex accepted the cigarette without a word of thanks, placed it between his lips and waited for Lacy to light it for him.

"You know, Coulter, that's really no way to treat someone who's about to do you a favor."

Alex hated the sound of that voice, so sickeningly sweet and southern. "Just tell me what you came here to tell me, Hawkins." He took a long deep drag on the cigarette and shuffled back to the cot.

"I thought you'd like to know who's responsible for your being here." Lacy studied him for a sign of interest but saw nothing except a sarcastic sneer on his face.

"What difference does it make? Or have you forgotten that I'm to die at dawn?"

"I haven't forgotten. Nothing I can do about that. But there is something I can do to, shall we say, even up the score?"

In a half-interested tone, Alex asked, "Yeah, like what?"

"It would seem to me that a man who's about to be executed might like nothing better than to get even with the man who put him in this spot in the fist place."

"I told you, Hawkins," Alex snapped, "I want no games. If you've got something to say, then say it. If not, get the hell out of here and leave me alone."

"All right, all right." Lacy licked his lips and decided that skirting the issue would only make the arrogant bastard angrier, then he'd never get Coulter to believe the lie he was about to tell him. "Look, I just thought you'd like to know

that it was Austin Fleming who engineered your capture.
Why look so surprised? Don't tell me you didn't even suspect
it?" He gave a short contemptuous laugh and hoped it
sounded convincing. "I guess you don't fit in with the Fleming
plan for the universe. But who knows, I could be wrong.
Maybe he hates you for something else."

Alex's mind raged full steam ahead with startling and
conflicting thoughts, trying desperately to weigh what he'd
just heard against all he knew and felt in his heart. Austin was
his friend. Did he really have something to do with this?
Why?

The one answer seemed almost too preposterous—the
Lady Laura. Could it be that after all these years Austin was
no longer content to let the world think him the owner of the
mine, when in fact the rightful owner had always been Alex
Coulter? Could it be that after all this time, by a strange quirk
of fate, Alex's life should end so abruptly because of an even
stranger quirk of fate that had brought the two of them
together in the first place? Did Austin do it for himself, or did
he do it for her?

Suddenly Alex understood. Danielle Fleming was the kind
of woman who could drive a man to madness. She'd done it to
him, and here was proof that she'd done it to her own
brother. Yes, she had that power over men—the power to
turn them against one another in their insane obsession to
possess her. Could he blame Austin for betraying him if he
did it for her?

The shock and outrage of this monumental deception
stunned him. Over and over again all he could think of was
one thing—Austin Fleming had been his friend and he'd
trusted him. So, Austin wanted the Lady Laura because he
could not bare for Danny to find out that it had never really
belonged to her at all. Or, did she already know that? Jesus
Christ, was she in on this, too?

He ground the stub of his cigarette into the earth floor and
came forward. "What's your offer?" he asked in a low voice
that came from somewhere deep in his throat.

"I could arrange to leave a pistol . . . no, a knife. And
when Fleming comes to see you later, which he probably will,
you could . . ."

Alex drew close to the bars, silencing Lacy with his stare.
"What's in it for you, Hawkins?"

Lacy swallowed hard. "What makes you think there's

anything in it for me? Maybe I just don't like seeing a man double-crossed."

"I don't buy it. Not from you. There's got to be more. We both know it's not my honor you want to protect, so what's your reason for wanting Austin Fleming out of the way?"

Lacy could feel the beads of perspiration breaking out under his collar. "Look, Coulter, they're going to execute you at dawn one way or the other. Of course, if you're not interested in my offer, then we'll forget we had this little talk."

Turning away with the disgust evident on his face, Alex returned to the cot and slumped down onto it, elbows on his knees, face in his hands, retreating quickly behind an impenetrable curtain.

In an attempt to call him back, Lacy said idly, "If you'd care to write any letters, I could arrange—"

"I've got no letters to write," came the snarl of reply.

"Not even to your *wife?*"

Silver eyes flashed up at him. "You stay away from her, Hawkins."

"I don't think that's any of your business. Especially seeing as how after tomorrow morning you won't even be around anymore."

"So that's it! You stinking bastard!" He leapt for Lacy, thrusting a contorted grasping hand for his throat, only to miss by inches as Lacy sidestepped and placed a hand on his revolver in warning. "It's my wife you're after, you miserable dog! And you know damned well that you'll never have her if Austin is around to prevent it! Did you think I'd fall for your sordid plot and go to my grave knowing that she's lying in your arms?"

"But he betrayed you!" shouted Lacy, perpetuating the lie.

For Alex, it was irrelevant. Austin may have betrayed him, but the pain of that was slight compared to that of dying with the thought of Danny with this bastard. "Go peddle your goods somewhere else, Hawkins," he sneered. "I'm not interested."

Lacy knew it was useless. He should have expected as much from this heathen. "You know," he drawled venomously, "Danny and I would probably have been married if you hadn't come along and . . . Well, that's all water under the bridge. I guess it will just take a little longer than I planned, but I assure you, Coulter, she *will* be mine."

The expression on Alex's face remained unreadable, but there was no mistaking the ominous threat in his voice. "Hawkins," he said, his steely glare biting into the man, "you'd better hope they kill me tomorrow."

Lacy smiled, but it was not pleasant to see. His mouth formed a hard line as though it had been drawn on his face by a single pen stroke. His green eyes narrowed at Alex in contempt, while the threat echoed in his ears. He knew it was preposterous, and yet, as he walked from the guardhouse, he felt strangely relieved to be out of Coulter's presence.

As he walked slowly back to his quarters, a chill passed over him. What was there to fear? he asked himself. An idle threat uttered in desperation by a condemned man. But still the words rattled through his mind. 'You'd better hope they kill me . . .'

"Would you unlock the door and let me in?" Austin asked.

The guard looked at him in surprise. "I don't know, sir, it's unlikely you'd want to be in there with that murderer."

Austin shot him a heated look and his tone grew severe. "Do not presume, Corporal, to tell me where I would or would not wish to be. Just open that door and lock it behind me, then place yourself outside. Is that clear?" He was in no mood for this, least of all from some backwoods boy whose dreams of the world had landed him in a remote outpost in the middle of the Southwest.

"Yes, sir," the trooper snapped, and pulling the key ring from his pocket, he jangled it about until he found the one that fit the cell. Austin stepped inside, then waited until the guard had left the guardhouse and they were alone.

"We don't have much time," he whispered in haste. "I want you to listen carefully."

"Looks like you've got all the time in the world, don't you, Austin?" Alex muttered, his voice sounding strangely remote.

"We've got to hurry," he said, the urgency evident in his hushed tone.

"If you wanted the Lady Laura why didn't you just ask for it? Didn't you always know that I'd have given it to you at any time?"

Austin looked at him with a blank expression, unable to make sense out of his words or his strangely hostile behavior. "What are you talking about?"

Alex shook his head in disillusion. "It's funny, I never thought it would be you who would double-cross me. I guess you never really know how things will turn out."

He's upset, Austin decided. After all, what man to be executed in a few hours would not be and talking crazy at a time like this? Rubbing the weariness from his eyes, he said, "Look, when I call the guard back in, I want you to make a run for it. You'll have about thirty seconds to make it across the parade ground to where I have a horse waiting behind the adjutant's office. From there, you're on your own."

"I'd never make it out of this fort alive, and you know it."

"You might if the gate is opened," Austin replied. "And it will be."

"But how . . . ?"

"We don't have time for that, I'll explain later."

"There may not be a later," Alex remarked dispassionately.

"I know," said Austin, his expression grave, "but I figure you'd rather die trying."

There were so many things Austin wanted to say to him, but Alex placed a distance between them that was impossible for him to broach. He didn't understand it, nor did Alex's unexplained behavior help to alleviate his own mounting fears. If this thing failed . . . His mind could not complete the awful possibility.

He wanted to say more to the man he might never see alive again, but the words stuck in his throat and his tongue felt like it filled up his whole mouth. He was sure if he tried to speak, he would choke.

Alex broke the awful silence at last. "Call the guard."

Austin knew the moment of reckoning had arrived. Once the wheels were set in motion, there would be no turning back.

The iron-barred door swung open with a creak and Austin walked through. But when the corporal turned back to the cell to lock the door, the blow Austin delivered from behind tumbled him to the ground. Springing lightly over him, Alex bolted from the cell and followed Austin to the outside door.

Austin peeked his head out and glanced around. The coast was clear. It was time to move. A knot formed in his throat the size of an orange and a cold sweat broke out all over his body, chilling him down to his bones in spite of the balmy October night.

At his signal, Alex rushed past him and dashed across the open parade ground. Running silently, he shot a quick glance back over his shoulder at the man he'd left behind in the shadows. But the sight of Austin standing in the middle of the parade ground, illuminated by the moon, stunned him. The horrible sickening surprise of it sent shock waves through his body.

He felt the shot before he heard it. The momentum of the shell as it hit and exploded in his back sent him flying forward in a grotesque whiplash motion. The last thing he saw before he hit the ground was the pistol in Austin's hand, pointed directly at his back, its muzzle still smoking.

Seconds later shouts came from the barracks and a lamp was lit in the adjutant's office. From out of every doorway issued streams of men, some clad only in their longjohns, some less than that. In no time a crowd gathered, into the center of which strode the Commanding Officer, General Trench.

Austin stood as if drugged, the pistol dangling from his hand, barely able to distinguish words from sounds. From out of nowhere the post doctor rushed to Coulter's body and knelt on the ground beside it. He placed his fingers on one side of the man's throat, then the other. Neither side registered a pulse. Reaching forward, he pulled him over onto his back and rested an ear against his chest for any telltale sign of a heartbeat. He shook his head. The prisoner was dead. There would be no need for further examination.

Looking sickeningly at the body, Austin felt the color drain from his face and the life seep from his limbs. He followed dumbly behind General Trench who led him away from the scene.

For some of the men who milled about, it wasn't the gunshot that had roused them from their bunks and sent them racing, half-clothed. It was the screams that sent shivers down their spines.

Unable to sleep, Danny had stood at the window wishing she could hide from it all in the soft shadows that the moon sent shimmering across the earth. It happened so fast she barely had time to react. It sounded like a crackle of thunder, but there was no mistaking the sound for what it was, and a thin shrill scream tore from her throat when she saw the bullet rip through Alex's body and send him sprawling.

The violent thrust of her heart being wrenched from her chest made her knees crumble beneath her almost as if a bullet had torn through her body as well. And in the next instant she sank lifelessly to the floor.

Bright white-yellow sunlight poured in through the window, and gradually she awakened. Was it the next morning? Had she been asleep? Had it all been a cruel dream? She rose on wobbly legs and made it to the window only with the aid of the wall to lean against. Outside the parade ground was bleached from the glare of the afternoon sun. Moving as if in a trance, she went to the wash basin and splashed cold water on her face. She glanced down at the white dress she wore—yesterday, new and clean; today, rumpled and stained with dark splotches of blood—his blood. Suddenly the memory of last night came back to her in a painful rush.

Flinging herself onto the bed she sobbed helplessly, stifling the sounds of her grief within the pillow.

Oh, Alex, she cried, don't leave me . . . please don't leave me alone. Without the strength of his presence, she felt very weak and small, and so horribly alone.

Chapter 24

Emmett Fleming left at once for Fort Defiance in the wake of the explosive events that had his niece unaccountably delayed from returning to France as she had wished, and his nephew incarcerated in an army prison. The months since Danielle's abduction had taken their toll on him, but the last few days had aged him the most.

The whole affair was preposterous! Now they were actually talking about executing Austin! Hell, he did them a favor by killing that renegade!

"They don't see it that way," Carl Forrester told him.

"I thought a man was supposed to get a fair trial in this country before they executed him!" Emmett angrily exclaimed, puffing away on his cigar.

Carl shook his head. "Beats me. I can't get a straight answer out of anyone. Frankly, I don't think anyone really knows what's happening, but they're all afraid to admit it. I'm worried that because of it, they might see this thing through to the end."

"Who's the man in charge?"

"Reed," answered Carl. "General Payton Reed."

"That's why. Reed's a hard-ass soldier. Right by the book. God, it makes me sick."

Carl Forrester looked at his boss thoughtfully. "Do you think there's anything you can do?"

"Who the hell knows, Carl. Who the hell knows."

Three days later he walked into the general's office prepared to let the Army name its price in return for Austin's life. But they weren't buying. Austin Fleming had killed a man and for that he had to pay his own price. Emmett slunk from the commanding officer's quarters hating the sickening task he had to perform in telling Danny about her brother's fate. How could he tell her that as soon as the orders arrived from Washington, Austin would die?

Danny wept uncontrollably as he held a comforting arm around her shoulders. This was all too insane and she felt herself going mad. She hated him for killing Alex, of that she had no doubt, but not even in her contempt of him did she ever wish for *that!* She'd never forgive him for what he'd done, but she didn't want him dead!

Her tears spilled onto Emmett's shirt but he didn't mind. Stroking her hair he placed a tender kiss on her forehead. "Don't worry, honey; we'll do whatever we can to help Austin."

He hoped his reassuring words would calm her distress, but he had to admit secretly that the chance of getting the Army to reverse its decision was close to zero. Not when it was President Grant to whom he had to go begging.

It was no secret around the nation's capital that the Fleming name lent its powerful support to the Democrats, and with next year being an election year, any Democrat bearing Fleming support would be a formidable adversary. It was kept under wraps, of course, but among Democrats themselves it was widely acknowledged that a front-running contender for full support was George Custer. He was one of the most colorful men in the country, and a personal friend of Emmett Fleming in the bargain. That in itself was enough to turn a Republican Grant strongly against Emmett, since there was precious little about Custer that the President liked.

With elections just around the corner, the more scandals the Democrats could pin on the Grant administration, the better their chances of winning. So they had set about their task diligently, first uncovering a shocking situation within the War Department whereby the Army was selling trading post appointments with annual kickbacks deposited directly into the pocket of the Secretary of War. It was George Custer who unearthed the whole affair and exposed the Secretary of War for what he really was, a two-bit politician with very expensive tastes.

Then there was that little affair over the President's personal secretary who was accused of conspiring in fraud schemes against the Indians. True, there was insufficient evidence to bring the man to trial, but the pressure brought to bear against the President by men like Emmett Fleming and George Custer angered an already irate Grant.

The President disliked having his back against the wall. What did it matter to him if Austin Fleming met his end in front of a firing squad? Grant's chances of securing the Republican nomination were slim to say the least, since his fellow party members were already touting the names of several possible candidates, primarily that of Rutherford B. Hayes. So what did it matter whether Austin Fleming died? Maybe it would teach those damned arrogant Flemings a lesson!

Emmett Fleming didn't really think there was much of a possibility of convincing President Grant to supersede the orders for Austin's execution, but at this point, there didn't seem to be any other hope.

These were fears he could never voice to Danny, whose distress was already as much as she could bear. Turning her teary eyes up at him, she spoke between broken sobs.

"Maybe you could speak to General Trench. He might be able to—" But the tortured look on his face told her something was very wrong. "What is it? Please, tell me."

Emmett looked away, and taking a deep breath, he told her.

"General Trench is dead. He committed suicide the day after Austin's arrest. They found him with a bullet in his head and the gun still in his hand."

Collapsing into his arms, Danny wept in uncontrollable shudders at the horror of the nightmare that was increasing by terrifying proportions.

Lacy Hawkins gazed out the window at the approach of dusk. The sky was midnight blue with immense stretches of purple, and very soon it would glisten with millions of tiny sparkles. In about an hour the bugler would sound lights-out and the camp retire.

He reached for the blue jacket that hung on a peg close to the door and flung it over his shoulder as he let himself out. At Danny's door he slipped it on, buttoned it up neatly and smoothed down the wrinkles with the palms of his hands. His mind jumped back to the proposition he had vainly attempted to make with Coulter, and a tight smile curled his lip. What a damned fool Coulter was, he thought, refusing to kill the man

who killed him instead. Well, Lacy Hawkins was about to
make another proposition, but he felt fairly certain that this
one would not be turned down.

Her room was dimly lit by a single oil lamp set low so that
its lambent light cast long undulating shadows across the
walls, and dark red lights danced through her long auburn
hair.

All the hardships she'd been through had made her no less
beautiful. Oh, she was thinner, he could see that right off, but
it only enhanced her fine lines and sleek bone structure. And
those golden slanted cat-eyes of hers seemed to flash more
brilliantly than he remembered. When they'd parted company in Bennett, she'd been a girl. Now she was a woman.

"Do you mind if I smoke?" He pulled the small tobacco
pouch from his pocket without waiting for her approval.

Ignoring the question, Danny sat down at the table and
watched with only mild interest as he rolled the paper and
placed the cigarette between his lips. Striking a wooden
match on the sole of his boot, he said, "I heard about
Austin."

Danny sighed deeply. "Uncle Emmett was here yesterday.
He's promised to do whatever he can."

Taking a deep drag on his cigarette, Lacy let the smoke out
slowly through pursed lips. "I have to tell you, Danny, it
doesn't look good. There's a lot of people who wouldn't mind
seeing him executed." As he spoke, he watched her carefully
and noted with satisfaction that his words were achieving the
desired effect. Her eyes widened and her face looked worried
and confused. "Oh, I'm sure your uncle means well, Danny
honey, really I do. But it's high time you realized that the
Fleming name isn't the word of God, especially out here."

Danny rose from her seat and began to pace the floor,
wringing her hands and biting at the corner of her bottom lip.
"Oh, Lacy, sometimes I think I'm going mad," she exclaimed
with emotion. "They're going to kill Austin and I don't think
I can stand that." Her body began to tremble and once again
tears ran freely down her cheeks, as they seemed so often to
do these days.

He went to her and wrapped his arms protectively about
her and stroked her hair tenderly. Bending his head, he
brushed her ear with his lips. "Danny," he whispered, "I've
got a plan."

She straightened up instantly. "A plan? What kind of plan?"

"I'll tell you about it later. Right now I want you." Crushing her against his chest, he brought his lips down on hers with frightening force, holding her so tightly that she had no choice but to endure the feel of his lips on hers, as wet and sticky as the very first time, and filling her with as much distaste.

Finally able to squirm away, she protested, "Lacy, please don't."

Breathless from his surging desires, he could feel the blood racing through his veins, the pulse pounding in his temples and the constricting bulge in his trousers. Damn her, was she still playing hard to get? Her rejection roused instant anger in him.

"What's the matter, honey?" he drawled, snatching her by the wrist. "For all the others it was all right, but not for me?"

The remark hit her like a slap across the face. "I think you'd better leave."

"Not until you hear what I have to say." Dropping all pretense, his tone told her that he no longer saw any need to hide behind the cloak of a gentleman. "I want you to marry me."

Danielle was completely amazed. She could barely suppress the laugh that broke from her throat. "Marry you? You must be crazy!"

The corner of his mouth twitched and his eyes hardened into a piercing glare. His breath came quicker, but it had nothing to do with lust. "But you married that dog, didn't you? Or do you expect me to believe that he forced you into it?"

She hated Lacy and his sickening smile and southern drawl that slid over her like sticky hands. What a fool she'd been to have ever thought him handsome—or a gentleman! "You make me sick!" she spat at him. "Get out of here!" She whirled away to fling the door open, but he caught her by the arm and snapped her around with a painful twist of her arm.

"You should be happy someone's offering to marry you. What man would have you after the things you've done? Why, you're nothing but a cheap whore, aren't you, my fine, cultured lady? Just a common slut who'd sell her body as quick as she could to get what she wants. Those men back in

Caliente told me all about you, Danny. So what does that make you, my sweet thing? I'd say it makes you no better than a barroom tramp."

"No!" she screamed. "It's not true!"

But he would not cease his taunting, and her denials seemed only to spur him on to further cruelties. "All the while you were putting me off, pretending to be so innocent and virtuous, you were probably giving yourself to any man who asked. Why, you—!" His own anger got the best of him, and with one blinding movement, he brought the back of his hand crashing across her face.

She stumbled backward, her hand flying up to her bruised and stinging cheek, the tears hot and fresh in her eyes.

"Do you want to save Austin?" he demanded harshly. "Do you?" He was shaking her now, fingers digging deeply into the flesh at her shoulders, whipping her head about her neck like she was a lifeless rag doll. "Answer me! Do you want to save Austin?"

Confusion and fear clutched her. Her mind spun in circles and Lacy was relentlessly demanding an answer.

"Yes!" she shrieked. "Yes!"

He released her with a shove. "Well, my *chérie*, I am the only one who can help him. In return for marrying me, I'll save your precious brother."

What could she do? She couldn't let Austin die, but if saving him meant marrying a creature like Lacy Hawkins . . .

His impatient voice tore at her very sanity. "What's it going to be, Danny? You don't have much time. The orders have already arrived."

It was a lie, of course, but it worked.

Her voice emerged in a listless monotone, void of emotion. "Yes, Lacy," she whispered, "I'll marry you."

"Good," he said curtly as he strode for the door, adding with sarcasm, "Who knows, you may come to like it." The door slammed behind him.

He returned ten minutes later with the Reverend Meeker from the Episcopal mission and two bleary-eyed troopers who'd been rousted out of their bunks to act as witnesses.

The ceremony was brief and impersonal, the Reverend reciting his passages quickly, eager to return to the comfort of his night clothes. When it was Danny's turn to speak, she felt the pressure of Lacy's grip at her elbow, and mechanically, she mumbled some incoherent words that sounded vaguely like 'I do'. Then it was over. She had kept her part of the bargain. She'd become Mrs. Lacy Hawkins.

The orders for Austin Fleming's execution had not been received. That much was a lie. But Lacy had told Danny the truth when he claimed to be the only one who could save him. Selfish ambition made him sit down late that night and carefully compose the letter that would secure Austin's freedom.

When he was finished, he folded it and placed it inside a sealed envelope and sent it off to Fort Wingate with one of his best men.

At Fort Wingate one Major Arthur Tate wondered bitterly how Captain Lacy Hawkins had managed to learn those embarrassing secrets that could, if revealed, put an end to his military career. He, along with the rest of the world, had apparently underestimated Lacy's knack for sniffing out indiscretions.

Angrily, he crushed the letter in his whitened fist and tossed it into the fire. So, Captain Hawkins wanted a favor and if he didn't get it, he was going to bring some pretty unsavory events to light. Tate knew exactly where he had to go to effect this so-called favor. After all, he hadn't worked his way up in the military ranks to have some snot-nosed southern brat shoot his reputation full of holes.

Taking quill pen in hand, he composed a letter of his own, exercising little time to decide which of his acquaintances was deserving of some pressure at this time. As the words flowed across the paper, the wheels began to turn, setting in motion a chain of events and a series of confidential, highly personal orders whose inevitable end would set Austin Fleming free.

Lacy Hawkins had gambled, risking his position and his reputation, not to mention his aspirations for the future. He gambled and he won.

Within a matter of days, orders were received directly from Washington calling for the release of the prisoner.

Stepping into the bright, sunlit day from the dim interior of the guardhouse, Austin was informed that his sister had already returned to St. Louis and that his release was conditioned upon his returning to San Francisco at once. He supposed that Emmett had pulled the right strings, yet the day he left, a letter was placed in his hand and he learned how foolish he'd been to think it was Emmett's doing.

His face grew red with rage as he read Lacy's note saying that he and Danny had been married and that Austin had his new brother-in-law to thank for his freedom. Austin wanted to kill him. He wanted to wrap his fingers around Hawkins' throat and squeeze it until even the gurgling and choking ceased. To Austin, Lacy Hawkins was a conniving calculating man who'd stop at nothing to get what he wanted. He'd sensed it from the beginning and had thrown a shield of hostility between himself and Lacy, letting Lacy know that he did not wish friendship. Now, that man was married to his sister, and Austin felt himself grow weak at the thought of it.

One glance revealed a heavily armed guard congregated around the coach that was waiting to take him to California. He climbed inside, his mind in confusion. For the moment all he knew was that he was free to leave and that Danny wished never to see him again.

Lacy had managed to secure a couple of weeks' leave, pulling as many strings as he could to get even that much, and together they had left the lonely frontier outpost in the Arizona desert.

The house he had found for them on a pleasant street in St. Louis was perhaps small, but it possessed a commanding view of the river. It even had a garden in back where Danny could regain a bit of the color missing from her cheeks.

When Lacy made love to his bride, he did not expect much of a response at first, but his repeated attempts at tenderness failed to arouse any reaction. It angered him, and he found it difficult to be nice when she was making it so hard.

One night, however, as his hands glided over her silken body, her resistance seemed to break down, her body finally assuming control of her emotions. It was more than he'd ever hoped for.

He was amazed at her skill as a lover once she gave in to the urgings of her body. She seemed to exude passion, to crave it, hunger for it, and drove him to near madness. She was his now—totally and completely his, denying him nothing.

Soft moans and breathless mutterings escaped from her parted lips arousing him further. But then a single word erupted and shattered the rush of emotions surging through his body, leaving him seething with enough anger to sink his teeth savagely into her flesh.

Danny screamed and snapped abruptly out of her dream. Struggling furiously, she sprang out of the bed, rubbing the spot on her shoulder where his teeth had drawn blood.

Lacy's face was so twisted with raw emotion that it chilled her to the quick. He got up and walked toward her, green eyes menacing, jaws clamped tight, spitting the words out between gritted teeth.

"So, you haven't forgotten that dog, have you? What the hell do you think I am, stupid or something? You bitch!"

With that he brought his hand sharply across her cheek, spinning her around with force. Before she could regain her balance, he grabbed her by the shoulders and was shaking her senseless, shouting in her face.

"So it's me you lay with, but it's his name on your lips! Forget him, he's dead! You're mine now, *mine!* You belong to me!"

"It will never be you!" she screamed. "Never! You'll have to kill me first because I'll never give you what you want!"

He released her with a violent shove. "Kill you? Not on your life. You're too important to me. Or did you think I married you just because I needed a good lay? Hell, I could get that anywhere. No, lady, I did you a favor, remember?"

He sauntered back to the bed, leaving her trembling in the middle of the room. "Come here," he ordered.

Danny hesitated, fearful of what would happen next.

"Don't make me come over there and get you."

She approached the bed tremulously and laid down beside him. And with her warm tears spilling onto the sheets, she endured the rest of his repulsive lovemaking before she was allowed to turn over and drift into sleep.

When she awoke in the morning, she found him already dressed, a single bag packed waiting by the door.

"The honeymoon's over," he drawled, as she rubbed the sleep from her eyes. "I have to meet my company at Fort Lincoln. I'd take you with me but you'd only get in the way. I'll be back soon. I want you to stay here and be a good little wife, you hear?"

His voice sounded obnoxiously sweet. "Buy yourself some nice clothes to wear. Something respectable, not the kind of stuff you're used to running around in. I don't want people thinking I went and married some Indian squaw. Get that black wench up here to tend to your needs. The one who rode out to Bennett with you. I forget her name, but you get her up here. And tell that cousin of yours to stay where she is. I don't want to see her face around here."

He paused to study Danielle carefully. "I trust you've got enough money to take care of things while I'm away. I should be gone about a month, maybe two. Depends on how long it will take to wipe out those red animals." He reached for his coat and slung it over his shoulder.

"Is there anyone you like who isn't white?" Danny was surprised to hear her own voice ask the caustic question.

"No," he replied with a sneer as he bent to pick up his bag.

"Then why do you want me to send for Dossie?"

"Because it's not fitting for a lady to be seen around town without her maid, that's why. We may know you're not respectable, but no one else does, and I aim to keep it that way."

He walked to the bed and placed a wet kiss on her mouth, then turned and strode from the house.

Danny waited until he was gone before she wiped the slime off her lips. Then she dressed quickly and went to town. Her first stop was the telegraph office where she had a wire dispatched to the *Hacienda de Agua Azul*.

Her reunion with Dossie was taxing at the beginning, with both young women trying to pick up where they'd left off. But there were too many emotions in between to pretend nothing had happened. Dossie wisely did not push Danny to reveal anything, realizing that in time it would come out.

Late one night when Danny had awakened crying, her body bathed in perspiration, Dossie had crawled from her own bed and climbed softly into bed beside Danielle, holding her until, at last, the weeping subsided and the story came spilling out. The more horrible memories stayed locked tight inside, but Danny felt immense relief at having most of it in the open, and as the days went by, the women drew closer together because of it.

During the weeks that followed, Danny walked around in a state of limbo, initially unable to believe that she was far away from all the terror of the West, and that she was actually in St. Louis again with pretty new gowns to wear and someone to look after her who was also her friend.

One particularly brisk afternoon, Dossie burst into the room, breathless with excitement. She flung off her coat and pulled the woolen cap from her head, letting the snowflakes fall carelessly to the floor to melt on the carpet.

"Danny, you won't believe who just got into town!" she exclaimed, ebony eyes sparkling. "It's Zoe! Oh, Danny, it'll be just like old times, won't it?"

Would it ever be like old times again?

Zoe Fleming hadn't changed much. She was still the same pretty bubbling girl Danny remembered. "What's this I hear about you sitting cooped up in this dreadful house?" she scolded, shaking a stern finger at Danny. "Dossie tells me you never even go out. Is that true?"

Danny shrugged lifelessly. "Well, I—"

"Nonsense," interrupted Zoe. "I'm here now and I'm telling you that we shall have ourselves a grand time. We'll go shopping, attend the theater, concerts and parties. Maybe we'll even pay a midnight visit to the Bull's Head Tavern."

What a marvelous pair they made, Zoe with her sleek blond hair and bright green eyes, and Danny with her long, dark red tresses and alluring amber eyes. Together they became a familiar sight around the city of St. Louis, always surrounded by a flock of admirers, never lacking for an escort for dinner or a play. They had a wonderful time together laughing at the tongues they caused to wag so furiously. At moments Danny was even able to forget the memories that continued to haunt her.

Some nights, after returning from an evening of drinking too much champagne and dancing until dawn, she would cringe beneath her covers, struggling to keep her sobs to herself, plagued by the one stark memory that would not be shut out no matter how hard she tried. It was the memory of Alex Coulter, the feel of his arms around her and the image of countless nights spent in his embrace.

Zoe listened quietly when Danny tried to put it into words. "I can't say I know what you mean," she confessed. "But I do know that a woman never really forgets her first man—the one who made her a woman. But, to spend your whole life regretting is sad. There will be others, really there will. You must not let this thing hurt you anymore. You must put it out of your mind and learn to live for today. That's what I do, and it works."

Zoe was right, of course, and Danny tried to heed her advice by throwing herself into her social life with renewed vigor. Soon her name began to appear in the gossip columns of the city's newspapers and she was recognized wherever she went.

It succeeded in temporarily taking her mind off one obvious fact—Lacy would one day return. She knew when he did, he must not find Zoe there. She broached the subject very carefully, not wishing to hurt Zoe's feelings.

Zoe was plainly astonished, her pretty green eyes flashing and her mouth dropping open to protest.

"You don't understand," said Danny. "He's . . . he's changed. I think it would be best if you were not here. I'm sorry, Zoe, but you must leave. And very soon."

Zoe sank onto the velvet sofa, looking quite dejected. "When do you want me to go?"

"Tomorrow," Danny replied, and turned away so she would not have to witness her cousin's abject disappointment.

The next day Danielle and Dossie stood on a frozen train platform, their gloved hands snug inside fur muffs, their breath like white clouds mingling with the frosty air, watching as the train belched its way out of the station. Then they hurried home to warm their hands and feet by a toasty fire and fill their bellies with hot tea.

With Zoe gone and winter upon them, Danny retreated into the cozy warmth of the house she shared now only with Dossie. One wintry afternoon in December, with Christmas just a week away, she sat curled up in a deep armchair, her favorite afghan pulled up around her knees, the glow of the fire on her cheeks, when Dossie came in the front door. Her arms were laden with packages. Dumping the boxes onto the hallway table she reached into her pocket and pulled out an envelope.

"What is that?" Danny asked when she spied the letter in Dossie's outstretched hand. She reached for it with a frown growing on her features as soon as she recognized the words printed by hand across its upper corner. It was from Fort Lincoln.

Without ceremony she ripped open the flap and read the letter from Lacy. Jumping to her feet, she tossed the afghan aside, crying, "Don't just stand there, Dossie! Get some wine glasses from the shelf, we've got reason to celebrate!"

"Danny, what—!"

"He's not coming back, Dos! Not for a while anyway! There's too much snow out there and nothing can move—the trains, the horses, the wagons—nothing! It means he won't be back until at least the spring thaw!"

Dossie laughed out loud. "I don't believe it!" she cried, "Oh, Danny, I'm so happy!"

"So am I, Dos. And I'll tell you what we're going to do. You and I are going to spend Christmas at the *Hacienda*. How does that sound?"

Dossie went wild with excitement, dancing around the room and spilling wine on the carpet, and not caring.

Chapter 25

New York society was electric with the impending arrival of a legend—the most celebrated composer all of Europe had to offer.

The name of Anton Savanyu had spread across two continents as the darling of the musical community, and months prior to his arrival on American shores, the newspapers and periodicals were aglow with praise for the young pianist who had astounded audiences in Paris, Vienna, his native Poland—indeed, the world over.

His ability to enrapture the soul through his musical endeavors was surprising for one so young, and he'd achieved, at the age of twenty-eight, that which was seldom heard in a man's lifetime. His creative energy seemed oblivious to the fragility of his body, and in spite of an unusually slight physique, his entire being seemed characterized by refinement and dignity. He possessed a stubborn will that was difficult, if not impossible, to bend, and his natural reserve made him not one of the easiest people to know. Yet, even those who did not like him because of it, were compelled to acknowledge his abilities, and all recognized the passionate spirit. Few, if any, were impervious to his particular form of subdued magnetism.

His story was history. He was born in a small village near Warsaw, Poland, where, at the age of seven, after mastering the piano, he wrote his first composition, a polonaise, and made his first public appearance. At twelve he entered the prestigious Warsaw Conservatoire, and at fifteen, he was playing for the Royal Family of Austria at the personal request of Prince Sahan.

It soon became apparent that Poland could offer him little in terms of musical education and so he left the Conservatoire, his credentials putting his name into orbit. The obvious place to go was Vienna, the beautiful Austrian city that was second only to Paris as the musical center of Europe. His concerts there were so successful that the critics showered him with phrases such as 'indescribable perfection' and 'a genius for rapture'.

But he could not satisfy his audiences with concerts and follow his true path as a composer at the same time. His *Concerto in E-Flat Minor* was still incomplete and he found it difficult working in the charged atmosphere of the musical city. A year after arriving in Vienna, he left for home.

There he finished the *E-Flat Minor* and regained a bit of the strength that always seemed to slip from him so easily. Even his cough practically disappeared during the days he spent roaming the verdant Polish countryside. Finally, with the *E-Flat Minor* concerto finished, in October, 1867, Anton Savanyu left Poland forever.

This time he went straight to Paris where his reputation had preceded him, and it was there that his music flowered and flourished. As a composer and pianist par excellence, he revolutionized piano technique by introducing new dynamics, brilliant and daring virtuosity and new ranges of composition never heard before. One critic summed it all up by calling him a phoenix of intimacy with the piano.

Through the letters of introduction he'd brought to Paris, he met many influential people, among them the Katowice family, Polish émigrés, who remembered Anton as the child prodigy in Warsaw. They made certain that he came to the attention of wealthy and powerful families like the Rothschilds and the DeMallerays who accepted him into their fashionable world.

It led to private tutoring for the sons and daughters of rich patrons, and soon his income from teaching was handsome enough to accommodate an exceedingly comfortable lifestyle. Occasionally he still performed in public, but for the most part he was temperamentally unsuited for such performances, and eventually left the virtuoso's life behind to concentrate on teaching and composing.

He rarely left Paris those days, only once in the spring of 1870 for a visit to Lucerne, and again a year later to the sunny Spanish coast to heal the wounds of a broken love affair. His engagement to the girl, which was at first encouraged by her aristocratic family, was broken off abruptly when they viewed his failing health as a cause of concern and informed him, in a rather cold manner, that the wedding would not take place.

It deeply wounded the hypersensitive young man, severing his ability to work. At the urgings of friends, he traveled to southern Spain where time could heal his injured sensibilities and the warm Spanish sun could perform therapeutic wonders on his health, which was besieged by a hacking cough.

He returned to Paris and settled into a calm routine, spending his summers in the French countryside and performing during the concert season. Within himself he'd reached a plateau that placed him somewhere high above the pain of lost love. The choice was a simple one, he reasoned. You could either be in love and be vulnerable, or you could decide never to know love and so be able to stand on the outside and manipulate a relationship. With the decision never to love again locked away in his heart, Anton turned his attention to the only true love of his life—composing. It was during the peaceful days that followed that his genius reached its height.

However, it was not without its cost. Within a few years, with the state of his health rapidly declining, Anton found his funds dipping dangerously low. And so, with the clamor of voices calling his name, growing louder from across the Atlantic, he gave his final concert in Paris to a wild ovation and left for the United States. It did not seem to him that the surly Americans had any real appreciation for his art, but those who did were exceptionally monied and willing to pay handsomely to hear him perform.

Public concerts were out of the question, so it was arranged by his managers that he would perform privately for three or four of the most prominent families, with a final performance at the White House for President and Mrs. Grant and select members of Congress.

The ocean crossing had been difficult, but once docked in New York, he quickly regained his strength and prepared for his first performance at the Windsor Hotel in the private suite of the Cornelius Vanderbilts.

'Anton Savanyu glowed', was how *The New York Herald* described his performance. *The New York Times* was even more lavish.' Unequaled perfection. Savanyu takes us on a flight into rapture, then deposits us back on earth with our senses whirling and our souls still soaring'.

At the elegant Windsor, his suite was besieged with reporters and well-wishers. A steady stream of uniformed bellboys carried in bundles of flowers and telegrams from places as far away as San Francisco, Chicago and New Orleans.

Later that evening, when he was alone, he reached into the pocket of his waistcoat and extracted a piece of paper bearing a hastily scribbled reminder of his itinerary. His eyes skipped past the name at the top, that of the Vanderbilts, and settled on the second name on the page—Fleming.

Anton sighed and wondered what this place called Bennett, Colorado was like. His performance there would coincide with the Christmas holiday, and it would be his first spent in the company of strangers, with nothing but his own music for company. Shoving the unpleasant thought aside, his mind strayed back to the Fleming name. Hadn't he heard that there was a nephew from France? And a niece? He smiled. Perhaps there would be some company for him after all. It would be good to see a countryman again, for he'd long since considered France his adopted homeland. It made him feel, for the moment at least, not so very alone.

But Christmas was still a week away, and meanwhile, he had to endure the harsh and exceedingly wet winter days of New York City. Cooped up in his suite at the Windsor, his spirits grew weaker, and not even the heat of the fire was enough, at times, to chase the chill from his bones.

December, 1875, was a time of unbearable depression for the pensive man. Adrift in a strange land, plagued by the presence of winter, his emotional nature was barely sufficient to sustain him, let alone bear up under the weight of his rapidly declining health. Only this morning he had spit up some blood. Merely a speck of red, but it had not been the first time.

Idly, his slender fingers caressed the cold ivory keys of the piano the management had installed in his suite. The sounds that filled the room soon blossomed into a wordless realm of feeling, pulling the composer away from his depression so that every thought, feeling and fiber of his being was engulfed by it.

The music floated through the air infiltrating the tiniest places of the elegant hotel. Those who heard it paused from whatever they were doing to listen. Those who worked in the white-tiled kitchens several floors below stopped from their work to close their eyes to the divine sound. Even those who walked the wet streets of Fifth Avenue paused beneath their umbrellas to allow their souls to be caught and held by one who had such power over them.

He had the power to reach those inexpressible realms of feeling which were inaccessible to all logic and where the very act of speaking was frivolously incidental. Essentially, he was a romantic in his attempts to capture and express a variety of moods through his music. But he was, nonetheless, a perfectionist who was never satisfied with imitations or the kind of rhetorical expressions found so common among the artists of the day. He was a purist who sought within himself absolute perfection of his form. His gods were Bach and Mozart. But his inspiration sprang from the depths of his own soul.

A single oil lamp burned low in the room set three stories above Fifth Avenue as the twenty-eight-year-old composer sat at his piano, eyes haggard, face like glass, playing one of his preludes with tearful desperation.

Chapter 26

Wearing an elegant, bronze satin dressing gown, Danny was eating a breakfast of coffee and warm raisin biscuits in the glass-enclosed porch of Emmett Fleming's study. The sky was overcast with a thick covering of storm clouds. Soon, very soon snow will cover the earth like a shroud she thought, sipping coffee and gazing out the tall windows. She lounged back in the chaise, drawing her gown tighter around her.

"Would you mind if I joined you?" A voice from the doorway interrupted her thoughts.

She turned and looked into the dark brown eyes of a man whose face bore a serious expression and whose entire countenance seemed at once formal and yet relaxed.

"No, not at all," she replied. She swung her feet around to sit up, and as she did her gown slid open for just a moment exposing a bare slender thigh. She quickly replaced it, but not before he got a look at the creamy flesh. "Would you care for some coffee? If you would rather have tea, I could ring for some."

"Coffee would be fine," he said in a pleasant voice.

Danny poured a steaming cup for him from the pot that sat on the silver tray. "Please have a seat, Mr . . . ?"

"Savanyu. Anton Savanyu."

"Oh!" Danny's surprise plainly registered on her face. Anton Savanyu! Had she heard him correctly? Oh, she knew the brilliant composer was going to play for them, but she never thought he would pop up like this! She scolded herself shamelessly, knowing that if she had really been paying attention, she would have recognized him instantly from the countless pictures in the newspapers and the posters she had seen spread throughout Paris. Her embarrassment was obvious in the flush that turned her cheeks crimson. "Please, forgive me, Monsieur Savanyu."

"Forgive you, *mademoiselle?* What is there to forgive?" He smiled at her, his serious expression lost.

"For not recognizing you. I should have since I have long admired your music."

"For the compliment, I thank you," he said. "And for the late recognition, I also thank you. It is not often that I get a chance to be simply another person before someone recognizes me. And once they find out who I am, they always appear to be overcome with this strangely peculiar urge not to be themselves." He shrugged and sat down. "And whom do I have the pleasure of sitting with?"

"My name is Danielle Hawkins," she answered, feeling his eyes on her.

"You are an acquaintance of our host, Monsieur Fleming?" He felt no particular need to hide his curiosity about the beautiful woman he had stumbled across this morning quite by accident.

"Emmett Fleming is my uncle."

"Ah, yes," he remarked, his eyes lighting up. "So you are the French niece! And you have a brother, that is what I am told. Your brother is with you?"

Suddenly the young woman who seemed to overflow with grace, dropped the spoon into her cup and fumbled with it nervously. "Uh, well, no, he is not here. He is . . . that is, I believe he is in San Francisco."

Unaware of the intrusion into her privacy and oblivious to his lack of manners, he asked, "There is something between your brother and yourself that is not good?"

Danny looked up with surprise in her tawny eyes. "How did you— I mean, what makes you think so?"

He looked directly at her, his expression grave. "Do you think I could create the music I do if I did not possess a natural perception?"

Danny was speechless.

He added with a grin, "You looked as if you had seen a ghost when I mentioned him." He watched her carefully and saw a weak smile touch her lips at his attempt at humor. "I wonder what it is that would turn a sister's heart against her brother."

She was annoyed that he would not let the matter die.

"There are some hurts, Monsieur Savanyu, that know no limitations and are, indeed, heightened by the intimacy of the source."

He said nothing, but a shadow swept across his features as though he were remembering some of his own hurts.

"We appear to have gotten off to a poor start," Danny sourly remarked. She rose to her feet, bringing him immediately to his.

"You are leaving?" he asked, whipping a linen napkin from his knee.

"Yes, I am going to my room. I understand you are honoring us this evening by playing for us. I look forward to it." With that, she walked away, leaving Anton Savanyu alone in the glass-encased room with empty coffee cups and the scent of her perfume lingering in the air.

That evening Dossie helped Danny slip into the dress she had bought especially for this affair. It was an exquisite gown of green glacé silk, cut daringly low at the neck, with two thin straps holding it up and exposing the delicate skin at her shoulders which, by now, had lost its deep bronze and had returned to its fashionable alabaster hue. Light folds of silk draped across her abdomen and trailed off into a swirl of hidden pleats that revealed iridescent shimmers of the palest pastel shades when she walked. She descended the stairs feeling a bit reckless, as the stares on the faces in the room were enough to convince her that she'd done an excellent job of looking her best.

As she mingled with the guests, she brought embarrassingly obvious glances from men who kissed her hand and piercing glares of jealousy from their wives. The names that filled the guest list were those that appeared on the front pages of newspapers throughout the country; names like Aubrey Wells, the Texas cattleman, and the millionaire industrialist, Chester McVey, whose eyes lingered a trifle longer on her than they should have. Government was well represented also, proving to Danny that Senators and Congressmen were as wicked in their ways as anyone else.

Threading her way through the crowded salon, she spotted Zoe looking ravishing in a pale, ivory satin gown that made the emeralds at her throat and her eyes glisten. "It looks to me as though your father is on his way to Washington, Zoe," Danny teased her. "Are you ready to make the move to the capital?"

Zoe flashed her pretty green eyes. "What makes you think that if Father goes to Washington, I'll go with him?" There was the usual unmistakable hint of mischief in her voice.

Danielle shrugged fatalistically and gave Zoe a sympathetic look. "Well, Zoe," she said, almost apologetically, "you know that wherever he goes, you'll have to—"

"Yes, but that will all be over very soon." Zoe bit her lip, watching with excitement the way the question spread across Danny's face. "Oh, I can't keep it a secret any longer!" she exclaimed. "Look!" Slipping her hand out of an elbow-length satin glove, she held it up for Danny's inspection. A glittering diamond and ruby studded engagement ring adorned her finger. "I'm engaged," she announced, her face beaming. "My fiancé is here somewhere. You'll see him later. But Danny, I think you already know him." She cast a demure glance at her cousin through the thick lashes that fanned her eyes. "It's John Avery."

Danny broke into a smile. "Zoe! Why didn't you tell me?"

"It didn't officially happen until I returned from St. Louis, and since you were coming for Christmas, I thought I'd surprise you with the news in person. Don't you think it's wonderful?" Zoe's eyes were like sparkling green lights.

Squeezing Zoe's hand, Danny said, "Yes, I do. It's absolutely wonderful news and I'm so happy for you both. You must tell me all about it after the concert."

In the next room the guests were already seated and a hush had fallen over them. The concert was about to begin; they waited only for the composer to enter. Danny sat back in a tufted armchair and Zoe sat next to her, eyes still shining with excitement, a rosy tint to her white complexion. A strange tenseness could be felt as everybody waited for Anton Savanyu. A cough here, a muffled whisper there, a sigh, and then silence as the door opened.

He walked to the piano, staring straight ahead. In his head were the sounds that would soon flow from the piano. Those who had never seen him were surprised at his slight body and unusually pallid complexion, and it ran quickly across some minds that this was an imposter—that it was not possible for this frail creature to live up to the demands the world placed upon him. Yet their suspicions were soon dispersed as they watched him seat himself at the keyboard and stare at it for a long moment, as though contemplating its potential.

Anton had already decided that he would perform his

Polonaise in F-Sharp Minor, not the piece on the program. It was one which he felt very deeply about, and therefore he rarely shared it with others. Privately, he dedicated it to the lovely lady he had met earlier in the day. The one whose slanted amber eyes had made him feel so weak. The one whose grace and charm, even whose nervous fumbling, could not hide the fire he sensed beneath the surface. It was the same kind of fire that had created compositions such as this Polonaise. Anton dedicated it to her—to the siren whose very presence permeated the room as much as his own. Tonight he would play for her the piece he had written from his tortured soul as a confession.

He placed his fingers gently on the ivory keys and began to play.

Zoe leaned forward in her seat and placed a hand softly on Danny's shoulder. "What do you think of Mr. Savanyu?" she whispered.

Danny brought her fan discreetly to her face, replying behind it. "He plays beautifully."

"Nothing more?"

"He plays magnificently then."

"Really, Danny," Zoe huffed under her breath. "I'm afraid not even the smoke from Daddy's cigar can mask your expression. Why, to look at you, anyone would think he's the most handsome man in the world. He's so skinny!"

Danny shot an annoyed glance at her. "Mr. Savanyu *is* one of the handsomest men I've ever met, and I find it difficult to close my eyes and restrict myself to just one aspect of his beauty." As far as she was concerned, the matter was ended.

Zoe slid back in her seat, catching instantly her mother's smoldering glare. Soon, Zoe reminded herself, there will be no more of *that.* Soon she would be married and answerable to no one, least of all her mother and father. A small smile erupted on her lips and she closed her eyes again to let the music carry her away to beautiful places with its intimacy.

When Anton finished, he hurried out of the room to the sound of applause. Danny noticed that his face was deathly pale, void of color, his eyes glassy and distraught. She also saw his hand go up to his mouth to hide his coughs. She was tempted to follow him to inquire after him, when a hand reached for hers and hastily escorted her into the adjoining dining room where cocktails and a buffet were being served.

"He'll be back," Emmett told her, patting her smooth

white hand. "He told me he would join us for cocktails. I suspect with a performance like the one he gave here tonight he's in need of some rest."

"Uncle," she breathed, "I've never imagined it possible . . . I mean, what he did here tonight . . . it was so . . ."

"I know, honey, I know," Emmett said. He felt the same loss for words as his niece, unable to put into thoughts the surge of emotions the young composer had managed to stir inside of him . . . indeed, inside the breast of every person who left the sitting room behind, its walls still reverberating with the power of his music.

Emmett spied a face in the crowd and scurried off, leaving Danny in his usual negligent, but harmless, way.

A moment later a man in a blue uniform appeared at her side with two glasses of champagne. "Would you care for some, Mrs. Hawkins?" He placed a glass in her hand, not allowing her to refuse.

"Thank you, Major." She did not know who he was, but she recognized the markings of rank on his uniform. "You appear to have me at a disadvantage. I do not recall having met before."

"We haven't. I know your husband, Captain Hawkins."

"Oh, I see," Danny remarked, immediately uncomfortable. "Tell me, Major . . . what did you say your name was?"

"Armstrong, James Armstrong, at your service."

"Yes, well, tell me, Major Armstrong, what is the situation like out West at this point?" She was eager to know what was happening in the Dakota territory where people she knew were fighting for their lives.

"Oh, don't worry, ma'am, Captain Hawkins is a good soldier, one of the best. He'll take good care of himself and his troops, and as soon as this mess is cleaned up, I'm sure he'll be on the first train back." He lowered his voice and shook his head. "Although I've got to tell you that from reports we've received, the whole country out that way is frozen solid. Between you and me, I wouldn't expect him until the spring."

Danny wondered whether she saw a strange little smile dart across his mouth. "Yes, but what of the situation with the Sioux?" How could he know she cared not a fig about what happened to Lacy?

The major's expression turned grave. "The Indian Bureau's special inspector stated that the Indians living outside the reservations are well-fed and well-armed and recommended that troops be sent against them as soon as possible. Then, of course, there's the Black Hills mess. From what I understand, the Sioux and Cheyenne agents have been notified to order all Indians off the reservations to come in to surrender by January 31st."

Danny's eyes widened in disbelief. "But that's so soon! It's the middle of winter! How could they expect all those people to move? We both know they are *not* well-fed or well-armed. How many of them would die making the trip?"

"I don't know the answer to that," he answered, avoiding her eyes. "But I do know that if they don't make that trip and report to the agents, the Government is prepared to use military force to subdue them."

"What of the Black Hills?" she asked, brushing aside the awful threat. "What's going to happen to them?"

"Again, I don't know," he admitted. "But that commission Washington sent out in September failed. The Indians wouldn't sell. It's my guess the Government will disregard the wishes of the Sioux and appropriate a sum they feel is reasonable for the purchase."

Danny eyed him carefully, weighing not only his words but the feelings she sensed emerging along with them. "How is it, Major Armstrong, that you are not Indian fighting out West? How is it that you are able to enjoy the pleasures of a private dinner party when the others are doing the dirty work?" There was something strangely unsettling about this man and she aimed to find out what it was. It never occurred to her that her questions might anger him, and if he had been another man, they might well have done that.

But James Armstrong was not quick to anger. He could sense in her feelings a much different nature than what appeared on the surface. At first he had expected to meet a woman as cold and shallow as her husband, but in her presence, he knew it must have been through some unimaginable quirk of fate that such a despicable man as Hawkins could secure such a woman for himself. He had met the man on several occasions and each meeting only reinforced his distaste for the southern Army captain.

"You have not answered my question, Major. Why is it

that you are here while the others are out there?" She would not let him get away, and she expected him to try. But his reply shocked her in a way she did not anticipate.

"Because it *is* dirty work, Mrs. Hawkins, and because as long as there are men around like your husband who seem to enjoy all the killing so thoroughly, then at least *I'll* keep my hands clean and my conscience clear as long as I can."

Danny lowered her gaze. "Please forgive me," she said softly, ashamed of her needless attack on him. "It's been a while since I've met a man with a conscience. I guess I had to make a fool of myself in order to find out whether you had one."

He smiled at her tenderly. "I don't think there's anything a woman like you could do to appear foolish to a man like me."

"But surely there is, Major," she laughed back. "In fact, you said it yourself." His face remained blank. "My husband. I would say that's one thing I did of which I feel immensely foolish. And judging from your opinion of him, I'd say you quite agree with me but are too much of a gentleman to admit it."

He chuckled under his breath at her perceptiveness and wondered when he had ever met a woman so thoroughly engaging as this one.

"Are you married, Major?" Danny asked, as she drained her glass of the last of its bubbly liquid.

He blushed, misreading her thoughts. "Yes, I am."

The sound of her laughter put him back at ease. "You mustn't be so mischievous. I simply meant that when you and Mrs. Armstrong are in St. Louis, I would consider it my pleasure if you would call on me."

"I don't expect to be in St. Louis in the near future," he said, and something in his voice chased away her gayness. "As a matter of fact, this is my last night here. Tomorrow I leave to rejoin my company. I was only sent here to carry some papers."

"I see. And what is your destination?"

"Fort Lincoln."

"That's where my husband is stationed!"

"Yes, I know," he said, eyes sweeping the floor. "My company has been ordered to meet up with the Seventh. They're planning a big campaign against the Sioux this spring, and I suppose they need all the men they can get."

She gently placed a slender white hand on his sleeve. "I'm so sorry. It's such a shame that decent men have to get caught up in a thing like this."

"Yes, well, those are my orders," he replied stiffly.

"And you shall follow them to the letter." She forced a smile to her lips. "Well then, Major, you must say 'hello' to my husband when you see him. You might also mention that I am having a splendid time." She laughed and glided away from him, leaving him with a sad sort of smile on his face.

Her tawny eyes searched the room for the one face she wished would appear. But when at last it seemed apparent that the composer would not be joining them for cocktails as he had promised, she slipped quietly from the crowded room. She wanted to get away from the cigar smoke. It was too cold to venture outdoors, so she headed for the one place where she knew the frosty night air was allowed to enter through bare window panes. She closed the door to Emmett's study behind her and crossed the floor silently, her slippers sinking softly into the deep pile of the Oriental carpet that graced the hardwood floor. She opened the door to the small glass porch and felt the rush of cool air wash over her. Standing with her eyes closed, she breathed the fresh air deeply into her lungs.

"I thought you would not come." His voice came from the shadows. She could not see his face, but she could feel his presence all about her.

Her voice was weak, barely a whisper. "I didn't know at first, but then I knew I would find you here."

"I have taken the liberty of pouring some cognac. Will you have a glass with me?" He stepped forward, a glass in each hand. "I do not usually drink cognac, but the color of it so matches your eyes, I thought it an appropriate toast." He took a sip of the brandy. "It is a strange feeling, this," he said quietly, unafraid to reveal his emotions. "Drinking the amber liquid and feeling it warm my mouth and throat, as I look into your eyes and feel myself drowning. What would you suggest I do, Danielle?"

She gazed at him, trying to read his features. "Save yourself, Anton," she whispered. "I would suggest that you save yourself."

Hours later he was beyond saving. He returned to his bedroom, tired and needing rest. Without bothering to remove his clothing, he stretched his lean body across the bed, wondering how it was possible to know the things about Danielle Fleming that he did without their having spoken of them.

It was preposterous to think himself in love with a woman he scarcely knew. And yet he was fascinated by the strange paradox she presented. He found himself wondering whether it was possible for a young lady who had gained a racy reputation in St. Louis to appear so quiet and easily flustered as this one seemed to be. He decided that it was, because there was nothing false about Danielle Fleming. He guessed she had the capacity to be many different people in one, and it only served to increase her magnetism.

Of her beauty there was no doubt. Her softly parted lips played reckless games with his passions, making him ever so aware of the ache in his loins whenever he looked at her. Before meeting her he had been slightly put off by the somewhat notorious adventures he had heard of. At times Anton had an almost exaggerated regard for social conventions, a trait viewed by many as a counterbalance to his disregard for musical rules and regulations. His aversion, however, lasted only until he saw her for himself and was at once mesmerized by her charm, captured by those devastatingly good looks and drawn to the extreme vulnerability that lay bared beneath her gay exterior.

For her part, Danny saw Anton's polite reserve as a challenge to her own powers, and yet she quickly succumbed to the fascination of his personality and the power of his music. The same laconic presence and limited responses that made so many content to admire Anton Savanyu from afar, merely drew her closer.

On the surface it appeared as though they were the most unlikely couple to come into being, and yet, this evening, with only the light of the crescent moon bathing their faces, without a single touch being exchanged between them, they agreed that upon the completion of his tour Anton would join her in St. Louis. Yes, she assured him, she would arrange to have a piano moved into the house so he could practice. He would register at the hotel, of course, but she would give him the key to her home and she would be there whenever he needed her. It would be often, he had whispered as she turned to leave.

She was gone, but in her place he could still hear her breath close to his ear, and he could still smell the heady fragrance of her perfume lingering in his nostrils, turning his blood hot and his throat dry. Would she really be his? It was not the husband that frightened him. There was some elusive quality that told him otherwise.

A cough broke from Anton's lips, then another and another, until his frail body was constricted with spasms erupting from his chest. He grabbed for the handkerchief in his breast pocket and held it before his mouth until at last the coughing ceased and he could catch his breath again. But upon removing the white cloth, a gasp caught in his throat when he looked down and saw it spattered with blood.

Rising from the bed with difficulty, feeling especially weak in the legs, Anton began to undress, cursing in his native Polish tongue against the despicable weather that had brought this accursed bronchitis to him. That's what it was, he told himself . . . nothing more. The excitement of the tour and the strange foods that wreaked havoc on his sensitive stomach all helped trap the cold in his chest. He complained bitterly as he leaned over to poke the fire into flames. In the morning his party would leave for San Francisco where the climate would be kinder to him. From there they would go to Washington and the private performance at the White House. After that it was to be home to Paris. But all of a sudden there was a change in plans. The stop after the White House would not be home, it would be St. Louis, Missouri, where he would stay as long as he liked. Exhausted, he rolled over and drifted to sleep, his brown lashes closed over ashen cheeks.

Upon returning home, Danny found two letters waiting for her, one bearing Austin's familiar flowery scrawl. She carried the letter to her wardrobe and kneeling down, reached into a corner to pull out a small, hinged metal box that had not been touched since the last time one of Austin's letters had arrived. Now, as she had done the other times, she placed the envelope into the box, closed the lid and shoved it back into its nook. This letter, along with all the others from Austin, would remain unread.

She tore the flap open on the remaining envelope and cringed when she saw the seal of the United States Army at the top of the page. It was from Lacy. Reading it quickly, she smiled. Weather conditions and some unexpected trouble with the Sioux made his return to St. Louis indefinite, and as far as he could tell, he would not make it back until at least April. She read the half-apologetic, half-sarcastic letter and supposed she was happy. At least she was free of him for the time being. It should have made her glad, but it failed to do so.

None of it succeeded in making her happy—not the beautiful ball gowns and exquisite riding habits that filled her wardrobe, not the glittering parties, not the scores of men who sought her. What did any of it matter, she thought dismally, when Alex was dead? There was no bringing him back except in the recesses of her memory where she would never forget, or in the depths of her heart where she knew she would trade everything to have him again. She wondered whether she could love a man like Anton Savanyu. In her heart she knew she already did. But was she *in love* with him? That was something only time would tell. It remained to be seen whether he could fill the void in her life, whether he could fill her with the passion that only one other man had been able to do. Would she find in those soft brown eyes the brilliance she had once seen in a pair of silver ones?

The afternoon he arrived in St. Louis was laden with moisture, clouds about to break at any moment, with dampness creeping into every corner and the whole city looking like it was covered in a drab shroud. She helped him off with his coat and hurried to make some tea. He looked thinner and paler than she remembered. "Here, drink this," she said, offering a cup of hot fragrantly scented tea into his cold hands. Then she went to the fire and plunged the brass poker into it to revive the flames she'd allowed to grow too dim. When the fire was again throwing its warmth into the room, she sat down beside him on the sofa. "Perhaps it was not a good idea for you to come," she said, watching him sip the tea. "This dreadful weather is not good for your health."

He dismissed it with a wave of his hand. "No, do not worry about my health," he told her. "It's just a cold. It's nothing really."

"Anton, how long have you had this cold?" She recalled that he had had it at Christmas time. "Have you seen a doctor?"

"I told you not to worry about that, my darling." He placed the tea cup down and took her hand gently in his. "I have been plagued with colds all my life for which I have consulted many doctors. Indeed, one time it was so bad that friends called in a doctor and do you know what the stupid man suggested? That I be bled." He grimaced, wrinkling his nose at the prospect. "Needless to say, I would have none of it. So they called in another doctor who was of such dubious medical skill that I had him properly tossed out of my chambers. And so they brought in a third doctor who prescribed medicines that could be found in none of the pharmacies. So, you can well see that I have come to place little regard in the skills of medical men. According to one, I have already expired. According to a second, I am in the process of expiring, and according to a third, I shall one day expire. As you can see, here I am today, the same as ever."

Danny laughed, throwing her head back so that her hair fell softly over her shoulders and cascaded in long silken threads down her back. Suddenly she felt the touch of his lips at her throat and his hands behind her neck pulling her toward him. His fingers were cold when they caressed her flesh but as they moved over her body they began to grow warmer, hotter, and soon burned across her skin, proclaiming the true strength of the man next to her.

When they finished their lovemaking and picked up their clothes from the floor, both of them weak from their own passions, they settled in front of the fire to speak those words that could not be uttered until they had tasted each other's desires. As the evening wore on and all light except the orange glow of the flames faded from the room, Danny felt herself drawing closer to Anton. Gradually, all the fears she had, all the doubts of him, were dispelled, and at long last it was to this man she turned for the relief she so desperately craved.

It was to him she told her painful story . . . all of it, even the parts she had purposely kept hidden from Zoe and Dossie. It was to him she turned when words would not express the feelings that consumed her—when there was nothing left to do but sit in silence and allow the tears to spill unchecked, with only his smoldering presence beside her to tell her that she was no longer alone. And, it was through his body that she found a revival of the passion she thought had ceased long ago with another man's death.

Anton Savanyu wrapped his arms tightly around the trembling young woman. He loved her. He needed her. He knew now that the love which emanated from his being for this woman was equal in depth and height and breadth to that love attained when he sat at his piano and lost himself in the magic of his music. He loved her, and if there was any doubt in his mind before, there was no longer. There was something else he had discovered this evening which answered the question that had plagued him. Now he knew she would always belong to another.

Chapter 27

Alex awoke in a cell, alone, his arms manacled behind him and connected by a strip of heavy metal links to the shackles about his ankles. The hard dirt floor of the cell felt stone cold to his cheek, and he lay there feeling sickened by the stench that filled his nostrils. He was degraded by being forced to wallow in his own waste, but still too weak to lift himself out of it. He realized with a start that, in spite of himself, he was managing to stay alive. It revolted him, and he cursed his body for acting of its own volition. He had even been eating the food that was slipped in to him through a small opening at the bottom of the iron door. Mechanically, he crept toward it on his knees and lapped it up like a starving animal, oblivious to its rancid taste, uncaring about its awful smell, intent only on assuaging his awful hunger.

It went on like that for how long he did not know, until his mind realized what his body was up to, and then it triggered a reaction of retching so violent that it soon became physically impossible to take the nauseating slop into his mouth and swallow it. Each day after that the tray was removed from his cell by someone unmoved by his moans of agony. Each day, despite the fact that his wounds were healing, it became harder for him to lift himself out of the sickening muck.

Once awakened to the terrible truth of where he was, the efforts made by his body to sustain itself were obliterated by a single desire to die, as every fiber of his being rebelled at the cruelty of this living death. To a man like Alex Coulter, who had always possessed more pride than most men, this form of existence was perhaps the worst . . . a thousand times worse than the death he craved so desperately. But as soon as the guards discovered what he was up to, they came for him and taught him how they dealt with prisoners who were foolish enough to think they could take their own worthless lives. Through a succession of merciless beatings, Alex Coulter learned to do as he was told, and in his case, he was being ordered to stay alive.

So he did, but as his strength returned, the guards had a different reason to inflict their punishments on him. It was hard for them to believe that any man could be capable of the kind of resistance they were getting from this recalcitrant prisoner. No matter how many beatings Alex endured, he still rebelled against their authority. In the end it was the solitary confinement and the regular sting of the whip that broke him. When he ceased giving them trouble they returned him to his cell allowing him out only to work.

During the day he was moved with the other prisoners, each man chained by leg irons to the one in front and behind, forming a single file of ragged men, trudging in silence to the work site. They used shovels to dig deep trenches in the mud-soaked earth beneath the blistering Mexican sun. Their sweat-soaked bodies strained against the weight of the iron shackles and contorted beneath the razor-sharp whip, tearing the flesh from the bone and leaving gaping lacerations on their backs, arms and legs. Reality was the continuous sound of agonized groans that haunted the darkened cells at night.

With the thought of death out of reach, Alex turned his attention to escape in order to preserve what sanity he had left. The thought obsessed him, occupying his every waking moment until he thought he would go mad.

At night while the others slept his mind worked feverishly devising some elaborate plan that would win his freedom. Each day he sought to pick up a clue, but without a weapon, and shackled like an animal, he was powerless. His inability to escape threw him into a wild frenzy, igniting his dulled mind with a spark of its old brilliance, and the desperation that gripped him soon turned to stark rage. More than anything it was that that attributed to his survival, indeed, to his very growth. When most men were suffering with defeated spirits, Alex raged within himself, feeding off the energy of his own fury.

He followed orders blindly, ignoring as best he could the taunts and jeers of the guards who never addressed him as anything other than dog or swine, or the one that made his skin crawl—heathen. How long had he been here? Three months? Four? Time lost all meaning to him. He had long since given up trying to put some meaning into his state of affairs. Nothing made any sense anymore. Just when he thought his life had taken some recognizable form, his ears were still ringing from its awful shattering as it all broke up into a million irreparable fragments. He wondered bitterly whether he would ever be able to still this new wretched reminder of a painful past. Once again a trust had been broken—once again his love had been sent crashing to the ground. He was a fool to ever have thought it could be otherwise.

More than he hated the guards, he hated himself for the weakness that had deceived him into thinking that a man he once called friend could be trusted—that a woman he once thought he loved actually loved him. He could feel the venom flow through his veins at the thought of them, and always when their faces filtered into his mind, he cast them out viciously. The sting of the whip as it tore pieces of flesh from his back could not come close to the torment he suffered on account of that man and woman. The thought of his own ignorant serving of their cruel self-interests blinded him with white rage. There was only one purpose to his being now—escape.

Some days later the bearded ragged mess of a man, practically unrecognizable from the others except for the color of his eyes, stood before the desk of the Mexican colonel. Alex wondered why he had been dragged out of his cell in the middle of the night for this meeting. The man seated at the desk, with his shiny black boots propped up on its edge, waited a long time before he raised his eyes from the newspaper he had opened in front of him. At length he rose and came forward. "Do not worry," he assured the guards. "This *thing* will give us no trouble, but if he does, shoot him." His voice held no emotion, not even a sneer behind the contemptuous words. Even his eyes showed not a glimmer of hatred, disgust, satisfaction—nothing. "Look at you, you are filth," he said to the prisoner. "There is so much mud caked on you that I can't even see what you look like underneath. You stink, too. When you leave, I will have to open the window to let the smell out." He circled Alex as he spoke, eyeing him carefully. "And yet," he continued slowly, turning the new thought over in his mind, "and yet, you speak fluent French."

A spark ignited in the prisoner's silver eyes before they narrowed into suspicion.

"You were unconscious when they brought you here and you were ranting like a madman," the Colonel said. "But not in Spanish or English. Nor were you raving in Apache, since that is what you are supposed to be." He turned his look away to ponder the mumblings he had heard from an unconscious man. The colonel drew closer, enough to smell the sweat as it ran from the prisoner's pores. "No," he said, measuring his words carefully. "Instead, you spoke French. And not the type of French a man might learn in a brothel in New Orleans. It was fluent, despite the obscenities." He pivoted sharply and walked several paces away, then turned and faced Alex. "I am asking myself what kind of a man it is who is a killer, winds up in a place like this and speaks French. Yes, I wonder about a man like you, especially since, you see, *señor*, I, too, speak fluent French." He scratched at his black beard.

"You can learn a lot of things about a man from his ravings. For one thing, you can learn who he is not. For instance, I know that you are not the Apache Indian those idiots think you are. Tell me, *Señor* Coulter, how does a man of your cunning fall into a situation like this?"

Alex leveled his gaze on the man's dark-skinned face. "You seem to have all the answers already," he remarked dryly.

"Not quite," the colonel replied. "So perhaps you can enlighten me on a few points."

"Unless you like being told to go to hell, then I wouldn't ask if I were you." Alex's voice was tightly controlled, and even though the threat was a mild one, the hint of something worse sizzled hotly in the air between them.

The colonel's face turned white. "I must warn you that I will not tolerate threats, particularly from filth like you. You forget that I can have you killed at any moment!"

"But you won't."

"Now who has the answers?" the colonel asked angrily. Approaching Alex warily, he said, "There is a big price on your head up North." He was surprised to hear the prisoner laugh out loud.

"If you're thinking of turning me over to them for that lousy reward money, forget it. I've been through that already and I don't think the Army's going to want to pay twice for me." His laughter dripped with scorn.

"That is not what I had in mind." The colonel looked over his shoulder, mumbled some quick words to the guards and sent them marching briskly from the room. "As I was saying, it is not reward money that interests me. No, I am more interested in silver—the kind of silver that you have access to. I thought you might be persuaded to part with some of it in return for which you could buy anything you wanted." He walked to his desk and sat down.

"Such as?"

"Freedom," he replied matter-of-factly. It brought no response from the prisoner who stood silently with his lips drawn in a tight line. "I know your kind of man, Coulter. To a man like you freedom is something worth dying for. That is why I force you to go on living. Maybe if I dangle your freedom in front of you in return for what I want, we can both wind up with something."

"What makes you think I kept any of it for myself?"

"Because you would be a fool not to."

"Then I guess that makes me a bigger fool than you think, Colonel, because I kept none of it. If that's all you wanted from me, then I'll go back to my cell now."

The colonel jumped to his feet and smashed his fist down on the desk. "That will *not* be all!" he cried. "Your answers are unsatisfactory. Unless I hear the ones I want to hear, I will see to it that you never leave this prison alive and that each day of your life be more hideous until your death. Do I make myself clear?"

Alex remained tight-lipped.

"I take your silence as approval," the colonel declared. "Now, you will answer my questions. First, where is the silver?"

"Go to hell."

The blood rose quickly to the colonel's face, but he did not explode as he looked like he would. "How much of it is there?"

"Like I said, go to hell."

This time the man did react. He screamed for the guards who came bounding into the room expecting to find the prisoner at their colonel's throat. They were surprised to find him merely standing there with an amused grin on his face, while the colonel stormed about the room. "Take him back,

and see that he receives no food for the next seven days.
Perhaps when he is hungry, he will have the answers I want.
Get him out of here!"

As they closed around Alex, he suddenly wrenched himself
free and flung himself toward the colonel's desk. There,
opened to a center page was the newspaper, and even upside
down, Alex Coulter recognized the face of his wife.

It was Danny! Smiling radiantly for the camera, her
unspeakable beauty enhanced by the elegant gown she wore
and the sparkling jewels at her throat. Her arm was entwined
in that of a frail looking man who beamed at her with much,
too much, of his feelings revealed in his eyes.

The Mexican colonel saw the shock and outrage on the
prisoner's face and mistook its meaning. Seizing the opportunity to further taunt him, he strode forward and snatched
the paper away. "Here, you want to see?" He offered it to
Alex. "Have a look at the kind of woman a dog like you will
never know."

Alex took the paper into hands that trembled with rage.
His cold metallic eyes took in every bit of the picture, then
scanned the caption below. The photograph had been taken a
few weeks before when the wealthy silver heiress had
attended an opera in St. Louis on the arm of the world-
renowned Polish composer, Anton Savanyu. He glanced
again at the picture, and Alex thought he would snap in two
under the weight of his fury. So *that's* how she was spending
her time!

The colonel chuckled to himself and pulled the paper out of
his hands. "That's enough." Turning to the guards, he said,
"Remember, no food for a week and lash him every day for
his insolence. Get him out of my sight!"

He allowed himself to be led away, oblivious to everything
except the photograph that remained indelibly imprinted on
his furious mind. The picture of a radiant beauty smiling out
from the pages of a newspaper. How easily it all fell into place
now, and all it took was one glance at her smiling face to
convince him of her treachery.

If it didn't disgust him so much, he might have laughed out
loud at the thought that he had even married her, thereby
insuring her right, as his widow, to everything he owned. As
far as she knew, everything he owned was the Lady Laura.
That's what it was all about, wasn't it? The Lady Laura? She
and her miserable lying brother wanted to get their hands on

that mine so badly they resorted to their own dirty devices to do it. Jesus Christ, it sickened him to think that he played right into their murderous hands.

The days dragged by with a slow torturous tedium and since seeing that picture he had thought of nothing else. He would give anything just to have her once again, to feel her silky quivering flesh beneath his hands, to hear her soft moans, to feel her body clinging to his. Then, after he had filled himself with her, he would place his hands around her slim throat and squeeze hard until all breath of life was choked out of her. After that he would go to France to find Austin, and he would watch a bit of the man die each time he told him about the way he had taken Danny whenever and wherever he wanted. He wanted to see the hatred on his face, the outrage, the shock, but most of all the jealousy when he described for Austin the intimate ways he had known Danielle, ways in which Austin Fleming never would.

After the seventh day, he was brought to the colonel again. The man was surprised that Alex had endured so well in spite of the torture inflicted. "I wonder what it is that drives you," he said. "What keeps you hanging on to your miserable life? Hmm, it is a puzzle, this obsession you seem to have to remain alive. Could it be the thought of all that silver?"

"You know, I'm getting tired of hearing about it," Alex hotly declared. "I told you before, I didn't keep any of it for myself!"

"What kind of fool do you think I am!" The colonel was so furious he could have brought his fist crashing across the prisoner's insolent face. But he did not move his arm from his side, feeling instead the presence of something beyond his control that told him to beware. "Do you think I believe a word you say?"

"Frankly, Colonel," Alex replied, "I don't expect a man like you to believe anything, so I won't attempt to tell you why I never kept any of it. And as far as the kind of fool I think you are, I think you're the worst kind. You're an even bigger fool than I am for not lying and telling you the things you want to hear. Don't you think I know it's the quickest way to get out of here?"

"And you would not even lie for that?" the colonel questioned.

Suddenly, Alex's anger dropped and a cool smile spread across his lips. "Oh, I'd lie all right."

The remark puzzled the colonel. His black brows drew together in a questioning look and for a moment Alex could see the bewilderment racing through his dark eyes. "Then how do I know you are not lying now?"

Alex snarled back at him, "You don't. But we both know you're not going to have me killed until you find out for sure. You already know that you're not going to get the truth out of me by torturing me. At this point, you don't know whether that's because I'm the most stubborn man you've ever met or whether I really don't have the damned silver. No, Colonel, I'd say you and I are through playing games. You'll release me and you'll do it simply because if you don't, you'll never find out. Maybe when I leave here, I'll lead you to it, maybe not, but you've got to find out, don't you?" An arrogant smile tugged at the corners of his mouth and he stepped back to see the effect of his words on the other man.

The colonel turned his gaze away and scanned the floor. "Have you never in your life wanted anything badly?"

"Yes," Alex quietly answered, "once." Into his mind sprang the vision of a summer night when the stars glinted down on him and the earth sprawled hundreds of feet below—when there stood beside him a girl whose very presence sent tremors of fear through him, the kind of fear that comes from wanting something so badly that you find yourself doing things and saying things to drive it further away. He had been so cruel to her that day when she thought she could touch the sky, and when she had asked him what he saw in his dreams, he had turned on her like a vicious animal. How could he explain to her then when he did not even know himself the reasons he went out of his way to be so mean to her? Only later did he realize why. When it was too late for them and it no longer mattered—only then could he have told her how very much he wanted her.

Now, left in the wake of her scheming and betrayal, hating her, deploring her cruel revenge, he wanted her, damn it, still wanted her.

Chapter 28

It seemed as though the spring would never come again to St. Louis, but the flames burning steadily in the stone fireplaces warmed the house and helped keep the chill at the windows where it lay frosty white on the panes. The couple seldom ventured outdoors these days, for the harsh winds and ever constant dampness posed too much of a hazard to the diminishing strength of the fragile composer.

All attempts to have a doctor in to examine him were in vain and Danny finally relented and tried to pretend she did not hear him when he slipped out of bed in the middle of the night to hide his coughs. One morning she awoke to find his pillows plotched with blood, and she knew then the unspoken dread that had been laying heavily on her heart. How could she not help but notice how pale his complexion was these days? Nor how drawn his face had become, with his dark eyes set deeply into his face, ringed with shadows. Nor did she miss how his strength seemed to fail him so easily, not only when they made love . . . or tried to . . . but more and more now even when he sat at the piano.

The dreary winter days slipped by without a word exchanging between them, the physical aspect of their relationship ceased to be. No longer did the lambent glow of the fire play across their naked entwined bodies. Danny knew that the feelings which grew out of their closeness could never be diminished for lack of physical love, but the spark of passion he had briefly ignited in her left her with a dull ache of longing. The only time it didn't seem to matter was when she sat curled up in a corner of the plush sofa, her eyes closed as the sound of his music engulfed her, filling her with awe for his fascinating power to create beauty.

Their days fell into an easy routine where Anton spent much of the time composing and Danny found the time to write letters. She had even taken it upon herself to write to Major Armstrong. Their meeting at Emmett Fleming's house, although brief, was sufficient to convince her he had a sensitive nature borne of compassion. So it was to him she wrote for the information she sought on the situation as it progressed out in the Dakotas, where the people she once knew were struggling to be free.

The major had been pleased to hear from her, replying right away. He was happy to have found in the Frenchwoman feelings that ran parallel to his own, and he was only too glad to share with her some of the things he himself had difficulty dealing with. His years in command had landed him in the middle of the Dakota badlands, striving with guns and bullets to take away a land that was not his to begin with and which, he strongly believed, he had no right to. It was a difficult situation to be immersed in, for the Army was his life and he had always considered the relationship between a country and the man who had sworn to serve it as something rather special. But the gentle-mannered and quiet-tempered man could not easily come to terms with what he also considered to be his government's unthinking, unknowledgeable, and oft times unfeeling treatment of the Indians. It appalled his better senses, and yet, he himself perpetuated it by his very presence in the affair. It left him angry and confused, but mostly it made him sad.

It amused James Armstrong to know that Danielle Fleming was the wife of a man whose very countenance was a source of irritation to the major. He never dwelt on the question of how she wound up with such an insensitive person as Captain Lacy Hawkins, allowing that most people are permitted one great mistake in their lives.

One blustery day in late March, with still no hint of spring in the air, Anton struggled endlessly with his latest composition. Danny questioned him about his trouble. "It's only that I cannot seem to keep my attention focused on it long enough to develop the melody," he explained. "If I do not hear it here in my head, then I cannot recreate it here." He gestured with a sweep of his graceful hand toward the piano. "Oh well," he shrugged, "perhaps tomorrow. I was foolish to try so late in the day. Morning is always the best." He rose from the keyboard, picked up the newspaper and sat down on the sofa next to Danny.

He turned automatically to the international news section of the *St. Louis Chronicle*, bypassing the local news which had nothing to do with him at all. As far as Anton was concerned, his residence in America was temporary and would last only as long as it took to convince the young woman at his side to leave with him. Secretly he hoped that remembrances of Paris in the spring might be precisely what she needed to say yes. Perhaps then he would be able to convince her that her place was with him and not with that man she called her husband—the one she hated without having to say so. They did not speak much of Lacy, and at times even succeeded in erasing the image of the absentee husband completely from their private little world. But sooner or later the man must return, and then what? Would Danny make a choice between them? Anton hoped it would come down to that, for in his heart he knew she would choose him.

What Anton could not know, was that Danny could not simply play the adultress, and run off with him to Europe. Nor could she divorce her husband as Anton urged her to do. For she had neglected to tell him about the paper she had signed shortly after her marriage to Lacy, the one that said she would not divorce him for any reason, the one that bound her to Lacy Hawkins as his possession for as long as either of them lived. For the moment Anton was safe in his assumptions, secure in his trust of her love.

"Danielle, does the name of DeMalleray mean anything to you?" he asked, glancing up from the newspaper. "One of the oldest families in all of Europe," he recalled out loud. "I met some distant cousins in Paris." He glanced back down at the article. "It says here that the vast DeMalleray fortune lies virtually untouched. It seems that through some legal maze, the only ones who can touch it are the direct heirs of Pierre DeMalleray. The old gentleman died many years back and no one knows where the one surviving heir is. How curious." He stared intently at the page, his dark brows drawn together. "Hmm, all that money, what a shame." When he turned to her, all thought of the DeMalleray fortune passed through his mind. "What is it, my love?" he asked, seeing her grave expression.

"It's a letter from Major Armstrong," Danny replied. "It came in this morning's post." The expression on her face suggested that the letter brought with it few well wishes. "Oh, Anton!" She jumped to her feet with a cry. "They have attacked another peaceful village! James says that the soldiers completely destroyed a village of Sioux and Cheyenne and that they were on their way to surrender at the agencies. Oh, my God, how dreadful!" Her eyes reddened and welled with tears.

Anton sprang to his feet and went to her. "Are you certain of it?"

"Oh yes, it's all right here." She shook the letter in front of him in her small clenched fist.

"Did you know any of them? Were they your friends?"

She slumped back onto the sofa, the letter from James Armstrong laying loose in her lap. "I met some of them while I was with Crazy Horse's people. James says they escaped with just their lives. Everything else was destroyed. Can you imagine that they would want to kill those people?" She turned her shiny amber eyes on him. "Help me to understand why this is happening," she pleaded.

He sat down close beside her and placed an arm around her shoulders. "You have been exposed to many of life's uglier sides, Danielle," he said softly, cradling her in his embrace. "If you cannot find understanding out of all the things you have been through, then surely I, who have never been exposed to any of it, can find no meaning in it. I wish I could help you, dearest, but all I can do is be here when you need my comfort."

"Anton—" Her golden eyes, shiny with tears, turned up at him. "Anton, what would I do without you beside me?"

Winter seemed to abruptly disappear, leaving late one night while the city slept, and by the second week of April spring laced the air and the buds on the trees looked about to burst open. Spring also brought with it a change in their habits, as Anton reluctantly agreed to move back into his suite at the Hotel Pierre. Danny insisted that it would be best if he were not there when Lacy returned, but she came every day to sit with Anton while he added the finishing touches to his composition.

He worked feverishly, often late into the night, pouring into this new piece his strength to create something for her that his mere physical love could never equal. Around the melody of the Polish countryside that flavored his music and gave it its particular beauty, he had wrapped what he felt was the very essence of Danielle's soul—the intensity for survival. With it he added a new dimension to his music, an aspect so personal that only he could know its true nature.

That's what he told her when he finished playing it for her and rose shakily from the piano seat, exhausted and trembling from the passion that flooded through him. That was what he told her when he went to her and found her with tears in her eyes. There was no need for words between them, but he wanted to make sure that she knew it was for her. That if it had not been for her, there would have been no inspiration great enough for it, nor love strong enough to give it birth.

"Anton," she whispered, "I don't know what to say." She stood at the door, her cape over her shoulders.

"There is no need to say anything. Your eyes say it all."

He sent her home that evening with her eyes bright with tears, the feel of her lips, soft and warm, lingering on his.

It was the tenth of April and she had been in America for almost a full year. She sighed and settled back into her seat as the driver guided the shiny black carriage home. She took a deep breath and filled her lungs with the cool evening air, pulling her cape tighter about her to keep out the chill that spiked the air. Above, the stars were strung like Christmas lights across the sky.

She pulled the key from her purse and let herself in. First she lit the oil lamp, setting it on a low flame, then went to stoke the logs in the fireplace. Perhaps some hot tea and then she'd go to bed.

"Where the hell have you been?"

The instant familiarity of the voice turned her blood to ice. Whirling around in its direction, she saw him. His sudden appearance paralyzed her speech and all she could do was watch with widened eyes as he came closer.

"I've been here since six o'clock," he said, his drawl thick as ever. He glanced at the clock on the mantle which read eleven thirty, then looked back at her as if waiting for an explanation."

"I was out."

"I can see that." The sarcasm was building in his voice, spiking that sickeningly sweet southern accent with a hint of the cruelty she knew him capable of. "Would you mind telling me why I should have to wait five-and-a-half hours for my wife to come home?"

"Lacy, you didn't tell me. If I knew you were coming, I would have been here."

"Yeah, I'll bet," he said, catching her by the arm as she tried to slip by him. "Wait a minute, don't you have a kiss for your husband?"

Before she could reply, he smothered her mouth with his. He tasted of liquor. She stood stiffly against him, waiting for the kiss to end. When he got no response from her, he released her abruptly. "You really missed me, huh?"

"What did you expect me to do? Run to you with open arms?" Danny pulled herself away and went to sit on the sofa.

Lacy followed right behind her. "You still haven't answered my question."

"Yes, I did, I told you I was out. I owe you no explanations, Lacy, so don't expect any."

"No explanations?" he echoed. "I see. I come home after being away for months and find my wife out until very late in the evening. I find that she is living without the maid I instructed her to send for. I find a man's gloves in the hallway and a walking stick by the door. And the strangest thing of all is that!" He pointed to the piano. "Have you recently learned to play, Danny?" he asked. "Have you injured your ankle perhaps so that you'd need a walking stick? Tell me, if I searched this house further, what other things would I find that don't belong to you?"

Danny jumped to her feet. "How dare you," she cried. "How dare you come in here and snoop through my things." She guessed that he had already familiarized himself with all of the drawers and closets, so his question was that much more insulting to her.

"I might remind you that I live here too. This is my home too!" He yelled at her, his green eyes narrowed into slivers. "As far as explanations are concerned, you'd better come up with some, Danny, because I want to know where the hell you were tonight!"

"I was with a friend," she snapped. "I do have some, you know."

"Does *that* belong to your friend?" Once again he cast a quick scornful look at the piano.

Danny tilted her chin up, no longer willing to back down, prepared to meet him head on. "Yes, it does," she answered. "So do the gloves, and the walking stick." She watched the sparks of anger ignite anew in his eyes.

"Are you having an affair with him?" Lacy demanded.

"I suppose in your terms you could say so."

"What in the hell does that mean?"

Danny was not about to go into detail of her intimacies, physical or otherwise, with Anton Savanyu. Lacy would never believe her anyway. How could she expect him to understand the type of relationship she had with a man like Anton Savanyu? Rather than risk explaining, she let him think the worst, knowing that he had already tried and sentenced her in his own mind. She shivered and moved closer to the fire.

"I asked you what you meant. Are you having an affair with this man or not?" Lacy's impatient and caustic voice rose behind her.

"Yes, Lacy, I am having an affair," she loudly declared, watching with a smile the way Lacy's features changed at her admission. "But I assure you we have been very discreet, so you have no need to fear that your good name has been tainted. Why, I believe the only people who know are the maid at his hotel, my driver and, let me see . . . oh yes, the man who sells papers. I really did have your best interests in mind." She sidled past him, the sneer plainly written on her face. "If you are thinking of hitting me," she told him, "I would advise against it. I may be your wife but I am not your whipping post. I assure you that if you ever strike me, I'll see you destroyed, regardless of what agreements we may have made. You're an ambitious man, Lacy, and I could so easily squash your ambitions beneath my thumb like the dirty little gnat that you really are. You need me, Lacy, my name, I should say. But you also need me in one piece, and as content as possible. And *that*, my dear husband, means that you will never interfere with my affairs."

Lacy remained silent, his face red with rage, the veins visible at his temples.

"There is something else," she went on, unable to stop the

momentum of her wrath. "You will never again make love to
me." She saw the flash in his eyes and heard the sharp intake
of air through his nostrils. "I never want to have your hands
on me again," she said. "Do you hear me, Lacy? Never
again! You married me for my name, damn it, and that is *all*
you are going to get! From now on, if it's intercourse you
want, I would suggest you go elsewhere and pay for it—better
still, *I'll* pay for it. After all, I'm paying for everything else
around here, aren't I? I paid for the house, which is why it's
so laughable to hear you refer to this as your home. I paid for
the furnishings. I pay for the food in the pantry and the
clothes in the closets. I suppose one day, when you have
reached the pinnacle you're after and you have no further
need for me, then I suppose I'll even be able to pay for my
freedom from you. Until then it's just a free ride for you, isn't
it, Lacy? Tell me, what is it you are really after? What have
you set your sights on that has turned you into such a poor
excuse for a man? God, you must hate yourself so!" She
turned away from him, an expression of disgust evident on
her face, unable to look him in the eyes any longer . . .
unable to stand the sight of him.

A hand on her arm snapped her around, and when her eyes
stopped rocking from the force, she gasped at the sight of his
face. His features were contorted and wrought with rage, his
eyes blazed fiercely. His grip on her arm was painfully tight,
and as he spoke, it grew tighter and tighter until Danny felt
her hand turning blue. But no matter how hard she struggled,
she could not escape him. She was forced to listen to the whip
of his words and his breath hot against her cheek.

"You want to know what it is I'm after, you slut? All right,
I'll tell you! I'm after something my daddy never had—
something my daddy never found on that goddamned chicken
farm! Yeah, that's right, it was chickens, not tobacco.
Goddamned chickens! I'm after something he never even
knew existed. Well, I'm about to get it any way I can. I'll tell
you something else, Miss high and mighty, fancy-assed lady,
you didn't fool me for a minute. I knew you were a slut the
minute I set eyes on you. But I also knew you would fit in with
my plans real nice. And so, here we are. Only I'm not
finished yet, not by a long shot! I've got my eye on something
bigger than this, and I'm not about to let your whoring ruin it
for me! I'm on my way to the White House, and you're not
about to—"

"The White House!" Danny exclaimed. "You really *are* mad! Why, you're nothing but a Cavalry captain. What on earth makes you think—" The pressure he applied to her arm silenced her instantly.

"I'll tell you what makes me think it," he snarled. "I haven't worked myself up close to George Custer for nothing. And when you're up close, you get to hear things that others don't."

"Like what?"

He released her sharply and stalked to the liquor cabinet. Withdrawing a bottle of brandy he poured some into a crystal glass. "Like the fact that Grant holds Custer directly responsible for Congress' decision to impeach Secretary of War Belknap. Like the fact that Custer testified at Congressional hearings against the Grant administration. Like the plain fact that Grant hates Custer's guts." He lifted the glass to his lips and swallowed the contents without ceremony. "That's got to make Custer look pretty damned good to a lot of people. Good enough to maybe win the nomination in this year's elections. If he wins that nomination, he's got it clinched. That Big Horn Expedition the Army brass is planning against the Sioux this summer will be a major campaign, and one good defeat of those savages is all Custer needs to get that nomination."

"One good massacre you mean."

"I don't care what *you* call it," Lacy retorted, "but the papers back East will call it a victory, and that's all that matters."

"Doesn't it matter that all those lives will have been lost for it?" She was incredulous at his matter-of-factness about it.

His voice was strangely void of emotion. "It's a plain fact of war that people die. Since warfare is something you know nothing about, I'd suggest you mind your own business."

"But, Lacy, have you no compassion for them? Have you no feelings when you send your men blindly tearing through their villages on a rampage of death and destruction?"

"Compassion?" He sounded surprised to hear the word. "Tell me, was it compassion that was flowing through those Yankees' veins during the war? Do you suppose that Yankee that laid my brother Brett in his grave did it out of compassion? What kind of compassion do you think those damned niggers had when they just up and left the place after the war? Do you think they cared that the old man couldn't

handle the farm without them? Do you think they remembered how he had fed them and sheltered them and gave them the clothes on their backs?" He turned and walked away to refill his glass.

"So you perpetuate it," Danny accused. "You take all the wrongs done to you and you do them to others, only worse. I hate to think what kind of man you would be if you ever did realize your ambitions."

"You mean when," Lacy corrected her. "*When* I realize my ambitions."

"You're so very sure, aren't you?"

"Yes," he replied. He walked to the sofa and sat with one leg crossed over the other, twirling the stem of the glass in his fingers. "Well now," he drawled, "we haven't discussed our plans for the future, have we?" He patted the seat beside him. "Come sit down, Danny. That's right, come on. Good." When she was seated stiffly beside him, he said, "Now, I say that we can forget all about this little tryst you're having and talk about our plans. Here I am back in town not a day and already we've had a nasty argument, and because of it, I completely forgot to tell you what we're going to do. Would you like to hear?" He paused as though she really might care. "I've made arrangements to return to Fort Lincoln where I have to rejoin my company. You'll be coming with me." He saw her eyes widen and her mouth drop open. "Do you think I'm going to leave you here! Not on your life! You're coming with me, whether you like it or not. In fact, your bags are already packed." He gestured toward the dark shapes sitting in the shadows against the wall. "I took the liberty of packing some of your things. Of course, Fort Lincoln's not the Hotel Pierre, but I think you'll get used to that pretty quick. After all, you've seen worse accommodations than that." A sickening smile spread across his lips.

Danny could not believe her ears. Was he really telling her that she had to go out there with him? Would he really force her to accompany him? In the morning her questions were answered, her doubts confirmed. She awoke to find him already dressed.

"You'd better hurry," he said coldly, "we have a train to catch."

They rode in silence, she sitting stiffly beside him. The only sound between them was that of the carriage wheels and the drumming of his fingers on the armrest. Glancing up as they passed the Hotel Pierre, she could see Anton's window from the street. She lowered her eyes, blinking back a tear that stung at the corner of her eye.

If ever there was to be another, she whispered to him in her heart, it would have been you, Anton, my very dear lover. She didn't even have a way of letting him know what had happened. If only she could see him one more time, however brief, just long enough to tell him that she had made up her mind to run away with him after all. Today was the day she was going to tell him that she had decided to leave St. Louis to return with him to France, regardless of the consequences. It was to be her last gift to him, after the splendid one he had given her last night. Little could she have known that it was never to be.

Once again she was a prisoner, and the thought sent a tremor racing through her that nothing could chase away . . . not the remembrances of the beautiful wild hills that she would see again, nor the feel of the hot dry wind against her cheeks that she had once come to love. This time her wrists were not bound in rawhide, her hair did not hang in snarled ringlets down her back, nor was she dressed in tattered remnants or quilled buckskin. She was returning with silver bracelets adorning her wrists, her hair piled fashionably atop her head beneath a wide-brimmed hat with a flowing plume that caught the spring breezes, her slender body clothed in a delicate swirl of velvet and lace and the intoxicating fragrance of expensive perfume scenting her skin. But she was no freer than the last time to do as she pleased. Only this time it was far, far worse. This time the man was Lacy Hawkins and this time she could not even lose herself in the depths of passion as she once did with Alex Coulter.

Storm clouds were starting to roll across the valley when they arrived at Fort Abraham Lincoln. When they entered the small cabin that was to be their private quarters, there was already a fire burning low. She stood at the window while Lacy issued curt orders to his aide. The sky immediately overhead was still clear, its midnight blue streaked with color the way it never seemed to be in St. Louis. The sight of it made Danny's mouth go dry and her breath quicken. She had almost forgotten how magnificent it could be. Closing her eyes, she let its lingering vision carry her far from this spot back to a time not so very long ago when she stood as still as the air looking up at the same orange-streaked sky, feeling its beauty seeping into her, filling her senses, drawing her closer to the man at her side whose silver eyes blazed out across the open land. 'I keep my visions to myself'. Her heart jumped at the sound of the voice she knew from light-years ago. The suddenness of it, popping up like that when she least expected it, snapped her out of the semi-dream. She turned from the window and began to unpack her bags.

That evening they attended a private dinner party at the home of General and Mrs. Custer. Danny was pleasantly surprised to see a familiar face in the crowd and after dinner managed to catch him alone for a few minutes of conversation. Instantly, she noticed the dark circles beneath James Armstrong's eyes. "You haven't been getting much sleep," she scolded him.

A sour expression came over his face. "Now that you're here, you won't either. I've put in for a transfer," he confided. "I don't know how much longer I can continue like this."

"James, are you all right?" She placed a hand lightly on his sleeve at the desperation she heard flooding his voice.

"Yes, yes," he assured her, patting her hand. "I've been guaranteed a transfer sometime this summer. They can't let me go sooner than that because they're in the middle of a big campaign against the Sioux. In fact, in a week or so we'll be riding out. Everything is ready, we're just waiting for the final orders to march. Colonel Gibbon will march from the west, Terry and Custer from the east. I'll be moving my men with the Seventh along with Major Reno and Captain Benteen and . . . Captain Hawkins." He passed his hand in front of his eyes as if erasing a vision. "I hate to think what we're going to find."

She could not read the strange look on his face. "What do you mean?"

"I don't know," he replied, doubt sifting through his words. "Custer seems to think we'll have an easy time of it, but the reports we've been getting are that there's a lot of Sioux out there." He shook his head as though he sensed impending danger.

"Custer needs this one, doesn't he?"

James Armstrong snorted in answer to the question. "I'm surprised he made it back here in time. He must really want it bad."

"Yes, I heard of some trouble with President Grant, but to

tell the truth, James, I didn't really pay much attention. What was that all about?"

"Oh, I don't know, Danny. There's so much going on it's hard to keep on top of everything. From what I understand, Grant was furious with Custer over the whole Belknap thing, not to mention those Congressional hearings. So he issued strict orders that Custer was not permitted to leave Washington, and that, of course, meant that he was stripped of his command in the Big Horn Expedition." He sighed deeply. "So naturally, Custer did what he wanted to anyway. He left Washington, disobeyed the President's orders and infuriated him, and then Custer had the nerve to ask Grant to let him come back here to command the Seventh in the campaign. Naturally Grant refused. Ordered Custer to remain where he was, and for a while it looked like Custer was done for."

"But he is here."

"Oh, yes," the major commented, "but that's because he had to go begging to General Terry. Fortunately, Terry knows that we all need Custer on this one and he was able to convince the powers that be." His feelings of foreboding did not need to be spoken.

That night Danny had trouble falling asleep. She slipped from bed and walked barefooted to the window. The storm that had threatened earlier had never materialized. Dusty streamers of moonlight filtered in through the open window, seemingly carried along by the gentle summer air. Soon the daybreak star would appear and the sky would grow pearly. As she stood there a voice from a time gone by passed through her thoughts. It was a soft voice, quiet, almost shy.

She saw him as she had seen him last, his slender, smooth-skinned body, bare to the waist, soft brown hair braided and wrapped in otter fur, hanging far below his belt. Falling Sun was what he had named her because her hair was the color of the sunset. She could feel his closeness despite the fact that he was probably over a hundred miles away camped on the bank of some hidden creek.

How has it been with you, my friend, she asked him in her heart. The whole country reverberates with your presence, she told him even though he was not there to hear her. It is your spirit alone that keeps these men trembling in their shoes, even though few of them will admit it. She closed her eyes and pressed a fevered cheek against the cool glass. This winter must have been terribly hard on you, she sighed. But it is not over, not yet, she warned him. I wonder whether you know that at this very moment plans are being made to destroy you.

She walked from the window and crawled back into bed, pulling the covers up over her head. Into her dream she carried the face of the man she met last summer. The quiet, light-skinned Indian whose very name of Tasunke-Witko was enough to strike terror into the hearts of the white men who would destroy him, and love into the hearts of his people who would follow him wherever he went.

Chapter 29

Suddenly, the country erupted with Indian scouts racing back and forth from village to village, crying that the Rosebud Valley was covered black with soldiers. In less time than it took to council, a thousand warriors were ready to fight, dressed in full regalia. Some had rifles, most were equipped with only bows, arrows and war clubs. Their guns and spear tips glistening in the sun, they rode around the great campfires, circling to the sound of drums that made the earth rumble and the voices of the women who cried out their names sang strong heart songs for them. At their head rode a man with a splattering of hailstone spots on his chest, a zigzag streak of lightning painted across his face and a single feather from a red-backed hawk behind his head.

On June 17, 1876 the two opposing forces collided. At the onset Crazy Horse held his warriors back, but the soldiers were many and the rifle fire so close that the Indians were forced to retreat to the rocks. From there, gathering force, the Sioux warchief led a charge descending on both sides of the hill. In the choking curtain of dust and smoke it was difficult to tell friend from foe, white man from red, and by the time the sun had climbed high in the sky, there were charges spread all along the miles of rough ground.

Unexpectedly a rush of warriors, Crazy Horse at their head yelling frantic encouragement to them, charged directly into the sea of bluecoats, thundering up behind them and sending the soldiers' horses scattering. Sensing an abrupt shift in the tide of the battle, the warriors pressed even harder, charging straight through, some shooting from under the necks of their horses, others racing in with spears and war clubs lifted high over their heads. The entire party of soldiers was forced to retreat into the valley like frightened deer where they ran to hide amongst the safety of the bushes and rocks.

Picking up dropped carbines and whatever shells were on the ground for the taking, the warriors continued, turning around over the creek and sweeping down the side. As their horses pounded past, they could see the dead and wounded lying in the settling dust, and it made their hearts strong to see that many had died so bravely. They returned to their camp on the Rosebud River just as a new day was beginning to break. Their horses were worn out and their shells were gone. Yet it had been a good fight, and it left little doubt as to who the victors were that day. That evening the victory dances began, the drumming and singing and feasting lasting long into the dark night. Even those who had lost a man of their family could find some words of joy to sing as they mourned.

The officer in command, General Crook, returned to his base camp to await reinforcements from the detachments of Terry, Gibbon and Custer. The startling defeat he had just experienced was proof enough that the Indians on the Rosebud were far too strong for him to conquer alone.

With the battle over, the great Sioux encampment moved to a spot where there was enough grazing land for the immense pony herds and where the game was plentiful. There they spread their camp circles along the shores of the river they called the Greasy Grass, their lodges covering the twisting shore. To the whites, the delightfully sparkling river was called the Little Big Horn.

The day broke hot and clear with the people rising lazily to greet it. In the great camp the kettles were full from the meat the hunters had packed in from the buffalo herds that still roamed west of the river. Nighttime brought much dancing and feasting and courting, while the ensuing sunny days saw the children splashing naked in the cool waters of the river, the young men racing their ponies through the camp circles and the women cooking and chatting. Scouts were posted to keep an eye on the movements of Crook's soldiers, but as that threat posed no immediate danger, they settled into a calm and easy life. What they did not know was that the soldier chief they called Long Hair Custer was already prowling the shores of the Rosebud. Nor did they suspect that Custer had sent Major Marcus Reno to approach them from behind in the hope of catching them unaware. Custer on one side, Reno on the other, each with a single goal in mind.

From the surrounding hillsides, the women could see the flash of sabers as Reno's men swept down upon the Hunkpapas who were camped at the upper edge of the valley. Everywhere the air filled with the firing of guns as bullets tore through the lodges striking whatever lay in the path, without discrimination as to old women or young children. The echo of the guns roared through the camp as the bluecoats pushed through and the people fled to the river for safety.

From out on the plains the pony herds came racing in, the stunned young men catching any horse they could get their hands on, jumping on their backs and charging into the fight with wild war cries on their lips, stark raging anger in their black eyes. "Be strong, my friends!" Crazy Horse cried. He signaled for some to remain behind to fight Reno's men, then raised his loaded Winchester high into the air above his head and led his storm of warriors across the river to meet the troops of Long Hair Custer. With the songs of war in their hearts and the sound of the drums in their ears, they rode to meet the two-hundred-and-twenty-five men of Custer's regiment. The warriors fell behind their leader in formation, moving like a great tide across the ground, two thousand strong.

The initial charge cut through the soldiers' lines, separating them from their horses. In the charges that followed, the dust and black powder smoke grew so dense that men rode blindly into the thick of it or stumbled around on the ground, deafened to everything except the roar of the battle. Many men fought bravely amidst the bullets whistling hotly all around them, and Crazy Horse felt proud in his heart to see his fighting men. It was not mere honors they were after this day, not in this battle. In this battle, they were striking to kill.

He circled his fevered warriors and charged, then circled and charged again and again, catching sight of many brave deeds being done by his men and the whites alike. But there was no time to sit and watch. The great wail of men dying rose into the air, intermingling with the whooping war cries.

The angry warriors chased down the bluecoats that had managed to get away somehow. The soldiers were struck as they ran, and the ferocity of the Indians' determination caused several troopers to point their guns to their own heads and pull the triggers. Inch by inch the pressing warriors forced

the remaining soldiers up a rising slope. But with the top of
the rise just yards away, it appeared at last that the soldiers
had gained the miraculous advantage they so desperately
needed. If they could only get to the top of the rise, if they
could make it over! Through the clouds of swirling dust and
stinging gunpowder, George Custer's eyes caught a fleeting
glimpse of the safety that lay not more than twenty-five yards
away. He shouted furiously to his remaining men to hold on.
"To the rise!" he yelled. "To the rise!" But all at once it
seemed as though the curtain of dense black dust was lifted,
and the sight he saw turned his blood to ice.

There, fanned out across its breadth, stood over a thousand
mounted Sioux, all painted for war, astride their best war
ponies. For just the barest instant the two men faced each
other, the look of the fate about to be sealed written in their
eyes. Then the dust descended again and engulfed the entire
hill in its murky depths.

Much as an eagle sweeps down from the sky, so it was that
Crazy Horse's Sioux and Cheyenne warriors swarmed over
the hill, their hearts bad from the many sadnesses they had
endured, their blood hot from the losses they had suffered on
the white man's account. They fought until there were no
more men to fight.

Crazy Horse rode back to the ridge over which he had only
moments before looked down upon the Long Hair. Already
his men had gone back to strip the bodies. Lying naked in the
sun with their blood drying on their white flesh, they looked
as helpless as those of his own people who had not made it out
of the way in time. Searching a time out of his memory,
Crazy Horse could not remember when it was not so. In his
span of thirty-three years, he could not recall a time when
his people had truly been avenged for all the wrongful acts
against them. But today his breast swelled with pride at being a Sioux warrior, while within his heart beat the pulse of
the people. Ah, but it was a sad and foolish thing for so many
to die like this, he thought. Suddenly he felt tired and weak—
indeed, as though he were as dead inside. Pulling his eyes
from the scene, he turned his pony's head for home, his
warriors falling in place behind him and at his sides.

That night Crazy Horse slept with his head beneath his
buffalo robes to keep out the sounds of mourning that arose
from across the river where the death lodges had been placed.
The following morning, with the sun bouncing off the east
side of the hills, the great camps of the Oglalas, the

Hunkpapas, the Brulés, the Minniconjous, Cheyennes and all the others moved onto the trail. This time they did not sing as they went. The women were not decked out in their fine saddle trappings, there was no showing off or playing of tricks. Leaving the scaffolds of their dead behind, they traveled slowly and silently out of the little valley that was so pretty and fertile at this time of year and made their way toward the shelter of the mountains.

Behind the people rode the warriors—the ones who watched the rear—and with the warriors rode a man, indistinguishable from the rest unless one looked closely. Then you could see how light his hair was and how fair his complexion, and how slender his body—almost like a boy's. He rode with the others, eyes guarded, but blushing quietly whenever one of them attempted to praise him or single him out for their victory over the bluecoats. "This was not something done by one man," he told them, his voice low as ever. One would never have guessed him capable of rallying his fighting men with heated cries as he had done. "This thing was done by many who followed the plans as they were made."

Yes, they knew this, they told him, but the planning had come from only one. And while this one man could not bring himself to admit to his greatness, they would follow his trail until the song of death was in their hearts.

Chapter 30

On June 27, 1876 the Democrats nominated Samuel J. Tilden for President, and the newspapers were filled with the ghastly details of what was termed the bloodiest massacre in the nation's history. Everywhere voices roared for vengeance against the bloodthirsty savages that had totally wiped out Custer and his regiment.

Preparations were begun immediately to deal with the hostile Sioux and Cheyenne Indians, now regarded by an inflamed United States Government as prisoners of war and to be dealt with as such. With General William T. Sherman ready to assume military control over all the reservations, the Indians who had fought so strongly were about to see the true strength of the Army against them.

On July 7th, a small handful of Oglalas and Cheyennes wandered across some of General Crook's soldiers. They approached as friends and were fired upon.

On July 17th, a small group of Cheyennes left the reservation in search of some meat. They were met and driven back by troops at Warbonnet Creek.

One week later, on July 24th, Danielle Fleming packed her bags and left Fort Lincoln and the Dakota territory by coach, accompanied by the widow of James Armstrong.

She tried to find it in her heart to say some words of comfort to women like Caroline Armstrong who had lost a husband in the battle. What kind of true comfort could she offer any of the widows, Danny wondered sadly. How could she tell them at a time like this that Lacy's death on that hill was the key to her freedom? How could she tell them that her heart wept also, but not for him?

She stopped briefly in St. Louis to settle some matters. There was the house to get rid of, and some legal matters concerning Lacy's property, which she flatly refused to take title of, turning it over instead to her attorneys to dispose of as they thought best. She also paid a visit to the Hotel Pierre.

"No, madam," the clerk informed her, "Monsieur Savanyu is no longer registered. He left many weeks ago. He came back to the hotel one morning and said he was leaving." The man shook his head. "I don't quite understand, Monsieur Savanyu seemed so upset about something. I had no idea he was unhappy. Why only the night before everyone in the hotel could hear him playing. It was glorious, the most beautiful thing I have ever heard. The next morning he walked out of here so courteous and pleasant, humming to himself as he went. I thought, surely there goes a happy man. But then, just like that—" he snapped his fingers in the air, "he leaves. I wonder what could have upset him like that."

"Thank you," Danny mumbled, not surprised to find Anton gone, guessing dismally that he had most likely returned to France.

She searched the newspapers for a hint of his name, but there was nothing. Not a trace of the name that had appeared so frequently just months before.

She could not know that on that morning when she left St Louis Anton Savanyu had left the Hotel Pierre in splendid spirits, stopping on the way to her house to buy a small bouquet of wild flowers from a corner cart.

There was nothing about the house to suggest that anything was amiss. Danny was out shopping, he had assumed, so he settled himself on the sofa to read the newspaper. Gradually, a strange sensation had crept over him. It was a feeling of something incomplete . . . pending, and it made him shift nervously crossing one leg over the other. Suddenly he became aware that all was not as it seemed.

A sickening feeling seeped into his stomach, but it was the sight of her bed, empty and unmade, and the bare hangers in the closet that confirmed the dreaded suspicion. She was gone! He turned on his heels and stalked back to the parlor, his eyes ripping the scene apart for a sign, a clue, a hint as to her whereabouts. Nothing!

On his way out, Anton spotted a pair of kid gloves on the hallway table—his own. His walking stick was propped against the wall. Best to leave them behind, he told himself, trying desperately to steel himself against the onrush of pain. He would want nothing around to remind him of this. It was then he noticed the bouquet of violets, and picking them up, dropped them into the wastepaper basket at his feet. Not even these, he thought. Then he had walked out and left it all behind him.

Once in New York, Danny dispatched a letter to her uncle, explaining to him why she was leaving for France. She knew Emmett would argue that America was her home now, that her place was with the Fleming family. This could have been her home once she wrote, but since coming here she had learned about things that only wounded her deeply and reminded her time and time again what an inhospitable place this really was. Each time she came close, something she loved died or was taken from her.

She did not disclose to Emmett exactly what had happened since her abduction, not in so many words, that is. But she did admit that, yes, she had been in love with Alex Coulter, and that yes, she still was. Any further delay in this country would be a reminder of what she had lost. She did not necessarily feel that returning to France was the answer, but for now the distance seemed important. She begged his forgiveness and understanding, wished him love and sent the letter off to Colorado. Then she addressed a letter to her grandmother informing her of her arrival and asking to have a carriage meet her at the train station.

Standing on the platform at the *Gare L'Est*, gazing anxiously into the crowd, she spotted a familiar face and heard a friendly voice. It was Johnny—the stableman from Chateaudun—who had come to pick her up.

The ride back was just as she remembered it to be. It was the middle of August and everything was in full bloom. The valleys were lush with vegetation, the vines hanging heavy with grapes. As the carriage turned off the main road onto the private tree-lined path that wound its way another half mile to the stately stone house, the surrounding groves rang with the laughter of one whose voice had not been heard for a long time.

If Danny had allowed the peacefulness of Chateaudun to lull her into forgetting at first, then she soon learned there was no escape . . . not beneath the branches of the graceful

mimosa trees in the solarium, nor anywhere along the serene
French countryside, nor even beneath the covers of her bed.
In a few short weeks things began to bother her that had
always brought her pleasure. Small things grated on her
nerves and at times even the soothing atmosphere that she
thought would be so healing only forced her further into
herself, where she faced things she never wished to see again.
In an effort to divert the surge of memories, and despite her
grandmother's strenuous protests, she took an apartment in
Paris on the Boulevard St. Germain where she had easy
access to the theatres and concert halls. And where, too, she
could frequent the fashionable salons in hope of catching
word of Anton Savanyu. It was the only way she knew to find
him since his name no longer appeared in the papers and the
posters around town were quite old.

She didn't know what she would say to him if she ever
found him again, or even if he wanted to see her at all. When
she had returned to the house in St. Louis, she had found his
gloves and walking stick untouched. She had also found
something else. A small bouquet of violets, dried and
crumbling from age. She had to find him to explain what went
wrong. She had felt his pain and his anger when she saw the
wild flowers in the trash basket. There should be no misun-
derstandings between them. But her searches through the
Parisian salons failed to turn up any word of him, and it
seemed as though the man had vanished off the face of the
earth.

Rarely did she attend a concert unescorted these days, for
no sooner had she arrived back in Paris, than her name was
heard around the fashionable circles of French aristocracy.
The Fleming name had gained considerable influence in the
French capital and Danny found herself flocked by people
who wished to meet her, men who wished to have her. They
were some of Europe's wealthiest and most eligible young
men, France's oldest and most distinguished gentlemen. They
called on her, promising her the world if she would accompany them to the theatre or go for a ride in the park on a Sunday
morning. Sometimes she accepted, sometimes she refused, as
the mood struck her. Some of her escorts were more likable
than others, a few were downright charming, wealthy and
handsome. Yet always, there was something missing.

She would permit them to kiss her goodnight, even to wrap
their arms around her supple body and whisper naughty

things in her ear. But her responses were always contrived, always the same for each man. She even accepted their gifts of flowers and candies and precious stones. Long dangling earrings of emeralds sparkled at her earlobes, fiery opals graced her throat and blood-red rubies were wrapped around her slim wrists. She never promised them anything in return, not even with her eyes. She was prepared to give them nothing more than her company. Few men were lucky enough to show up at the opera with such a devastating beauty on their arms, or to take a wealthy heiress to dinner at a fine restaurant. And for those who did suspect that her ardor was less than she pretended, it was all forgotten when they had the chance to embrace such a woman.

For her part, Danny no longer continued to spend weekends in Paris searching for the man she had come to find, but she still needed the forced gaiety and bright night life of the city to take her mind off the forbidding memories that waited in her bedroom back at Chateaudun.

"There was a gentleman here to see you today, Danielle. He came all the way from Paris."

The enthusiasm in Sophie's voice was lost on Danny, who could summon a mild curiosity at best. She had just returned from an early morning ride with Destiny through the countryside. The mare proved difficult, probably because it was such a long time since she had a frequent rider on her back. Danny was slightly out of breath and had an awful headache when Sophie greeted her at the door.

"It must have been important to bring him from Paris, don't you think, dear?"

"Oh? Did he leave his name?"

"No, but he did leave this for you." Sophie handed her the small white business card.

Danielle read the name aloud, in the disinterested tone she had adopted since returning from America, one which Sophie found annoying. "*Societé Industrielle de Française et Americaine.*" Danny shrugged and handed the card back to Sophie. "I don't know anyone from this firm."

"He asked specifically for you, dear. I asked if he cared to leave a message, but he said no, that he would have to check with his superior about sending a letter. I wonder what he wanted."

"I'm sure I don't know, Grandmother," Danny answered.

She wanted only to go to her room and lie down. Maybe she could sleep off the pounding in her head. But Sophie was in one of her talkative moods, and Danny knew relief would have to wait.

"You know, dear," Sophie commented, holding up the card, "this is one of the largest enterprises in France—in all of Europe in fact. I seem to recall having read something about it." She bit her lower lip, trying to jar her memory. Her pensive expression changed to one of instant recollection. "Oh yes, of course, the name is DeMalleray. You remember, dear, that rich old gentleman who owned all that property in Chartre—the one who died some years ago, leaving everything to his grandson. We spoke about it at breakfast one morning. Of course, it was several years ago, but in any case, the young man never even came to claim his fortune, can you imagine that! It's been laying there all this time, getting bigger and bigger."

Danny listened with growing impatience. The story sounded vaguely familiar, but her thoughts at the moment were concentrated on the throbbing at her temples.

Sophie seemed oblivious to the grimace on Danny's face. "I read something very recently about that firm, now let me see. Silver, that's it! Yes, now I remember, they have acquired vast silver holdings in America. What an odd coincidence, don't you agree, dear?"

"Odd indeed," Danny muttered. She turned away before Sophie could see the shadow pass over her face. Silver. America. She wanted nothing to do with any of that—with anything that would remind her of the past and the ever present agony of loving a ghost.

Sophie picked up her wide-brimmed straw hat on her way outside. Pulling shears from her apron, she pruned the rosebushes and azaleas, her mind often darting back to Danielle. It broke Sophie's heart to know that her granddaughter was suffering and that there was nothing she could do to help. Nothing she did or said seemed to satisfy the girl. When she asked questions, Danny retreated into herself, shutting Sophie out. Once when she suggested that they send for Austin, thinking that his presence would snap Danny out of her depression, the girl had flown into a violent rage. She longed to be taken into her granddaughter's confidence, but Danielle would reveal nothing. The letters Sophie received from Austin were always brief and ever so vague, never mentioning what had happened to send his sister running back to France. Why hadn't Austin returned with her? What was going on between them? What was it about that godforsaken country that had claimed her own daughter's life and now threatened her granddaughter's? Sophie Le Hoult did not like being kept in the dark, but her grandchildren had seen to it that she remain ignorant of the events that tormented them both.

Once in her own room, Danny eyed the white envelope with Austin's familiar handwriting on it. She picked it up gingerly and placed it in her top drawer, unopened, with all the others that she had allowed to remain in sealed envelopes. She closed the drawer and locked it with the small key she kept hidden beneath the lacy runner. Then she flopped down on the bed, not even bothering to remove her riding clothes or boots. Within seconds she fell asleep.

When she awoke, her headache was gone, but she felt laden with drowsiness, the kind that results from too much sleep. She stumbled to the window, but when she flung the curtains aside, the flash of light that leapt into the room blinded her with its brilliance. It was morning! She had slept the entire night.

Danielle went downstairs to join her grandmother for breakfast. When she entered the dining room, Sophie looked up from her tea and noticed something different about the girl. It was an undeniable presence that hovered around Danielle—a new aura of self-assurance. Danny was no longer a child; she was a woman with the body, grace, emotions, and the stark sensuality of a very beautiful woman at that. The shock of it sent Sophie's spoon clattering into her teacup.

"I'm sorry if I startled you. I thought we would have breakfast together this morning."

"Of course, dear." Sophie rang the silver bell that sat by her plate and within seconds the imposing figure of Anna, the German cook, was at her side. "Anna, dear, would you please get Danielle some breakfast?"

The fair-haired Anna grinned widely. "I set two places or one?"

"One will be fine, Anna, thank you."

"Grandmother, if I knew you were having a guest for breakfast I wouldn't have intruded. I can have mine in the solarium, I don't mind."

"Nonsense," Sophie huffed. "I wouldn't hear of it. Besides, it's only you and me, dear." She laughed a little too easily Danny thought to herself. But she waved it aside when Anna returned and set a delicious plate of croissants and butter in front of her.

"What's the matter, dear?" Sophie asked when she saw Danny eye with distaste the tea Anna had also brought.

A sheepish grin crept over her face. "Well, I'd really prefer to have coffee." She handed the cup back to Anna, explaining, "I seem to have acquired a taste for it."

When the cup of steaming coffee was set before her, Danielle realized something was going on. She spied the guilty look on Sophie's face and felt an immediate need to run from the room—from whatever it was that Sophie was trying to hide and doing such a poor job at. She started to rise, leaving all thought of breakfast behind, when a voice stopped her cold.

"Good morning, Sophie. Good morning, Danielle."

Danny flashed a dark look at her grandmother who had not said a word, but before she could say anything to Sophie, she felt Austin bend over and gently place a kiss on her forehead.

He felt her body stiffen when he touched her. "I'm sorry if I frightened you, Danny." His voice sounded warm and friendly, but she refused to respond to it. "You're looking well."

She fixed her eyes on one of the embroidered appliqués on the lace table cloth. "Thank you," she said through gritted teeth.

Austin shot an apprehensive look at Sophie, sighed and took his seat at the table.

"You knew! You planned this behind my back!" Danny's voice was aimed at Sophie, who was shocked by the sharpness of the accusation. Even Austin looked at his sister in surprise. Her eyes blazed as she leaned over in her seat to glare at Sophie. "How could you do this!" Her voice rose to a shrill pitch, demanding an answer. "Why did you? Why did you?"

Austin's voice rose above hers with a thunderous velocity. "Stop it, damn it! Stop it!"

Sophie and Danny were both startled by it, and they turned simultaneously to look at him.

Austin rose to his feet, slapping his linen napkin down on the table. "My arrival was certainly no secret to anyone, Danny, so don't pretend ignorance of it as an excuse to vent your childish rage at Sophie. I won't have it!"

Danny looked frantically back to Sophie. "But *I* didn't know," she cried. "*I* didn't know!" She slumped back into her chair, her strength suddenly dissipated. "Why did you come here, Austin?"

"You haven't answered my letters," he said, ignoring the question. "Didn't you receive them?"

She took a deep breath. "Yes, but I haven't read them."

Austin stared at her, surprise plainly evident on his face. "Then . . . Oh my God, then you don't know!"

"Austin, please, let's not make a game of this. If you've come all the way from America to hear that I haven't read your letters, then you can just turn around and go back to—"

"He's alive."

She didn't hear him. The words slipped by unnoticed. "St. Louis or San Francisco or wherever and forget—"

"Danny, he's alive!" This time he shouted.

"Do you think I care? What kind of marriage do you think Lacy and I had anyway? Ha! The fact that he is alive means nothing more to me than the trouble I must go through to obtain a divorce. If you think I am going to remain married to that insidious hypocrite, then you're very much mistaken!"

"No," Austin said, shaking his head at her angrily, "not Lacy." He uttered the name with obvious distaste. "I mean *Alex*."

She stared at him blankly, her face growing paler by the second, the words slowly seeping into her numbed brain. Alive. Alex was alive. She turned on him viciously, seeking to tear him into shreds. "Don't lie to me, Austin, not about this! Don't do this to me!"

"Danny, I'm not—"

"But I saw it!" She shrieked at him, her cheeks flushed with rage. "I saw you kill him! I watched him die before my eyes, and I wished and prayed that you would kill me too, that I could die with him." She collapsed with her head in her hands, sobbing helplessly.

Sophie sat at the opposite end of the table, tears visible in her eyes, the pain of understanding breaking her heart in two. Austin went to Danny immediately and wrapped his arms around her, holding her tightly; comforting and soothing her with whispers. He stroked her hair tenderly, feeling once again the silky softness of its texture and tasting the salt of her tears against his cheek. With a firm arm about her waist, he led her from the room.

He guided Danielle to the solarium where her sobs contrasted to the perfect stillness of the glass room. After the moment of impact passed, Danny was left trembling. She walked in a trance-like state to the wicker loveseat beneath the feathery mimosas and sat next to Austin.

At length, after he felt her sobs subside and the tenseness ease out of her body, he spoke. "I never really expected you to answer my letters," he whispered, "but I never doubted that you would read them." His voice stiffened a little. "If you had, you would have learned sooner than this that Alex is alive."

There it was again, that name, like an explosion in her brain. She looked at Austin through squinted eyes as if to detect any hint of a lie, but there was none. "Would you tell me," she said, steadying her voice, "how Alex is alive when I saw him die?"

Austin sighed. "I think it's time you knew the truth about what happened that night."

"You think it's time! I think you owe me an explanation for your sudden interruption into my life, Austin, and I'd damn well better get it! I've waited long enough for this so-called truth of yours!"

"Austin slumped back into the loveseat, his hands laying listlessly in his lap. For several minutes he stared at the floor. He cleared his throat and spoke slowly in an effort to keep his voice from cracking. "I've been over this in my mind hundreds of times, and sitting here now, I don't know where to begin."

"Try at the beginning," she said, her voice flat. "He was your friend and you shot him."

He jerked his head up sharply. "How did you know that?"

"I saw it," she snapped.

He grabbed her harshly by the wrist and pulled her close. "What else do you know?"

"Nothing." She wrenched free of him, then rose and looked down at him. "I'll leave for America in the morning."

Austin opened his mouth to protest, but she stopped him before he could utter a sound. "No, Austin," she declared, "I must go to him, and you cannot stop me. You'll make it a lot easier if you'll tell me where he is."

"I don't know where he is."

"Surely you don't expect me to believe that!"

"I tell you I don't know!" He was beginning to lose his self-control. "I haven't seen him since . . . that night."

"Then how on earth do you know he's alive? Oh God, Austin, why did you come here? What do you hope to gain by telling me Alex is alive if you don't even know that for certain?"

"I *told* you he's alive!" His face turned livid with anger, and small blue veins stood out at his temples. "I told you that night I would take care of it, and I did, damn it, I did!"

"The doctor said Alex was dead." She flung the words at him, daring him to refute them.

"I arranged it with him," Austin replied disgustedly. He laughed, a short haughty sound that sent a chill through her. "Every man has his price, Danny. The good doctor's price was a bit more than I anticipated, but certainly not out of reach. For the sum of five thousand dollars, he agreed to sign his name to a false death certificate. It's simple as that."

She was bewildered now. Was he lying to her? "But the others, there were others who saw it too."

"There were no others. No one else saw it. In the confusion the stockade guard was knocked unconscious. That left just me and Alex."

"Then why didn't you let him escape? Why did you shoot him?"

"You still refuse to believe that I didn't shoot him out of some deep hatred, is that it, Danny? Or would you prefer to think that my insane jealousy over you drove me to kill the only man I've ever really called my friend, the only man who ever—!" He wanted to grab her by the throat and strangle her, silencing her accusations. Forcing himself to be controlled, he swallowed hard and went on. "Alex would never have made it out of that fort alive. I knew it and he knew it. He was willing to take that chance, but I was not. So I shot him, in the back, the way a man would shoot an enemy he despised." He saw the shock on her face. "I had to make it *look* that way, don't you see! The wound wasn't nearly as bad as it looked, and later the doctor gave Alex laudanum to keep him unconscious."

Danny stared at him incredulously, one moment hoping in her heart for confidence, but the next fearing treachery.

"I knew the fort commander, General Trench, from the visit I had made to Defiance on my way to San Francisco. I also knew about his . . . well . . ." He gulped down the lump in his throat. "Sometimes we have to do things that make us sick inside, but there was no way I could avoid it."

"I don't understand," Danny whispered, afraid to hear the rest.

"Trench had led his company on a campaign against some hostile Apaches the summer before. He was the only one to come back alive. He said he was thrown from his horse and knocked unconscious during the attack." Austin snorted sharply, a look of distaste on his face. "But that's not the story the Indians tell. He deserted his men in the face of battle, after deliberately disobeying written orders. When Trench ran from that fight he thought he was leaving behind any trace of his disgusting deed, but I guess he never counted on anyone finding out about it."

"How did you?"

"News travels fast on the plains," Austin answered. "In no time the Sioux knew about the cowardly soldier chief who left his men to die at the hands of the Apaches." He did not have to explain further. She knew that if the Sioux knew, then Alex did too, and that was probably how Austin found out.

"General Trench paid for my silence with Alex's life," Austin said. "Yes, that's right, he was in on it, too. He had to be. Otherwise, I could not have gotten Alex out of Fort Defiance."

"But Austin, the doctor, what if he ever tells what he knows?"

"That's hardly possible, my dear," he stiffly replied. "He's dead too."

She held her breath waiting for the explanation. He spoke with his eyes averted from hers, his voice breaking under the pressure. "When they placed me under arrest, they decided to move me, along with Alex's body, to Fort Wingate because they have better prison facilities there. At dawn the day after we left we were hit by a small raiding party of Apaches." He forced a strained laugh from his throat. "I think all they wanted was some coffee and tobacco, but the soldiers opened fire on them, killing four or five and sending the rest scattering. About noon they were back, only this time they were ready for battle. They came at us from all directions, and in the confusion to dismount and find something to hide behind, I stumbled over a rifle laying on the ground beside one of the fallen soldiers. I picked it up as I ran and then, all of a sudden, without thinking, I . . . I . . ." The faraway, tortured look in his eyes told her that he was reliving that moment over again. "I saw the doctor just standing there, frozen with fear, and I . . . I . . ." The words tore from his throat in an agonized scream. "I aimed the rifle at his heart and shot him!"

Danny threw herself at Austin, arms going up around his neck, pulling him close to her. She wanted to tell him that she understood and that she didn't hate him, but the words would not come. In their place, blinding tears fell over her cheeks and mingled with his own.

Hours later, when the room was no longer brightened by sunlight, when she could see the shadows of dusk dancing over Austin's features, only then did she kneel at his feet and place her head gently on his knee. "So many things have happened. So many things have changed."

He felt her warm breath through the fabric of his trousers. Letting his head fall back, he closed his eyes to the complete stillness of the night. He heard only the sound of his own faint pulse in his ears, growing stronger, steadier, quicker at her touch. "Yes, so many things have happened," he quietly agreed. But nothing has changed, he added in the privacy of his mind.

"I have to find him," she said. "You know that."

"Yes, I do, but it may not be that easy. I made inquiries after I returned to San Francisco. I had my best men working on it, but—"

"But what?"

"We couldn't find him. I know he's alive, but I don't know where he is. The last I heard, there was this mix-up."

"What kind of mix-up? For God's sake, Austin, what are you trying to say?"

"Something went wrong and I don't know where he is!"

She grasped him firmly by the hand. "All right, Austin, tell me from the beginning everything you know."

"When we got to Wingate, I wasn't permitted to see Alex. All I know is that Trench sent word ahead to expect us. Trench listed some minor offense for Alex, and I figured the worst that would happen was that Alex would spend some time in an army cell and then be released. That was the plan I worked out with Trench. At least Alex wouldn't have been killed." He paused to collect his thoughts. "When I was released I discovered Alex had escaped. Apparently, he headed toward Apache territory figuring that the first place the Army would look for him would be among the Sioux. Anyway, it must not have worked too well, because it seems the Mexicans picked up Alex, mistaking him for some Chiricahua Apache who had been giving them a lot of trouble."

"Do you think they'll execute him in Mexico?" Danielle asked, fearful of the answer.

Austin shrugged fatalistically. "Eventually, when they can't get any information out of him, they'll realize they have the wrong man and will have to release him. That's my guess. But until they do, there's no telling what they'll put him through."

"If he's alive, I'll find him."

"But how? I've tried! One of my men made contact with an official of the Mexican Government and told him to name his price for any information he could furnish about Alex Coulter, or an Apache prisoner that might be in one of their prisons. He came up with nothing. They don't even have a man down there who fits Alex's description. I tell you, it's hopeless."

"Don't say that!" she yelled. "You may think it's hopeless, but I don't. He's my husband, Austin, and I've got to find him!"

"There's something else."

Danny glared at him, amber eyes blazing. "More surprises, Austin? Come on, let's hear it."

"Suppose he's not in prison? Suppose he's free somewhere and doesn't want to be found?"

"Well, that's something I'll simply have to find out."

"Where will you begin?"

Danny contemplated the question several moments before replying. "I've got a couple of ideas," she said, "but other than that . . ." she sighed, "I don't know."

Chapter 31

The woman sat hunched over the ledger. With a sweep of a quill-tipped pen, she inscribed the date at the top of the page. April 14, 1877. Beneath it she penned the results of the day's profits. A gentle knock on the door drew her attention away from her work. "Come in," she mumbled.

"Sorry to bother you, Miss Unity," the girl said, wrinkling her nose at the heavy sweet smell of lilacs that permeated the room.

"What is it, Kitty? I'm busy."

"There's a lady to see you downstairs. She didn't leave her name, but I'd have to say she's just about the prettiest thing I've ever seen. She's . . . she's—"

"Kitty, *please*," Unity exclaimed, a touch of exasperation to her voice. "It's been a long day and I'm beat. Just tell me what she looks like."

"Well, she's got the most incredible eyes I've ever seen. They're gold. And her hair is dark red, and she's got—"

Unity snapped the pen down on the writing table at hearing the description. "Never mind, I know her. Send her up."

Unity remembered Danielle Fleming as a beautiful girl, but she was hardly prepared for what she saw when the young woman was escorted into the room. Was it possible for her to have grown more magnificent? Unity let out a loud, hearty laugh and took Danny's hand. "Honey, I didn't think it was possible," she exclaimed. "I declare, if I had a girl like you working for me, I'd have the West sewn up." She stood back to admire her, noting first the fine clothes Danielle wore and the way her hair was perfectly arranged behind her neck, and

335

the tiny but elegant jewels at her ears. She looked so much the lady that Unity feared her declaration might have offended Danny.

"Tell you what," Danny said, her voice a purr, "if I ever decide to enter the business, I'll let you know."

"Not on your life, honey, Alex would have my hide," Unity laughed.

Danny began to remove her gloves. "I'm glad you mentioned Alex, because he's the reason I'm here."

Unity gestured toward the loveseat and they both sat down. Pouring some coffee from the silver pot on the tray in front of them, she said, "You were saying about Alex?"

"I'd like to know where he is," Danny said, and saw a faint look of surprise register on Unity's powdered face.

"You mean you don't know?"

Danny cleared her throat nervously. "No, I haven't seen him for over a year."

"That's funny," Unity muttered, "I would have figured maybe you'd have stuck with him. Guess I was wrong."

"I didn't leave him. I can't explain to you how or why it happened, but you must believe me, Unity." She looked down at her hands. "No," she said quietly, "I couldn't have done that. It took me a while, but I learned that I could not have left him."

"What makes you think he wants to see you?" Unity realized the question had a sound of cruelty to it, but she reasoned that the possibility was strong and wondered whether Danny had given it much thought.

"I don't know," she answered, "but I've got to find out."

Unity dropped two lumps of sugar into her coffee. "I've got to hand it to you, honey, you've got guts. When Alex brought you up here, I figured there was something special about you that made him go along with that wedding. Alex Coulter's not the kind of man who does something he doesn't want to do, and I figure if he let himself get tricked into marriage, then maybe he knew what he was getting into. But to tell you the truth, hon, I don't know where he is. Saw him a couple of months back, though." Her expression turned serious and she stared into the coffee swirling in her cup. "He didn't look too good. Oh, handsomest devil I ever did see, but he looked kind of wild-eyed. Hard. Bitter. Like I've never seen him before. I was thinking that it might be dangerous for you to

see him again. He's changed." She shook her head dismally.
"He always was an unreachable man, but now he seems to
have retreated further into himself. Won't let anyone near.
Frankly, honey, I'm worried sick about him. Don't even
know if he's still in one piece. When he left here, he looked
like he was capable of almost anything."

Danny spoke up timidly. "Did he say where he was going?"

"Not a word. But then, Alex never seemed to have any
particular destination in mind. He just kind of wandered
wherever it pleased him. Indians are like that."

"Well then, did he say where he had been? If I knew that,
then maybe . . ."

Unity gave her an apologetic smile. "Sorry, he was here
only for a night and he didn't have much to say. Not that I
didn't ask, mind you, but he wasn't talking. He wouldn't even
tell me where he got those awful scars on his back." She
stared off into space for a moment. "Something sure is
troubling that man," she sighed. "It's eating away at him
along with all those other things he keeps locked up inside of
him. But this one is fresh, the scars are new, and I don't just
mean the ones on his back. Wish I knew myself where he was,
but like I told you—Hey, wait a minute!" She sprang to her
feet. "I think I know someone who might know. Wait here."

Several minutes later there was a gentle rapping on the
door and Pierce Morgan stepped into the room. His soft
brown eyes, the ones Danny had always remembered as kind
and warm, opened wide. "Well, I'll be," was all he could say.

"I'm just as surprised to see you," Danny said, tugging him
gently into the room.

"I thought you were . . . I figured you weren't in these
parts anymore," he exclaimed. "I thought you went back to
France."

"You could only have known that from Alex!" she cried.
"Have you seen him, Pierce?"

Morgan stared at her. The last time he saw her she was
dressed in a bright red skirt with a white blouse that dipped
over her shoulders, emphasizing the brownness of her skin.
She was barefooted and her hair hung in long curls down her
back. Even then there was no mistaking her beauty. But now,
seeing her dressed in lush green velvet that enhanced the
whiteness of her skin, she was exquisite. Despite her elegance, he sensed in her the same wildness he had seen when

she was riding astride the Indian pony, casting long looks of hatred at the man who would become her husband.

"Pierce, please," she begged him, "can you tell me where he is?"

He turned away and ran a hand nervously through his sandy brown hair. "I don't know."

"I think there are some things you must know," Danny said, taking his hand and leading him to the sofa. "If by knowing, I can gain your confidence, then I have to tell you."

He listened quietly as she told her story. When she finished, she turned her shiny eyes upon him, pleading with her look. "Please, I must find him. I must see him again. Can you help me?"

He rose to his feet and paced the floor. "Nando, he's . . . I don't think he wants to see you again. He thinks . . . well, there's no telling what he'd do if he saw you."

"If you'll just tell me where he is, I'll get there myself, and I won't tell him where I found out. I'm not asking any more than that. Will you help me?"

He drew in his breath and let it out slowly. "Yes, but I can't let you do it alone. You'd never make it there alive. There's too much scum roaming around, hostiles all over the place. Be ready, we'll leave in the morning." At the door, he turned back to her. "And another thing, see if the girls can come up with some clothes for you. You can't do hard riding in that outfit."

Their journey was slow and unbearable because Pierce insisted that they travel only a couple of hours during the early morning, then hide themselves away for the remainder of the day. There were signs of activity everywhere—tracks on the ground, flattened grasslands where men had camped and allowed their horses to graze, broken branches on thickets, an absence of wildlife in the area. It told Danny that the country they rode through was crawling with activity, but she saw no one, nothing. "What is it?" she asked Pierce one evening when they were sitting by the camp fire. "I can feel it all around me."

"This part of the country is a bad place to be at a time like this," he told her. "This past January, the Army attacked Crazy Horse's village north of here. They're really coming down hard, and—"

Danny gasped. "Crazy Horse? Did they—"

"No, they didn't get him, but they sure are trying. They're hoping at Fort Robinson to get him to surrender this summer."

"Do you think he'll do it?" she asked tremulously.

Pierce shrugged. "I don't know the man myself, although from what Nando says, he's thinking about it. Don't see how his people can take much more of this fighting and running all the time. From what I hear, they're already starving and half-naked." He thought about her question again. "Yeah, I think he'll surrender."

"When did you see Alex last?"

"Couple of months ago. Look, I don't even know if he'll be there. He doesn't come south much anymore—been spending his time up north with the hostiles, riding and fighting with them. But it's the only place I know of."

Danny mustered her courage to ask, "Did he speak at all about me?"

"Yes, briefly. Only to say that you were no longer around and that he believed you double-crossed him."

Danny put a hand on his arm. "Do you think I betrayed him?"

She looked almost like the innocent girl she had been when he first met her. "No," he answered softly, "I don't." He plunged a crooked stick into the fire and poked at the red coals. "But it doesn't matter what I think," he added. "It'll be harder to convince Nando. He's changed from the last time you saw him. He's just as stubborn and strong-willed as ever, but now that's laced with bitterness like I've never seen. There's still time to change your mind."

"No!" she cried. "I won't. Don't you see, Pierce? All the time I thought he was dead, I felt dead inside, too. And then to find out that he was alive, it was like a rebirth for me! Can you imagine what it was like all those months of merely existing, and then to have something once again to live for? I've got to do this! If he hates me, then I don't suppose there's anything I can do about it, but I must find out!"

She was a tough little fighter, all right, but he wondered how tough she would be when it came time to stand up to Nando.

The days grew warmer the further south they rode. "I think

you'll recognize the place," Pierce said when he turned his horse's head through the same wall of thickets that Tomas Alvarez and Matt Turner had led her an eternity ago. Once again her eyes looked upon the green valley that lay spread out before them with four small cabins situated among a grove of pine trees. She could almost hear the bellow of Jake Alvarez's voice come roaring from the cabin the way it had done that day.

"He hasn't been here for a while," Pierce said, after he had gone into the cabin to have a look around. Danny followed right behind him. "That could mean he'll be back soon. It could also mean he won't ever be back. Are you sure you want to wait?"

"Yes," she replied, trying to gather her strength. This place brought back so many memories she felt suddenly weak and tired and felt she should run from here as fast as her legs could carry her. "You don't have to wait with me," she offered. She knew that he too was apprehensive.

"I've got nowhere to go," he said simply. "Maybe I'll stick around a couple of days. If he doesn't show by then, I'll get one of the local farmers to come over and stay with you. This place is as safe as any, though."

The next day he returned with a rabbit slung over his saddle and glanced inside the cabin she had spent the entire morning cleaning. "I don't know if Nando's gonna like this," he laughed.

"That would be exactly like him," Danny said. "Sometimes I think that man loves to hate the world."

"Yeah, well, I guess he's got reason to."

"Like what?"

"You know Nando, he doesn't talk much about what's bothering him, but I've known him awhile and I think that it goes back a long way."

She was eager to learn more and pushed him to explain.

"I always thought maybe something happened to him when he was young. People aren't usually born that way."

"Aren't you forgetting that he's part Indian," Danny reminded him. "That alone is enough to give a man reason to be bitter. It must be a hard way to live."

"I'm not forgetting that for a minute. But I'm not talking about his being a half-breed. I'm talking about the other thing I've seen come over him when he thought I wasn't looking. I really do believe there's not a damned thing in this world that man fears other than himself. No, there's something he doesn't speak about . . ."

Pierce Morgan was a rare man. He was kindhearted when a man in his position—outlaw, outcast—almost had no right to be. He was considerate of her comfort when he owed her nothing at all. He had helped her at great risk to himself, perhaps at the loss of a friendship with someone he clearly cared a great deal about. Pierce had a settling quality about him, and while she had seen him at times laughing heartily and at times saddened and dismayed, she had never seen him angry. He seemed not to possess that capacity, and she wondered how on earth Pierce had come to live the life of a wanted bandit.

Concealed in her past lay the remains of men so much better suited for criminals than this one with the gentle brown eyes. Orders and insults, that's all they knew, and you could expect no compassion or understanding from them. But this one was different. He was sensitive and tender and yet, he was an outlaw, no different really from any of the others whose faces hung on posters in the offices of lawmen throughout the country.

She stood barefooted outside the cabin, watching him saddle his horse. "I don't expect we'll be seeing each other again," he said.

On impulse she threw her arms around his neck, hugging him tightly and burying her face against his shoulder.

"Hey, what's this?" he said, taking hold of her chin and guiding her eyes to his. "If you do that, you're gonna shatter all my illusions about you."

Danny sniffed back the tears and managed a weak smile.

"I'll stop by the Ramirez farm on my way out and ask old Ramon to come over to look after you. He sometimes takes care of this place when none of the men are around." He grasped the reins tightly in his hand. "Take care of yourself, Danny," he said as his horse began to prance about, eager to be on the move.

"I will, and you do the same," she smiled.

He spurred his horse around and rode out of the valley.

Chapter 32

Despite Danny's efforts to scrub the cabin clean, the lingering traces of perfume that filtered into her nostrils reminded her of whose home this had been. That bitch! That black-haired gypsy! Danielle put a kettle over the fire to boil while she heaped more angry words upon the memory of Bianca Alvarez.

Later that night, as she lay in the same bed she knew had once been occupied by another woman, she felt tired and longed for sleep to take her away from the conscious world.

It was not only the presence of Bianca Alvarez that lingered in the tiny cabin. There was someone else here too. Danny closed her eyes but the image would not depart. How many nights? she wondered. How many nights had Alex lain in this bed with his arms around that wench? How many times had he kissed her and stroked her voluptuous body? His masculine presence was everywhere, even though there was nothing in the room that belonged to him, no clothing left behind, nothing except the unmistakable hint in the musty air that he had been a frequent visitor to this room . . . to this bed.

At length she drifted into a fitful sleep. It was not until dawn that she ceased tossing and settled into an almost calm repose. Her breathing returned to its normal pitch and the perspiration evaporated from her body, leaving her skin silky. Disrupting the peace that had been so long in coming came a sudden thunderous interruption, and she awoke with a start as the door to the cabin crashed open from a forceful kick, shattering it against the wall. In an instant her eyes were wide awake and large with terror.

"God damn it!"

He had returned! She watched with eyes growing wider as he staggered in the doorway, muttering unintelligibly under his breath. "What the—!" His eyes strained to make out the shape on the bed. "What the hell is going on here?" he cursed angrily. "Who the hell—!"

"Alex." His name sprang from her lips in a desperate whisper.

Even through the darkness she saw his face turn white. "What the hell are *you* doing here?"

Alex Coulter was gripped by a blinding rage. He was overtaken by an impulse to run to her, but not to take her into his arms and hold her. He wanted to murder the lying, whoring little bitch. All the nerves in his body were tensed, ready to spring for her if she dared utter another sound.

Danny shrank back involuntarily at the cold fury she saw in his face, her terror so great that she could not have said a word if she wanted to.

He remained in the doorway, silhouetted against the opalescent light, glaring at her, his buckskin jacket dangling from one hand, a bottle of whiskey held recklessly in the other. He tilted the bottle to his mouth and drank greedily in long gulps, spilling some down the front of his shirt. He whipped the jacket into the corner and took a step toward her.

Danny bit her bottom lip so hard she tasted blood. If she had any sense, she'd run away as fast as she could. But she willed herself desperately to see this through.

Alex took one step, then stopped. Why didn't she run, or scream, or do something? Couldn't she see he meant to kill her? Even now she defies me, he thought, damning that defiance of hers that had sent him into uncontrollable rages in the past. It surprised him to see it now and he backed off. He walked to the washstand where he poured some water into the basin, then splashed it on his face with cupped hands. The icy water washed away the heaviness that clouded his eyes from too much whiskey, and when he looked at her again, it was as if seeing her for the first time in many long, agonizing months. There she was, looking exactly like the last time he had touched her. He realized, almost with regret, that even his dreams did not do justice to her beauty. She radiated in the darkness, spilling over with such sensuality that he found himself cursing her and himself for having fallen victim to it.

Well, it would never happen again, he sternly vowed. He'd never let her blind him again.

It infuriated Alex that she could appear out of the blue looking unscathed and unscarred, while he died a slow hideous death, consumed by a festering cancer in his very soul. Before she had come along, he had always chosen to live a solitary existence, coming and going as he pleased. These past months, however, he was living a self-enforced isolation. His world was crumbling around him and in his aloneness, he was powerless to deal with it. In his frustration, he struck out violently at anything that got in his way. His Indian friends said that he was a man whose blood had turned hot and whose heart had turned bad. The white men called him a renegade and much worse.

His friends left him pretty much to himself, warily responding to him only when he ventured the first overture. He had become a brooding creature, at times going off by himself and returning days later in a drunken stupor. Sometimes there would be scalps strung carelessly from his saddle horn. Other times he would lead a strange horse into camp and leave it for whoever wanted it. Always, he issued orders no one dared disobey.

Danny seemed to have bounced back with a resilience borne of some inner strength. She seemed to have managed quite nicely, and he hated her all the more for it, almost as much as he hated himself. Here she was, appearing out of nowhere, clutching the blankets in front of her like a nervous virgin. Well, one thing about Danny, she was never without a lot of nerve. Finally, he could no longer suppress his curiosity. "What brings you back to these parts? Have you tired of your brother's arms so soon, or has he finally succumbed to his own guilt?" He flung the words at her viciously and immediately brought her to her feet.

"Alex, why will you never give me a chance to explain anything to you? Why do you always—"

"*Explain*, madam? Even an illiterate half-breed like me can comprehend some things. Do you think I need you to show up here to explain the reasons for your conniving, scheming betrayal of me!"

"Alex, please," she cried. "It's not fair of you to attack me like this when you don't know what you're saying!"

"I'll tell you what I know, you bitch. I know how it feels to lie with a bullet burning in my back, a bullet put there by someone I *thought* was my friend. Christ! I should have known the minute I saw you that Austin couldn't be trusted. Oh yes, madam, I know a lot of other things, too. Like how it feels to wake up every morning in a stinking hellhole, cursing the very life that flows through your veins. Even death would have been better than the rotten existence I endured at your hands, you and that traitorous brother of yours! I assure you there's little that even us Indians forget, so you can take your black heart and your lying words and get the hell out of here before I—"

Danny ran to him, flinging herself at him, clutching him fiercely around the neck. "Alex, it's not true! It's not true!"

He flung her away with one sweep of his arm. She landed on the floor with a thud, then scrambled quickly to her feet a second before he grabbed for her. "You think you know what makes people do things?" she yelled. "There are things I know too . . . things I would never have had to endure if it hadn't been for you, for your intrusion in my life! And you stand there like some horribly wronged victim. All you care about is telling me how I've hurt you! You don't want to hear about your betrayal of me, do you, Alex? You don't want to hear about the man broken in France, do you? He's barely a shell of a person!" She was hysterical, half-screaming, half-sobbing the caustic accusations. Like sharp daggers, they hit home. "Is your hatred of me so great that you won't even listen to the truth simply because it comes from me?" she demanded.

"Truth!" His voice bellowed above hers. "The truth from your lips would certainly be a change of pace, wouldn't it?" He turned his back on her and stalked to the washstand where he had left the half-empty bottle of whiskey. He held it to his mouth a long time. When he had enough, he ran the back of his hand roughly over his mouth and looked at her. The metallic gleam of his gray eyes pierced the duskiness of the room. He shoved the bottle at her. "Here, you look like you need this as much as I do," he said harshly. "Drink it, damn it. If there's anything I can't stand, it's a hysterical woman."

Danny obeyed, placing the bottle haltingly to her lips and grimacing as the hot liquid scorched past her mouth and down her throat. It provided her with renewed strength in spite of herself. "Alex," she said, her voice husky from the whiskey, "you and I spent too much time hating each other. You said it yourself once, it's a thin line we walk between love and hate. We always seem to be on opposite sides of that line. There's so much we don't know about each other, we're like strangers with nothing to like."

"The only thing I'd like at this point is to never have to see you again."

"I know you're saying that to hurt me, and believe me, it does. Everything you say hurts me when you intend it to. But it doesn't stop me from loving you."

"Love!" he cried with incredulous shock. "Love? Is *that* what you call it? Was it love that led you to stand by while they carted me off to prison? Was it love that drove you to your southern army captain as soon as I was out of the way? Don't make me laugh, Danny, you've never done anything out of love in your life. I've known countless women like you. You're all the same. You'll play with a man and embed yourself in his very soul to get at the one thing you've set your designs on. Tell me, you scheming demon, was it out of love that you and your brother arranged to have me killed? And when that didn't work, thrown into prison? Too bad your little plan backfired. I'm sorry to disappoint you, but as you can see, I survived after all. It's too bad Austin is such a poor shot."

"He didn't aim to kill you. If he had wanted to, he could have done it easily. Austin is one of the best marksmen in all of France. Surely you know that!"

"Even the best marksmen make mistakes," Alex said contemptuously. "The moon that night left a lot of shadows to lose a target in. I saw him!" he shouted. "When I looked over my shoulder, he had a gun pointed right at my back. Do you think I didn't see it!"

"Yes, but he wasn't—"

"And do you know what else I saw when I looked back? I saw you, Danny, at the window watching. How did you like the show, my *wife*? Did you and Austin spend the rest of the night in each other's arms?"

She clapped her hands over her ears to block out the cruel words. "No! No!" she shrieked. Her own fury burst upon her like a tidal wave, and in one quick leap she went for him, a savage cry escaping her lips as she raked her fingernails across his face. Satisfaction filled her at the sight of the blood welling up from the scratches. Blinded to everything else, she beat his chest furiously with her small clenched fists. "It's not true! It's not true!" A sharp kick aimed at his shin brought an angry growl from Alex, and in the next second he successfully subdued his flailing attacker by wrapping his arms mercilessly tight around her and choking the breath sharply out of her lungs.

He lifted her off the floor and flung her down harshly on the bed as though she were nothing more than a sack of flour. He stood back, thumbs hooked in his belt, looking down at her with a sardonic smile on his face.

She lay there with her shift twisted about her hips, panting heavily, her bare legs parted in an unconsciously seductive manner. Alex felt a gnawing in his loins and backed away. *Even now she has this power over me. Damn her for the lying whore she really is!* "That position suits you best." he said caustically. "Sometimes you were so eager to spread your legs for me, I almost believed you liked it."

"I did," she said, "because it was you, and because you're the only man who has ever satisfied me." She scrambled to her knees. "Oh, you stand there laughing at me, Alex Coulter, but at least I can admit to it. What's the matter, Alex, you want me as much as you ever did, yet you stand there paralyzed. Have you lost your capacity as a man?"

Her taunting jeers filled him with disgust. "You won't stop at anything, will you?"

"That's right," Danny declared triumphantly. "I've found that out the hard way. I've done things I never thought I could do, but they were never so horribly final as when I thought you were dead. My life was totally empty and meaningless when I thought you were no longer alive. It doesn't matter now that I say these things to you, Alex. I've learned the hard way that love has no pride."

"Does Austin's love have any pride?" he asked scornfully. "Is his love for you so without honor that he would kill me himself to win back the Lady Laura for you? You two really had me fooled for a while," he confessed. "Who would have guessed that you planned together to rob my silver mine."

She stared at him in disbelief at the crazy things he was saying. "What are you talking about? The Lady Laura, *yours?* You know damned well that mine belongs to—"

"Don't say it!" The ice-cold warning stopped her in mid-sentence. "Because if you do, you will be wrong."

Danny looked away nervously, unable to meet the glare of his eyes. Suddenly a shiver seized her. She opened her mouth and could barely get the words out, so tight was the knot in her throat. "I . . . I . . . didn't . . . know."

There was something about her perplexed expression that told Alex she could not be lying. He sighed deeply and closed his eyes. "I see," he muttered, feeling a rush of disgust. "So, he used you too." He shook his head in dismay.

Immediately, she snapped out of her confusion. "No, Alex, no! I know what you're thinking, but you mustn't. Austin would never do anything to hurt either of us. Please, you must believe that! He did what he had to do. He's no different from you and I after all, only he's probably suffered more than we have. He did it knowing that one day, if he succeeded, he would risk losing it all. And he has. He could not have done that for himself, don't you see? He's not that kind of man. It had to be for us. I suppose he just never wanted to hurt me with the truth that the Lady Laura was not mine. Oh God, I can't stand it!" She sank back onto the bed, her face in her hands.

"Your torment over his state of affairs is touching," Alex remarked. "I might even be tempted to believe what you say about him, if it weren't for the fact that it's proven difficult for me to believe anything you say."

Things were rapidly falling apart before Alex's eyes. All the pictures, images, scenes he had etched into his memory were distorted, shattering into fragments. All right, so she didn't know about the Lady Laura, so what? That was possible after all. But she *did* know about Austin's little death plot; she had even conspired in it. It would take a lot of hard talking and plain cold facts to convince him otherwise. "You were always such a good little liar, I almost believed that story about Austin being a crack shot." He laughed, a short bitter sound from his throat.

"He won the national championship three years in a row," she mumbled. "He's better with a gun than you are."

"What else is he better at than me?" The cruel question was precisely aimed.

"I wouldn't know," she said, "only you won't believe that."

"I wish I could believe you." Alex's desperate whisper filtered across the room.

"And why can't you?" she demanded.

"Because I don't know what to believe anymore. I've lost faith in so much."

"You had no faith to lose, Alex, and you know it."

"Don't presume to tell me what I know. What would you know about it anyway?"

"Nothing! That's just the point! There's not much I do know about you. You've allowed so precious little of it to escape from that prison you hold it all in. Whenever I try to reach out to you, you shut yourself off."

His voice was low and sounded like a growl. "You should not have come here."

"I came here to find my husband,"

"You're full of jokes, aren't you?" Alex snapped. "Which one, may I ask? I seem to recall you had two of them—at the same time! Oh, that's right, wait a minute. I believe husband number two was killed in battle. Died bravely, I hear, at the hands of some savage along the banks of the Little Big Horn River. Isn't that right, Danny?" He snorted in contempt. "I certainly hope you mourned his death a little more fervently than you did mine."

"Oh, Alex Coulter, you can be the most detestable man I know!" She was exasperated with his stubbornness.

"And I dare say, you've known many."

The remark stung her deeply.

"You'll notice, my love," he drawled, "that I said he died bravely. That *is* what the papers said, isn't it?" He paused for effect, raising one eyebrow. "Would you care to hear how he really died?

"Do you know who the last man was at Little Big Horn, Danny? Care to guess who crawled around on his knees in the dirt crying and begging for his life? They all died bravely except one. I was there. I saw it."

"My God, Alex, don't you see it only saved me the trouble of doing it myself? Do you think I could have endured living with that wretched man any longer? I only married him to save Austin, because Lacy was the only one who could help. As much as I despised Austin for shooting you, I couldn't stand by and watch them execute him!" She paused to take a deep breath and gather her strength. "I did that for him, but for you I've done more."

"You're just doing things for everybody, aren't you?" he taunted. "Reminds me of the time a couple of months back when I was up north and I heard a fellow talking about some whore his buddies had picked up. From the way he described that little lady, not to mention the things they did with her, he had every man in the place frothing at the mouth. What's the matter, don't you want to hear this?"

Danny clasped her hands over her ears, shaking her head from side to side. He could be so devastatingly cruel when he wanted to be. "No," she protested, "I won't listen."

Alex covered the distance between them quickly and caught her by the arm. "You will listen," he ordered. "You didn't think I knew about your escapades, did you? Well, I found out all right, along with every other man in that saloon. How do you think I felt hearing about my wife's infidelities in front of a roomful of men?" His grip tightened painfully. "Turns out they were the same lousy bastards that turned me in for the reward money. Ironic, isn't it?"

"You have no right!" she screamed at him. "You don't know what really went on at all! You have no right to judge me!" Her voice rose to an agonized scream so she didn't even notice that Alex's hold on her wrists had loosened to where she could easily have broken away. All she could see were the faces of those men who had violated her. Her slender body was wracked with sobs, and watching her, Alex felt the color drain rapidly from his face. Unconsciously he let go of her, a knot growing inside his stomach.

"Danny . . ."

She looked at him sharply with amber eyes narrowed into slits. "Don't come near me," she warned breathlessly.

Alex ignored her, and pulled Danielle to him again. He looked down past her glazed eyes to her parted gasping lips and all of a sudden he became acutely aware of the feel of her body molded to his, her firm round breasts against his chest, the soft richness of her hair, the scent of her perfume.

Despite the haze in her eyes, Danielle's fingers inched their way around his neck until she had him in her grasp, and then she clung to him fiercely. Without realizing it, Alex's fingers tangled in her mass of auburn hair. Without further warning for either of them, his mouth was on hers and he was kissing her hungrily, as a man who has been on the verge of starvation. The desire that overwhelmed him made him moan out loud, and all he could think of at the moment was possessing her, having her again. It had been so long!

He felt her tongue push its way between his lips and dart

about his mouth as she kissed him back with a fervor that excited him. How many other men had kissed her like he was kissing her now? Partly from desperation, partly from self-disgust, he tore his mouth from hers and pushed her away with a savage thrust. She stumbled backward and caught her balance, her eyes welling up with glistening tears that came spilling over her lashes. "Why, Alex, why?"

His voice was flat and dry. "I think this meeting is at an end. You'd do best to leave for France as soon as you can. If you don't, I'll simply leave you here and go away myself. I'll have the divorce papers sent to your home in France again."

"Divorce! But Alex—" She stopped short when the word rang in her ear. "What do you mean *again?*"

"I sent my man to your house to deliver the papers personally, but I understand you weren't home that day."

Danny examined him quizzically, trying to make sense out of his riddles. "I don't remember any such man. What are you talking about?"

"That's funny," Alex said, "He told me he left his card for you, but then, I guess you must have lots of gentlemen callers who leave their cards." His remark was spiked with that familiar old sarcasm.

"What do you mean that you sent *your* man?"

"Nothing," he said quickly. "Nothing at all. I just hired someone to deliver the papers. I wasn't about to take off for France to do it myself, so I hired a firm that does that kind of thing."

Danny gave him a look of total contempt. "You really are a brute of a man, do you know that? You speak to me of divorce as though I've done some unspeakable thing to you. But what about you, Alex? Isn't there something you're hiding from me? Oh, I know there is because I've seen you pull it out of sight often enough whenever I get too close. What makes you think that if I knew the truth about you, that it would not be me who'd be demanding a divorce because I found you as contemptible and repulsive as you find me?"

Alex laughed abruptly. "I don't think myself any better than you," he advised her. "As a matter of fact, it has often amazed me how much alike we really are. Unfortunately, the only time we seem to get along is when we're in bed and—" His words broke off sharply. He hadn't meant to say that, and once again he was reminded of the strange hold she had on him.

"That bothers you, doesn't it, Alex? You won't admit how much you want me, but don't you think I could tell before when you held me? You want me as much as I want you, and we both know it." She looked up at him through thick black lashes that framed her tawny eyes.

She was close . . . so close again, and he could feel her breath, soft and warm, against his chest, penetrating the fabric of his shirt.

"Alex, please . . ."

Her whisper reached his ears and sent faint tremors down his spine. Fighting against his own muscle reaction, he willed his body to remain rigid and firm. She placed a hand timidly on his chest to test his reaction, but when he did not strike out at her, she slid it slowly to his shoulder. Reaching around his neck, she clasped it there, feeling the thick black curls at her fingertips. Finding his hand at his side, she took it gently and placed it on her breast. Feeling his resistance and hearing the increased pitch of his breathing, she ignored the warning.

Alex Coulter was torn by an uncontrollable impulse to send her flying across the room. Was there no limit to the tenacity of this woman? How could she persist in flinging herself at him in spite of his efforts to repel her? Each time she only seemed to bounce back stronger than before. He hated her for doing this to him, but Christ, she smelled so sweet. And he could still taste her lips from before, and beneath his palm he could feel her hard little nipple. She knew the extent of his anger and still she continued to defy him. Of all the women he'd known, she was the only one who could defeat him . . . the only one who could prove to be his downfall. From the day he'd met her, she had been his one fatal weakness, and Alex Coulter was incapable of resisting her any longer.

A groan escaped from his throat as he brought his mouth down on hers with crushing force. He forced his tongue between her lips and ravaged the inside of her mouth as thoroughly as his hands raked over her body, leaving not a single inch free from his desperate caresses. He could hear her whimper beneath his kiss, but it only increased his frenzy. He was beside himself with lust, obsessed with consuming her.

Sweeping her up into his arms without removing his lips from hers, he carried her effortlessly to the bed. This time when he threw her down, he landed on top of her. He held her arms pinned above her head even though she was giving him no struggle, and he forced his way between her legs even though they parted easily for him. In one tear, the nightdress came ripping off her body as though it were made of nothing more than the silk of a spider's web. She gasped at the force of his passion, but gave no resistance.

The length of his hard muscular body covered hers. He was kissing her lips, eyes, cheeks, throat, shoulders, breasts, belly. And Danny responded to every caress with an increased pitch of her own. Her body rocked in unison with his until she thought she would go mad with the throbbing excitement that was about to burst from her.

His lips brushed past her ear and she heard his voice like a feathery whisper sending waves of tumult rolling over her and a savage quiver down her spine. "Oh God, Danny, I've wanted you."

They made love to each other as two people starving for nothing but each other, with only their own passionate appetites to feed. In all their lovemaking, he had never known her to respond with such fervor. She called to him with tender words of love, intimate urgings, heated demands, igniting his desire into a roaring flame and carrying him to infinite heights. The months of waiting and longing seemed to melt away when each, at long last, had the one thing they could not live without.

Chapter 33

His. She was his. No matter what had happened during those months when they were apart, he had once again enforced his claim on her. My God, he muttered to himself, only a witch could have crawled beneath his skin the way this golden-eyed she-demon had done. When had he let his guard down long enough for her to slip in, making herself as much a part of him as the blood that flowed through his veins? She was trouble for him. He'd known that since the day he met her. She alone could destroy him. She almost did once, she could do it again. He rolled off her moist body and lay next to her, his head propped up on one elbow watching her.

How perfect her breasts are, he thought. Lightly he ran his finger over her taut pink nipples, raising goose bumps on her flesh. "I suppose I should be grateful that you've come back to me," he said softly, "but somehow I don't think it's all over yet. It's still hanging there between us." He got up and walked, naked, to the window.

Her gaze followed him, watching the way the muscles worked as he moved. She felt her throat go dry as her eyes swept across his hips, over firm buttocks and down long lean legs. As worn out as she was from their lovemaking, she felt the familiar stirrings for him begin anew in her loins. She was like putty in his hands, she thought dismally, under the spell of his touch and he knew it. He alone had the ability to reduce her to an animal, with an animal's naked hungers. When he turned to face her, it was easy to banish all thought of passion, for his voice, when he spoke, bore none of the desire that had surged through him minutes before. It was flat and cuttingly to the point.

"I'm heading out of here in the morning," he said. "I only came back to gather some of my gear. I didn't plan on staying." From across the room he saw the look of pain spring into her eyes. "Don't look at me like that. What did you expect? That we should live happily ever after? It doesn't work like that." He turned away, unable to bear the hurt written on her face. "Look, I've got to go north for a while. Maybe I'll be back, but I don't know when. You can stay here if you want to. There's Ramon around to look after the place. Matt Turner might ride in, I heard he's in the area."

"I see," Danny said stiffly. "Does it matter at all to you whether I'm here *if* you come back?"

His voice roughened. "Don't ask me how things are going to be because I don't know. Neither of us is used to being owned. We're too much alike, and I wonder whether it wouldn't get in the way. I don't know if it would work between us." He gave a fatalistic shrug and added, "Or if it even could work."

"What's up north?" she asked, forcing a casual tone.

"Crazy Horse."

She tried to keep the emotion out of her voice. "Couldn't you take me with you?"

"No, not this time, it's not safe for you. There's too much going on. Crazy Horse is on his way to the Red Cloud Agency to surrender, and there's likely to be some trouble along the way."

Her amber eyes grew large. "You mean he's surrendering his freedom, the freedom of his people, for life on a reservation? How could he do that?"

Alex approached her cautiously, calculating her reaction. "How would you know about that?" he asked sharply. "How would you know about the hunger and the suffering those people have seen this past winter? How would you know what it's like to run from the soldiers who pop up at every turn, ready to destroy your villages and kill innocent women and children who get in the way? If Crazy Horse is surrendering his people and compromising their freedom, then it's only so that they can live. None of them has to follow him into captivity. If they do, it's because they choose to."

He returned to the bed and lay down again beside her. "I figure to be gone a couple of months, probably less. If you're still here when I get back, then maybe we'll see if things can be worked out." He rolled over, closed his eyes and forced himself to sleep.

When Danny opened her eyes to the sunlight that streamed in through the open window the next day, the spot on the bed beside her was vacant. She raced to the window. The sun was already high in the sky and she knew that Alex had been gone for hours. Turning dejectedly back to the room, she searched for a note he might have left, but there was nothing.

A sound outside caught her ear and she stiffened. Someone was approaching. She darted to the window and crouched beneath it, afraid to peek out, listening intently to the sound of a horse's steps drawing closer at a steady pace. She heard singing in a friendly voice and finally summoned the courage to look.

Ramon Ramirez was not surprised to find the woman there. He'd been told by Morgan to ride over and check on her, and to be especially nice to the lady, since she was Nando's wife. The old man had whistled between his teeth at that bit of news, and decided to come over to see her for himself. Nando's wife. *Por Dios.*

Ramirez was no longer a young man but even if he could not literally enjoy the pleasures of a beautiful woman, he had never ceased to appreciate a fine thing. Even a self-proclaimed connoisseur of lovely ladies such as he, however, was not prepared for the one he met at the hideout. The old man chuckled to himself as he watched her approach. He knew Nando always picked the prettiest ones, but this one, *ay caramba,* this one was a prize!

In no time at all he was charmed by her and he knew Nando had chosen well. In the days that followed Ramon came to realize what it was, along with her looks, that gave her this special status in Nando's life, for the girl seemed to possess a rare spirit. She was such a skinny one, Ramon thought, secretly preferring the ample proportions of his own wife to the sleek lines of this little gypsy. Still he could easily see how many men would fall all over themselves for her.

The days passed slowly and uneventfully, and gradually Ramon saw Danielle's glow fade. Something seemed to be troubling the woman, although he could tell she was making a valiant attempt to hide it from him. He did not ask and she did not offer to tell him, but it was there and growing stronger each day.

For some days now an uneasy feeling had begun to nag in the recesses of Danny's mind, growing more irritable the more she could not put her finger on its source. What was it? she demanded of herself, growing impatient at its elusiveness. Gradually, she realized it was a feeling of doom, though not for herself. She could not see it, nor hear it approaching, and yet she felt danger lurking about, with a definite foreboding in the air. She could not even guess from which direction it would spring, nor what shape it would take. Austin came to mind and a strange twist developed in her stomach at the thought of him, alarming her.

Ramon Ramirez glanced at her from beneath the wide brim of his tattered straw hat. He could never have guessed that while she went through the motions of preparing dinner, her mind was on a distant shore.

The room where Ramirez and Danielle sat quietly eating their dinner of rabbit stew was rough-hewn and bare except for the most essential pieces of furniture. The room in her thoughts was elegantly furnished. The man who sat with her was an illiterate Mexican farmer who had had little luck in his life. The man in her thoughts was young, handsome and had had many opportunities—enough to make the head of a man like Ramon Ramirez spin wildly.

The spitting flames cast a strange orange glow over Austin's face as he sat motionless before them, staring with empty eyes into the fiery depths, feeling neither the warmth of the burning logs, nor the chill as the flames gradually began to die.

The only part of Austin Fleming's plan that had succeeded was that which kept Alex Coulter alive. Yet knowing that his best friend lived did little to alleviate Austin's overwrought conscience when, in his heart, he knew that Alex would have chosen to die a free man than live confined to a prison cell for any length of time.

Austin had failed miserably and the shame which filled his heart made it that much harder to bear his self-incriminations. As the flames flickered and grew dimmer in the hearth, so too did Austin's reasons for living.

He had succeeded only in bringing torment into the lives of those he loved the most, and the weight of it laid heavily on his conscience, clouding his judgments and marring his sensibilities. Eventually, the intentions which had once seemed so good, had turned against him and now lay at the pit of his stomach like some awful disease eating away at him.

He rose from the sofa and walked with heavy steps to the decanter of cognac on the table. He seemed to move as if by some outward force, as though someone had pulled his strings and set him in motion. The soothing warmth of the liquor as it washed down his throat went unnoticed. He was sitting at his desk, although how he got there he did not know. Casting a dispassionate look downward, he wondered how he had come to be holding the quill-tipped pen in his hand, and who had put the sheet of blank paper before him. He lifted his hand with effort, placed the tip of the pen at the upper corner and wrote in a flowery script with as steady a hand as he could, 'Chateaudun, 24th June 1877'.

Without prior thought as to what he would write, how he would begin, or if indeed he could even find the words to express the feelings in his heart, he watched the pen glide across the naked page. The room was silent except for the scratch sounds of the pen and the beating of his heart. Sitting hunched over for an indeterminate amount of time, his eyes strained against the darkened room to see the words, not really grasping their meaning, but trusting they sprang from his heart. At the close of a very long time, when there seemed no more to say, the pen dropped from his fingers and he slumped back in the chair exhausted, tapped of all physical strength and emotionally drained. The fire had gone out and the room was dark, but the final words he had written radiated off the page, 'Your loving brother, Austin'.

When the ink on his signature was dry, he folded the letter in half, tucked it into an envelope and scrawled her name across it. He propped up the envelope on the desk so that her name shone out at him. Then, mechanically, without thinking, for it had already been decided, his hand moved to the drawer at his right. Sliding it open, he reached inside and felt around its interior until his fingers rested on a familiar object. He lifted it out and closed the drawer again.

His mind was blank, his emotions were suspended somewhere above the earth. His eyes lingered on the name penned on the envelope, and without removing his gaze, he raised the pistol to his head and pulled the trigger.

Sophie Le Hoult managed to remain remarkably calm in spite of the fact that she felt herself falling apart. She had known that Austin was depressed, she'd seen him moping around the house for weeks ever since Danielle left for America. But she never thought, that is, she never even imagined . . .

He even seemed to be in better spirits during the past few days. Just that morning at breakfast he had chided her on her fastidious manners and they had laughed about something trivial, although she could no longer recall what it was. He seemed so at ease with himself which should have told her that something was wrong. Yet it failed to attract her attention then, and she let his good mood slip by without questioning it, relieved that he had climbed out of his morbid depression. She had eaten dinner alone that evening, assuming that Austin would eat when, and if, he wanted to. He had never been the kind of person one could tell what to do. Instead of bothering him with her foolish insistence that he come to supper, she had instructed Anna to keep a dish warm for him should he decide to emerge from his study. Sophie could not know then that he would never come out of that room again.

It was the sound of the shot that broke the stillness of the night, followed in minutes by the most awful bloodcurdling screams she'd ever heard which she recognized instantly as Anna's hysterical shrieking. She threw on her robe and ran from her bedroom, her mind whirling. When she reached the study, Anna was clutching the door screaming and pointing inside. Sophie had squinted into the darkened room and saw a figure slumped over the desk. Leaving Anna outside, she entered the room and closed the door behind her. When she emerged, the front of her robe was crimson and the tears that ran from her eyes mixed with the streaks of blood on her cheeks.

Sophie had handled all of the arrangements herself, finding in herself a strength she did not know existed, but it was not until nearly three weeks later that she could bring herself to enter that room again. Haltingly, she had unlocked the door to the study and stepped inside. The curtains were pulled tight. It was daylight outside, but stepping into the morose tomb-like room was like stepping into nighttime. Rather than draw the curtains, Sophie lit the lamp and glanced around, afraid to let her eyes go by the desk. She feared the shadows might play tricks on her failing sight and force her to see the horrors of that night all over again. Skirting the room, she saw nothing out of the ordinary. Finally, she found the courage to look at the desk. As she approached it warily, she saw what she was looking for . . .

The letter was still where he had placed it, with Danielle's name written across its face. Sophie reached out a shaky hand for it, and held in her fingers her grandson's last words. It was not difficult for her to guess what those words were, and she gazed long and hard at the envelope struggling with her conscience over what she knew she should not do, and yet which she knew she would. What purpose would be served in giving this letter to Danielle? The question ravaged Sophie's mind, finding no easy answers. None, she decided and slipped the letter into her pocket. This time when she left the room, there was no reason to lock the door behind her. The danger was gone.

She went directly to her bedchamber where a low fire burned in the corner fireplace. Without hesitating, and with only one quick final glance at the familiar script, she tossed the letter into the flames and watched it die. Later she would sit down and write to her granddaughter, and in her letter she'd tell her of the unfortunate, fatal 'accident' that had befallen Austin. Poor Danielle would be inconsolable, but only Sophie would know how much more her grief would be if she knew that she were the ultimate reason for this thing that had happened.

Sophie shook her head sadly. Poor, poor Austin, my poor darling, if only you had not loved her so much. If ever I was impatient with you, my dear, it was only because you did so little to dissuade your own emotions, emotions that you knew to be wrongful yet harbored nonetheless.

Chapter 34

A light summer shower sprinkled over the dried earth and gave the grass the moisture it needed to keep from turning brown and dull. The cool slanting droplets provided the heat-drowsy creatures with a refreshing bath, luring them out from under the rocks and brushes of sage where the heat of the day had chased them. Without warning, the force of the rain increased with a full wind that blew in from out of nowhere, once again proving the complete unpredictability of nature and its total mastery over everything.

Sitting outside, enjoying the feel of the soft raindrops splattering against her dust-streaked cheeks, Danny watched the skies open up. By the time she reached the safety of the cabin, she was drenched, and there was no telling what time it was. The sun was blocked out of the sky by dark forbidding clouds and it may well have been the dead of night. Her hair hung in damp curls down her back and fell into her eyes. Grasping thick handfuls, she piled it on top of her head and fastened it there with some hairpins. She slipped quickly into some dry clothes and put a pot over the fire for coffee. Staring listlessly into the flames, she waited for the water to boil, while outside the storm was rapidly subsiding, as quickly as it had developed. She knew that a sunny winter day could change abruptly into a terrifying blizzard, bringing winds that caused snowdrifts covering buildings.

A whinny from the corral snapped her away from the frightening thought of families suffocating in their homes, and she went to the window to see what the matter was. He was just dismounting when she threw the door open to daylight. She hadn't even heard him ride up. The rain had made the ground so soft that his horse's steps had been muffled in the mud.

She ran to Alex, her hair still damp and coming loose from the pins. She stopped a few feet short of him, suddenly remembering how angry she was at him, torn between the desire to fling herself into his embrace or to curse him violently for staying away so long.

With saddlebags dangling from one hand and his rifle from the other, Alex turned finally to look at her. His silver eyes sparkled as he cocked his head to one side. "Are you going to just stand there, or are you going to help me with this stuff?" The sound of his voice was like sweet music to her ears.

"Oh, yes," she said, as she accepted the pack he slung into her arms.

"Wait a minute. Here, take this one too." He fitted a package beneath her arm. "And keep your nose out of it."

She flung her head up at him, amber eyes shining. "Have I ever snooped through your things?" she asked, scowling.

Alex rolled his eyes upward and shook his head. "No," he admitted, a touch of annoyance in his tone. "No, you've never done that. Now would you please take those things inside?"

Danny wheeled around and stalked away, her skirts swirling about her ankles. When her back was turned, Alex broke out into a wide grin, exposing flashing white teeth. So, she still had the old fight in her, he thought, amused that she refused to take his guff. She sure could spit, that little hellcat, he laughed to himself, but as soon as he entered the cabin and saw his belongings laying in a heap in the middle of the floor, he ceased to be amused. He picked up his things and threw them down on the table. "Are you through playing games?" he tersely asked.

"Are you through giving orders?"

There were no longer traces of a smile on his face. "You're beginning to try my patience, Danny."

"I'm really sorry about that," she said with the sarcasm dripping from her honey-sweet voice. "I suppose my patience was not tried when I had to wait here all these weeks not knowing whether you would return or not!"

"No one told you to wait." His comment silenced her, and she walked away quickly. He was instantly sorry for what he'd said. Sure, he hadn't really asked her to stay in so many words, but he had implied it. During the time he'd been away, he asked himself repeatedly why he had not given her a thicker thread to cling to. He knew she'd be angry with him. Underneath it all he had to admit that he loved to see her when she was all fired up. When her eyes blazed golden daggers at him and her cheeks flushed scarlet, she reminded him of a gypsy, and it was at those times that he desired her the most. He moved toward her and in two long strides was at her side. Encircling her waist with one arm, he pulled her to him and kissed her thoroughly, as if claiming her all over again and sealing his brand on her. Sweeping her up into the air, he carried her to the bed.

There were no words between them, save the soft murmurings of love and the breathless whispers of passion and desire that filled the silent room as they discovered each other once again. She lay with the weight of his body half covering hers, listening to the sound of his breathing returning to normal, filling her nostrils with his male smell and gently running the tips of her fingers over the rough uneven scars on his back. They had healed further in the past weeks, but she knew that the whip had cut too deeply to ever eradicate its mark from his flesh.

She lay contented and drowsy in his arms. He had come back to her, having offered no excuses for his heartless indifference and she, for the moment at least, didn't care. She stirred, nudging Alex awake.

He sat up and looked at her nude body stretched out close to his. "What's the matter? You're nervous about something, baby? Is anything wrong?"

"I guess that storm shook me up a little," she confessed. "Were you caught in it?"

Alex nibbled at her breasts, teasing her pink nipples erect. "No," he said quietly as he moved his mouth along her body. "I rode in just behind it." She writhed beneath his touch. "I'm pleased to see that something besides that storm can shake you up," he teased. His mouth found hers. "You'll never convince me that you don't love it as much as I do," he said, brushing her ear with his lips.

Danny squirmed out from under him. "You presumptuous brute!" she cried. "I know you only say those things to make me angry."

Alex laughed heartily. "And it works every time."

"Oh!" She turned on him in a flurry of movement, until he caught her wrists and stopped her. "What the hell are you trying to do, kill me?"

"I should have killed you long ago. You're insufferable, and if you don't let go of me this instant, I'll . . . I'll . . ."

Alex cocked an eyebrow at her. "You'll what, my love? You hardly look in a position to do anything."

The reminder of her absurd threats dissolved her ire into giggles. Alex smiled and kissed her, long and deep, while his hands caressed her body with a new tenderness. When the desires that burned in her matched his own, there was nothing she would not have done for him.

Later that evening she cooked some meat and potatoes and watched Alex wolf down the food on his plate. "When was the last time you ate?" she asked, amazed at his appetite.

Alex looked up from his plate, a wry grin playing at his lips, and a teasing glimmer in his gray eyes. "Lots of good loving always makes me hungry."

Danny blushed involuntarily and lowered her eyes. Having him back again had brought a resurgence to her own appetite, and they finished their meal in silence. When the dishes were cleared off the table, Alex reached for a bottle of wine and drank in long gulps. Danny stared at him in wonder. There was something strange about him this evening, about the way he drank so intently. Almost as though he were trying to get drunk in a hurry. Was it her imagination, or did he seem impatient to swallow down the entire bottle of wine?

Alex sat back in his chair and stretched out his hard-muscled legs in front of him. "What's the matter," he asked, nodding at the glass that was untouched in front of her, "aren't you going to drink to our reunion?"

"You seem to be doing enough of that for both of us," Danny remarked dryly.

Alex scrutinized her carefully. "Where did you put that package I had on the table?"

Danny glanced to the corner. He got up, the sound of his bootheels heavy on the wooden floor. When he returned to the table there was a half-smile on his face. "It's for you," he said, placing in front of her the package wrapped in plain brown paper. "Open it."

She fumbled with the string nervously, trying to guess what could be inside. When she succeeded in working the knots loose, she opened the paper and gasped.

A pair of pistols lay on the bed of crumpled brown paper. Her astonishment turned gradually to fear and then to wary caution. "Why did you give me these?"

Alex flicked his silver eyes over the guns scornfully. "Don't you recognize them?"

"What are you talking about? They're only guns."

"Look closer."

Danny looked closer, but still failed to see anything remotely recognizable about them.

"The handle," Alex whispered.

She nudged one of the guns aside to reveal the pearl-handled pistol beneath. Her eyes swept over the weapon searching for something familiar about it, and all at once alighted upon a sickening sight. The handle was inscribed with the initials WG—William Garvey. "I don't understand. Why . . . ?"

Alex slammed the bottle of wine down on the table. "I could have brought you their scalps. Would you have preferred that?"

Danny's eyes widened at him as he paced the floor of the tiny cabin. "No, no, I don't want their scalps," she cried. "I don't even want these." She shot a scornful look down at the cold objects on the table.

"Well, they're yours now, do what you want with them," he snapped.

A sudden thought brought Danny to her feet and at his side in a hurry. "How did you get them?"

Alex whipped his head around to face her and his reply sounded like a snarl to her ears. "How do you *think* I got them?"

Danny's hand flew up to her mouth as though to stifle her words. "You killed them." It brought no response from Alex who neither admitted nor denied anything. "You killed them!" The accusation brought an instant response.

"What did you expect me to do," he shouted. "Did you expect me to let them live? Did you think I could live knowing that they walked somewhere on this earth?"

Danny was too stunned to cry. "My God," she said, "a man like you must have many enemies, do you plan on hunting down all of them and murdering them one by one?"

Alex looked at her with an astonished raise of his dark brows. "You think I killed them because of what they did to me? No, baby, I did it for you. Doesn't that please you?" He turned and walked away, leaving her speechless. "I knew I was probably walking into a trap," he said, "but you couldn't have known what those men were capable of. That's why what they did to you was so much worse than what they did to me. That's why I hated them, and that's why I hunted them down."

She closed her eyes and thought of all the raw rage he had directed at Will Garvey and Del Grass. Oh, she hated them all right. She despised them with every ounce of strength she had in her body, and to the end of her days she would live in fear of the memories evoked by them. Yet somewhere in the bottom of her heart, in a spot that she seldom thought existed anymore, a trace of pity was to be found—even for them. As the victims of a man like Alex Coulter, she knew without being told that their deaths had come hard.

The silence in the cabin almost deafened her with its roar. Somewhere outside a night owl hooted and in the lonely distance a coyote called to its mate beneath a full moon. Alex's voice was husky from too much wine. "When I was tracking them, I asked around and found out a couple of things I wasn't after. I learned for instance that there was another one who rode with them. Seems Will Garvey had himself a younger brother." He shot a sidelong glance at her and saw her stiffen. "His name was Lonny and they say he was gut shot at close range."

Danny felt her blood quicken, and shut her eyes tightly to the awful remembrance.

"They say he was shot by a woman with auburn hair and eyes of gold. You didn't tell me about that, Danny. Makes me wonder what else you're hiding."

She ran to him and flung herself at him in a flurry of movement, fists pommeling him, shrieking wildly. "How dare you! How dare you! You keep yourself hidden from me at all costs and you dare to wonder what I'm hiding!"

Alex caught her by the wrists and stifled her wild flailing. With one strong maneuver, he whipped her around and brought her down sharply on his lap, pinning her arms to her sides so that she could not use her sharp nails against him. In that position she was helpless, and she sat panting heavily from her struggles and cursing him in the most vile words she knew. "Do you think it comforts me now to know that I have been avenged?" she asked through gritted teeth. "Am I supposed to thank you for your gift?" She whipped her head back, tossing her dark red hair about her shoulders, and laughed loudly. "Avenged! You think in those terms, Alex, not I. Those are memories I will carry with me for the rest of my life, whether those men are alive or dead. All you've done is add to your list of killings!"

"Then why did you kill Lonny Garvey?" he demanded.

Danny's bottom lip began to tremble and she bit it to keep it still. The face of Lonny Garvey loomed up before her frightened eyes and she shrank inwardly from it. She had warned him to stay away from her, to keep his distance. He wouldn't listen—he kept coming toward her. She could still hear his taunting words, and she could still feel the stinging slaps of his open palm over and over again until there were no more tears left to shed. And still he came for her. It was the fear, the gut-shaking fear that had led her to pull the trigger.

She sobbed hysterically. "I couldn't let him touch me again . . ."

Alex swallowed hard and pulled her close. "This is why I killed them," he whispered. "Because of this." He turned her face to his. "I know what it's like to carry the past around inside of you," he said, keeping his voice low to keep it from breaking. "And I know how it feels to have to live with it. I hate Garvey and his gang!"

Alex sighed and walked to the fireplace. Sitting back on his heels in front of it, he poked amongst the flames with a branch, jabbing here and there carelessly, not mindful of his actions. "I will hate those men each time you wake up screaming from the things they've done."

Danny knew there was no talking to him when he felt so emotionally about something. She left him to his own private hatreds, wondering whether she would ever know what they were all about.

On a bright afternoon she sat with her hands spread out behind her on the ground, her feet dipped in the rushing water of the stream that ran the length of the valley. A faint, almost imperceptible rustle behind her caught her ear and she turned quickly to see what it was.

"Not bad," Alex said as he approached and knelt down beside her. "I see you've developed the reflexes of an Indian."

"It's hard not to out here."

Alex laughed softly. "You'd be surprised how many don't.

It's what makes the difference between dying and staying alive. I'd say you've learned well."

"I've had a good teacher," she replied simply.

His hand caressed her shoulder and tangled itself in her red tresses. "Your hair has grown quite a bit," he observed, crushing its silky softness in his hand. "Stay still," he ordered gently, and then, with the utmost precision he worked her hair into two long braids. Over each one he slipped an intricately beaded covering of the most supple deerskin, and leaned back to admire his work.

Danny ran her fingers lightly over the hundreds of tiny glass seed beads that went into the stunning geometric design which she recognized instantly as Sioux. "They're gorgeous," she exclaimed.

"So are you," Alex whispered, as he slipped his arms around her and carried her to the shade beneath the mammoth ponderosa pines. Laying her down on a bed of green grass, he dropped to his knees and began to undress her, his silver eyes roaming over her perfect flesh. Without removing his own clothes, he excited her with a tenderness that showed another side to the man. With caresses so soft and so smooth they made her flesh jump in a hundred places, he kissed the hollow at her throat, then her lips, her eyes, her ears, her breasts.

"Danny . . ." The sound of her name stirred the fires that simmered inside of her. "Danny, you've become a sickness with me."

Her mind whirled and she thought she heard a note of desperation in his breathless whisper. "You're like a drug to me . . . something I can't do without. I crave your body. I want to feel you writhing beneath my hands, to hear you moaning with pleasure. I want to fill myself with all of you . . . every part."

Her body strained and arched against his, aching for him to put a final end to her delirious passion. At last, he too couldn't bear putting it off any longer. Fumbling with his trousers, he succeeded in getting them opened and part way down to his knees. "Oh, Danny," he groaned, as he placed himself between her legs. She moved to accept him, greedily.

He was gentle at first, moving with a slow, steady motion, almost lulling her into a delicious dream. He stayed inside of her for a while without moving, feeling her around him, feeling his body a part of hers. Then he began to move faster and stronger until he drove into her maddeningly, demandingly, and the world around them ceased to exist. Afterward, Danny was so weak from their heated lovemaking that she could barely summon the strength to return his kisses.

He put out a hand and helped her to her feet, then announced that he was going for a ride.

"*Now?*" she asked, in disbelief.

"Of course, now," he replied. "When did you think I meant?"

In no time he was back to his usual insufferable self. She tried to keep the urgency out of her voice. "Where are you going?"

Alex did not alter his stride. "I told you," he said over his shoulder as he walked back to the cabin, "I'm going for a ride. And, no," he added, "you can't come."

Danny went off by herself while he threw his saddle on the Appaloosa stallion's back, mounted fluidly and spurred the horse out of the valley. Over the countryside he rode, with the stallion beneath him, feeling the uneven ground pass beneath the flying hooves. He could easily recall other times they had ridden like this. With subtle movements of his taut leg muscles, a faint tensing of his knees, he guided the horse in and out of canyons, deep into gullies and ravines, flat out upon the unbroken prairie, following the path of the moon that had illuminated on the ground before them.

He needed time to think about what was happening or he might do the wrong thing. Alex Coulter had never been a very patient man, and his confusion set him ill at ease. His thoughts would not stay straight in his mind and no matter how he tried to arrange them, they still went off in different directions. Only the exhilaration of a ride through the mountains, only the air against his face, could clear his head long enough for him to think things out.

Anything that could hurt you was real, was his theory, while anything that gave pleasure, even in the smallest measures, could not be. His indifference toward his women reminded him of that because they were no better really than a hot bath after a long dusty ride, or a delicious dessert after a good meal—things a man could live without if he had to, things a man picked up along the way if he was lucky.

Before Danielle Fleming came into his life, he had not

allowed a woman to dictate his actions nor change his emotions. Bianca Alvarez had come close, but only because it amused him to let her have her way. He liked to see her stomping about, her red skirts swirling around her ankles, ebony eyes glaring at him, red lips pouting seductively. Since his release from prison, he had even thought of heading south to find her. He supposed he could be happy with Bianca, and Lord knows, she wouldn't have balked at riding around the country with him from place to place like a nomad. She had done enough of that herself to feel at home in a saddle, beneath a tent, even in a cave. And, she knew exactly where she stood with him, knowing she'd be a fool to place any restrictions on him or seek commitments.

But in spite of all the trouble it had brought him, Alex Coulter could not keep his mind off the woman with the eyes like amber stones. He thought of her constantly. He puzzled over how she managed to steal his soul in a way no other woman had done, and he cursed himself violently and incessantly at his utter lack of resistance to her. She was in his blood like a poison, sealing his fate against his will.

Each time he thought of her lying in another man's arms he nearly went insane with jealousy. At times he unleashed it blindly, even against her, when he would have killed any other person in the world for hurting her the way he was doing. He damned her bitterly for causing him to display his weakness to the world, and he hated himself for being incapable of forming a sufficient defense against her. She was a nuisance in his life! She was the sole woman he knew who could louse up his thinking like this.

Out here one stark truth was evident to him as though he had suddenly discovered it for the first time. He loved her. He adored Danielle as surely as she had popped into his life and made him do things he'd never in his right mind do. He had taken damned fool chances and acted like a lovesick school-boy. As surely as he could hear her voice and feel her warm breath against his chest and lose himself in the depths of her eyes, he loved her.

Maybe she really was a witch as he had so often accused her of being. Whatever she was, it didn't matter. He had side-stepped the truth about his feelings for Danny too long. Yet, before he could allow himself to admit it to her, he had to take care of another matter. Otherwise, he'd lose his sharpness and not be able to return to her. He needed to concentrate on hatred in order to carry out this last act of revenge.

He returned hours later, long after the sun had fallen below the horizon, and had no intention of offering excuses for why it had taken so long. He was in an ill mood, and the sound of his footsteps on the porch awakened Danny from a fitful sleep. He walked in and kicked the door closed behind him, and one menacing look from his gray eyes warned her that she'd better not give him any trouble. His face wore an angry scowl and his black brows were drawn in a straight line across his forehead. "I'm leaving at dawn."

Danny stared at him as though she had not heard.

"There's something I have to do," Alex said, removing his leather jacket and tossing it aside.

"Going north again?" she asked. Contempt rifled through her voice.

"No," he replied. "South. To Mexico."

"What's in Mexico?"

He shot her a look of caution. "Do you really want to know?" he asked. "Let's just say there's something I have to do, and this one's for me." A muscle at the corner of his mouth twitched unconsciously. There were still some scores to settle before he could think about anything else, and he knew it would be useless to try to explain that to her.

Danny found it impossible to read the expression in his eyes as he packed his saddlebags. That night he did not make love to her, nor would she have let him. She crawled into bed, feeling angry and hurt, and eventually fell asleep. The last thing she remembered seeing was his figure at the table, sitting back with the chair tilted off the floor, his boots up, silhouetted in the moonlight. He appeared to be lost in his thoughts, a thousand miles and a million years away.

Chapter 35

"Still no word on the boat, ma'am?" the desk clerk of the Hotel Pierre inquired when Danielle returned from the levee looking greatly displeased.

"No, nothing," she replied dismally. "They don't even know how long the delay will be. Now they tell me that it may be more than a week before the *Lilly Martin* gets in."

"That's what they said days ago," the clerk recalled.

"Yes, I know." She cast a dejected look at him. It certainly seemed as though luck was running against her. First, there was the unexpected explosion that had ripped up several hundred feet of rail track that was going to take her to New Orleans where her ship waited in port to sail for France. Then, when she had resigned herself to the dismal prospect of taking a slow steamboat from St. Louis to New Orleans, she was greeted with the news that for some unexplained reason, the *Lilly Martin* was unavoidably detained somewhere along the Mississippi. Of course, no one could say where the boat was at this time because no one really knew what was wrong. These things happened and there wasn't anything they could do except wait. The quicker she got out of St. Louis the better, and this unbearable delay was doing precious little to put her into good spirits.

Mere words could not even express the sheer frustration she felt, when all she had hoped for at this point was to flee this country with all possible haste, to leave it all behind her forever. Nor could words define the awful feelings of rejection after sitting confined to a tiny wooden cabin for weeks on end expecting Alex Coulter to walk in the door at any moment, only to eventually realize that he was never coming back. Could she ever possibly express the torment she felt the day she rode out of the valley leaving it all behind? Or the awful indecision over whether to leave a note in case he ever came by that way again?

Danny wondered whether she would ever be able to stop thinking about him—whether one day she would no longer feel the burn of his hands across her naked flesh, nor hear his voice whisper love words in her ear as he lost himself inside of her. Could she ever erase from her mind the image of his handsome features; his smile, taunting one moment, tender and mischievous the next; and his eyes, eyes like she'd never seen before in her life, so full of life, and so soft they could melt away any of her resistance?

She tried to shake his image loose, but to no avail. It followed her everywhere she went. Each and every glimpse of a black-haired stranger on the streets of St. Louis brought her heart to an immediate halt. She spent her days waiting, longing with desperation for an end to the torturous delay. Sometimes Danielle did not even bother to venture out of her suite at the Pierre, taking her meals alone and glancing out the stately windows for signs of the life that went on outside in spite of her own miserable existence.

The truth of the matter was that he had wanted one thing from her. How could she ever forget her first encounter with the man? He had raped her, hadn't he? What further proof could she ever need than that? To him, she was no better than any other woman, any other whore, he'd ever had. She was merely a convenience to him, an amusement for as long as it tickled his fancy. When she was no longer of any use, he had abandoned her like any other thing that was used up. The bitterness welled up inside of her until she could feel her temperature rise, and she walked around for days with a flush to her cheeks.

The few remaining days of August dragged by, pulling in September, and Danny thought she would go mad from the wait. Each morning she went down to the levee and endured the bustling crowds that flocked the piers, only to return with the same apologetic answers to her questions.

The desk clerk smiled sympathetically. "You know how those things are," he said in an effort to console her.

Danny glanced up at him sharply. Yes, she knew how those things were and she was getting pretty sick and tired of them all. She would have told him so, too, using the well-meaning man as a vent for her unhappiness, had not an early morning edition of the *St. Louis Chronicle* caught her eye. The headline in large black letters glared out at her, screaming for her attention, tearing through her heart. **CRAZY HORSE DEAD.**

With trembling hands, Danny lifted the paper to her eyes. Hot salty tears streamed uncontrollably down her cheeks as she read the account of the Sioux war leader's death. Death! Murder was more like it! She threw the paper to the ground in a furious gesture, sobbing openly and not caring who might see.

She stumbled back to her room through the blinding veil of tears, speechless from the constricting lump in her throat. Why? Why, damn it, why? Her mind rang with the words she had just read, but in her heart she knew how the story should have been printed, and the awful sadness of it brought with it a pain and bitterness that went far beyond her own sorrows.

An exceedingly harsh winter, his people tired of running, starving, barely clothed, all led the young Sioux chief to the sole source of their salvation—surrender. But there had waited for him at Fort Robinson not the understanding and peace he sought for himself and his people. Instead, he found only lies and broken promises. He had been arrested while trying to flee the reservation. It was claimed that he was wounded with his own knife when he resisted the guards, but the newspaper account also mentioned stabs in his back. One nearly pierced his heart and the other had punctured a kidney. Could a man have stabbed himself like that with his own weapon, a hunting knife concealed in his leggings? A soldier's bayonet was more likely responsible. Stinging tears rolled down Danny's cheeks for the life that had ended in the mid-thirties, and for the vulnerable people Crazy Horse had left behind.

Danny shut her eyes tightly. How was Alex taking this news? He must be grieving. He was so totally alone within himself. He had cast her out of his life along with everyone else, and now he did not even have his lifelong friend.

Oh, it was all so wretched! The torturous delays detaining her departure, and now this awful news. Tasunke-Witko. He had been the very essence of the Sioux defense and without him, what would happen? Danny suspected the question would have no easy answer.

Unable to face the prospect of eating in public, she went

down to the lobby only long enough to ask that dinner be served in her suite. Once back in her room, she faced the problem of what to do with herself when, once again in the morning, she would take a carriage to the river to see if the *Lilly Martin* had arrived. She knew steamboats were in the habit of banking along the river's edge to purchase cords of wood from the Indians to propel them on their journeys. Perhaps the *Lilly Martin* had been waylaid. Maybe the boat would never come at all. Oh, what did it matter, she would get out of St. Louis if she had to walk clear to the port of New Orleans!

Her mood grew sullen as she reclined in a corner of the plush velvet sofa with her feet curled under her. A knock on the door reminded her that she was not hungry, but she supposed she should accept the dinner since they were kind enough to bring it up. "Come in," she called, and rose with a dejected shrug of her shoulders. Digging into her purse for a coin to give the bellboy, she gestured with a limp wave. "You can leave it over there." Her purse turned up nothing and she was overcome with embarrassment that she had forgotten to stop at the bank and could give the boy nothing for his trouble. She rummaged through the pockets concealed in the folds of her skirt. "I'm sorry," she apologized. "I don't seem to have any money."

"I'll take care of it."

She whirled around at the familiar mocking tone of voice, and saw Alex in the open doorway. She flew to him and threw herself into his arms. "Alex!"

That was all she could say before she found his lips on hers.

A discreet cough interrupted their embrace, though only long enough for Alex to tip the bellboy who made sure he closed the door behind him as he left.

The man who stood before Danielle was dressed like a gentleman of the highest caliber. Alex wore an expensive black velvet-collared suit that fit his body like a second skin, and a brocaded waistcoat set off a white silk shirt that had lace ruffles cascading down the front.

His hair had been trimmed so that it curled slightly at the base of his neck, tapering just over his collar. He was clean shaven, but had allowed his sideburns to grow along the sides of his face, giving him a roguish look to add intriguingly to his elegance. Danny blinked at him, unable to believe the transformation. Alex had always been an incredibly handsome devil, but now, dressed in fine tailored clothing, appearing so much like a European aristocrat instead of an Indian brave or a common bandit, she was taken aback by the extent of his dazzling looks. The more she gazed at him, the more she liked what she saw, and the smile that broadened across his face told her he was having no difficulty reading her thoughts. He gestured toward the crystal decanter that sat on the mahogany-lustered table. "Brandy?"

"Yes," she said, collecting herself. She hoped it would clear her head of its confusion. Was this some kind of game he was playing? He could be so damned full of surprises, she did not know what to expect of him.

She had wished, and even caught herself praying, that he would come for her, but she'd quite given up on ever seeing him again.

Alex Coulter's gray eyes raked over her thoroughly, even noting the absence of a few pounds. "You look as if skipping meals has become a habit with you," he said. He advanced toward her slowly. "But I like it." He brushed her hair behind her shoulder. Running his index finger lightly across her cheek, he said, "It suits you. Gives your cheeks a slight hollow and brings out the color of your eyes. Makes you look as wicked as you really are." His smile did not prepare her for his question, when he asked in a soft voice, "Why'd you run out on me, baby?"

The question seemed absurd to Danny, and it angered her instantly that he should have asked for an explanation when he gave so little reason for the things he did. "Why did *I* run out on *you?* I can't believe what I'm hearing." She pushed away from him. "How can you stand there looking so damned smug and ask me why I ran out on you? Alex, if I asked you that question, would I get an answer?"

The reversion back to his usual self was instantaneous. "I thought you knew I was coming back," he snapped.

Danny could see now that he'd come prepared for a fight, and was surprised not to see a gun at his hip. She was sorely tempted to make some caustic remark about it, but didn't. "Well, I *didn't* know. How could I have known, you never gave me anything to even cling to. Or maybe you thought I could hang on indefinitely to invisible threads?" She turned away with a scowl on her face.

She could sense his tenseness, and knew that he was trying to curb his temper. But even the threat of unleashing it on her did not frighten her, not when her own vexation was as great as his. "I presume you did what you had to do in Mexico," she said tersely.

Alex stiffened at the mention of his trip back into hell. "Yes." The icy chill of his voice turned Danny's blood cold, but still it did not curb her mounting indignation. She paced about the room like a stalking lioness, forcing his eyes to follow her. "You're beautiful when you're angry like this."

She ignored the compliment. "Why have you come here?" she asked, and then, in answer to her own question, she flung her head around and glared at him, her chin tilted and her fists tightly clenched at her sides. "Surely if it was just for a tumble in bed, then you could have found a willing female without having come all this way!"

He covered the distance between them quickly and grabbed her by the arm. "Is *that* what you think? All this time, is that what you've thought?"

"You've left me little else to think. Let go of my arm, you're hurting me!" She was furious, and with hidden strength wrenched free of him.

Alex laughed, a short bitter sound from his throat and his voice emerged like a sneer. "I always thought that was one of your favorite pastimes, baby. Don't tell me you've changed your habits."

"Did you come here to insult me, then? Because if you did—"

Suddenly his hands were moving over her shoulders and against her will she found herself being smothered against him. Against her cheek she felt the brocade cloth of his waistcoat, and involuntary sobs began to break from her lips.

His touch was tender, but his voice was not, as though he were holding a tight rein on his emotions. "Don't cry," he said, although it sounded more like a command. "Besides, I see you've been doing enough of that. Your eyes are all red and—"

"Yes, that's right!" She put her fists against his chest and pushed herself away forcefully. "I have been crying— something *you* would know nothing about! Or perhaps you haven't read the newspapers." She eyed him carefully to test his reaction, and as soon as she saw the pain written on his features, she regretted her callousness.

"I've read them." His voice was a bare whisper but in it she heard all the hurt and outrage he felt at losing his friend.

Danny sighed heavily and closed her eyes. "Why did you come here, Alex?"

"Because I want you," he answered. "You're right. I do want your body. I crave it. But it's more than that, and I've only just begun to understand what it is. I want all of you, every part, every inch. You've succeeded in capturing not only my passion, but my mind and soul as well."

"Do you love me?" She wondered where she'd ever gotten the nerve to ask aloud the question whose answer had escaped her for so very long.

The answer was yes, but he could not bring himself to tell Danielle directly. "I want you, Danny. I want to be with you and to bury myself in you and become a part of you. Isn't that enough?"

Danny laughed, but it was a forced sound, nervous and tense. "Would it be for you? I know all about people like you, Alex. People who never say I love you, but who all their lives are dying to be told."

He shot a glance at her, cursing himself for allowing this woman close enough to know him better than he knew himself. "Look, what do you want of me?" he demanded. "I've never in my life met a woman like you—a woman who could do these things to me, make me run counter to my very instincts."

"Is that why you treat me the way you do?"

"That's right," he admitted grudgingly. "And because other men have taught you things I haven't."

"Whose fault was that?"

He had no answer.

Alex's lack of a fast retort made them both stop and think. Simultaneously they realized the issue was a foolish one to pursue. They reveled in each other. That was all that was important. It did not matter from whom they had learned how to give sexual satisfaction.

Their eyes locked, Danielle and Alex sensing they had reached the same conclusion. They met in a tender and profound embrace, and Alex lifted her into his arms and carried her effortlessly to the bed.

They lay on the bed together, unfastening one another's clothing as though it was a fresh and mystical experience. Gently, Alex lowered himself between her already spread thighs. Alex's breath was raspy, and Danielle placed her hands on his hips, guiding his penetration of her.

Their bodies did the talking, speaking of all the desire that raged within them. And when his passion reached a degree he had never thought attainable, when Alex felt himself soaring from the sheer power of it, he knew he would tell Danny how very much he loved her.

Later they lay drowsily content in each other's arms, the room darkened, shadows playing across their naked bodies. Propping himself up on one elbow, Alex teasingly traced light patterns across her breasts with his fingertip. "When I got back and you weren't there, I went crazy," he confessed. Through the dimness she saw the sheepish grin on his face. "I even went to see your uncle thinking you might be there."

"Uncle Emmett? Oh!" Danny sat up with a start. "What did he say to your visit?"

"He was polite, but it was obvious he didn't want me there, if that's what you mean." He flipped onto his back, both arms crooked behind his head. "Dossie told me where to find you, and once I knew where you were, I rode like the devil to Bennett and caught the first train for St. Louis. I didn't know if I'd make it in time before your boat pulled out, but I had to try." Reaching forward, he traced the curve of her spine with an airy caress. "Did you think I could stand to lose you a second time?"

Danny slipped out from beneath the white linen sheet and walked nude to the wardrobe. He watched her silhouette, so slender and supple, as she slid on a mauve silk blouse and stepped into a full skirt. Only when she lit the lamp did he tear his eyes away from her mesmerizing figure and get dressed himself.

"When I found out that the *Lilly Martin* wasn't in yet, I did some shopping," he said as he buttoned the silk shirt and fastened its ruffled stock about his neck. "I also arranged for us to move into a larger suite. Thought we'd spend a few days in St. Louis and then . . . well, I thought we could talk about that."

Danny sat down on the sofa and stared at her hands. "Oh, Alex," she sighed, "I don't know." At this point she was uncertain of whether anyone's feelings were to be trusted. "Maybe this can't work. There are so many things standing between us."

"I know there are," he said as he sat down beside her. "But I thought maybe between us we could somehow work them out. Maybe if we try together, we could forget—"

"Forget? Forget what? How can I forget what I've never

known? Don't you see, Alex? There are still questions left unanswered—huge, gaping spaces that must be filled before you and I can begin to find any true understanding of each other." She slipped her hand from his and rose. "I've told you all of my ugliest secrets—the ones I'm most ashamed of. Yet you still refuse to let me share yours. No, Alex, it can never work, not if you're going to keep me on the outside. I love you, Alex Coulter. I love you so much it frightens me at times. But I want to love all of you, every bit, even that which you yourself think is horrible. How can I love what you won't let me know?"

She walked to the window and drew the heavy drapes aside. For several long moments she stared at the gaslit street below, hoping that somewhere out there she would find the strength she needed to continue.

Alex poured himself a drink and raised the glass to his lips. From the corner of his eye, he saw her turn back to the room.

"Where did you get the name, Nando? Tell me this time."

The glass froze in midair and when he did not answer, Danny suddenly felt dread begin to fill up inside of her at his silence. She could barely get the words out a second time, and all that she could summon was a hoarse whisper. "What is your real name?"

He looked at her squarely, gray eyes sparkling brightly.

"Fernando DeMalleray."

Danny stared at him blankly, the name resounding in her mind. *"DeMalleray, DeMalleray,"* she repeated over and over again. How many shocks were still in store for her, she wondered. She could not help but shake her head incredulously at him at this latest startling discovery. Oh, how stupid she had been all along not to even have suspected something like this.

"Would you tell me why one of Europe's wealthiest men would turn desperado?" she asked.

"Because all of that never really had anything to do with me or with who *I* was or what *I* wanted. It was simply there, an ocean away, as if it never even existed. This is what was real for me, what was happening here. I wanted my own identity, not French or Indian, so I used Alex Coulter."

Danny's mind reeled as the pieces began to fall into place. Suddenly things began to make sense. "The man who came to serve the divorce papers," she said, "he was *your* man." Her tone was sharply accusing.

"Yes," Alex admitted. "After I got out of prison I decided

to make use of, shall we say, the resources at my disposal? And I'm not talking now about the Lady Laura. I made a few contacts and identified myself to certain individuals, and there it was, a vast empire, laying at my feet. I've only used it once though, and that was to send a man over with the papers. I never wanted any of the DeMalleray money for myself. All I ever wanted was what came out of the Lady Laura so that I could help my friends." He snorted at the irony of his intentions that had somehow gone awry. "It didn't exactly work out the way I thought it would. All it did was prolong the inevitable. And now Crazy Horse is dead and his people are scattered on reservations. There's no reason to keep any of it a secret any longer."

He poured more brandy into his glass and swirled it around. "Austin helped me because it was something he believed in also, although from what I gather, it wasn't something he wanted to tell you about." He shrugged fatalistically. "I don't know his reasons for keeping you in the dark, but if he hadn't, well, who knows, maybe all this wouldn't have happened."

"Does Austin know who you are?" she inquired, trying to keep up with him.

Alex nodded his head, rustling the black curls at his forehead, "But it had nothing to do with him. All that concerned him was the Lady Laura, and he was perfectly willing to go along with the charade as long as no one got hurt. Strange how things work out."

The bitterness was easily detected behind his words as his mind recalled the horrors that had been forced upon all of them because of this secret he had vowed to share with only one person. "Of course," he continued, "I never realized Austin never told you about the Lady Laura and that it really belonged to me." His gaze dropped to his half-empty glass. "Nor did I figure on you popping into the picture . . . and into my life." In one gulp he downed the remainder of the brandy. "I've booked passage on the *Lilly Martin*," he announced. "I'll be returning to France with you."

Danny shot a surprised look at him.

"I'm going back to administer my inheritance," Alex said.

"But why?" she exclaimed. "I thought you didn't want any of that. You have the Lady Laura. Surely that's enough for you."

"Well, it's not," he said with a grin. "Women like you need

to be clothed in lace and satin, and I thought I'd like to see some rubies dangling from your ears and maybe some emeralds draped around your throat."

"Oh, Alex, please don't tease me, not at a time like this. Even if I did want those things," she added, "you know perfectly well that the income from the Lady Laura is enough to buy all the jewels in the world."

Alex turned away to avoid her gaze, the smile disappearing. "I'm getting rid of the mine."

"What!"

"I'm turning the deed over to you." The shock on her face forced him to laugh. Quickly he checked it and forced a serious note into his voice. "I figured the Lady Laura belongs to the Fleming family. Let's just say I sort of borrowed it for a while. It's the wedding present I never gave you."

Danny grew flustered and searched the room as if for an answer to this unexpected gesture. Wringing her hands, she looked at him tremulously and said, "Alex, there is something I must know. All those years, when Uncle Emmett was having that problem with the shipments leaving Winslow and never making their destination . . . It was you, wasn't it? You were robbing your own silver mine, weren't you?"

"Yes."

"You did it for the arms and ammunition it would help buy the Indians?"

He nodded. "And to help feed them."

"And the man Uncle Emmett suspected of helping you . . . the one he thought was working on the inside . . . the one who told you when and where to strike . . ." She wet her lips and swallowed. "It was Austin, wasn't it?"

"Yes."

She shut her eyes tightly and tried to force some strength into her limbs. "So," she said, turning back to him with a fiery glow in her golden eyes. "So, you turn out to be one of the wealthiest men in all of Europe, not to mention the sizable fortune you've amassed from the Lady Laura, and here you are parading around this country like a desperado. Meanwhile, despite your arrogant airs and false mask of bravado, you shake inside from your own private fears." She glanced up at him through her lashes to see his reaction, and sure enough, a spark of brilliance ignited in those silver eyes. But he would not take the bait. "Oh come now, Alex," Danny said, "don't you think I can guess that there's more to this than what you've told me? I'm not referring to Austin's role in it, nor am I talking about my own part. I'm talking about *you*—Alex Coulter or Fernando DeMalleray, or whatever your name is." She shook her head of dark red hair at him suspiciously. "No, Alex, my woman's intuition tells me there's more lurking beneath your surface than you're willing to reveal. Why? Are you afraid that I will hate you for it? Believe me, I won't, but since there's no way I can convince you of that, you'll have to take the risk."

Danny studied him intently while he continued to say nothing. "You've always been the kind of man who likes to take chances," she said, "always flirting with danger. You would not go through so much trouble and effort to hide it if it didn't pose such a danger to you to expose it."

Alex looked up at her. "Does it show that much?"

"No," she replied. "You bruise too easily to let it show that much."

Alex turned away to hide the smile he was forced to part with at her understanding his nature. In the next moment he felt her touch, as light as a feather, at his back. The feel of her hand sent a faint tremor through his muscles.

"Every form of refuge has its price, Alex. Haven't you paid a high enough price for yours? Isn't it time to stop paying?"

All the muscles in Alex Coulter's body tensed into one constricting knot for a fleeting instant when faced with the ultimate question. Then, strangely, they began to ease, and with the relaxation came an unfamiliar feeling of calm. He walked to the sofa and flopped down on it, stretching his body out, one arm dangling listlessly to the carpet, the other propped behind his head. After a while he opened his eyes and turned to look at her. Raising his head, he gestured for her to come sit beside him.

Danny obeyed wordlessly. Gathering up her skirts she dropped to the floor at his side. He looked to be asleep but beneath his eyelids she detected faint movements, as though he were seeing things. His breathing deepened, growing stronger and quicker, telling her that he was battling with himself.

For a long time Alex and Danny remained silent. Then he began to tell the story that he had never allowed to be spoken.

Chapter 36

Flashes of light pierced the blackness of Alex's memory and he grimaced at the familiar faces that sprang into his dulled mind. They took him back to a time he would have given his life to forget.

He was a man divided within himself, and that division had erupted into his being long before he even knew its rightful name. It had come with an explosion that rocked his very being, sending his senses flying in all directions and his mind shattering into a thousand pieces. For the first time in his life he had known the meaning of inner conflict, but at the age of eight, he could not fully comprehend the meaning of it. Any other child would surely have crumbled from the weight of such inner turmoil, but Alex seemed to grow stronger as pain slowly ate away at him. Even at eight years old he was able to survive. From that day on, that's what his life had been all about. Surviving, and staying one step ahead of the memories.

As a child growing up in a raw land, he had been taught many things by the people who loved him. From his mother's people, the Oglala Sioux, he had learned the ageless culture of the red man. Everything he did and thought was geared toward one thing, whether consciously or otherwise—self-preservation. In a land that was at times so inhospitable that only the strongest in body and spirit could prevail, Alex Coulter had been equipped with all the essential tools for staying alive. Food, clothing, shelter, weapons—all were there at his disposal in places where others would never even have thought to look. He was deeply indebted to his red brothers for sharing their ways and their lore with him.

His white brothers had been generous with him also. From Jake Alvarez, in particular, Alex had learned how to stay alive by one's wits. Jake had passed on every trick he knew. He taught Alex to think his way out of tight spots, to use what was around him the way even his Indian friends could not. From Jake, Alex learned the essential value of planning. Alex learned to calculate his moves and control his hot impatience.

Over the years, his Indian's finely honed instincts and feel for the land, and his white man's capacity for shrewdness equipped him to face the dangers of the path it was his fate to follow. Always he managed to stay barely ahead of that decision that laid in the pit of his stomach, growing larger every day, every year, tearing him apart with its uncertainty. Red world or white? To which did he rightfully belong?

Once, he had tasted the white man's life. Not the kind that Jake Alvarez lived, running from hideout to hideout, pursued by posses out of El Paso or Tucson or Bennett. It was when Alex had been picked up and deposited amidst all the wealth and opulence of one of Europe's oldest families, where he remained for five years. To him they were the saddest, most tormented years of his life, and the boy longed to return to his homeland, to his people, in spite of the agonizing memories the place conjured up in his young mind. One moment he had been living peacefully, as happy as a child could possibly be, surrounded by the love and affection that radiated between him and his parents. But suddenly one day, it had all come to an abrupt end.

Everything he had become stemmed from that single day nineteen years ago. A gray December day, bitterly cold and pregnant with storm clouds. He and his father had returned to their lodge and found his mother's body lying in a huge pool of blood, mutilated beyond distinction.

"White men! White men!" he had shrieked at his father, the hysteria mounting shrilly in his little voice. The impact of the horrible scene had yet to explode fully in his mind.

Jacques DeMalleray had stood wide-eyed in the middle of the lodge, his eyes transfixed on a single object that Nando had not yet seen, unable to move, unable to think, unable to feel.

Nando had raced to his father and had begun to pull on Jacques' buckskin leggings, but the big man did not budge. With frustration tearing away at him, Nando had beat at Jacques with his small hands clenched into whitened fists, but

Jacques was oblivious to the assault. It only served to infuriate the boy into a hysterical frenzy. "White men did this! *You* did this!"

He had whipped the hunting knife from its sheath at his side and plunged it into his father's leg. In his frantic young mind the boy was oblivious to the absurdity of his awful accusations. He knew only that whoever did this thing to his mother was white, and the man who stood in the room with him was white. It was impossible for Nando to see beyond that.

The sharp pain had seared through Jacques, snapping him quickly out of his horror-induced trance. He had let out an enormous bellow and grabbed for his son, but Nando kept slashing, drawing blood wherever the sharp blade struck. Jacques could have knocked the boy across the room into oblivion, but instead of protecting himself, he tried to calm Nando. But Nando was all over the place at once, kicking, biting, slashing with the razor-sharp weapon. Suddenly, Jacques felt the hot sting of the blade slice through the palm of his outstretched hand, severing a tendon and sending blood spurting into the air, spraying Nando in the face.

Jacques had stumbled backward and gasped sharply at the sight of eight-year-old Nando standing there wild-eyed, knife in hand ready to kill; his blood-splattered face looking like he had just painted it for war. Even the shiny glare of his steel gray eyes could not detract from what he was . . . an Indian. Jacques let out an agonized scream and lunged for his son. In a blinding flash, he had brought the palm of his bloody hand squarely across the boy's face with an impact that even a grown man would have found difficult to withstand.

A rude red welt sprang up on Nando's face, but he did not falter. The piercing glint of his stare never wavered, and although knocked back several paces, he remained miraculously on his feet, glaring at his father, lips curled back over his white teeth in a snarl. Switching easily from the language of the Sioux back and forth to French, he lashed out verbally at his father in a string of searing accusations. Soon he was breathless and he glared at his father, panting heavily, unconscious of everything now except the emotions pounding in his temples.

An unearthly quiet pervaded the lodge as father and son stood not five feet apart, neither any longer aware of the dead woman in the corner. The only things existing in the world were one man and one small boy, each paralyzed by the conflicting thoughts stampeding through his dazed mind. To Jacques, the scene was like some horrific comedy. Oh God, that such a peaceful and happy existence could have been shattered so abruptly, without cause or reason. His mind reeled at the thought, and his mouth stung from the bitter taste of bile. His heart cried out angrily at the finality of this crude, horrendous joke. *Why? Why?* No answers came to him. "Why, damn it!" The scream tore through his throat, piercing the stillness of the lodge and shattering the web of tension strung between him and his child.

Nando began to tremble, and when Jacques opened his eyes he saw him cowering like a bewildered animal, tears streaming down his bronzed cheeks, mingling with the splotches of blood. Jacques had taken a step toward him, but like lightning the boy sprang away, all reflex and motion. For Jacques, the hateful moments had passed and he wished desperately to penetrate the awful black curtain that had descended between him and his son. But Nando resisted his attempts. Slowly Jacques forced Nando backward in a semicircle until they stood at opposite sides of the single-room lodge. "You want to know who killed your mother?"

Nando did not answer. He already knew who did it. It was those white men who had stumbled across their lodge the night before in the midst of a blinding snow storm . . . the ones they had fed and warmed and spoken to as friends . . . the ones who claimed to be trappers working the Upper Missouri for beaver and otter. Nando had listened to their talk without speaking, taking in everything about them. They didn't look like trappers, and his young eyes had watched them suspiciously.

Later that evening, Nando had spotted the quiver of arrows one of the men had concealed beneath his shirt. It was dark in the lodge, for the fire had grown dim, and it was difficult to see what kind of arrows they were. There was something else, though, that was very easy to see. It was the way one of them looked at Wind Song whenever he thought Jacques was not paying attention. Nando had noticed it instantly from his place at his mother's feet as he sat waxing a bowstring, and he did not like the way the white man's eyes swept over her, lingering too long.

The next morning, at dawn's first light, his eyes had popped open and he sprang from his sleeping robes. The men were gone . . . so was Jacques' Winchester rifle and all of the beaver pelts they had collected over the preceding weeks. He had rushed to his parents' mat to shake them awake and tell them of his discovery. "Well, boy," Jacques had yawned, "looks like you and I will have to go hunting today." Wind Song had just giggled and gone back to sleep.

Later, dressed in his coat of buffalo fur, thick and warm, with double-soled moccasins to protect his feet from the cold snow, and heavy buckskin leggings, Nando had followed Jacques into the wilderness in search of game. A couple of hours later they had some hefty hares for Wind Song to turn into a sumptuous stew, and all thought of the thieves was gone from their minds. As they had approached the lodge, Nando felt Jacques quicken his pace and the boy soon had to run to keep up with him. The lodge stood with its door wide open, and Nando found himself racing breathlessly after his father, feeling an evil presence.

When Nando had reached the door, panting heavily and gasping for breath in the thin frozen air, the first thing he saw when he looked past his father's paralyzed figure was the body of Wind Song sprawled grotesquely in her own blood. Instantly Nando knew what had happened, and he knew who had done it.

"You want to know who killed your mother?"

The question was meaningless to the boy. He already knew.

Jacques' face was no longer menacing. It had softened toward the boy and shown plainly of sadness. Nando was unsure of the look in his father's eyes and inwardly shrank from it. It told him something he could not understand. He looked at Jacques with frightened eyes.

"*That's* who killed your mother." Jacques nodded stiffly to a spot to Nando's left and a little behind him.

The boy pulled his eyes away from Jacques and swung around. There, planted not a foot from him, was a plumed lance jutting out of a crack in the hard earth floor of the lodge. At its head, a red and black feather trimmed with bands of white flicked about in the wind. Crow! The recognition was immediate and sickening in its certainty. *Indians* had killed his mother!

Nando had fallen back on his heels and reeled around, throwing his hands up to his mouth in a futile attempt to stop the gush of vomit that sprang from his mouth. Then he had turned and run outside before Jacques could stop him.

If Jacques DeMalleray had possessed the strength, he would have gone after his son. Nando returned to the lodge hours later after the sky had turned menacing again, with another storm threatening. Jacques had already wrapped Wind Song's body in whitened deerskin and erected a scaffold to place her on. When the boy came in, he was sitting in the darkness, shivering from the cold, having made no fire to keep warm by, staring blankly into space.

Nando had removed his heavy coat and threw some sticks into the cold fire. In a few minutes the flames were alive again. Not a single word had been spoken between father and son, and only the sound of the spitting flames broke the deathly stillness of the dwelling. The fire felt warm and the penetrating heat was like medicine to Nando's bruised and aching body as he sat in front of it. It felt good. It was the only thing that did. Only eight years old and he could find no relief for his bruised and aching mind.

After an eternity Jacques lifted his empty eyes to the small figure sitting before the fire. "In the morning we ride out. Pack your things tonight, we'll be leaving early."

Nando had not asked where they were going. If he had, and if Jacques had told him that he planned to send him to France to live with the DeMallerays, Nando would surely have run away during the night, and in all probability, he would have frozen to death on the icy plains. As it was, the slow death that followed, in the form of five torturous years in a strange country across the ocean proved to be a death much worse than any he could have suffered on the prairie or alone in the frozen mountains.

Chapter 37

In the heavy winter of 1860, when the snow lay twenty feet deep in the valleys, Jacques DeMalleray spent the long weeks in a cave whose entrance was blocked by an enormous drift, without even once seeing the light of day. In the blackness of the cave, disconsolate with grief, he stayed alone without the sound of another human voice for company. He prayed it would snow even more, burying him beneath its suffocating blanket, snuffing out his life slowly and horribly. It didn't.

On the day he emerged the sun shone like a brilliant diamond, but no sooner had he dug his way out of his snowy dungeon than he became gripped with a new feeling that twisted his gut. Everything was silent as though frozen in time and space beneath a thick layer of ice. Not even the wind moved. For a few moments time stood still and then it closed over Jacques. The quiet was shattered by a long agonized wail, crying out for the one thing he longed for most.

"Nando . . . !"

His lonely voice resounded against the white-faced walls of the mountains, echoing in all directions with a deafening magnitude. It sounded like the voice of a stranger. But it was his voice . . . the voice of Jacques DeMalleray, thirty-two years old, voluntarily exiled to a snowy wilderness, aching for the one part of him that still existed. His son. He wanted his son.

In the morning he headed out of the mountains and found Black Crow's Oglalas with their lodges spread along the banks of the Sweet Medicine Creek. The people had heard of his tragedy and wanted to know why he had sent his son away. It was inconceivable to them that the father should remain on one side of the big water while the son remained on the other, when all the while the grief of both would have been so much more bearable had they remained together. Jacques grew tired of their grumblings and eventually packed his gear into a bundle and headed back to the mountains.

It was different there after that. Hour upon hour, day after day, year after year of aloneness had gotten to him. In the end, five years away from his son was all he could bear. He became obsessed with seeing once again the only thing that was left of his union with Wind Song. So greatly had he loved her that in his own pathetic grief he had blindly turned away from his son. Once implanted, the desperate desire to see Nando again began to grow until he could bear it no longer.

The boy had changed little except to grow taller and broader in the shoulders. At almost fourteen he was big, but it would be a while before he stood eye to eye with Jacques.

At the beginning Nando spoke little, only bothering to answer Jacques' questions when the mood struck him and never offering anything on his own. Gradually, however, father and son formed a tentative relationship based on a mutual accommodation, a grudging respect and an unspoken love for the memory that kept them together at all.

One evening, some months after his return, Nando was rummaging through some bags piled carelessly in the corner searching for some wax for his bowstring.

"Try that one there," Jacques suggested, pointing to the big, brightly painted parfleche beneath the others. "Might be some in there, don't know."

"Nothing in here except this," Nando said, drawing out his hand with an envelope in his fingers. The paper was frayed at the corners and its face was soiled with smudged fingerprints of age. "What's this?" he asked, curiously examining it. When Jacques failed to reply, he went ahead and opened it.

The paper inside was a deed. "Where'd you get this?" He turned to his father, his eyes narrowing in suspicion.

"Won it in a poker game."

"You won a deed to a silver mine in a poker game?" Nando asked incredulously.

Jacques raised an eyebrow at his son. "Do you doubt me, boy?"

"No, no, I don't." He didn't really, it just seemed so amazing. "How long have you had it?"

"About a year. Got it last time I took my pelts down to trade. Met a fellow there I'll never forget. Name of Fleming . . . Richard Fleming. You can see it right there on that paper. Was about my age. Well-educated, good family upbringing, I'd say, but mad as a hatter and getting crazier every day. Heard his wife died. Guess that and working in the closeness of the mine, not seeing much daylight, got to him. I've never seen a man so intent on destroying himself as that one was. I won that deed from him fair and square, but I'll never help thinking that he meant for me to . . . almost like he was just begging me to take it from him. Isn't that strange?"

"Not so," Nando replied. "Where is he now, this Richard Fleming?"

"Dead."

"What are you going to do with it—the mine?"

Jacques sighed deeply and shrugged. "Who knows, I don't much want it, so I guess it doesn't really matter what happens to it. You saw for yourself firsthand the wealthy background from which I fled. What possible use would that mine be to me? If I turned my back on all of that, why should I want this?" He shook his head at the irony of it.

The reference to the DeMalleray fortune and Nando's five-year immersion in it was allowed to pass. "I want it," Nando said.

Jacques stared at his son, carefully weighing the words.

"Give it to me if you don't want it." There was no mistaking the seriousness of his request.

"What do you want with it?"

Nando cocked his head to one side and smiled. "Do I need a reason?"

Jacques did not answer him, leaving the matter far from settled.

The following morning they rode south to do some trading with the Sioux along the Belle Fourche, and for the next few weeks the mine went unmentioned. It was the end of summer and most of the scattered bands of Sioux had gathered at the foot of Bear Butte for the autumn hunt. Everyone had a good time, and Jacques noticed with pride that Nando was among the quickest of the boys he ran with. Secretly, he was pleased that the boy had lost none of his Indian skills over the past five years.

Weeks later they were back in the north country, having

obtained enough shells to insure a plentiful supply of food through the long winter months ahead. Unpacking the provisions they had purchased at the small trading post they'd stopped at along the way home, Nando looked over his shoulder at Jacques, forcing a casual tone into his voice. "So, how about the mine?"

Jacques kept his eyes on the rifle he was cleaning. "Over in my saddlebag," he said.

Nando shoved his hand in and came out with a crisp white envelope. Opening it up, he read the words on the paper inside. It was his! The Lady Laura! "Some day it will *all* be yours," Jacques said, "so why not, huh?"

The smile dropped from the boy's face. "I don't want any of *that,*" he said with a sneer. "Just this. This is all I want."

In early May of the year 1866, when the spring thaw was just beginning in the north country, Nando and his father packed their saddlebags and headed out of the frozen mountains. The further south they rode, the longer the days became, and they soon discarded their heavy fur robes in favor of lightweight shirts and leggings. Nando's shirt was of whitened deerskin, decorated with a chest bib of green-stained porcupine quills, and the hair from the tail of his pony hanging in fringes down the length of each sleeve and across the open neck. He had spent countless hours on its creation as he had waited the passing of winter. Even Buffalo Woman, the Brulé squaw known for her excellent and intricate beadwork, could not have produced a finer shirt. Jacques tested the newly formed relationship by boldly chiding him about it, laughing that Nando would surely now be the envy of all the Sioux women. Secretly, he was pleased that Nando possessed the ability to focus his energies on so delicate an undertaking as the shirt, proving that there was more to his son than just a hellion on horseback. Nando accepted his father's gentle teasing, and responded with a little easy ribbing of his own, careful to stop at the point where the game could become dangerous. It was still too soon to wade into deeper waters, where memories were still vivid and wounds still fresh for each of them.

On the thirteenth day out they reached the Holy Road, the rutted trail the whites called the Oregon Trail. From there the journey grew progressively easier. The land over which they now rode was hard and smooth, tamped down by the constant traffic of hooves and wagon wheels churning across it, and they made good time. The following day they met and overtook four horsemen moving in the same direction, the first men they'd seen in many long months. "Where ya headed?" one of the men called out.

"Wherever they're trading pelts," Jacques cheerfully replied.

"That'd be up along the North Platt," the stranger called back. "Place called Arrow Rock Creek. Couple of days' ride."

"Much obliged, friend," Jacques shouted over his shoulder, and spurred his horse on to catch up with Nando who did not bother to stop for conversation. Damn, but that boy sure is a moody one, Jacques complained to himself, cursing his son's unnerving ability to place himself far away from reach, to the point where he neither wished nor sought contact with anyone. A day later they passed a group of some twenty covered wagons moving west, and as Jacques waved eagerly, he noticed from the corner of his eye the way Nando nodded politely, but stiffly, to the people who poked their heads out to say hello.

Finally, on the twentieth day they reached the town of Arrow Rock Creek that sat like a sore spot on the bank of the North Platt River, due south of the Sand Hills. Jacques had passed this spot some eighteen years earlier, having followed the Platt from its birth at the great Missouri northwestward into the Wyoming territory where it trailed off into a dribbling stream. And he could remember no such town as Arrow Rock Creek. Had the civilization he'd left behind reached this far already?

They rode into Arrow Rock Creek unnoticed in what appeared to be the middle of a great celebration. Their first stop was the large tent that stood erected at the far end of the town, just off the river's edge. A lot of noise and bawdy music came from within and as they dismounted, they saw a man come flying out of the tent. Sliding several feet on his face in the mud, he rose shakily to his feet and stumbled back inside. Several seconds later the same figure came hurling past them. Again the man rose on wobbly legs, but only to his knees, before collapsing on the ground where he stayed. Jacques and Nando looked at each other, Nando's handsome face breaking into a wide grin and a hearty laugh spilling from Jacques. Slapping Nando on the back, he slung an arm around his shoulder and they entered the tent.

They saw a throng of men. Some like themselves, others better, not but a few worse. The whiskey was flowing freely and seemed to be about the only thing all these people had in common, all assembled for the annual rendezvous that Jacques and Nando had unexpectedly walked in on.

"I've been in the mountains for too long," Jacques said, "to have missed all this." He could feel the electricity in the air and he watched anxiously, licking his lips as a bottle of whiskey passed through several hands until it reached Nando. The boy stared at it, making no move to take it, mistrusting the strange hand that offered it. "Go on," Jacques said, "take it. Could use some of that myself."

Nando took the bottle and swallowed a quick gulp of the cheap liquor. It stung his lips and flamed its way down his throat to his stomach. With its heat still sizzling, he handed it to his father, glad to be rid of it, and watched as Jacques took his swallows in turn and passed it down the line until it disappeared in the flurry of hands.

"Hey, *amigo,* so we meet again!"

Nando turned around to see a man approach and slap Jacques sharply on the back.

Jacques responded heartily, a smile of instant recognition overtaking his face. "Jake, Jake Alvarez, why you old—What are you doing here?"

The boy eyed the man cautiously, taking in everything about him. He was dark-skinned, smaller than Jacques, but thin and wiry. His face did not look old, but there was a hardness about it that suggested a great many years behind it. He spoke with a thick accent that Nando could not place but which told him the man was not American.

He stood by silently as the two men went through the ritualistic greetings and backslapping that follows a surprise reunion. Apparently Jacques knew the man well, but Nando could not recall ever hearing the name before. Well, it didn't matter, he'd find out soon enough who he was. He nudged his way forward, making his presence known.

"Hey, Jake, this is my son, Nando." Jacques made the introduction but did not wait for either of them to acknowledge it, before he grabbed Jake Alvarez by the arm and led him away from the crowd to an unoccupied spot along the wall. Nando followed grudgingly behind, resenting instantly this man who had the power to steal his father's attention so easily. He stood off by himself, refusing to be drawn into their conversation or their merriment, making his displeasure greatly known. As far as Jacques was concerned, Nando was just being his usual brooding reticent self, sizing up the situation and watching everything intently. When he feels like it, thought Jacques, he'll come out of himself.

Jake Alvarez interpreted Nando's behavior differently. The wily Mexican felt the nervous energy radiating from the boy and something in his keen mind told him to beware. Indian, he thought to himself, careful not to look the boy in the eye. The boy's part Indian, no doubt about that. The thought of it sent a faint tremor of fear rushing down his spine. Did Jacques know what he was doing by bringing the boy here? Jake was not about to offer his opinion on the matter, not with the boy staring at him like he was ready to pounce on him if he did or said the wrong thing. Jake tried to force an easiness into his voice. He was glad to see his old friend again after twelve years. *Por Dios!* If the boy weren't there, they could really celebrate. But as it was, things were apt to get a bit sticky when it was discovered there was an Indian in their midst.

Nando was not doing much to help the situation. As Jake talked with his father, he could see the way the boy stiffened whenever someone came too close, as though he felt threatened by every person in the place. At one point Jake held his breath when he saw a miner brush too close to the boy and Nando's hand move swiftly to the knife that lay sheathed at his belt. His movement was fluid, hardly noticeable except to one who was watching intently. He even moves like an Indian, thought Jake, feeling the anxiety mounting and trying to conceal it from Jacques who seemed oblivious to everything except the whiskey.

"Nando," Jacques called, the effect of the whiskey evident in his speech. "Come here, boy, I want to tell you something." He slung a heavy arm over his son's shoulders and Nando knew from the weight of it how drunk his father really was. He looked at him impatiently. "Boy, this here is Jake Alvarez, and you hear my words now. If you ever need a man to trust, this is him." He turned to the Mexican and said, "Jake, the boy's a bit wild." He paused and shook his head. "But then, I guess he's got reason to be."

Nando looked at his father in amazement. Although the words had been spoken to Jake, he knew they had been meant for him, and it was the first time he'd heard Jacques speak like that. It bothered him that Jacques did not utter these words to him when they were alone. Why did this other man have to be present? Nando clung to the words desperately, his outward stoicism never once betraying the rush of emotions swelling inside of him. He shook himself loose from Jacques' heavy hold and moved off to a corner where he could repeat the words in private to himself where they belonged, and not out in the open for strange ears to hear.

Jake turned back to his friend. It was not long, however, before he heard a commotion over in the corner. He tried to turn in its direction, but Jacques stopped him with a strong hand on his arm. "Never mind that," he said. "Say, Jake, how are those boys of yours? They must be about Nando's age, I guess."

"Tomas and Cisco are well, *amigo*," Jake replied. "I leave them in El Paso with the other men to look after their little sister while their Papa goes off to celebrate with friends."

"You old fox," exclaimed Jacques. "So you got yourself a daughter. If she's half as pretty as her mother, then I hope the boys keep a good eye on her. How's your wife anyway?" Jacques' eyelids drooped and he teetered unsteadily on his feet.

"She died," Jake answered. "Eight years ago."

It was something Jacques had not expected. It hit him sharply, rudely reminding him of things even his drunkenness would not allow him to forget. It forced him into a reluctant sobriety. "I'm sorry to hear that, really I am."

The change was astounding. All of a sudden he was standing upright and steady, his eyes clear, all traces of drunkenness having vanished. Jake sensed he had touched a hidden nerve, but he could not guess what it was. He never had a chance to find out.

A few quick words from the corner caught his ear, and he heard a thin and mocking voice rise above the others, sending a chill through Jake's body, standing the hair at the back of his neck on end. "Well, lookey here, Amos," it said. "Lookey what we got usselves here." Jake whirled in its direction but couldn't see over the heads that formed a half circle in the corner. Another voice rose in pitch to meet the first. "Well, boys, looks like we got us an Injun."

The first voice piped up again. "I ain't never seen no Injun with silver eyes before, have you, Amos? Whadda ya make of that?"

"Well, Luke, I'd say it's a breed." In the next instant the tone changed and Jake heard the scathing question asked with a hateful force behind it. "Whadda ya doing here, breed?"

The question was met with a flurry of angry demands and vituperations from the others. "Hey, there's a breed over in the corner," someone shouted.

"Get the breed!"

"Get that Injun. Don't let him get away!"

In a flash the happy drunken crowd turned into an angry mob. Before Jake could react, they descended upon Nando, closing over him quickly, surrounding him, making any attempt to escape impossible.

The boy felt himself backed into a dangerous corner, the worst possible place for him to be. Like a frightened animal he stood poised, ready to fight his way out rather than die quietly at their hands. Guns were drawn at him but he didn't even see them. All he could see were the dozens of angry faces, all strangers to him, all taunting and jeering with vicious insults, calling him names and screaming for his blood. Swiftly, his knife was loosened from its sheath and he held it menacingly before them. Its blade glinted brightly as he waved it around, holding off the turbulent crowd.

"Look out, he's got a knife!" a voice yelled. "Get the knife! Somebody get the knife!"

In a rush the man called Luke made a lunge toward the boy and before Nando even felt the pain, he saw the flash of the man's knife as it sliced into the flesh of his forearm, ripping through his shirt and laying the skin open. Nando let out a scream and dove for the man, but his stab missed its target. Turning on his heels he lunged again to attack, but once again the man sidestepped.

"Ya got him now, Luke. The breed can't even use a knife!" his companion shouted, and the other men howled in laughter. They all waited anxiously for the moment when Luke would put the Indian away.

Nando surprised them all and drove them further into their fury against him. In a flash, with one terrifying backward sweep of his hand, he dealt the man a near mortal wound across the neck. The sudden sight of blood spurting from one of their own incensed the others and as the first man fell to the ground clutching his throat, another jumped into the circle to finish the boy off. Before he even landed with his feet on the ground, Nando attacked him with deadly intent. Nando's movements were swift and sure . . . a blur before the crowd's eyes. He knew how to gouge and draw blood with what seemed to be only a flick of the blade.

Jake pushed his way through the thick throng and watched with horror-stricken eyes. His gun was drawn and ready in his hand, but it was difficult to get close enough to take a shot . . . should it come down to that. He continued to shove his way in closer, pushing shoulders out of his way, but a glimpse of the boy's face stopped him cold. The awful rage and hatred stamped there was enforced by the wild piercing glare of his steel gray eyes. Jake stared hard at him, unable to take his eyes from the boy's face. Suddenly, he saw Nando make a quick movement to the left, throwing the man off guard. And in a fleeting instant he lunged, plunging his knife to its hilt deep into the man's side, catching him below the left lung.

The wounded man let out a muffled howl and flung himself around, but as he did so, Nando grabbed him sharply by the arm and wrenched him around forcibly, flipping him over in a quick movement and dropping him to the ground. He landed on top of him, his knife at the man's throat.

Jake's mouth dropped open and he gasped when he saw the boy land on top of the man. As soon as the boy's hand drew back, knife poised for the kill, he knew he had to do something! If Nando killed that man, the rest of the men would go crazy. They would kill him right then and there.

All eyes widened as the knife drew back high into the air above Nando's head, paused there momentarily, and then began its downward descent with vicious speed toward the man's throat.

All of a sudden, a strong hand appeared from out of nowhere, catching Nando's arm by the wrist just as it fell inches above its target.

"*No!*" Nando let out an agonized scream and whirled his head around to see who stopped him from doing what he had to do.

It was Jacques who stood towering over him, his grip on Nando's wrist like a vice.

"Let me finish him!" Nando shrieked at his father. To

everyone else it sounded like an order, but to Jacques it was a plea.

He tightened his hold and pulled Nando up stiffly to his feet so that he stood astride the bleeding man. The eyes of father and son locked for a long moment, then Nando jerked his arm loose, stepped angrily over the man, shoved his way through the speechless crowd and left the tent.

The Frenchman looked at the man lying in a puddle of blood at his feet. The man peered back at him with glassy eyes out of a chalk-white face. Coughing and sputtering blood, he spoke in a broken whisper. "Thanks, friend."

Jacques grimaced and spat at the man's face. "I'm no friend of *yours*," he said coldly. "I didn't do it for you, you scum. I did it for *him*." With that he turned away to follow after his son. Pushing through the crowd, tears visible in his eyes, he walked blindly by Jake Alvarez without seeing him.

Jake let him go without saying a word and turned back to the others. The man who lay wounded in the middle of the tent was trying with difficulty to raise himself up onto one elbow, and before anyone knew what was happening, he had pulled a gun out of his pants. Jake opened his mouth to yell, but it was too late. The shot rang out like a miniature explosion and Jacques stumbled forward, his momentum carrying him through the tent flying out into the street. In the next instant a second shot was fired and the man on the floor jerked convulsively several times before slumping back to the ground with a dull thud, splattering the pool of blood. Jake replaced his smoking revolver and turned away.

Nando had stormed from the tent and was standing about twenty feet away when he heard the sharp sounds of the pistols. He also heard his name called out behind him, and turning abruptly he gasped at the sight of his father staggering out of the tent, the look on his milk-white face a strange mixture of pain and desperation. Nando watched speechlessly as Jacques took several steps forward, dragging his feet. Then Jacques's eyes rolled backward as he sank onto his knees and fell forward, dead.

A long silent wail pierced Nando's very soul, and a cry tore through his frenzied mind.

Jake Alvarez raced to the scene and looked at the body of his friend, then over at the boy. He felt the lump forming in his own throat, and knew if he dared try to speak at this moment, the words would never come out. His heart was heavy as he stood between them and he felt an overwhelming grief spring into it. But was it for Jacques that he silently grieved? Or was it for Jacques' son? The boy looked so pitiful . . . with a strange unreadable look on his ashen face.

Jake forced himself to approach the boy. In spite of the knife still gripped tightly in the boy's hand, Jake knew he was defenseless. Placing a strong hand on Nando's shoulder and feeling no resistance, he asked softly, "Do you have anyone you can go to?"

Nando's voice was low and icy-cold. One word cut through the stillness of the afternoon. "No."

Jake Alvarez smiled at him. "Then, *amigo*, you come with me."

Nando picked up his father's body, his legs hardly able to sustain the weight of the big man who had stood over six feet tall, and carried Jacques away. That night Jake accompanied him on his silent ride north into the Sand Hills. Together they laid Jacques DeMalleray to rest in a neat grave around which they piled some smooth white rocks. From there, without even returning to Arrow Rock Creek to collect his things, Nando rode south following dumbly behind Jake Alvarez on his Indian pony.

His mother had been slain by Indians. His father was murdered by a white man. Nando was a part of both worlds, and a stranger to each. Now the scales were evenly balanced against him. Only the future would tell which path he would follow. The nightmare that had commenced on a cold, cloud-filled December day six years earlier, had been forever sealed inside of him on a day when the sun had shone brightly in the perfectly blue sky.

Chapter 38

His shirt was soaked with perspiration, but he could do nothing about it. He could not find the strength to lift himself up. He felt drained and exhausted, as though he had just finished an enormous labor. His throat was dry and he needed a drink.

A glass was put before his blurred eyes and numbly he reached out to take it. It was not until the heat of the brandy started his blood pumping again that he realized he was not alone. Blinking several times to erase the shadows that lingered across his vision, he was surprised to see Danny standing over him, her face pale, her eyes worried. She had heard it all. She was still here.

Alex rose to a sitting position and shook his head to free it of its heaviness. Thick black curls tossed about and settled down again. "I feel like I've been to hell," he said in a hoarse voice, managing a weak smile.

"You have," Danny whispered. "But I've been there with you and you're out of it now."

He inhaled deeply and let the air escape slowly through his full lips. "I wonder," he muttered to the air. Slumping back against the sofa, and retreated once again into his thoughts. At length he spoke again, his voice a whisper, almost as though it hurt too much to say the words out loud. "God, I hated him."

Danny closed her eyes and said nothing, lest she shatter his attention and drive back the words that had to be confronted at last, after so many torturous years of repression. The awful wound had to be cleansed and she sat silently by listening to the painful healing process.

"All those years," he said in a muffled whisper. "All those years without him . . . when it was killing me to be alone . . . when I needed him so badly." He shook his head slowly in sad disillusionment. "He sent me away when I needed him the most."

The room became quiet as Alex withdrew into himself again. After an unbearably long time he spoke and his voice was soft, without anger or bitterness spiking his tone. "I could never have hated him so much for what he did to me if I didn't love him so much." He rose to his feet, a crimson flush giving his complexion the color it needed. Back were the familiar features—the startlingly bright eyes of silver and the rakish smile that swept across his face. There was also something else that she had never seen before. This time when he smiled, it softened the hardness of his eyes and refined his rugged features to near perfection.

He moved toward her with his usual grace, but also with an easiness that had been absent before. In an instant Danny felt herself encircled in his embrace. His strong browned hands caressing her back, weaving his fingers into her hair and drawing her face up to meet his. He gazed down at her tenderly, cradling her face in his warm hands.

"I know now that I could not have hated *you* as much as I did if I did not love you so insanely." He shook his head in disbelief. "Everything I've done since meeting you has revolved around you, and at times I thought I'd go mad if I could not have you." He dropped his hands and looked away, recalling the harsh realities of his life. "Not a damned thing in this world has come easy to me, Danny, and I've grown accustomed to taking what I want . . . by force if necessary. The first time I saw you, I knew I had to have you for myself no matter what it meant in the long run." A smile erupted on his lips and he laughed softly. "You impossible woman, don't you know that you've had me utterly bewitched from the very beginning?" Without waiting for a reply, he pulled her to him and kissed her delicately on the lips. "I think in your heart you always knew it as much as I did," he whispered against her ear.

A tiny giggle escaped Danny's lips at the thought that, yes, in her heart she had always known.

Forcing sternness into his voice, Alex said, "I'll tell you something though, if you ever run away from me again, you little demon, I'll tan your hide until it's black and blue and you can't sit down for a month."

Danny lowered her eyes, black lashes fanning across her cheeks and a guilty little blush tinting her complexion.

"Go and change your clothes now," said Alex, "I'm taking you out to dinner. Are you hungry?"

"Oh, yes," Danny laughed. Spinning around she pulled a dress from the closet, one she knew he would like. After allowing her to slip out of her skirt and blouse, he stopped her before she could put it on. His hands were all over her and once again she was swept into his arms. "But Alex, I thought you said—"

"I know what I said," he laughed, as he slung her over his shoulder and carried her to the bed. "But right now my hunger is only for you."

He dropped her onto the brass-posted bed and stradled her with his knees, silver eyes raking over her naked body, memorizing each seductive curve, every hollow, every inch of her gorgeous silken flesh. His mouth went dry, as it always did, at the closeness of her, and the smell of her oiled body drifted to his nostrils making him heady with its intoxicating fragrance. His voice was scratchy with mounting passion. "Long before you came here I knew about you," he said. "Austin described you to me so many times, so thoroughly, that I felt I knew you. I guess I always sensed that I'd have to take you from him. It was something I agonized over without really knowing it, until the day you walked smack dab into my life. Then it didn't matter any longer who got in the way . . . not even him."

"Alex, I—" But his lips silenced her words. She closed her eyes and clasped his body to her, feeling his thick curls at her fingertips, pulling him closer still so that she could feel his male hardness against her.

When their bodies joined and became one—when she felt him deep inside of her—when everything else in the world ceased to exist, she heard the words she had longed to hear spoken into her ear in breathless whispers.

"Danny . . . Danny," he breathed, "you golden-eyed creature, from the very beginning you've been the fire in my blood, the flower of my soul, the reason for my existence. I love you . . . I love you . . ."

A pale moon shadowed the earth, and across the dark

midnight sky was spread a blanket of stars—a million, tiny shining faces smiling brilliantly down upon two naked bodies. Danielle felt the strength of Alex's presence beside her, safe and reassuring, as they lay together listening to the rise and fall of their breathing. Alex found her hand and gripped it tightly in his own, his warm touch telling her everything and promising even more. He committed his destiny to hers. Without words he vowed to love her as long as they lived.

Golden eyes fluttered closed and a smile touched the corners of her lips. As of this moment, her world was just beginning.

About the Author

Nancy Morse began her writing career rather modestly at the age of nine by entering a Twenty-five Words or Less contest on why she liked Rin-Tin-Tin. She won. Encouraged by her success, she immediately began publication of a newspaper which she distributed to her friends. This was accompanied over the years by countless volumes of short stories written to satisfy a child's imagination in addition to special writing classes in school.

Serious writing came in her late twenties, when, after a brief gambit into the free-lance market, she decided that her particular path was as a novelist where she could continue to indulge her imagination.

A lifetime love of reading led to an early curiosity about American Indians. This has been cultivated into the formation of a collection of Indian antiquities and an indelible interest in the history and culture of the native American.

Nancy Morse has been married for twelve years to a free-lance film technician and they live in the same suburb of New York City where she has spent most of her life.

The Silver Lady is Nancy's first book. She is currently working on a second, which will take place largely in Europe.